Beneath the Rock

Tommy Birk

**CALUMET
EDITIONS**

Minneapolis, Minnesota

**CALUMET
EDITIONS**

Minneapolis, Minnesota

SECOND EDITION JANUARY 2015
BENEATH THE ROCK.

This is a work of fiction. All of the characters, names, incidents, organizations, and dialogue are either the products of the author's imagination or are used fictiously.

Printed in the United States of America.
10 9 8 7 6 5 4 3 2

ISBN: 978-939548-24-5

Book and cover design by Gary Lindberg

To my father, PFC Elmer Birk, who was with the 2nd Battalion on Hill 314 at Mortain and survived, but died a little inside. And to my mother, Mary Ann, who tried to reach that dead spot, but couldn't.

Beneath the Rock

Tommy Birk

Epigraphs

"Thousands of our men will be returning to you. They have been gone a long time and they have seen and done and felt things you cannot know. They will be changed. They will have to learn how to adjust themselves to peace."

—Ernie Pyle, World War II Correspondent, in *Brave Men*, 1944

The wounded [of the 2nd Battaalion] were the inspiration that kept the battalion fighting [on Hill 314 at Mortain] long after many had given up hope of coming out alive. Aid men were helpless without medical supplies and the wounded were comforted more with words than with treatment. But it was the wounded who shouted, "No, no, no surrender!" when the German officer demanded surrender.

—"The Saga of the Last Battalion," front page story in the August 21, 1944 edition of The Stars & Stripes, the daily newspaper of the U.S. Armed Forces.

Acknowledgements

He is a worldly man, a great teacher, one with the gift of knowledge, inspiration and courage—the courage to always demand better. To him I owe much. I am proud to call him my mentor and friend. His name is Ian Graham Leask, and he lives in Minneapolis, Minnesota.

PART 1

Chapter 1

The short German soldier ordered Ernie Balbach to place his hands on his head and stand with his feet apart, and then searched him. The guttural snipings of German soldiers searching other members of Ernie's patrol buzzed around the clearing in the forest. Some of the patrol sobbed from fear of their captors, or maybe helplessness, like during a German artillery barrage. The short German's hands fluttering around Ernie's body violated him and pounded deep into his psyche, his own helplessness, his own fears.

Then the German soldier, in a small voice, asked, "Sprechen Sie Deutsch?"

"Ja, I speak *Deutsch*," Ernie sneered.

"What is your name?" the soldier continued in German.

"Ernie Balbach."

"Where in America do you live?"

"Dubain, Indiana."

"My name is Gunther Balbach." Then, in a whisper, "We will talk later."

"About what?" asked Ernie.

"We are under the command of the SS," said Gunther Balbach, continuing in German. "Waffen. They will be here shortly."

"Do...do they take prisoners?"

Gunther Balbach put his finger to his lips and muttered, "Later."

"But..."

"There will be time, but not much. Sit on the edge of the group."

"What gr—"

"You will see."

There had been a lull in German armored attacks on Hill 314, and the American battalion commander on the hill wanted to know why. So he had ordered Ernie's patrol to reconnoiter the woods at the bottom of Hill 314 nearest Mortain and send back intelligence on the positions and numbers of German soldiers and tanks hidden there. The Germans had spotted the patrol, which had hidden in the woods. Ernie wasn't sure what had happened to his sergeant and if he was alive or not, but more of the patrol might have escaped were it not for local French boys who searched the woods, found the Americans, and pointed them out to the enemy. The Americans had no choice but to surrender. Ernie, Jimmy Franken, and Fred Patterson concealed themselves in a small gulch behind two medium-sized trees that were uprooted and laid over by an artillery shell. A French boy with a scar down the right side of his face found them. They were taken last.

The German soldiers gathered the American prisoners in a unit and suggested they sit and rest. "Your war is over," a few of the younger German soldiers told them. They were ragged, dirty, hollow-eyed, and teenaged. Ernie sensed that they wished their war was over. Two more guarded the Americans. The GIs had little food and no water, and so were grateful when the Germans sat in a kind of semi-circle around them and gave them German rations and water. Ernie stayed on the perimeter of the group of American prisoners. Gunther Balbach rested near him. Many of the GIs, now assured of their safety, fell asleep. Ernie, who desperately wanted sleep, did not. He watched Gunther Balbach out of the corner of his eye and then brushed his fingertips against the ammo pocket of his dungarees. Ernie blamed fatigue for why the German Balbach failed to find the small Beretta pistol nestled there.

Then a panicked voice in his head said, Ernie, the German Balbach has a special hatred for Americans and is tricking you! At the moment of your capture, the Beretta turned from a weapon of war to a weapon of concealment. They'll find it and shoot you at the entrance to the POW camp. Hand it over to the German Balbach, now, before it's too late!

Then an icy voice said, No, Ernie. Keep your wits and the gun. Look at this German Balbach. See? He and you look alike. Something is up with him. Rely on your instincts. Go with your gut. You'll need the gun before this day is out.

Ernie kept the gun.

Gunther Balbach handed Ernie a cigarette and lit it for him, then lit another for himself. "We have the same last name," said Gunther in German without looking at Ernie. "We are the same height and have common features. Perhaps we are related, as are many Germans and Americans. I am from the town of Pfaffenweiler, which is located on the lower east side of the Black Forest, not far from Switzerland. My great-great grandfather, Joseph Balbach, left Pfaffenweiler about a hundred years ago to move to this town, Dubain, in America."

Ernie didn't acknowledge the German. The panicked voice said, Ignore him and give up the gun. Whoever heard of sketching family trees in the middle of a war?

The icy voice said, Precisely, Ernie. This man's got nothing to gain by tracing common blood between you and him except family. Family's important to him. He's probably lost some in this war. He wants to befriend you. All this sounds crazy, and might be, but go with it.

He wished the sergeant were there to offer his support. But Ernie was on his own. He made the decision to continue the conversation in German. "Joseph Balbach moved to Dubain from Pfaffenweiler in the 1830s. He is also my great-great grandfather." Then Ernie, perhaps sensing the German Balbach's need for closeness, even to an enemy soldier, added another, more intimate detail. "He's buried first on the right in the St. Augustine Cathedral cemetery in Dubain."

"Well, then, GI Ernie Balbach," said Gunther, "we are fourth cousins."

A group of French boys entered the clearing and pointed at and ridiculed the American prisoners. The boy with the jagged scar on his face led the jeers.

"Ach, that one with the scar," said Gunther Balbach. "You are not the first."

"The first what?"

"Since the attack started," said Gunther, "he and his friends have found other Americans hiding in the woods. They do this at the instigation of the SS."

"Why?"

"Their families work for the SS. They spy on the French Underground and report American enemy troop movements. Some sabotage. 'Collaborators,' you Americans call them. The SS rewards them with food—sausages, cheese, even fresh meat. Ach, not even we German regulars get the meat!"

An SS man entered the clearing.

"That SS man is Stresseman, Colonel Peiper's adjutant. I must go! You are on your own now."

"On my own?" Ernie blurted. "What—" By that time, Gunther had risen. Ernie watched him walk to the edge of the clearing about twenty feet away, place his rifle stock under his arm, and stand guard over the prisoners.

Ernie turned to the boys and watched Scarface point to him and hoot. The SS man laughed and joked with Scarface and patted him on the head. Then he walked to the Wehrmacht sergeant and loudly berated him. In the next few moments, Ernie grasped the meanings of Gunther Balbach, his cousin—and the Beretta, his weapon. Because Ernie understood every word of German from the SS adjutant.

"What," the SS man, Stresseman, asked, "do you intend to do with these cowardly Americans?"

"Sir," replied the sergeant, "we have searched, disarmed, and interrogated them. Two of our men will march them to the POW enclosure on the other side of the woods." The sergeant pointed south.

"Ach, we don't have time for such foolishness, sergeant. We took no prisoners in Russia. It is no different in France." The adjutant pointed at Gunther Balbach and then at several other German soldiers. "Line up the prisoners."

The German soldiers moved to follow orders, but as Gunther Balbach passed by Ernie, the SS man eerily flashed his eyes between them. "Well, well, what do we have here? An American and German who very much look alike." He pointed at Ernie, "Do you speak Deutsch? What is your name?"

In the second that Ernie had to decide, the icy voice said, Tell the bastard the truth. Many German and American soldiers have the same last names, and many Americans of German descent speak German.

"Ja, ich spreche Deutsch. Mein name ist Ernie Balbach."

"This is remarkable," said the adjutant. "His name is Gunther Balbach. It would be interesting to see if you are related, but we have no time for such pleasantries."

A group of SS men, one of them an officer, walked into the clearing. The adjutant saluted the officer and said, "Major Peiper, sir, we are preparing the prisoners for execution, as you ordered."

Suddenly, Major Peiper shot Chambers in the back of the head. Ernie, watching in line with other captured Americans, wet himself. His entire body, though numb, trembled in a way he had not felt even at St. Lo. The panicked voice said, This is it. This is it.

The icy voice said, Wait, watch for developments—you have the gun.

Major Peiper was working his way down the line. Fred Patterson from Maryland would go next. Then Joe O'Reilly, also from Maryland. Then Ernie. Fred had probably saved Ernie's life on Omaha Beach by shooting a German sniper who'd drawn a bead on Ernie. Beside Ernie, Hightower, a redheaded Texan, wept murmured prayers to the holy mother and murmured, "How can anyone just kill me?" Beside Hightower, Jimmy Franken—eighteen years old and who didn't smoke, drink, or swear—whimpered for his momma. Fred stood straight, his shoulders back. A smell of shit came off him. Major Peiper pointed to two Wehrmacht soldiers—no more than boys, ragged, dirty, and hollow-eyed—to haul Chambers to a brush pile a French farmer had mounded in the clearing. Ernie looked at Chambers lying on the top of the brush pile and couldn't push out of his mind the vision of the whole patrol lying on the pile with him.

The major took off his cap and wiped his forehead with his sleeve. His blond hair, cut short in the back and down the sides, sprang up on the top as if the cap had been suppressing it. His hair looked beautiful in the hot sun, almost like a girl's. The panicked voice inside Ernie said, You'll never again see you're sweetheart, Maymie, back home.

Bullshit, said the icy voice. You will because you've got a plan, so fuck these bastards.

When Fred stepped forward, Ernie would pull out the Beretta, shoot both the SS major and his adjutant, and run for the woods.

The panicked voice said, Ernie, it won't work.

The icy voice said, Ernie, it might work. You've got nothing to lose. The others will break for it too, and there'll be chaos. If it doesn't work, what's the difference between being dead and being dead? Besides, you made it this far from Omaha Beach. You're a lucky sonofabitch and don't forget it!

The officer turned and looked at the prisoners. He put his cap back on and, followed by his adjutant, walked toward them. "Straighten yourselves up!" he ordered. "Try to show some bravery, even though you are Americans." The German's use of English caught Ernie's attention. It sounded almost like the accent he'd heard while training with the local Tommies in the countryside outside Southampton. Just to be there again in the Kings Head with a pint of warm dark ale! He remembered how Jimmy Franken had been sweet on the barmaid there, although the other privates, especially the Tommies, called her dogface.

The officer looked over each of the Americans in turn. This was it. Ernie nearly pulled out the Beretta when the officer's blue eyes locked onto his.

The panicked voice in Ernie said, Oh shit!

The icy voice said, Your chance is coming. Watch for it.

"Du hast ein kommischen gesicht," said the officer as he examined Ernie.

Ernie could never handle abusive authority. "No funnier than your face, you murderin' bastard." It came out in German before he could stop it. Oh shit, what have you said, Ernie thought to himself. Ernie, you're a dead man.

The major frowned, then smiled. He continued in German, "Ach, you understand German, and you are insolent."

Ernie, the top of his head only just level with the officer's chin, could find no answer so he drew himself completely to attention and looked the officer in the eyes. The officer leaned in close enough so that his breath, a sour mixture of strong cigarette smoke and days of battle scum, turned Ernie's stomach, making him draw back slightly.

"Are you a Jew?" Peiper asked in German.

"Nein." Ernie replied.

"Are there any Jews in your unfortunate patrol?"

Ernie, speaking in German, said, "None. We are American soldiers, protected by the Geneva Convention." The panicked voice said, Ernie, remember the rules. Only your name, rank, and serial number.

The icy voice said, No, Ernie, you're a good talker. Keep it going. Give him a line of shit. Peiper's SS, but he's no superman. Get him to relax his guard. Then pull him in and shoot him.

The officer laughed and looked at his adjutant, who also laughed. "Ah, the Geneva Conventions. Mere scraps of paper, like the Fuehrer says." The officer pushed his face even closer to Ernie's. Without looking away, he pointed to Jimmy and said, "You lied. That one is a Jew. He looks like a Jew, and one of your 'brave' Americans told us his last name is Franken. We are saving him for last." The major pulled back and smiled. "I forgive you for the lie, but you are a little like him. Perhaps you count shekels too. Do you?"

"I'm a Roman Catholic and I count dollars," said Ernie, thrusting his own face forward.

"I believe you, my friend," said the major. "Oh, I've forgotten my manners. Private Ernie Balbach, I am Major Hans Peiper of the Waffen SS."

Ernie refused to salute the major. The major nodded, smiled at Ernie, and let the snub pass.

"I am also a Roman Catholic, so you and I have something else in common, other than a command of German, the most beautiful language in the world. Where did you learn to speak German?"

Fuck this, the icy voice told Ernie. Don't speak any more German.

"Many people in my hometown speak German. I'm one of 'em," replied Ernie in English.

"Warum?"

"You ask why? I can tell you why. They emigrated from Germany to a better country to get away from murdering bastards like you."

The men on either side of him groaned. Ernie knew what they were thinking: You and your big mouth, Balbach. Shut the fuck up. Maybe he'll show us mercy and spare us.

But the icy voice said, Ernie, there's no mercy here and you know it. Only the gun'll save you, and maybe some of the others.

The officer pulled back, his eyes furious for a second, then they dimmed. He smiled at Ernie. "What is the name of your hometown?"

"Fuck you."

The major drew his Luger and placed the muzzle against Hightower's forehead. Hightower sobbed.

"What is the name of your hometown?"

"Dubain," Ernie almost yelled. "Dubain, Indiana!" The major lowered his gun.

"So, a German-American settlement?"

"It's an American town of Americans. It ain't a German settlement."

"But you're proud of it, aren't you?"

"Yes."

"Where is this place you call Dubain, In—what you say—Indiana?"

"In Southwestern Indiana," said Ernie through clenched teeth, "close to the Ohio River."

"Indiana is an American state in what you call the Midwest, isn't it?"

"Yes."

"How many people live in Dubain?"

Ernie hesitated.

The panicked voice said, Stick to the rules. Only your name rank, and serial number and nothing else!

The icy voice said, Keep talking. Get him to trust you. Then shoot the bastard.

Ernie thought a moment longer while he weighed his options. "About five thousand," he said.

"Your American Midwest is large and fertile and grows many crops."

"Yes."

"I look forward to the day when my countrymen make their farms in your Midwest and your mongrel American comrades work there as slaves. Perhaps I might own a farm near your town, Dubain, and live out my days working hard to make it more productive than it is now."

Ernie said nothing. The major smiled again. He's happy about something, thought Ernie, but what does Dubain have to do with it? The major became more pleasant, as though he and Ernie were neighbors roasting hotdogs over a fire and sipping beer in the backyard on a Sunday afternoon. The major holstered his Luger as if to say, All is forgiven. Let's have peace. Live and let live. Ernie thought, What the hell's going on. He glanced at Fred and Joe, then at Hightower. He glanced at the adjutant. The icy voice said, It's right in front of you, Ernie. See?

Ernie didn't see.

"Where did you learn to speak German?"

"At home. From Mom and Dad."

"Do others in this town, Dubain, of the state of Indiana, speak German?"

"Yes."

"How many others."

"Most of them."

"How many Roman Catholics live in Dubain?"

"All of them are Catholic. Maybe a few not."

"Are any of those not Catholic, Jews, or Africans?"

"No Black folk. Maybe several Jews. I'm not sure," Ernie added, bewildered that he was having such an easy conversation with a man who could kill him at any moment.

"Ah, my American friend," the major said. "My subject at the University of Heidelberg was history. I am quite fond of American history, what little of it there is. I admire your war of independence from the arrogant British. I do not admire your Northern war of aggression against the South, whose people quite rightly owned the Africans as slaves, which you call 'Black folk.' Clearly an inferior race. The Northerners foolishly freed the Africans." Then, abruptly he added, "You are intelligent. So what do you think of that war? Did your people fight for the Africans?"

"My teacher talked about the Civil War. I don't know much about it," Ernie said.

"My next most favorite stories are those of my countrymen who went to the frontier of America and became—what do you Americans say—pioneers. They killed your American savages and founded new settlements. Is Dubain one of these?"

"I guess so."

"When was Dubain founded?"

"About a hundred years ago. Most of the Indians were gone."

"Who started it?"

"Germans."

"Which Germans?"

"My grandma said they were from Pfaffenweiler."

"Well, well, my friend. We have something else in common. My hometown is Ulm, which is on the east side of the Black Forest. Pfaffenweiler is near the lower west part of the forest. One of my teachers at the University observed that all things in life revolve in circles. You and I. We're parts of a circle."

Ernie said nothing but thought, Good for you, you blond fish-eyed fucker.

"Are you and your family descendants of these Germans?"

"Yes."

"And Dubain and its neighboring towns. Are they clean and well run? Prosperous, with honest citizens, well-trimmed parks, plenty of trees? Bierstubes and sports facilities?"

"Yes."

"It is like my Ulm. Perhaps I will visit after the war."

Ernie thought, If you do, and if I don't get killed here, I'll shoot you first chance I get.

The icy voice said, Dammit, look! You're getting your chance. Ernie thought, My chance? Godammit! Where?

But then one of the voices said, He's in a good mood, so try it. Try it now. It can't hurt. Ernie hesitated, then turned his head both ways to look at his buddies. Their faces stared back with—what? Definitely fear and anguish. But maybe a bit of hope?

"Major, sir, can I ask you something? One German descendant to a native German?"

"Of course. And I'll try to answer."

"Sir, you may not put much stock in the Geneva Convention, but our side treats German prisoners well. We are your prisoners of war, and we hear that you Germans treat American prisoners just the same. We won't put up a fight if you send us to one of your prison camps. Someday there'll be an exchange of prisoners between your side and ours and we can go home. Please, sir. Our families want us safely home just as, I'm sure, your family wants you. Will you let us go and join the other American prisoners of war?"

The major grinned and slapped Ernie on the shoulder. "You make a fair and reasonable proposal, my little American. It is worthy of consideration." The SS officer put his head down for a few seconds as if to ponder Ernie's request.

Then Ernie saw what the icy voice was trying to tell him. The Lugers of the major and adjutant were holstered!

The major raised his head and, still smiling, said, "Unfortunately, I cannot accept it. You, my friend, and the rest of your friends here shall not survive this war, I'm afraid."

The officer stepped back three paces, glanced at his adjutant, and nodded towards the brush pile.

Something resembling electricity shot from the nape of Ernie's neck to his sphincter.

"Step forward, private."

"Major Peiper," said the adjutant, "there is an interesting connection between this soldier, Ernie, and—"

Ernie took one step forward. It was now. Now! Ernie pulled the gun out of his pocket and aimed it at the adjutant Stresseman first.

Perhaps he wanted to protect Gunther Balbach's secret or maybe to give the major time to know that it was he who would not survive the war. Everyone froze for a second. Ernie loved the fear on their faces. He shot the adjutant in the chest. Then he fired at the major, who did a sort of back flip. There was no more time to aim and shoot. Ernie took off for the woods. He felt the others running behind him. There was yelling and firing. Ernie only saw ahead to the line of trees and undergrowth.

The panicked voice said, Ernie, remember your training. You've got to zigzag to avoid the bullets.

The icy voice said, You ain't got time to zigzag. Get to the woods as fast as you can. They are your safety. Your life!

Ernie listened to the second voice as bullets snapped around him. Hightower, the fastest guy in their platoon, passed Ernie on the left but went down. In one panicked but strangely graceful movement, Ernie jumped over Hightower, dove into the overgrowth of weeds and briars, rolled three times into the woods, used the energy to pop to his feet, and kept going. He ran lightly and flat-footed so as to leave as small a trail as possible. Ernie heard the wood-crackling sprints of others of the patrol who made it to the forest. He couldn't tell how many there were. He heard the Germans enter the woods and their yells of "Halt! Halt! Halt!" Then came the sound of automatic weapons firing.

Chapter 2

Ernie ran southeast, crossed a creek, and headed west until he came to a large pin oak tree. Then all of it cascaded onto Ernie, a gripping fatigue from the past four days of no sleep inside a cauldron of confused, desperate fighting born of orders from commanders to "hold your positions at all costs" against an enemy that surrounded you and outnumbered you ten to one. Then the patrol, then capture, and then murder by the SS. Ernie leaned over, dry-heaving, sobbing, and gasping. Momma, help me! Daddy, come down from heaven and save me! The Germans...they're closing in on me. I'm done. I can't take any more of this. It's too much. Just too much. Momma can't help me. Daddy's not here. I'm giving up. Death is peace, the end of this pain, this fucking war. No more SS. No more hedgerows. No more St. Lo's. No more massacres.

But then the icy voice, now calmer, said, No, Ernie, it's not over for you. You're not done. Momma can help you, even now, even here, at this place. Think of her, of going home to her, of hugging her on the front porch in your clean sparkling uniform. Think of hiking the forest again. Think of your daddy who, right this minute, beseeches God for you. Stop this foolishness! You can't give up. You can't die. You must live. You were the best tree climber of your gang. Remember?

Ernie heeded the icy voice. He ran and jumped into the pin oak's lowest branches, curled his legs around a limb, pulled himself upright, and moved up the tree, squirrel-like and quiet. He reached a large limb about seventy-five feet from the base of the tree. The leaves and branches below Ernie concealed him from anyone looking up from the ground. Ernie sat on the limb and hugged the giant trunk. By God, I'm alive, he thought. Ernie willed his body to catch up on breath, to stop its dry-heaving, to slow its heart, to call on instinct, to survive. Ernie saw that the limb—about fifteen inches in diameter, rare for a limb that high in any tree—was almost as wide as his body. Ernie lay face down on the limb, put the top of his head against the trunk to keep from rolling off, and held on. Some uplifting suckers helped hold his body in place although a small one poked his stomach.

The Germans moved noisily through the woods. Ernie heard them call out and track their positions to each other by noting large trees and rock formations. Then a familiar voice, Jimmy Franken's. Jimmy cried and coughed up something that wasn't sputum. "Ernie, help me! I know you're up there. Help me!"

The icy voice said, Ernie, if you try to save Jimmy, you'll only get killed yourself. Ernie said and did nothing.

Jimmy cried for help several times more, but his pleas grew fainter. Then Ernie heard Jimmy crawl behind the oak, probably to hide. It didn't matter because a group of Germans, including Major Peiper, found Jimmy. In a calm voice devoid of the effects of the chase, Peiper ordered his men to stand Jimmy against the tree.

"No blindfold for this Jew swine. Shoot!"

A small volley of rifle fire, a groan, a short pause, then two quick pistol shots. Jimmy was gone.

The sounds of the Germans faded in the distance. For a little while, at least, Ernie felt safe. The Germans, never totally out of Ernie's hearing, reached the other edge of the woods. They turned back for a slower and quieter search for Ernie and the few Americans who had escaped but were not yet recaptured. The major ordered the others to search the trees. Then, in a sweet and soothing voice, he called to Ernie in English. "Oh, my American friend Private Ernie Balbach, where are you? I know you are here somewhere. I forgive you for killing my adjutant. I forgive you for shooting me. It's only a flesh wound, a little pain, but it will heal. Come on out, my little friend. I am reconsidering your proposition. There's been enough death today. Perhaps you can go home to Dubain." The major and his group stopped under Ernie's tree. "Ernie, we are friends, you and I. We have so much in common. You love forests, don't you? I love them too. Show yourself and I promise you will eat steak before this day is done."

Eat steak? Like hell, Ernie thought. The only food I'll get from this murderous sonofabitch is lead.

"Well, I offer you friendship and you reject it. So I ask, why did your little Jew comrade struggle so hard to come to this tree? Did you talk to him, guide him here? Are you up there, hiding in the branches? We shall find out."

This was it. The end was coming. Ernie scrunched on the branch, moved his arms from the trunk, and wrapped them around the back of his head. He made himself as small a target as possible, but doing so multiplied many times over his chances of rolling off the limb. Oh, he thought, to be a squirrel, or even a cat, with claws to dig in, to hold me here!

Bullets zipped through the leaves around Ernie and slapped against the limb under him. After ten seconds, maybe twenty, the shooting stopped.

"Private Ernie," Peiper cried, "if you are in this tree, you are no doubt wounded. Yet you do not fall. We shall try again."

There was another eruption of bullets. Crazily Ernie thought, at least my balls are safe. The shooting stopped. Ernie turned his head and looked over his body. For a moment, he was drawn back to his army physical when the army doctors probed every piece of him. He detected no wounds, felt no loss of blood.

Then the major ordered a soldier to climb the tree. The soldier protested the order. "Major, Sir, es ist Niemand da oben." Major, sir, there's no one up there.

"Du wirst meine Befehle folgen!" You will follow my orders!

Ernie heard the soldier swing to the first branch, catch himself on the trunk, and climb. Maybe he'll stop before he gets to me, thought Ernie. But he won't. What the hell can I do?

The soldier—a good climber himself, Ernie could tell—grunted his way up. The German grabbed a branch facing east and level with Ernie. The top of the German's helmet appeared. Then his arms, face, and head. He looked up, then down, then across at Ernie. Ernie and the German stared at each other in recognition, one hearkening back to his American family, the other to his German. It was Gunther Balbach.

Ernie raised himself bit by bit to a sitting position on the branch. The German Balbach reached down with his right hand, touched the handle of a .45 pistol in his belt, then raised the hand, put a finger to his lips, and nodded. Ernie felt an overwhelming urge to blink but fought it off. Locking his eyes onto the German's, Ernie touched the gun in his pocket and shook his head. I don't understand.

The major, impatient at the silence, called out, "Was zum Teufel ist los da oben?" What the hell is going on up there? Gunther Balbach shouted down, "Ich bin an der Spitze des Baumes. Es ist Niemand hier!" I'm at the top of the tree. There is no one here!

The major ordered Gunther down. "Goddammit," he said in German, "if the American bastard isn't up there, where in the hell can he be?"

Gunther shook the limbs around him, looked again at Ernie, then moved his head in agitation, like a dog shaking water from his fur. He pointed to himself and, still shaking the limbs, whispered in German, "Prisoner."

Ernie pointed to himself and equally whispered, "Ich bin deinen Gefangene?"

"Nein! Nein! Ich bin *deinen* Gefangene!"

Ernie nodded in understanding. "You are my prisoner. But why?"

The German pointed towards the northeast so those below wouldn't see what he was doing. Then he pointed at his head and then his eyes.

Ernie got it. This German Balbach knew the way out of there.

But Ernie then asked, "How?"

The German pointed in the direction from which Ernie had fled, tightly shut his eyes for several seconds, then opened them. Ernie

gave the American A-okay sign, pointed in the direction of the clearing, and said in German, "I will meet you there at dark." The German
nodded, then climbed to the ground. The major ordered several soldiers to carry Jimmy's body to the brush pile in the clearing. The
Germans left.

Chapter 3

Private First Class Ernest J. Balbach of the Second Battalion, 120th Regiment, United States 30th Infantry Division, straddled the limb with his legs and leaned back against the tree trunk. Artillery shells—from the Americans east to west and from the Germans west to east—whistled over his head. The din of small arms fire inched up Hill 314. He picked out the rumbles of German tanks and winced for his battalion each time one fired its mounted 88 mm gun.

It was dangerous for soldiers in combat to think, but Ernie, for the time being, was in a tree seventy-five feet from the ground, alone, and with no war to fight. It was then he realized that memory *of* war was different from memory *in* war. The 30th had waded ashore at Omaha Beach on June 13, 1944, seven days after D-Day, and picked its way through the devastation of smashed vehicles, bits of landing craft, discarded equipment, and dead men and pieces of them. Ernie and other 30th soldiers had looked at each other and asked, Will this be us? They then assured each other, No, it will not be us. But a day later it was, and the 30th had been on the line without letup since. The hedgerow country in Normandy was pure hell. Ernie had watched buddies die right before his eyes—one of these, Herman Steltenhof from Ferdinand, a town south of Dubain, was killed by concussion from a German shell. There had been dead American paratroopers in trees with their dicks cut off and hanging out of their mouths. Ernie and his buddies asked each other how any human could do such things. A week of combat drove the question away with an answer: I can do such things. Ernie was amazed at how quickly a dead body invaded the nostrils of a living body with that sickly sweet smell of death, and he was more amazed that dead Germans and dead Americans smelled differently. Was it because Americans and Germans ate different food? Or was there a simpler, yet more complicated reason: Did Americans and Germans differ in death because they differed in life?

Ernie had spent two days in a field hospital when a sliver of shrapnel entered the calf of his right leg, but he sneaked out the second night to rejoin his outfit, which he knew needed him. The leg healed with the sliver still inside and ached occasionally. That was five weeks ago. Or was it six weeks, or four? Ernie didn't know and didn't give a good goddamn. He loved two things and two things only: his life and his buddies' lives. Ernie lived, fought, and killed for them, and they for him. There was room only for these things and nothing else, not even tenderness or patriotic memory. Did he kiss his mother goodbye? When was the last letter from home? When had he last written? What was the name of the movie he and Maymie saw on their last date before he left home? Did he have a hot meal in the past week? What was the name of his seventh grade teacher? The name of the priest who said Daddy's funeral mass? When did he last see the old guys at Piankashaw Rock?

The war had pushed everything else away. Ernie dimly recalled last November when someone from the local newspaper took a picture of his "draft class" on the courthouse steps in Dubain before they boarded the military bus to basic training in Louisiana. The concepts of "fighting for America," "freedom," and the "Great Crusade" proclaimed by Eisenhower a few hours before the landings were now as foreign to Ernie as a distant galaxy. War, Ernie learned, didn't work that way. The war Ernie experienced with his senses was simple. That which occurred in his head was not. And so Ernie cried in grief for Chambers, Joe, Fred, Jimmy, and all the others; in guilt for having, so far, survived; in anger at the Germans, the SS, Peiper, and his own commanders; in helplessness and rage, which, Ernie learned, were two faces of the same card; and in fear for his own life. Ernie never wanted to live so much as right then, when death stared at his youth, and after he'd survived so much.

Ernie raged at his country and the folks back home because they'd cheated him. They gave him peace, but stole it with war. They tendered him decency, but withdrew it with hatred. They bestowed on him health and youth and life and heroism, then transformed him into a dead man walking. They filled him with love of family and nation, then replaced it with the mindset of survival at its lowest primal level. They covered Ernie with Catholicism and faith in God, but sent him to a time and place that perverted religion and destroyed faith, and then belief. In quieter moments, like this one, Ernie mused that he was fighting on the very lands where medieval priests and monks locked away in monasteries had conjured up all the cathedral and God and religion bullshit. And all this might explain his strangest thought. He was certain he could kill his dad, a kind and gentle soul who died on Pearl Harbor day, if he appeared as an enemy soldier. His mother was made of sterner stuff, but he could also kill her if he had to.

He remembered the breakout from St. Lo and the hedgerow country, when Ernie and the 30th had moved east to Mortain, a sleepy little French town that lay in a valley surrounded by hills. The commanders said they had to have Mortain and ordered the 30th to take it. Ernie's battalion relieved an outfit of the 1st Infantry Division on Hill 314, which overlooked Mortain to the southwest. The rest of the 30th set up behind Ernie's battalion. All had been quiet on Hill 314, and Mortain lay in front of Ernie's battalion, easily within reach. The battalion, about seven hundred men in all, thought themselves lucky for a change. But neither the quiet nor the luck held.

The Germans attacked with two Waffen SS Panzer Divisions, but the battalion drove them off. The Germans attacked twice more, and twice more the battalion held. Then the Germans switched their tactics from the mailed fist to the open hand of reason and accommodation. It was clear that the battalion's position, which deteriorated hourly, was becoming desperate, and that the Panzers would eventually succeed in taking Hill 314, but at great cost in lives to both armies. So the

Germans sent an officer through the lines under a truce flag to meet with the American commander and arrange the battalion's surrender.

Ernie was near the battalion command post and saw and heard the whole thing. The German officer had told Ernie's commander that the Americans had fought bravely and honorably, but their position was hopeless and they were running out of food, water, medical supplies, and ammunition. He demanded the Americans' surrender and promised the battalion good treatment in captivity and medical care for its wounded. Before the American commander could reply, an American private stepped forward and told the German officer the battalion would not surrender but would continue to fight until the last American bullet was shot in a German neck and the last American bayonet was stuck in a German belly. He told the German officer to go fuck himself and to get the fuck off the hill before the private shot him off.

The German had then looked in astonishment at the battalion commander, who smiled but said nothing, then to the private, then back to the commander. In the German army, he protested, it was unthinkable to allow a lowly and impudent private to respond to the surrender demand of an officer from an opposing army. The American commander smiled and shrugged his shoulders. The private raised his rifle. The German officer concluded that the private would carry out his threat, dropped the lecture, turned, and hurried off the hill. That was the end of surrender talk. The next day, the battalion commander sent Ernie and the patrol to the bottom of Hill 314 and into the arms of the Waffen SS.

Night fell. Once he was sure the coast was clear, Ernie climbed down, jumped to the ground, and stretched his body. Ernie smelled like a French outhouse that had been blown up by artillery. He'd shit his pants but didn't remember when. Ernie cleaned his uniform with handfuls of dead leaves, then smeared dirt on his face, hands, and arms. Ernie remembered his skill at sneaking up on his friends in the forest back home and scaring the hell out of them. He'd honed these skills when he hunted squirrels in the same forest. Goddammit! What he wouldn't give to trade the insane death embrace between armies in

France for his familiar forest back home, substitute his M-1 combat rifle for his twelve gauge hunting shotgun, and hunt squirrels instead of humans. He imagined the rich aroma of squirrel and dumplings cooking slowly in his mother's kitchen, and the pleasure of eating them at the supper table.

Ernie moved cat-like from tree to tree. He broke no twigs, shook no leaves, scraped no briars. He stopped behind a maple about twenty-five feet from the edge of the clearing and about the same distance to the east of the brush pile. Ernie, just barely able to see through the briars and undergrowth, could make out some of the bodies that lay on the pile. There were Fred and Joe. Most of Hightower's head was gone, but it was Hightower. Franken lay on the other side of Chambers, whose head seemed to float on water. Did I get them killed to save myself, Ernie thought. No, they would have died anyway because the major said so.

Ernie looked beyond the brush pile to the SS soldiers and German regulars, then beyond them to the dead adjutant who lay about twenty feet from where Ernie had killed him. Major Peiper, a sling around his right arm, directed the ending scene of the day's murders. Ernie saw the glow on the major's face, as though he was certain the gods favored him, made him invincible, anointed his mission, blessed his crimes. The major ordered the men to drench the bodies and brush pile with gasoline. The German regulars, about nine in all, doused the pile. They moved slowly, their shoulders sagging and their faces screwed in anguish. They never so much as glanced at the major or his SS.

But where was Gunther Balbach? Ernie was risking his life to take Gunther prisoner. Wouldn't it be better if he soloed his way back to the American lines? Why risk the added burden of a German prisoner? What if Gunny, though "family," had another plan where he would sacrifice Ernie to save himself? Ernie turned to leave the area but then stopped. He couldn't leave Gunther because he'd risked his life for Ernie, not once but several times: when he allowed Ernie to keep the Beretta, when he hinted to Ernie to prepare for the murderous Waffen SS, when he lied to

Major Peiper while facing Ernie in the tree, and when he broke faith with his own side to surrender to Ernie and lead him back to the American lines.

A truck engine started somewhere in the distance. The major motioned the SS men away from the bodies. The truck wound its way through the forest, entered the clearing, turned around, and backed toward the brush pile and out of Ernie's sight. The motor stopped. Ernie heard some voices, a few seconds of silence, and then the cries of men in anguish and panic, all this followed by the ripping buzz saw-like sound of a German machine gun in action and the thuds of dozens of slugs entering human bodies. Bullets snapped in the woods to Ernie's left but none came close to him. Ernie stood on his tiptoes, peeked around the maple tree, and peered through the chaos of the underbrush to the clearing. There, he watched the frantic movements of the German regulars being machine-gunned to death by their own SS at point-blank range. The shooting ceased when there was no more movement from the German regulars. The SS soldiers then threw the bodies on top of Joe, Fred, Jimmy, and the others of Ernie's patrol. They poured the remaining gasoline on the heap and stepped back. One of them lit a dry leaf, dropped it on the brush pile, and backed away. *Phoomph!*

Ernie saw the machine gunner shake hands with Major Peiper and the other SS men. Peiper opened a bottle and handed it to the gunner who took a swig, then passed it to the other SS soldiers. The major toasted his men, turned and toasted his dead adjutant Stresseman, then emptied the bottle and tossed it into the fire. It was quiet but for the snapping of the flames and the popping of fat deposits in the bodies. The men's eyes bore into the fire, and their faces, mesmerized and proud, reflected the flames. They'd become one with the fire, and the fire one with them. Ernie retched slightly at the stench of gasoline fumes and burning flesh, but then a force, ancient, primitive, instinctive, indescribable, welled from inside Ernie and forced him to move towards the fire. The fire!

Ernie sensed motion to his left, then a hand shot out and grabbed his wrist. "Bist du verruckt?"

Fearing nothing and no one, Ernie turned his head and came eye-to-eye with Gunther Balbach. Then Gunther's eyes looked past Ernie and he mumbled, "Death, away from here!"

In German, Ernie rasped, "No Death! I am not crazy and I don't want you as my prisoner!"

"My God, you must!" Gunther responded back in German. "My comrades. See? All dead. We—you and I—are in the same boat now. We must live to bear witness." Gunther wept without blinking, and then stuttered, "There must be justice,"—Gunther waved towards the SS men—"for these swine. Justice!"

Ernie gawked at Gunther, then at the fire, then again at Gunther. "Justice?"

"We must go now," said Gunther. "Hurry!"

Ernie wanted to escape, now more than ever, but with all his running earlier, he knew that even if he didn't want the German for a prisoner, Gunther Balbach was his best chance of making it back to the American lines alive.

"Help me, Gunther. You must help me."

Chapter 4

Gunther's oldest war companion, Death, came back to him.

Death: The American is crazy. I almost had him in my clutches but you stole him away from me. Why did you not let me harvest him?

Gunther: The American saved my life from you. Go away. Do not come back.

Death: Gunther, the secrets you carry will never get out of these woods.

Gunther: I have outwitted you all these years of war, Death. I will do so again.

Death, laughing: You know me and yourself too well to believe in your bravado. But your soul is deep, Gunther. I admire that.

Gunther: So?

Death: Your soul does not speak to you as I do, yet it speaks.

Gunther: You talk nonsense!

Death: Do I? Gunther, you are unlike your foolish American cousin, whose soul is shallow and leads him to believe he can will his destiny. This, even after I—

Gunther woke to darkness. Without moving his head, he rotated his eyes in circles and saw the earliest glimmers of sun filtering from the tops of trees into their lower parts. He reached down to touch his pistol. It was there. He reached left to touch Ernie. He wasn't there.

He slowly removed the pistol with his right hand and rested it on his chest, his finger on the trigger. Then Gunther heard a grunt and a splotch. He stood and replaced the pistol. There was a rustling of leaves and the closing of a belt buckle, then Ernie stepped from behind his tree. Without breaking eye contact with Ernie, Gunther walked to another tree, reached behind it, brought out an M1, the

GI's rifle, and rested its stock on the ground in front of him. Gunther allowed Ernie to lift the rifle from his hands.

They conversed in German.

"We must start," said Gunther, "so we can cover as much distance as possible before the Americans begin bombing and strafing."

"I haven't eaten since yesterday morning," said Ernie. "You got anything?"

"No," replied Gunther. "But water is more important, so we'll have to drink from the creek, no matter how foul it may be from soldier shit. But there is another matter, Ernie, that is much more important than food and water. Under no circumstances can either of us be taken prisoner. You must understand this above all things."

"Because of yesterday? The killings?" asked Ernie.

"Those also, but they are trivial in comparison to the information I have. So it is most important that I talk to your commanders. I am your prisoner, but we must be certain. If we reach the American lines on Hill 314, will they hold out or surrender? If they surrender, the SS will torture you and me for information and then kill us, and this war, which will soon end, may come back in a much more terrible form."

"Our orders are to hold Hill 314 at all costs," said Ernie. "If we make it to the hill alive, there's a good chance that we may die on it or be taken prisoner."

"Then we must bypass Hill 314 and enter the American lines at another place."

"Which direction?"

"We first head southeast, along the direction of the creek," Gunther pointed, "then execute a large semicircle to get to your American lines. Ten to fifteen kilometers. This will take two days at least."

They moved through the woods along the creek in a walking crouch, Gunther in front, his pistol in his waistband, and Ernie behind, the rifle stock under his right arm and the Beretta in his belt. They ducked down to avoid German patrols and stopped at intervals to listen and look around them. Then the first faint humming came from the west, grew into a drone, changed to a rumbling, and climaxed with explosions. American artillery screeched over their heads to the German concentrations on the other side of the woods. Allied strafers laid down their bullets on the German positions.

Gunther and Ernie took cover as best they could when the strafing and bombing moved from the edge of the forest towards its center, and them. Shells with timed fuses blasted away the tops of trees. Others gouged the forest floor and ripped trees—some decades old, and some, Gunther was certain, over a century old—from their roots and sent them crashing down or against other trees.

The forest reeked of cordite and high explosives. Dense and suffocating wood smoke from forest fires ignited by the bombs snaked along the ground and coiled upward into canopies of limbs and leaves. Gunther and Ernie gagged at the smoke. The explosions reverberated through the woods and concussed through their bodies. The forest darkened and closed around them. Gunther told Ernie they had no choice but to walk in the creek bed and risk discovery by others likely doing the same. They drank its water and breathed the fresher air that lay on it.

The fires spread. Flames jumped across the creek banks above them. The smoke worsened, so they breathed through their shirts. Their eyes teared and their world blurred. They moved like old skin divers who scour the sea's bottom for pearls they know are there but can no longer see. Gunther detected Death and watched him. Death sneaked through the woods, sometimes coming close to Gunther, other times slipping away. But always Death returned. The war was reduced to its vilest yet purest form, stripping Death of his pretenses.

Death: Your journey is dangerous. You and your cousin must come to me.

Gunther: We will talk later, Death. Now go.

Death: Do not fear me. I am your friend.

Gunther: You are my sworn enemy!

Death: All people pray to a god when I appear. Why do you not pray to yours?

Gunther: Because my God is not here!

Death: Of course not, Gunther. He is never here. I have tried to impress this on you, but you have not listened. Your God is an absentee who ignores you, who cares nothing for you. But I am with you all your days, and all your nights. I will never desert you. This is my promise. I come to you when you have no hope. I am your best friend, your most trusted companion, your kindest giver, your sweetest lover, your only hope in a place of no hope. Hear my song, taste my cool water, feel my warm embrace. I give you peace.

Gunther: You've been with me these five years. Many friends have gone to you. My brother and cousins went to you in frozen bits and pieces at Stalingrad. Famine, Black Death, and the sword dispatched my ancestors in Bavaria to you. Your mortal embraces, nothing more than fire and bullets and bombs, cannot have me. Not until I fulfill my mission in this war. Leave me!

"What did you say?" Ernie asked between explosions.

"Nothing. You are hearing voices, perhaps."

Death: Why should I leave?

Gunther: I have no time for you.

Death: No one has time for me, so I make time for them. I shall follow and harvest you and your American cousin before you share your secret with others.

Gunther: Why both of us? Why not take the American and leave me?

Death: Ah, Gunther, you and your American cousin, Ernie, meet on a battlefield in a country foreign to both you and him. You and he discover that you are descended from a common egg. You join together at this moment, in this place and time. Is this by accident, Gunther?

Gunther: Yes!

Death: No! Two fates, yours and the American's, have merged into one. You know that fate is unalterable, and the fate for you and him is me, and soon. The American's severance by ocean and continent and one hundred years does not alter this. But there is humor here. Ernie, an American after all, believes in luck. You attempt to join his luck, all the time certain, deep down, that luck is a chimera that exists only in the American's head.

Gunther: You lie about our fates, Death, and you bluff!

Death: We shall see.

Gunther stopped and held up his hand, then he and Ernie scrambled up the bank to hide behind a large cottonwood tree. A German patrol stopped about twenty feet downstream.

"We must find them before it is too late," said Major Peiper.

"How do we know they are together?" asked an SS soldier.

"They must get to the American lines," Peiper replied, "and this creek is the only way there. That traitor, Gunther Balbach, deserted because he knows our plans and intends to disclose them to our enemies. I never trusted him and should have shot him months ago. Corporal, take two men and search upstream for two kilometers. I and the others will move downstream and search the areas on both sides of the creek. We will meet at the command post at 1900 hours. If you find them, take them alive. They may have already told someone about us, so we must make them talk before we kill them."

The corporal's patrol stopped not fifteen feet from Gunther and Ernie, looked around, and then moved on. Gunther and Ernie waited another five minutes before resuming their journey downstream along the banks of the creek. Gunther led Ernie from tree to tree, from undergrowth to undergrowth, from one part of the inferno to another.

Then Gunther asked himself, Have I died? Has this American behind me died? Has Death taken us? Have our souls been judged and cast into hell? This hell? Then Gunther felt his pistol. Death and Hell do not have guns because neither has use for them, he mused with relief. My weapon is my life, and my life is my weapon. I and my American are alive!

They crawled under a briar patch for the night.

"We are hungry and exhausted, Ernie," said Gunther, speaking in German. "But now we must talk, and perhaps this will give us the strength to complete our mission."

"I'm listening."

"All of us—me, my comrades, Major Peiper, the SS—pledged a personal oath of loyalty to the Fuehrer. We swore to him our unconditional obedience and promised to give our lives for him, if need be."

"We know about the fuckin' Hitler oath," said Ernie.

"Obedience and dying are only parts of the oath," continued Gunther. "The rest is unspeakable! But we must speak. I must speak. And then you. Ach! I was on the Eastern front. I saw it. Tens of thousands. Russian prisoners, the commissars, Jews, whole villages whose only crimes were that they lay in the path of the SS. Even children, crying behind their peasant mothers' skirts. Goddamn the oath! Major Peiper's unit murdered thousands! Then they shipped us to France. More SS cruelty. You saw it yourself yester—"

"Did you do these things, too?" Ernie retorted. "Because of your oath? Have you murdered unarmed American soldiers? Is that part of your secret too?"

"No. That is my answer. It must be my answer."

"Damn you German fucker Gunther Balbach!"

"Damn you American fucker Ernie Balbach! You have no right to judge! Your soldiers have killed German prisoners, no? Have you? Your soldiers have killed innocent civilians, no? Have you? You Americans and British bomb German cities and kill tens of thousands of helpless people. Do you condone these things?"

Ernie looked away from Gunther, much of his resolve abandoning him. Gunther thought, Ah, I struck a mean chord in my cousin.

"Go on," said Ernie.

"I overheard them talking in their tent. Major Peiper said there has been a change, that Hitler is insane, that the war is lost and, because of these things, they are released from their oaths. He said the Allies will avenge themselves against all Germans, but most of all SS Germans. They formed a group they call 'Werewolves.' That is their codename. They not only plan to escape the Allies' rage, but to continue the work of the Nazis. Only this time it will be different, Peiper said. They will build not a 'Fourth Reich,' but a 'Great Reich,' not just in Germany, but all over the world. I heard them:

Britain, France, Brazil, Japan, Australia, Canada, many countries, but above all, America."

"Us? America?"

"Yes," said Gunther. "Peiper said they must have America and its enormous resources."

"But that means another war. We'll have to fight them again!"

"No. No war, my friend. That would be too easy...for us."

"I don't get it," cried Ernie. "How can you take over the world without war?"

"The Werewolves," said Gunther, "will escape from Germany and they and their families will start new lives in nations around the world. They will live undercover and hide their true identities. None of Hitler's mistakes, Peiper said. They plan no armies, no tanks, no planes, no bombs, no guns. At least not at first. No. Their plan is much worse. It is deeper, darker, uglier. They will be good citizens, obey the laws, work hard, raise their families, worship in churches, even in synagogues! They will rise to positions of power in business, universities, churches, governments. They will recruit like-minded people along the way. The people will come to trust them, to follow them. Then, when the Werewolves believe the time is right, they will consolidate the power the people have given them and present themselves to these same people as the saviors of the world. All strictly according to law."

"What will they do then?"

"Ach, must I draw a picture for you?"

"No," said Ernie after a pause. "But these things can never happen in America."

"Please, Ernie, please. None of your American bullshit. Your America is open, free, chaotic. America is large and there is much opportunity. The Werewolves will easily blend in. The Werewolves will run in American elections, and you Americans will vote for them. They said America is their first target. They believe it will be their easiest conquest.

"The plan goes into effect when the Russians enter Germany from the east and the Allies from the west. The Werewolves will move to secret places in the Black Forest and hide there. Major Peiper said this will happen soon, maybe in a few months.

"I must meet with the American commanders. Only they can stop this! I tell you that Goebbels' rubbish about a so-called 'alpine redoubt' is a hoax! Hans Peiper and his SS Werewolves are real, and they must be arrested or hunted down and killed before they can escape. The Americans must occupy all the Black Forest at the earliest opportunity and stop them!"

"But we are only privates in enemy armies," said Ernie. "Why would any American commander listen to us? Your story of the Werewolves, Gunther, will sound foolish to them."

"They must believe us! There is no alternative. We must try, Ernie! We—must—try."

After resting for some time, they moved on at dawn.

They continued their way through the forest and crossed a small rise in the trees. Gunther suddenly heard voices, this time not guttural spurts of his native German, but soft and flowing sounds. Gunther threw his pistol away.

About ten Frenchmen stepped out of the trees and surrounded Gunther and Ernie. Gunther raised his arms up in surrender, opting for a chance at survival rather than confrontation. Ernie trained his rifle on the men one after the other. The Frenchmen seemed unconcerned. "Ah, what do we have here?" exclaimed one of the group, apparently their leader, in English. "An American with a gun on a German soldier."

"My name is Ernie Balbach, Private First Class, American 30th Infantry Division." Ernie replied. "This man is my prisoner."

"Well, well, Ernie, my ally. We shall do you a favor and take your prisoner off your hands. Then you can go to your lines without the burden of him. We already have quite the collection."

Gunther glimpsed a French woman and a child standing behind the group. They'd sheared the woman's head, a common French resistance punishment for any adult female who consorted with the Germans. But it was the boy, probably the woman's son, who caught Gunther's attention. An ugly scar marred the boy's face.

The leader gave an order. Two Frenchmen yanked Gunther hard from behind and shoved him up against a tree. Death appeared and snickered, but Gunther ignored him. Instead, Gunther turned his head to the right to look at the boy again, then to the left where Ernie stood. He watched Ernie focus on the boy, widen his eyes in recognition, and then narrow them in revulsion, hatred, and revenge. One of the Frenchmen lifted a gun to Gunther's head. Gunther, his head swiveled to Ernie, vaguely felt the Frenchman's gun against his temple. Then he heard the French leader order the executioner to stand down. Gunther turned and looked at his would-be killer, then the leader, and then the other Frenchmen, all of whom themselves now stared, not at Gunther, but at Ernie, and at the boy.

"You goddamn little French sonofabitch!" Ernie screamed. "You got them killed!" Ernie dropped the Beretta, lifted the M1, and ran to the woman and boy. Gunther saw the boy's face change from worry to recognition to terror. Ernie stopped about ten feet from the boy and shot him in the stomach. The mother screamed and threw herself on her son. Gunther saw Ernie run to the mother, grab her arm, yank her off the boy, and shoot her through the head. Ernie held the M1 muzzle inches from the boy's face. The boy tried to scream but couldn't. Ernie waited for ten seconds, pulled the trigger, and then stepped to the side and dry-heaved.

Later, Gunther would ask himself why he didn't escape in all the confusion caused by Ernie. He could have. He was certain of it. Instead, Gunther walked with the Frenchmen to the bodies, and then to Ernie, who stood shaking and sobbing, and held Ernie in his arms. Gunther lowered Ernie to the ground, sat beside him, and whispered in his ear.

The French leader turned to Ernie, then Gunther, and then to the woman and boy before making his decision. He ordered his men to bury the bodies and left two men behind to watch over Gunther, still rocking Ernie in his arms. A number of minutes passed as the men dug into the ground with their hand spades. In that time, Ernie stopped crying and his shaking decreased. Ernie stood, swayed a few times, and coughed. This got the French leader's attention from supervising the digging. Ernie motioned him over.

"Thi...this...man...his name is Gunther. Balbach. Gunther Balbach," Ernie managed. "He... is my prisoner. But he is also my friend." Ernie swallowed several times. "Yesterday, the SS captured my patrol and...and executed...all of 'em. But me—I got away. This man saved me from the SS three times, each time at great risk to himself."

"The SS? How can this be?" asked the leader.

"Don't matter," Ernie replied in a stronger voice. "You must take my word for it. Gunther has information on the plans of the SS for after the war. We must get him through the American lines so he can brief the American commanders."

"Why did you kill the boy and his mother?"

"That boy got my patrol killed," said Ernie. "We'd hidden from the enemy and might have escaped. The boy and his friends found us and turned us over to the SS."

"I see." The French leader smiled. "Revenge. It is good! My name is Jacques. We are La Resistance."

"We understand," said Ernie, still shaking. "Can you help me help my friend?"

Jacques turned to his men and they spoke in French for several minutes. Then he turned back to Gunther and Ernie and said in English, "Your friend Gunther, as you call him, is a German soldier and should be shot. But he is also a brave man, and maybe a good man if any such German exists. We believe you, Ernie. We will finish the burials. Then my men and I will accompany you and him to the American lines."

Chapter 5

The American MP led Gunther from the stockade to a fenced-in interrogation area. Gunther smiled when Ernie rose from the wooden bench to shake hands. It was the first Gunther had seen of his American cousin in days. They sat side-by-side at one of the tables in the area.

"Gunther, I got a promotion, and you got a new job," said Ernie, speaking in German. "I'm an official interpreter for the 30th Division, United States Army, and you will be my assistant."

The French resistance leader had been true to his word. Three days ago, Gunther, his hands on his head, marched with Ernie into the American lines. By then, the 2nd Battalion had fought its way out of the encirclement into the arms of the American 35th Division, and safety. The MPs on the hill took Gunther into custody before Ernie could escort him to the battalion command post. Ernie protested, but the MPs, including one called Frenchie, ignored him. As the MPs led Gunther away, laughing and kicking at him, Gunther eyed Ernie, who nodded, I'll do my best, Gunther.

"I have a question, Ernie. You told Jacques that I saved you from the SS three times. How—how did you know?"

Ernie smiled. "I suspected, but wasn't sure until just now. You saved me in the tree and again at the bonfire. However, when you searched me, you felt the gun in my pocket but didn't take it away from me. The gun saved my life. I thank you, Gunther. I... I owe you a lot."

Gunther smiled back. "Ach, Ernie, I only wish your aim at Peiper would have been better."

"So do I."

Gunther watched Ernie rise, walk to the fence, and stand there. After a few minutes, Ernie walked back, took his seat beside Gunther, and looked down, his elbows on his knees.

"Gunther, I tried," Ernie whispered to the ground.

"What happened?"

"I found the 30th Division headquarters in a farmhouse about two miles north of here. I told the sentries that I had to see the division commander on urgent business. An hour later they escorted me inside. I spent approximately five minutes with the general and his adjutant."

"And?"

"I told them about you, the Werewolves, and Peiper. They didn't believe me. The adjutant said your information is inaccurate. He said they are well aware of the SS's intentions and that the SS would be fools to rendezvous in the Black Forest. The pompous bastard told me the Black Forest is much too obvious and the SS much too smart to congregate there."

"The alpine redoubt?" asked Gunther.

"Yeah."

"They are fooled by Goebbels, then," said Gunther.

They both stared at the ground.

"The bastards!" exclaimed Ernie. "They told me not to worry, that General Patton and the 3rd Army will find and kill any SS who try to escape to the mountains. After all we'd been through, Gunther! It was for nothing!"

"You did your best, Ernie. That is all any man can do."

Ernie raised his head and turned to Gunther. "What happens if your best isn't good enough?"

When their time outside wrapped up, Ernie and the MP Frenchie escorted Gunther back to the stockade.

"This man's name is Gunther Balbach," said Ernie to Frenchie. "I want you to take good care of him."

"Why?" asked Frenchie, a half-head taller than Ernie. "He's just a Kraut. We got thousands of 'em. Ain't none of 'em get special treatment in my book."

"Where you from?" Ernie demanded.

"New York," said Frenchie, "and damn proud of it!"

"Look, you goddamn high-talking baton-twirling sonofabitch!" Ernie exclaimed. "My name is Ernie Balbach, PFC, 30th Infantry Division, 120th Regiment, 2nd Battalion. Yeah, I was on Hill 314. Don't remember seeing your ass there. This man's my cousin, and he saved my life."

Gunther saw the MP back away a few steps, and Ernie walk two steps towards him.

"I'm now an interpreter and Gunther is my assistant. Show you the orders if you don't believe it."

"Listen here, pipsqueak," said Frenchie, "I'll look after this bastard because it's my job, and not because some midget asshole's telling me. Got it?"

"You sonofabitch," said Ernie, "I know your kind. You ain't never had a bullet snap an inch from your ear. You sit back here on your fat MP ass and lord it over everybody. Your name ain't Frenchie to me. It's Chicken shit. And know what else? My buddies—the ones who made it alive off Hill 314—know about this particular Kraut here, and they know what he's done to save me. If you don't treat him like King Fuckin' Solomon, I'll pass the word to them. And some night, you'll be alone. You might be takin' a shit in the latrine. Or maybe you're tight and staggerin' home after a few too many. Don't matter. You'll just disappear. Into thin air. They'll look for you, but they won't find you. Then your mama'll get a telegram that says something like 'missing in action and presumed dead.' Am I gettin' through to you, you pansy-ass?"

Gunther hid his smile.

"Balbach, you and your mouth are coming damn close to gettin' you arrested. I'm warnin' you."

"Fuck you," said Ernie. "Go ahead and arrest me. I'll take the fuckin' stockade over the fightin' any day. I saw you kick and slap

Gunther when I brought him in. So I'm tellin' you now. If Gunther's hungry, you get him food. If he's thirsty, you get him water. If he wants his uniform pressed, you iron it. If he says 'shit,' you say 'what color?' If he says 'jump,' you say 'how high?' And you make sure all the other chicken shit limp-wrists in this place get the message. If they don't, I'll hold you responsible, and your mama'll get that telegram."

Frenchie didn't have anything to say to Ernie after that, but the message hit home. When it was mealtime for the German prisoners, Gunther stood in the chow line and grinned at Frenchie, who glared back at him. Gunther's grin widened. He nodded at Frenchie as if to say, Ernie's dead serious about his threats. You cannot touch me. Frenchie just glared at him even more.

Gunther took his tray of food, sat down, and started eating. Death popped up and sat next to him.

Death: Go ahead, laugh at Frenchie. Have your fun. Doesn't change anything. I sometimes lose, but I always win. You're now on my special target list. I'll visit you from time-to-time. And the last time I visit, you'll lose.

Gunther: I am hungry. I shall eat. And you cannot stop me.

PART 2

Chapter 6

Tim Balbach speed-shifted from third to second gear and gunned the Jeep around a sharp left curve on a switchback halfway up the mountain. The Jeep, in four wheel drive, spun all four tires to keep from sliding off the right side of the pavement into the two hundred foot drop to the mountain floor below. The road straightened and Tim up-shifted to third to gain speed for the upcoming steep hill. The Jeep's four cylinder engine wound out until its RPMs reached well into the red area of the gauge.

The Jeep said, Back off, Tim, or I may shoot one of these rods clear through the top of the front hood. Do you want that?

Tim, thrilled with the ride, the race, the rain, the slippery road, and the gray dark clouds snaking around the mountains, replied, Shoot the goddamn rod if you want to.

Tim swerved the Jeep back and forth across both lanes of the road so the smartass in the navy blue Porsche behind him couldn't pass. As the Jeep neared the top of the hill, Tim rammed the stick shift into second, this time not even bothering to depress the clutch. The gears ground until they synchronized and locked, jerking the Jeep down in speed but making it easier for Tim to hog both lanes of the highway as he reached the summit. It was a blind hill, and neither driver could see whether there was oncoming traffic. The Porsche played it safe. It settled in the right lane and dropped far behind the Jeep. Tim and his Jeep did not.

They straddled the centerline as they reached the top. If they met a vehicle traveling the other way, they would either crash head-on or the small-wheel based Jeep would flip and roll when Tim tried to whip it into the right lane. The road dropped steeply, and the Jeep lifted all four tires off the road to jump into the air. "We're flying!" roared Tim to the Jeep.

But Jeeps weren't built to fly. Or land.

The Jeep's right wheels crashed onto the road, its left wheels still in the air. Tim pushed the clutch, which disengaged the motor from the tires. He wheeled right to stop the rollover and brought the left wheels down. By then the Jeep was headed off the right side of the road toward the drop beyond. Tim popped the clutch, wheeled left, and slammed the accelerator to the floor. The front wheels grabbed the pavement, pulled the Jeep back onto the road, and straightened it in its lane with the help of a few more skillful turns of the steering wheel by Tim. But the race couldn't last. The Porsche approached, then backed away, waited until a truck and two cars going the opposite direction cleared, and then easily passed Tim. Tim gave the Porsche driver the finger. The Porsche pulled away and eventually disappeared in the hills, rain, and fog.

Tim lost the race with the Porsche, but that was okay. For the first time in months he felt alive, almost happy, as the scenes played out his action role in Tim and Jeep Versus the Road and Mountains and Rain and Fog and then, even better, Tim and Jeep Versus the Porsche and Smartass. These scenes pushed away the other scenes, the "haunts," as Tim told his shrink at Landstuhl Hospital.

Tim was driving across the Palatinate to visit his "uncle" Gunny Balbach in Mannheim. Tim hadn't seen Gunny since he abruptly left Dubain in 1960. Tim had part of the story from snippets he'd picked up over the years from his mom and dad, Maymie and Ernie Balbach. In 1944, Gunther Balbach, a German regular under the command of the German SS in France, along with several German divisions attacked the American 30th Infantry Division, Tim's dad's division, at Mortain. Somehow, Ernie took Gunther prisoner and, because they looked alike and had the same last name, discovered they were fourth cousins. After the war, in 1948, Gunny moved from Germany to Dubain with the help of Tim's parents. Gunny married Mary June Schmitt and they had a son, Henry, in 1956. Then, in 1960, Gunny abandoned Mary June and Henry, left Dubain, and returned to Germany. Mary June turned to the bottle at the desertion of her husband. She lost her job, and then her house. In 1963, Tim's parents fixed up the basement in their home and allowed Mary June and Henry to live there rent free. However, Maymie told Tim in her letters to Da Nang that Mary June now spent some of her time at Piankashaw Rock drinking with Tim's dad and the other Piankashaw drunks. Henry had left the basement and now shared a bedroom with Joey, Tim's younger brother, on the top floor.

Tim had started his trip from Landstuhl, located on the western edge of the Palatinate Forest, about an hour ago. The Palatinate was a low mountain area that Tim estimated to be about twenty-file miles wide as the crow flies from Landstuhl to Bad Durkheim, a town on its eastern edge. He drove on Landstuhl Road L395 to Kaiserlautern, then turned onto Road 37. Road 37 meandered through the Palatinate to Bad Durkheim, then took a mostly straight course fifteen miles east to Mannheim. Tim would meet Gunny at 1900 hours that evening, so he had plenty of time. Tim planned it that way so he could have fun with the Jeep and mountains, grab a few drinks along the way, and maybe see a pretty girl or two.

Tim saddened at the thought that looking at a woman was the best he could do for now. It wasn't something he wanted to dwell on, let alone talk about. When Tim's shrink had asked Tim about girlfriends, Tim clammed up and the session ended early. The hospital had granted Tim leave and assigned him the Jeep from the motor pool on the advice of Tim's shrink. "Timmy is not a danger to himself or anyone else," the shrink said. Tim smiled while remembering the shrink's words but swallowed a bitter laugh, which moved deep inside to that secret and desperate place known only to him and unapproachable to anyone else.

Tim stopped at Bad Durkheim at a bierstube along Road 37 because he saw the blue Porsche he'd raced earlier parked in front. The jarring aroma of strong and bitter coffee intertwined with stale beer struck Tim as he entered the bierstube. Tim eyed the Porsche driver at a small table, a newspaper in his hands and a stein of beer and cup of coffee beside him. Tim studied Porsche Man for a moment. He was between twenty-five and thirty, blond, and about six inches taller and forty pounds heavier than Tim. The man wore an expensive suit and exuded the quiet confidence of muscularity tinged with self-discipline. Tim passed the table, sat at the bar, and ordered a double schnapps neat from the elderly bartender.

Tim sipped his drink, turned to Porsche Man, and on a hunch said in English, "You drive a nice car, sir. But I suggest you take lessons driving a Jeep."

The man looked up and smiled at Tim. "I admire your driving," he said back in a thick German accent.

"You're pissed, aren't you," Tim said, "because an American and his Jeep got the best of you and your fancy ass Porsche."

"Nein, I am quite happy."

"About what?"

"Sir American soldier, I thank you to enjoy your drink so that I can drink my beer and coffee and read this newspaper." Porsche Man smirked a bit and raised his glass in Tim's direction before returning to his paper.

You German sonofabitch, Tim thought. You're not about to get the best of me. "We Americans beat the piss out of you Germans twice in twenty-seven years. I'm a US Marine. Semper Fi. And I can kick the shit out of every German in this bar, you especially. You Germans are good at bullying weaker people, but you aren't worth a shit at true courage."

"You Americans confuse courage with lunacy, as you did back there." Porsche Man thumbed over his shoulder, pointing west on Road 37.

"We may be loony," Tim replied, "but we're here now, protecting your sorry German asses from the Russians."

"You fought in Vietnam, yes? Sir American soldier?"

Tim stiffened at the comment. "That's none of your damn business."

"Ah, so you were there."

"Fuck you, Hitler."

"Ach, you Americans are lawless," replied the German. "It is forbidden to talk about that man in Germany."

"I'll talk about that sonofabitch anytime and anywhere I want."

"As you wish, friend." The German turned away and went back to his coffee and paper.

Tim drank the remainder of his schnapps in two gulps, paid the bartender, and walked out. He couldn't wait to get back onto the open road.

Tim parked in front of Apartment 13, 4545 West Kurpfalzstrabe, Mannheim. He exited the Jeep, sniffed the raw air, and scanned the heavily overcast sky. He tossed his cigarette in the gutter and crossed the street towards Gunny's apartment. Just then, three young men, all about Tim's age, walked by on the sidewalk.

One of them said, "Amerikaner, du machst Deutschland schmutzig mit deine zigarette."

Tim glared back at his Jeep, which must have been a dead giveaway for being an American. He didn't need this. All he wanted was to meet his uncle. He pointed at the German. "To hell with Deutschland and you. Deutschland is already dirty."

The three turned and approached Tim. Another threatened, "Sonofabitch Amerikaner GI."

"Nein GI!" retorted Tim, pointing at his uniform. "Unites States Marine Corps."

The second German asked, "Chicago gangster?"

The other Germans laughed. They dared to laugh at him after everything Germany had done? Tim couldn't imagine ever laughing again, not after what he'd seen in Vietnam.

"Go to hell," said Tim. "Why don't you kill—toten—Juden?"

"Amerikaner, Ich bin Juden," said the third German, pointing to himself. Gently, he added, "Vietnam?"

Tim thought he heard some kind of sympathy in the German's tone. No way was he going to accept any sympathy from a country of mass murderers, especially from one of its would-be victims. Tim raised his arms and went into the Marine hand-to-hand fight stance. He'd fight every one of them to prove he wasn't one of them.

"Ja," said the first German. "Verruckt!" They laughed but came no closer to Tim.

Just then, Gunny Balbach emerged from his apartment. He walked to Tim and grinned. "Ah, Timmy Balbach! It's so nice to see you. Come in. Please."

His English was still as good as the last time Tim saw him, and it was a comfort to hear his native language spoken by a German. Gunny motioned the three young men to move away down the street, and then he gently turned Tim and led him into the apartment. He motioned for the three young men to move away down the street. Gunny ushered Tim into his apartment and shut the door after him.

"Timmy, take a seat and relax. Can I get you coffee? A drink?"

"I'll have both. Schnapps, neat."

Gunny went to the kitchen, and Tim slumped into one of two easy chairs near a small coffee table. He tried to ease his anger by looking around Gunny's living room. It was small, probably wouldn't fit the two men comfortably for long, but it was tidy. Gunny's bookcases took up half the space. One light by the door cast shadows on the few pieces of furniture in the rest of the room. His uncle lived light with few mementos or clutter. Tim did notice a photo of Mary June Balbach and Henry on a table stand in one corner of the room. He thought the photo looked recent but couldn't be sure. He'd been away from home too long.

Gunny returned with the coffee and two drinks. He set the drinks on the table by Tim and sat in the chair opposite him. "I was surprised when you called, Tim. What can I do for you?"

"I need your help, Uncle Gunny."

"For what, Timmy?"

Tim hesitated. He threw back the schnapps and waited for the burning taste to reach his stomach before he picked up the mug of coffee and took a sip.

"To save my family. Save my dad. Me."

"From what? Whom?"

"War. Wars, Uncle Gunny."

"Timmy, what do you mean by, 'wars?'" Gunny switched on the lamp beside his chair.

"Turn that off," commanded Tim.

"Why? It's dark in here."

"I like the dark," replied Tim. They settled on turning on a small nightlight by Gunny's chair. The dim shadows it cast would allow Tim to hide in them if he felt the need to.

"Tim, start at the beginning."

"My dad's drinking got worse and worse after you left Dubain. Mom and I could do nothing with him. Dad and Mom fought all the time. Weekends were pure hell because Dad would be drunk and nasty from Friday afternoon until Monday morning. Sometimes longer. Holidays—Thanksgiving and Christmas—were worse. Dad got mean, and I mean real mean."

"How mean?"

"Well, I can put it this way. One time he pushed Mom so hard she fell and hit her head on the floor. She was knocked out and bleeding bad. I drove her to the emergency room where they stitched her head and diagnosed a slight concussion. We made up a story that she'd slipped and fallen down the basement steps.

"After this, when Dad got drunk, I stepped in front of him so he wouldn't hurt Mom or Joey. I'd take the blows from his fists."

"I'm sorry to hear this, Tim. I'm quite fond of your dad and mom."

"Sorry? Fond? Is that all you can say, Uncle Gunny? After all this time? Goddammit it all to hell!"

"Calm, Junge."

"I want another schnapps," Tim demanded. "Make it a double."

"Timmy, I think it's best that you drink your coffee and—"

"Uncle Gunny, if you won't fix me a drink I have a bottle in the Jeep and I'll just get that." Tim rose halfway out of his seat.

"Easy, Timmy. I'll get the drink."

Gunny returned to the kitchen, but by then Tim started feeling restless. He rose, moved to Gunny's bookcase, and started to search it.

Gunny returned with the schnapps. "Timmy, are you looking for something?"

"Yeah. Looking for your guns."

"Why?" asked Gunny.

"Everybody's got guns. I feel better if I know where they're at," Tim replied.

"I have guns, Tim, but they're not on the bookcase. Now you sit and calm down. If I have to get a gun, I will. Are we clear?"

"Yeah." Tim sat. "Loud and clear."

"Now go on."

Tim lit a crinkled cigarette he pulled from his pocket. "Many times, when he got drunk, Dad would go to the garage, sit on a stack of old tires he keeps there, and cry. I'd sometimes spy on him, and it'd always be the same. Dad would rub and bang his head with his hands while he bawled his eyes out. Like there was something in him that he was trying to get out but couldn't. But, he—Dad—wasn't there. In the garage, I mean. He'd go to another place in his head. A few times I tried to talk to him but I might as well have not been there. He'd mumble things. Really bizarre shit. He'd scream the same stuff at night. The strangest part is, you couldn't tell whether he was awake or having a nightmare."

"What stuff?" Gunny asked, just like how the shrink had prodded Tim on when he'd brought up his father.

"He'd jumble the words like he was dreaming, and I couldn't hear him clearly, but always certain things came through: 'Mortain.' 'Peiper fucker.' 'Jimmy, die.' 'Jimmy, go away.' Then other stuff: 'Mortain scar boy.' 'You killed Hightower.' 'Haircut the frog bitch.' 'Three-fourteen hills at Mortain.' 'Cut off.' 'Fire burn the meat.' 'Shoot 'em off the hill.' Then always, 'Kill, kill, kill.' 'I kill you killin' me.' It goes on and on."

Gunny stuffed his pipe with tobacco and lit it. Then he rose, walked to the window on the other side of the bookcase, and stared outside, puffing on his pipe. Tim lit another cigarette and took a long drag.

"Something happened at Mortain, didn't it, Uncle Gunny?

Something more than Dad taking you prisoner and making it back to the American lines. I need to know."

It was why he'd traveled so far. That need consumed him, but Gunny just stared out the window, silent.

Chapter 7

"I'm right, aren't I?"

Gunny turned his head away from the window. "It's raining again, Timmy."

"So?"

"The temperature is dropping and turning the rain into sleet and snow. It's best that you return to Landstuhl before the roads freeze over."

"I have two days' leave, Uncle Gunny."

"Ah, I see."

"See what?"

"Timmy, there's a nice little bed and breakfast one half kilometer north of Road 37 in Grethen, just on the other side of Bad Durkheim. You can stay there tonight. It's warm and cozy, and the proprietor has a daughter. You could meet her."

"I can't be with a woman. I mean, just now."

"Why not?"

"It's not like I haven't tried. The guys even took me to a... Look, I don't want to talk about it, okay? Shouldn't have even mentioned it."

"Ah, I see." Gunny's forehead wrinkled and he ran his hand through his thinning hair several times. Gunny's pipe smoke and Tim's cigarette smoke curled upwards and merged near the ceiling. Sleet and rain beat on the roof, and the wind, now gusting, whistled through the gables.

"What happened at Mortain, Uncle Gunny?"

Gunny looked away from the window towards the bookcase as though he, this time, was the one searching for something. Then he turned, walked back to his chair, and sat.

"Tim. Let the past go. Let it lie. Do not wake these sleeping dogs. They are not nice dogs."

"They're already awake! My dad lives under Piankashaw Rock, Uncle Gunny. You know the place. It's in the forest. It's where my grandpa lived and then killed himself. Two days before I left for the Marines, I moved Dad there and told him to stay until I got back. He cried, Gunny. Mom cried. I cried. But I had no choice! I had to get him away from Mom and Joey because I wouldn't be there to protect them from him. I'll ask again. What happened at Mortain?" Tim almost pleaded. "I have to know!"

"Why?"

"I don't know why! I just do!"

"Did you ever ask your father to tell you about it?"

"Yeah. Once. He slapped me then got real drunk and the shit hit the fan. Do I have to draw you a picture?"

"You were in Vietnam."

"Yeah. How did you know?"

"Never mind that. What was your job?"

"Counter intelligence. Uncle Gunny, 'Nam has nothing to do with—"

"Answer my questions or you get nothing from me. Understand?" Tim nodded.

"Where were you based?"

"Da Nang, in the north."

"Have you served your tour?"

"Yeah."

"Why are you in Germany? Why aren't you discharged and at home in Dubain?"

"I'll be discharged soon."

"But still you are in Germany. There is no American Marine base near Mannheim that I know of. You are here for another reason, no?"

"Yeah. I'm training others in counter-intelligence."

"Don't lie, Timmy," said Gunther. "You're not good at it. You aren't training anybody. You're being treated at a hospital for your problems, aren't you?"

"I'm at Landstuhl."

"The American hospital," said Gunny. It wasn't a question.

Tim looked away from Gunny.

Gunny continued, "This job of yours. Tell me about it."

Tim lit another cigarette. "Uncle Gunny, forget Vietnam. Tell me about Mor—"

"Were you a rat man?"

"Do you mean tunnel rat?"

"Yes. Tunnel rat. Was that part of your job?"

"Yeah." Tim thought, I have to know about Mortain. Get it out of him one way or another.

Again Gunny rose and strolled to the window. With his back to Tim, he gently spoke. "Timmy, you carry your own war now."

"Yeah. But what does that have to do with Mortain?"

"Let me count," said Gunny. "You fight your tunnel rat war. That's one. You fight your father's war. That's two."

"I've been fighting my dad's war since I was born, Gunny. Hell, for all I know, I'm probably fighting Grandpa's war in Flanders!"

"But if I tell you about Mortain, you will take on another war. No man can fight three wars at the same time. Certainly not four, if you are fighting in Flanders, as you say."

"What is this about another war, Gunny?"

"One with an enemy that is powerful and cunning. One you can neither fight nor defeat. One you need not know about."

Tim's mouth turned to ice. "I've fought wars all my life. I'm still in Vietnam fighting the gooks. I'll never leave the fuckin' place! Do you really think I'm afraid of another enemy?"

"This is a cursed day!" cried Gunny. "It is the day I have feared. It can only be bad for you, Timmy. Bad for our families."

"All my days are cursed! You ran away. I won't."

"Do not judge me, Timmy!"

"Oh yeah?" Tim sneered. "My mom and dad helped you get out of the hellhole that was Germany in 1948. They brought you to America. To Dubain. You worked at a good job. You and Mary June married and had Henry. You bought a house, and our families were mostly happy. Then you tore ass out! I remember these things, Uncle Gunny."

"They will crush you!"

"Goddammit, Gunny, no one can crush me because I'm already crushed! You think your war was bad? Well, move over, Mister German I-Follow-Hitler-My-Precious-Fatherland-We-Kill-Millions-In-Cold-Blood-Take-Over-The-World-But-Instead-Get-Blown-To-Hell! Your war led to my war!"

"I watch Vietnam on TV."

"You don't watch shit!"

"I know more about your war than you think, Timmy."

"You know nothing about my war! Do you know that the bank foreclosed on your house? Do you know that your wife is a drunk and sometimes lives at Piankashaw Rock with Dad and the others? Do you know that your own son, Henry, lives with Joey and Mom? You abandoned them like they were so much trash and ran away without even sayin' goodbye."

"You know nothing of my reasons for leaving!"

"Then tell them to me. I got all night, Uncle Gunny."

"You are a young marine hothead, Timmy Balbach. You don't want the truth, believe me. Go home and take care of your family. Marry a pretty girl. Make babies. Live a quiet life and leave it at that. That is the best you can do."

"Uncle Gunny," Tim's voice trembled, "I've hidden a pistol in the night stand beside my bed at Landstuhl. Every minute of every day— yeah, even at night—I have to think of a reason not to put it in my mouth and pull the trigger. I do this day after fucking day. So don't you dare talk to me about watching my war on TV or living a quiet life and pretty girls and making babies. Don't you dare!"

"Timmy, the truth will get you and your family killed."

"My family? Killed?" Tim leaned forward in his chair. His head spun and the room heaved.

"You heard me. If you raise your hand against them, they will either kill you or let you live until you kill yourself out of guilt."

"Who is 'them'?"

Gunther Balbach walked to the kitchen and returned with two beers. He handed one to Tim, left the room, and walked to what Tim assumed was his bedroom or a study. Gunny returned with a holstered gun in his hand. He drew the gun, laid it and one bullet on the small table beside Tim, and then took his seat. He repacked his pipe and sipped his beer. Tim eyed the gun and the one bullet. Again the room heaved. Vomit rose in Tim's throat, but he forced it back down.

"If you want to shoot yourself, do it here. Now."

"Don't tempt me, Gunny."

"I'm not. Do it. Chamber the bullet, put the gun to the side of your head, and pull the trigger. Your life is hell, but suicide is painless, they tell me, and easy. Go ahead. Death always gets us in the end, so it does not matter. I will clean up the mess and see to it that you get a Catholic burial."

Tim kept his eye on the gun. Death was nothing in Vietnam. He'd seen plenty of it. He'd seen buddies pull the trigger against their own heads. Sometimes he wanted death, but he had to live for his family. Still, his whole body shook.

"Won't...can't do it."

"Ah, Timmy. You refuse my offer. Why?"

"My family. They need me. I have to live for them. Mom has no husband. Joey has no father. I have to get Dad out from under that rock. And I can't abandon Mary June and Henry like you did."

Gunny put his head down for a few minutes while he puffed on his pipe. Then he placed his pipe aside, straightened in his chair, raised his head, and looked at Tim through narrow, piercing eyes.

"Timothy, tell me. Vietnam. Your war, as you say. How many people did you kill?"

Tim leapt from his seat and lunged for Gunny, but the older man was faster. Gunny jumped out of his chair and Tim missed him. Before Tim could recover, Gunny placed a knee on Tim's back, twisted his arms, and forced his face into the chair stuffing.

"You sonofabitch." Tim's voice muffled against the cushion. "You bastard!" Tim struggled to get out of Gunny's grip.

"Calm down, Timmy. I won't hurt you. Easy. Easy does it, Junge. I'll let you up, but you must be peaceful. Can you do that?"

Tim tried to relax his muscles, and counted to five. "Yeah."

Gunny released Tim, who stood up. Then Gunny took Tim in his arms and hugged him.

Tim sat, put his face in his hands, and talked through them. "Why did you do that?"

"I had to know, Timmy."

"Know what?"

"Everyone has secrets," Gunny said, sitting back into his own chair. "You have a secret and when I voiced it you confirmed it. You know the truth. You tell the truth. I think I can trust you with the story of Mortain. I'll tell it, but only under one condition—a promise from you."

Tim opened his mouth to speak, but Gunny held his hand up. "Timmy, for once you must talk little and listen much. You will have questions, of course. I will answer them if I can."

Tim nodded.

"First, you can cry, Timmy. There is nothing wrong with it. I've cried—over my war and those I killed in it."

"Uncle Gunny, I don't dare cry."

"Why not, Junge? It is a harmless human emotion."

"Because if I start, I'll never stop."

"That isn't true, Timmy. Your instinct is correct. Your daddy's pain—the torment in his heart, his rage and its partners, insanity, drinking, the violence in your family—are about his war and especially what happened at Mortain, and what has happened since. Many men who experience war can put it behind them. I can mostly do so. Your daddy, whose heart is too soft, cannot."

"And my heart?" Tim looked for hope.

"Your heart is that of your daddy's. You, like he, suffer from it. You cannot control your heart, but you can choose your actions."

"Not sure what you mean. But go on."

"The war and Mortain and the events since then burden him. Most of the time his burden is pain, which he can mostly hide, and some of the time the burden is torment, which he cannot. It overwhelms him, and so he drinks to dull it. The alcohol helps for a short time, but then awakens the nasty brutish dogs. These are the dogs of war, Timmy. They force Ernie to refight his war, especially that of Mortain. It goes even further. During these times, deep deep down, your daddy hopes—maybe believes—that he can change the outcomes, that he can transform the evil of the past into good. He fights desperately to do so, but he must ultimately fail. When these spells come on him, his family and friends and all things around him become the enemy. And so there is his drunken meanness, nastiness, and fists. Ernie intends no harm. The dogs inside him do."

Tim lifted his head to speak, but Gunny held his hand up. "There is another dimension to Ernie's torment. Mortain is not only about Ernie's war and what he did in it. It's about something much worse. It's about evil."

"Evil?"

"Yes, Junge," said Gunny. "Germany has much experience in these things. For hundreds of years, Germany has both given and taken evil. America has little experience of this. Americans believe they can re-make the world as they want it. America's capacity to fathom true malice—that is, malice on a world-wide scale—is so small. Americans sing 'thine alabaster cities gleam, undimmed by human tears.' This is the America of innocence. But America is not so innocent and this torments your daddy who knows America is not so innocent because he is not innocent. There is a price for this unintended hypocrisy, and men like Ernie and so many of those who fought with him pay it.

"The price is pain and torment. It cannot be helped that some of this passes on to the families of these men. These are shadows over those we love - Maymie, Joey, Henry, Mary June. None of them understand, but you, Timmy, are catching on. You have seen true evil. You struggle to understand it but you cannot. No one can. I am German and I accept this as fate. You are American and cannot accept fate because you refuse to believe it."

Tim leaned forward in his chair. "You fought in the war, Gunny. First the Russian front, then in France. You were with Dad at Mortain. Seems to me it'd be worse for you. But you say you do not suffer because you accept it and move on."

"Mostly true. However, sometimes even I suffer. It is rare but it happens. I am luckier than your father, however. It is easier for me to accept these things because I am a native German. Germany's long history lives inside of me and mostly inoculates me against Ernie's fate, but not entirely.

"Anyway, what matters now is that I am certain of your trustworthiness. You told me everything about your war when you came at me. You held nothing back. You have your father's soft heart but your mother's deep-down toughness. You are also stubborn and bullheaded, I'm afraid. You will find it very difficult to accept the truth in Dubain. Your instinct is to fight it, which you must not do. This is where the promise comes in."

"What is it?"

"There is a man in Dubain who lives in disguise. He is at the center of your father's illness and many other terrible things. So the condition is this: You must promise me that you will never mention his name, never try to unmask his disguise, and never attempt to fight him or his confederates. Can you promise me this?"

"I do."

"Then I will tell you the story of Mortain."

Chapter 8

"The man's name is Hans Peiper," Gunny started. "Yes, it is the same Peiper that Ernie shouts in his bad times. Hans Peiper lives in Dubain in disguise. It is he who holds hostage my family and yours. It is he who forced me to leave Dubain. It is he who blackmails your father into silence. And it is he who will destroy you and your family if you give him the slightest reason. Peiper has allies in Dubain. Some are spies, others are henchmen who enforce Peiper's orders. Peiper watches our families always because we are a danger to him. Indeed, your dad will not move home when you return to Dubain. Shortly after you left for the Marines, Peiper forbade your father to ever leave Piankashaw Rock."

Tim wondered how Gunny, thousands of miles away, would know something like that, but what Gunny said about spies concerned him even more. "This man—Peiper—has this kind of power?" Tim asked.

"He certainly does," said Gunny. "You find this incredible, and that is understandable."

"Well," said Tim. "If it's true, I owe you an apology for accusing you of running away."

"No apology is necessary. I would have concluded the same were I in your position. But there's more that you must be aware of. I'm certain Peiper watches you even now, here in Germany."

"Why?"

"Because he no doubt considers you a threat to his plans. You are intelligent, battle tested, and not easily scared or bluffed."

"How can—"

"A spy, Timmy," Gunny interjected. "Right here in Germany. This person no doubt is very good at his job and watches you intimately, but from a distance, and reports your activities in Germany to Peiper."

Tim thought about all the people he'd been in contact with in Germany: his shrink, the staffers at the hospital, people he'd talked to on the road. "This spy," said Tim, "I think I've met him. Tall, blond, muscular guy. Drives a late model navy blue Porsche."

"You've seen him?"

"Yeah. We raced in the Palatinate. Then I mouthed off to him in a bar in Bad Durkheim."

"Well, then, Timmy, you are in elite company," said Gunny. "I happen to know this man also spies on me!"

For the first time all evening, the men laughed.

"Do you know his name or where he lives?" Tim asked.

"Neither, Timmy."

"When Peiper finds out I visited you, Uncle Gunny, why wouldn't he think we're plotting against him? Aren't we putting our families in even more danger?"

"No," said Gunny. "You and I have a common past in America, and it just so happens that Landstuhl is near Mannheim. To them, your presence here is only a social visit between friends. I am certain the spy will so report our meeting to Hans Peiper, who will come to that conclusion. If I had felt otherwise, I would have forbidden your visit when you phoned me from Landstuhl."

Gunny went on. "I and about twenty other Wehrmacht soldiers were attached to the Waffen SS unit commanded by Major Hans Peiper. The high command ordered us to Mortain to attack the American 30th Division, your dad's division, which was outside Mortain and on the verge of taking it. We attacked with four divisions, two of them Panzer armored divisions. Our first and most important objective was Hill 314, located to the northeast of Mortain. Why? Because it was high ground from which spotters for the army that held it could direct artillery fire on the army that did not. Your dad's 2nd Battalion held Hill 314 and, of course, directed American artillery on our positions. We surrounded the hill and cut the battalion off from the rest of the 30th Division and the American army. We attacked the 2nd Battalion on Hill 314 with every tank, armored car, and soldier we could get. We outnumbered the Americans by at least ten to one. The battalion's position was hopeless, but it turned down our surrender demands. Ernie later told me that the American command had ordered the battalion to hold the hill at all costs."

"I know what 'all costs' implies. Your life is less important than the objective. Your government considers you expendable and tells you point-blank."

"Yes." Gunny nodded.

"Go on."

"During a lull in the fighting, the Americans sent a patrol, which included Ernie, to reconnoiter the bottom of Hill 314. We spotted the patrol, which then hid in the woods. Several local French boys, whose families were loyal to the Germans, helped us find the Americans. A boy with a scar on his face found Ernie and two others hiding behind an uprooted tree. They were the last to be taken prisoner. We marched the Americans to a clearing in the woods and searched and disarmed them. I saw that Ernie resembled me, so I personally searched him and stayed close to him as we waited for our SS commanders to arrive. We traded backgrounds and found that we were related. It was then that I warned him."

"About what?" Tim asked.

"The SS," Gunny replied. "Timmy, SS Major Hans Peiper seldom took prisoners."

"Just like the fucking VC."

"A short time later the scar-face boy and his friends walked into the clearing. Scarface pointed at your dad and led the others in jeering at him and the other American prisoners. Then Fritz Stresseman, Major Peiper's adjutant, ordered us to line up the American prisoners for execution. It was then that the weasel-eyed Stresseman saw that Ernie and I looked alike and discovered that we had the same last name, Balbach.

"Major Peiper arrived with the rest of his SS command. With no warning, he killed the first American in Ernie's line with two shots to the back of the head. Ernie was third or fourth in line.

"However, for some reason Peiper spotted Ernie and walked to him instead of shooting the next American in line. Peiper and Ernie carried on a very strange conversation, given the circumstances. Peiper and your dad first spoke in German, then switched to English. Maybe this was part of Peiper's plan. I cannot say. Peiper was well aware that many American soldiers spoke German because they were descendants of German immigrants to America.

"I'd seen and heard Peiper so speak with other American soldiers in France. This time was different, however. At Peiper's order, your dad told him the name of his hometown, Dubain, Indiana. Peiper seemed fascinated by Dubain and interrogated Ernie about it. Was it a German settled town? How many in Dubain spoke German? Where was Dubain located? Was it clean, did it have sports facilities, did any Jews or negroes live there, and so on.

"Ernie gathered the courage to ask Peiper to release the remaining—that is, living—Americans into German captivity. Peiper considered Ernie's request, but then turned it down. He ordered Ernie to step forward for his execution."

"Did my dad say anything?"

"Not a word. Instead, he pulled a pistol from his pocket, shot Stresseman dead, and then shot Peiper in the shoulder."

Tim smiled and imagined his father as the hero of the moment, not the broken alcoholic living back home at Piankashaw Rock.

"The Americans broke and ran. Some, including Ernie, made it into the woods. We rounded up all the Americans except your dad. Peiper and the SS shot them and then went in search of Ernie."

"Just a minute," Tim broke in. "You said you searched Dad for weapons when you took him prisoner. How did you miss the gun he was carrying?"

"I didn't, Timmy."

"What were you thinking?"

"I'll get to that, Timmy. Let's not jump ahead. Okay?"

"Okay."

"Your dad climbed to the top of a very large oak tree and hid there. One of the Americans, Jimmy Franken, was badly wounded but somehow made it to the base of the same tree. We found him there."

"Is this the Jimmy Dad rants about?"

"Yes, Timmy. Jimmy was a Jew. One of the Americans hoped to seek favor and told an SS soldier about Franken. Peiper was with us when we found Jimmy. He ordered us to stand Jimmy against a tree and shoot him."

"How many shot Jimmy?" asked Tim.

"Four."

"Were you one of the four?"

"Yes."

"How old was Jimmy?"

"Eighteen, your father later told me."

Tim lit a cigarette and Gunny went on. "Major Peiper had a hunch that Ernie was in the tree because we found Jimmy lying at its base. Peiper ordered us to shoot up into the tree to kill Ernie. We did, but Ernie had scrunched his body on a thick limb and was protected from the bullets. I learned this a few minutes later."

"How?"

"Peiper ordered me to climb the tree to find your dad. Ernie and I met face-to-face in the tree, but I kept this a secret. In whispers and in sign language, I told Ernie to meet me near the clearing after dark and to take me prisoner. We made our way back to the clearing with Jimmy's body. The major ordered us to toss Jimmy and the other dead Americans on the French farmers' brush pile.

"I'd seen the Waffen SS's treachery many times, so I watched events very carefully. A truck engine started in the distance, so I sneaked into the woods and hid behind a large tree. It took some time for the truck to find its way into the clearing.

"I saw the truck enter the clearing, turn around, back towards the brush pile, and stop. Then a machine gunner pulled the curtain to one side, opened fire, and killed the German regulars. I could only watch."

"They killed their own soldiers to eliminate witnesses to their murders."

"Of course. Peiper was cruel but smart. He saw that Germany would lose the war and there would be retribution afterwards. This is the reason he tried so hard to kill Ernie and me. We were the last witnesses to his execution of the Americans.

"The SS tossed the dead Germans on the brush pile with the dead Americans, poured gasoline on all of them, and lit the fire. Mein Gott! The stench of burning human bodies! Peiper and his men toasted each other with a bottle of liquor while they watched the fire do its work. I cannot put into words the looks on their faces as they watched. All this time I was searching for Ernie in the dark. I found him just in time."

"Just in time for what?"

"I fear telling you this, Timmy, but you want all the truth and maybe you can make sense of it. Ernie was staring at the fire, but it was his eyes. His eyes, Timmy! They were the same as those of the others—Peiper and his men—who watched the fire offer its sacrifice and fulfill its purpose. I, too, felt the forces, the powers that had taken over their minds, their souls. It was a sensation of revelation, of clarity, that I experienced only that one time, and I know with certainty that only another German soul can ponder or even glimpse such a thing. Ernie had a piece of that soul in him. I resisted. Your father could not."

"His eyes?"

"Ernie's eyes blazed, not in reflection of the fire, but from a force that welled up deep inside of him. The force wound its way through the trees to the clearing and into the bowels of the fire, and then from the flames back to Ernie. It was a tightening band of annealing steel that wrapped around the fire and Ernie, calling them to unite and compelling them to do so. The fire could not move, so the force was pulling your dad from the safety of the woods to it, and certain death. Major Peiper and his men would not have offered Ernie a drink from the bottle.

"Timmy, forgive me, for I fail with the words. There probably are none for this, and those that I have just get in the way. But words are all that I have! It flashed before me in panoramic view. The fire and your dad, then even I—yes me!—reached back across centuries, millennia, to a time when great primeval forests populated with hooded, terrifying beings covered Germany. The hooded ones chanted in a strange language before great bonfires they had built in the forests. Druids, I believe they are called. On these fires they burned alive animals and humans as sacrifices to their gods. I myself felt the call of the flames and am sure they would have taken me had I not deliberately averted my eyes away from them.

"I reached Ernie just as he began walking towards the inferno and certain death. I grabbed his arm and handled him rather roughly to bring him back to his senses. He turned his head towards me and asked for my help. We moved deep into the woods and spent the night there."

Tim lifted his head and raised his eyes to Gunny. "You felt this thing?"

"Yes, Junge."

"But...Dad...you say he felt it also?"

"Yes. Ernie so admitted it to me later."

Tim stared at the floor. But for the sleet, rain, and wind, all was silent for a time. Then Tim looked up at Gunny. "I know about the fire and the smell. War is fire, and Vietnam is war. Sometimes, it seemed all of Vietnam was on fire, but I watched only a small part of the flames and pushed the rest out of my vision. I don't know why I'm telling you this. It has nothing to do with Mortain."

"Timmy, your Vietnam fires have everything to do with Mortain. I've been trying to impress you with this. Vietnam and Mortain are joined together. You, your dad, I, and other unlucky souls sense the union of war and fire. The rest of the world does not. They are the happy ones, and we the sad.

"You gave your promise, and I expect you to keep it. However, Timmy, I fear—I fear greatly—that someday the fire will again rise and confront you. Evil will open an infinitesimally small window to the universe for an infinitesimally small moment, at a time and place not of your choosing, and enter the world. It will gift you your own bonfire. The flames, like those at Mortain, will burn high with the magnificence and lusciousness of a wood nymph, which you will see, but with the darkness and evil of Satan, which you will not. If it comes, you must resist it."

Gunny rocked back and forth in his chair, moving for the first time in what seemed like hours. "That is enough of Mortain for tonight. It is late and the alcohol has its effect on me and, I see, on you. We must rest. Tomorrow, we take up the rest of the story."

Chapter 9

Gunny and Tim sat at a booth in one of Gunny's favorite Mannheim cafes. The snow and sleet had ended and the sun shone into the cafe from a clear blue sky. Gunny read the morning papers but perceived Tim's mood. His depression wanted nothing of sunny days. Tim kept his head down and his eyes hidden behind his sunglasses.

Gunny finished the paper and folded it on the table. Tim ate the rest of his ham and eggs, poured more coffee for him and Gunny, and lit a cigarette. How can I help him? Gunny asked himself. How can I tell him that from certain kinds of calamity there is no returning? Timmy, you will go home but never entirely get there. You will force your family to travel to and partake of your dark places. You will try to stop this, but you cannot. You will confront strange thoughts and hide them at all costs from your family. They must not see the apparition, the ghoul, that was you in Vietnam. You will confront histories—yours and those of others—and these will overpower you and cause you to care too deeply and well past the point of futility. You will think: I don't want my brother to enter the tunnel and stick a knife into the VC guerilla lurking there and see men's privates get blown off by VC mortars. I don't want my family to fight at Mortain and see murder and fire. I don't want my cousin, Henry, to land at Omaha beach and brush against dead men when he wades to shore. I don't want my mother to turn on flame-throwers and burn the enemy to death in the caves at Okinawa. I don't want Joey and Henry to have to piss on their machine guns so they can keep firing them in the terrible cold at the Chosin Reservoir.

And you, Timmy, Gunny thought, will soon discover that you will not get your daddy back from Piankashaw.

Timmy, Gunny wanted so much to say out loud but dared not, the veteran is helpless because he has to live, and a good part of his life is the calamity, the illness, the fire. These are a virus inside you. You will keep the virus mostly at bay but never defeat it because it so often mutates. And when it does, it will not offer you the flu or pneumonia. These are too easy. It will instead hand you the booze, drugs, cold, flashbacks, nightmares, and the anger, rage, confusion, and bitterness. It infects you now, thought Gunny, and explains the nervous flashing of your eyes that I can make out behind your sunglasses. This cafe is warm and safe and we both know it. Yet you watch for the disguised guerilla with a hidden AK-47, for the live grenade rolling between the tables, for the terrorist with the hidden bomb. Timmy, I also have the virus, and it has just this second mutated.

Death: Hello, Gunny. It's been a long time.

Gunny: Almost twenty-four years.

Death: You know that time means nothing to me. I follow your war, Gunny. Even now, I see you and Ernie and the armies at Mortain. I followed them to you yesterday when you dared speak of Mortain with Timmy.

Gunny: What—or who—do you want?

Death: I want you to choose.

Gunny: Choose what?

Death: Between the families and you.

Gunny: You bastard!

Death: Be careful of your language, Gunny. Eternity and Judgment can be your lot at any time, especially since I'm back.

Gunny: Stay away from my family, Death. You can have me.

Tim raised his head. "Gunny, you just said 'death' aloud. What the hell?"

"Nothing to worry about, Timothy. I was just thinking about the autobahn car crash in the paper. Three people were killed. It saddens me, I guess."

Death: Ah, Gunny, you try to protect Timmy from me. It is futile, you know. He's already seen me in his war.

Gunny: Of course he has. You deal with me and let him alone.

Death: You have chosen yourself over your family. However, it is not that easy. You foolishly trust Timmy. He will return home, he will uncover Hans Peiper, and he will fight. I will harvest many Balbachs. But even I must have amusement. So here is my real proposition: I promise to not bother the Balbach families so long as you are alive.

Gunny: You are but a figment of my imagination.

Death: You don't believe that and we both know it. But remember this: The past is past and now is now. You and the American Balbachs are Peiper's unfinished business. Others pressure Peiper to kill the Balbachs, but Peiper has thus far refused. Timmy will act rashly and force Peiper to act. You are alone and thousands of miles from Dubain. Your murder is the easiest to cover up. You are Peiper's first target.

Gunny: So? I've always been a target.

Death: Exactly. And therein lies my little game. It will be so much fun to chase you, Gunny. See you later.

Gunny: Wait! Get back here you bastard!

"What's wrong, Uncle Gunny?" asked Tim. "You just muttered something about a bastard."

"My boss at work. Just thinking out loud, Junge."

Enough of this, Gunny said to himself. Back to Mortain, the business at hand.

They returned to Gunny's apartment where Gunny filled two glasses of water for them and Tim massaged his temples without removing his sunglasses. Gunny tried not to smile at the younger man's hangover as he sat down in his chair.

"Timmy, in the months after the German surrender, I couldn't stand the light because it represented hope and happiness, two emotions I thought denied me. The doctors said I was okay but I wasn't. However, in time these emotions returned. It shall be the same for you."

"Uncle Gunny, nothing's changed. I get the same from my doctors at Landstuhl. The bastards've never been close to a war. They tell me to buck up and be a man. It's shell shock, they say. I'd like to take shells and shove them up their asses!"

"Timmy, I must warn you. The short-term treatment for the malady is alcohol, and lots of it. Many German veterans got stuck in the alcohol stage and died young, usually before age forty, of liver disease, cancer, suicide, or 'accidents.' The long-term treatments are talking with other veterans who suffer from the same illness. You must understand that our defeat made it worse for us German soldiers. We felt a bit better to learn that veterans from the victorious countries suffered as well. But I was luckier than most because I found much peace and happiness in America."

"What happened to you and America, Uncle Gunny?"

"It all ended in 1960 when Hans Peiper arrived in Dubain and forced me, at the price of blackmail and the loss of my family, to return to Germany. Peiper did the same to Ernie, although he allowed Ernie to stay in his hometown. Peiper not only promised to kill our families if either of us stepped out of line, but also to report us to German and American authorities for killing German regulars in cold blood, and killing French civilians."

"Just a minute, Gunny. It was Peiper who ordered the killings of his own soldiers, and the Gestapo who killed French civilians. Are you saying that Peiper threatened to pin these on you and Dad?"

"Yes. But the story gets more complicated, Timmy, as you will see."

"Peiper's a dirty sonofabitch!"

"But a highly intelligent dirty sonofabitch. I left Dubain, and that was the time, you might remember, when your dad started drinking heavily."

"How do you know this?"

"Ah, Junge, you will find out anyway. Your mother has been my point of contact since I left Dubain. She receives and mails letters between Mary June and me. She and I trade information. It is she who informed me of Mary June's drinking, and it is she who receives and deposits the money I send to my family."

Tim stared at him, looking at him in a new way than he had since their reunion the day before. "Uncle Gunny, I...I didn't know."

"Of course not, Junge. We planned your ignorance of these things."

"So, back to Mortain," said Tim. "You trusted Dad. You let him keep the Beretta and shared some secrets with him. You could've been court-martialed, especially after Dad shot Stresseman and Peiper with the gun. Why did you take these risks?"

"There is no risk when you have no other choice. I might have been killed or captured. Only the Americans could have stopped the scourge of Peiper and his gang of devils. Ernie believed me, but the American authorities did not believe him.

"Ernie and I became family the moment I searched him. I sensed Ernie's courage and, more importantly, his anger. As you know, survival in war sometimes requires courage, but all the time requires anger, even hatred. I had a hunch about your dad, and I was right."

"When did you and Dad reach the American lines?"

"Later the next day."

"But you haven't covered all the words Dad blurts when he's drinking," said Tim.

Gunny sighed. Tim moved forward in his chair.

"We encountered a group of French underground marching two prisoners, a woman with her hair shorn and her son, who had a distinct scar on his face. They wanted to execute me, but they did not. There was some confusion. The French decided to escort Ernie and me to the American lines."

"With the prisoners?"

"No, Junge. They died of gunshot wounds and the Frenchmen buried them there in the woods."

"Who killed them?"

"Your daddy."

Tim held Gunny's gaze. "It was the same boy who found Dad and others of the patrol in the woods and turned them over to Peiper to be executed. Am I right?"

"Yes. I noticed the boy's scar immediately. Ernie saw it a few moments later. I would have tried to stop Ernie, but there was a gun against my head, and Ernie was too fast for me in any event."

Gunny paused. Tim rose, walked to the window, stood in the sunlight, and removed his sunglasses. Tim's words from the night before resounded in Gunny's head: "I know about the smell and the fire, Uncle Gunny. War is fire, and Vietnam is war...but I watched only a small part of the flames and pushed the rest out of my vision." Gunny thought, Timmy has killed women and children in rage, the nasty devil-child conceived of the killings of buddies and born of vengeance.

Tim, his sunglasses back on, stared out the window and asked, "Where did you and Dad next meet up?"

"The 30th Division made your dad an interpreter, and he appointed me his assistant," Gunny replied. "The American commanders allowed it when Ernie vouched for me. I lost my job when Ernie was wounded in a mortar attack a couple months later. The Americans sent me to a prison camp in England."

Tim nodded. "You and Dad stayed in touch and met again in 1948."

"No, Timmy, we met one more time before 1948."

"When? Where?"

"Several months later, in England."

"England's a big place," said Tim. "Where in England?"

"In a London hospital. In the Section 8 ward."

"The ward for the crazies," said Tim. "The same ward I... at Landstuhl."

"Yes, Timmy. For those soldiers who see too much, feel too much, and kill too much."

"How long?" Tim asked.

"About two months. Now, Timmy, before you return to Landstuhl with all I have told you, you must hear one more thing. The hospital's treatments for your dad and I were worthless. Ernie and I treated each other and brought each other back. However, they discharged me back to my POW camp outside London and sent your dad home. We were separated, and had to deal with what we felt on our own. Your dad has been alone with this darkness inside him for too long. It has changed him into a different man. You, Timmy, must always watch so that your wars do not do the same to you."

Chapter 10

Ernie Balbach—with Jimmy Franken in tow—Mary June Balbach, Brute, Jack Trocksley, Abraham Bernstein, Frenchie, and Georgie huddled around the fire under the overhang of Piankashaw Rock, a hunk of granite two hundred yards wide and thirty-five feet above the fire at its highest point. They sat on makeshift seats of rock and wood, which widened the holes in the ass parts of their pants. A cold front had moved in the night before, bringing with it leaden gray skies and snow flurries whose flakes wound their way through the bare trees to the ground. The fire fought against the cold front and snow. It spit sparks and heaved wood smoke. Sometimes the sparks landed on the people huddled around it and the smoke teared their eyes, but mostly they didn't mind because they loved the fire's heat, cheered the fire's battle against the hated cold, and absorbed the fire's salve, which soothed their own hatred, their own bitterness, their own anguish.

Their shoulders sagged beneath layers of old and musty coats, so carefully pinched from clotheslines in town or so resentfully taken from Christmastime do-gooders. Body heat was life, and the loss of it was death, and most of the loss was from the neck, head, and feet. They wore an assortment of hats on their heads, filthy scarves around their necks, smelly socks on their feet covered by maybe one, maybe two shoes. A drunken bum quickly learned that nature's cold at Piankashaw Rock was not stayed by insulated walls and shingled roofs.

Ernie was used to the smell by now, the sour odor of unwashed people with unlaundered clothes. He couldn't remember a time when the smell didn't pervade his senses. Time for the Piankashaw bums stretched out in an infinite line of mostly drunk, sometimes hung over, and maybe an iota of sobriety. A day could be a week, or a year, or ten years. Ten years could be a minute, or a day, or a century. A century could be eons, as old and as big as Piankashaw Rock. They talked some around the fire, but there was little to say that hadn't been said over the days, weeks, months, and years past. Yet, amid the mostly aimless talk of bums, Ernie could pick out certain harmonics: cigarettes, old stogies smoked or chewed down by a lucky someone else, grapevines—small ones cut from the woods—as the smokes of last resort. He heard, in various tones, some clashing, some not, "Pass the hooch." "Gimme some a dat-der sloocum." "Hey, you be drinkin' too much o' my sloocum and hooch."

It was Ernie who entered "hooch" and "sloocum" into the Piankashaw Rock dictionary. "Hooch," said Ernie, "is any liquor harder than wine or beer. Sloocum is anything weaker than hooch."

Sometimes a new Piankashaw bum asked for more detailed definitions, and sometimes Mary June Balbach gave them, if it was a day when she was present at Piankashaw and could tell you where she was. "Hooch is whiskey, rum, gin, vodka, and rotgut," she'd tell the new guy. "All the rest is sloocum."

Georgie had then asked Mary June, "What's rotgut?" Georgie was new to Piankashaw and was on his first bum kick. The short, fat, long-haired, red-headed kid said he was hiding out from his draft board in Pennsylvania.

Mary June had taken a bum mama's liking to Georgie and replied, "Rotgut is sour mash whiskey, moonshine, cough syrup, shaving lotion, grain hooch, and wood hooch."

Georgie, smart enough to run from his draft board and not stupid enough to drink poison, had asked, "Don't wood hooch make you go blind?"

But by that time Mary June had run out of words and bum mama-hood, so Brute, a veteran of the AEF's trenches in Flanders, had answered Georgie, "Only if you drink it, dumb shit."

Georgie had been with them a few weeks now, and he'd become comfortable talking like the other Piankashaw bums. He asked for his turn with the bottle as often as the others.

It was their lucky night sitting around that fire. Someone, Ernie couldn't remember who, had pulled out a larger than normal-for-the-group quantity of booze: two gallons of hooch and three quarts of unmatured homemade wine sloocum. They passed the drinks around and exercised their ancient rights to stare into a fire and think thoughts they didn't need to voice because everyone else was thinking the same thoughts.

"Gimme that jug," said Ernie, who took a long draw, belched, and handed the jug to Mary June, who refused because she planned to return home the next day.

"Why're we out here shiverin' around this fuckin' fire when we can be under the rock where it's warm?" asked Brute.

"I'm out here because I don't gotta look at the goddamn sun or the blue sky," said Ernie. "And I don't gotta be under any rock, and I get more of the hooch."

Then another voice spoke up.

Jimmy: Ernie, I don't like Brute. He looks too much like the German bastards who killed me under your tree. Tell him to go inside.

Ernie: Brute's just old, ornery, and harmless. But I'll try.

"Brute," said Ernie, "the door to the cave is right there." Ernie pointed to a small contraption made of thin paint-flaked slats of wood, which now closed over the entrance to the caves. "All you gotta do is slide the door and go in. It's warm in there and you can take a nap."

"I wanna stay out here," said Brute, suddenly stubborn.

Brute hated, in order, niggers, queers, Jews, and government. There were other Brute hates down the list, but he rarely got to them. To Brute, any sign of authority at Piankashaw Rock was government, and so he rebelled with the fanaticism of the master shit-stirrer. But Ernie had taught the others the tactics of rope-counter-attack against Brute when he shit-stirred. "Rope," Ernie had explained, "can be just that, rope. Or rope can be Brute rope, made up of time and Brute's mouth. If you give Brute enough Brute rope, Brute hangs himself." Even Brute, in rebellion at the time, had cackled at this.

"Brute, if you wanna stay out here, shut your toothless mouth," said Mary June.

"Look, bitch, this is a man's place. You don't belong here," Brute shit-stirred. "You should go home and cook something. Course," Brute continued, his head now cocked and an evilish grin on his face, "you ain't got a home. Mebbe you can stay with Maymie."

"Brute," said Ernie, suddenly angry, "don't you ever mention Maymie's name again, or I'll bash in your head. You got that?"

"I was gassed at Vimy Ridge," said Brute, sticking out his feeble chest. "I got the medal fightin' the Kaiser. I thought of that bastard every time I slit a Boche's throat in the trenches. There's Piankashaw injun in me. So this here rock was my place first. I ain't afraid of you, Balbach. I be on the warpath again, just like in the trenches. So shove it up your ass!"

Jimmy: Ernie, don't take that from Brute. Smack him!

Ernie: Why fight a half-crazy shell-shocked old man who actually believes Black Jack Pershing awarded him the Medal of Honor? Let him have his crazy delusions if they give him a bit of comfort against his misery.

"You tell 'em Brute!" Frenchie slurred as he rocked back and forth. "You saved my France back in '18."

"We did," said Brute in a softer voice and minus his shit-stirring grin. He lowered his head and stared at the ground. "That we did."

"And we thank you for it," Frenchie responded in that New York accent that so irritated Ernie because Frenchie lorded it over the ignorant rustics, the very people who'd saved Frenchie's ass. Sometimes, it seemed to Ernie, Frenchie was more proud of his ancestral France than his own country. After the war, Frenchie worked as a beat cop in New York City. He'd gotten caught selling drugs for organized crime and they threw him in jail. Then the mafia discovered that Frenchie had been skimming and put out a contract on him. Frenchie needed out of New York and a place to hide out, and fast. He jumped bail and contacted Gunny, of all people. Gunny directed him to Ernie and Piankashaw. The Piankashaws let Frenchie in because, Ernie told them, Frenchie had treated Gunny well at the POW stockade at Mortain, though Ernie left out the part about threatening Frenchie's life in the bargain.

Frenchie now pushed it too far. "But France didn't need no Americans in '44. France woulda whipped the Germans anyway. Americans just got in the way."

To Ernie and Mary June—and Jimmy—the combat in France in 1944 was altogether different than that in 1918. Ernie stood in front of Frenchie, and Mary June crouched behind him.

"Look, you asshole," said Ernie. "You say that again and I'll call your mafia buddies in New York!"

Jimmy: Atta boy, Ernie. You tell him! Now smack him!

Ernie seized Frenchie by the shirt, stood him up, and hit his mouth. Frenchie swung back and missed. Mary June pinned Frenchie's arms behind him and Ernie landed a few more punches. Frenchie, bleeding from his lip, dropped to the ground. "I…I'm sorry Ernie. It ain't true and I won't say it again. Cross my heart. I'm gonna leave for a while. Tend to some business. Gotta go!" Frenchie crawled towards the north end of Piankashaw Rock. Mary June kicked Frenchie in the rear.

"You fucking frog," Ernie yelled. "You say that again, I'll bust your dick and balls up your ass so far you'll have to take off your shirt to piss!"

Jimmy: Goddammit, Ernie, I died there, fightin' for 'em collaboratin' bastards. Be a man, and land a few more before he gets away!

Ernie looked across his left shoulder where Jimmy stood whenever he turned up.

Ernie: Jimmy, I've had enough of you today. Get lost!

Jimmy: Where should I go?

Ernie: Anywhere! Just get away from me. Hey, go to the cemetery down there where you belong. Ernie pointed down the hill towards the congregation of the Piankashaw dead.

Mary June didn't bat an eye as she looked at Ernie's shoulder. "Jimmy, you'd best go now. You can come back later."

Ernie looked to his left and saw Jimmy disappear. "He's gone," Ernie said to no one in particular.

"Ernie, don't you think you're being a little hard on Jimmy?" Jack Trocksley said. Jack was the Piankashaw peacemaker, even when he couldn't see the argument taking place.

"Maybe I am," said Ernie. "Maybe not. Goddammit, I don't know!" He'd tried explaining things to Jack and the others before, but every time he tried, Ernie lost himself in his days at Mortain. He had to push the words out to talk about it. "Couldn't help him. Mortain and the SS. Jimmy—he made it to the bottom of my tree. I woulda been killed too, like all the others. The fire, the smell. Scarface and his whore of a mother. Goddammit all to hell!" Ernie stared into the fire with bright eyes. He pleaded with it. Can't you burn it away, just this once?

Mary June and Ernie watched out for each other when she visited Piankashaw. Maymie wasn't there to comfort Ernie, so Mary June shuffled her log seat next to Ernie's, put her arm around him, and kept it there.

Jack got up and fetched another couple of logs for the fire.

"Abomination! Abomination I say!" Bernstein weaved on his feet, his filthy, matted white hair and beard quivering in the breeze.

"What's an abomination, you old kite?" asked Brute.

"Kike, not kite," Mary June corrected Brute.

"It's an abomination! Lyin' with another man's woman!"

Brute missed Bernstein's meaning. "Kike, Kite, Jew bastard,

whatever. What's the difference? They're all the same. Big nose slit-ty-eyed money grubbin' Jews."

"Abomination! Sin!"

"Now calm down, Brute," soothed Trocksley. "Bernstein's doing his best, just like all of us."

"Hitler's biggest mistake was not killin' em' all!" Brute warmed into his top three most loved hates. "Whaddya say there, Bernstein? You look like you got a little nigger in ya, you're a queer, and a kite."

"Sins! Talkin' to a false god on your shoulder. Runnin' down Yahweh's people. Sins! Man layin' with man. Abomination against Yahweh! Stone 'em to death, I say. All of ye'll be in hellfire, sure 'nuf!"

"Now, Abraham, be good and sit down before you fall in the fire," soothed Trocksley. "You're getting too old to drink that stuff."

Bernstein mumbled in Trocksley's ear. Jack helped Bernstein into the cave and rolled the door shut behind them.

The wind whipped harder. It was late evening now, and almost dark. Some of the snow turned into sleet. Brute, cussing out Georgie as a goddamn draft-dodger who oughta be stood up and shot, leaned on Georgie, who helped him into the cave.

"Get me in Radius's room," Brute muttered, Radius being Brute's buddy from their Kaiser trench fighting days. They shared a cave at Piankashaw Rock like roommates, the same way they'd shared the trenches together. "Gotta watch out for Radius cuz none a these other bastards'll do it." They shut the door behind them, leaving only Ernie and Mary June by the fire.

They talked little. Talk was mostly useless, Ernie knew from experience, as was hope and fear and grace. Only hooch and sloocum worked. Mary June called them the nectar of the gods. Ernie hated it when Mary June brought God up. He knew the truth. There ain't no goddamn God, Ernie thought. I worship the hooch.

Mary June held a heavy stick over the fire and poked it into the coals. This caused sparks to shoot up and land on Ernie's hair. Ernie, oblivious to them until they burned into his scalp, yelped until Mary June brushed them out with her hands and shushed him.

Ernie muttered, "Abomination!" They snickered like teenagers, and that act of laughing reminded Ernie that he had nothing to laugh about. "I gotta see Jimmy! We gotta find him down there in the grave-yard. I feel bad about sending him there."

They made their way to Piankashaw Cemetery, about a hundred yards below the rock and about twenty yards up from the Patoka River. They huddled against the sleet and cold on a log next to a grave. Mary June piled twigs and branches onto the remains of previous campfires by the grave. She lit it with the point of the stick, and the campfire burned into life.

"Jimmy?" Ernie said.

Only Ernie heard the *poof.*

Jimmy: Right here, Ernie.

Ernie: I...I'm sorry about kicking you away, Jimmy.

Jimmy: It's okay, Ernie. I visited with my friends here. Some of them are still hangin' around.

Ernie, Jimmy, and Mary June stared at the grave of Ernie's father, a lost and torn soul from Brute's war. Ernie remembered his daddy, a gentle soul who marched with the Bonus Army to Washington, D.C. in 1932. Doug MacArthur had burned Ernie's dad and his comrades out of their shacks, and killed a few for good measure. His dad returned a broken, bitter, and drunken man. He moved to Piankashaw Rock on November 11, 1932, Armistice Day, Ernie remembered. He died at the Rock on Sunday evening, December 7, 1941, after he got the news of Pearl Harbor. They found him with a hole in his head and a gun in his hand. Ernie knew why his dad had killed himself. Pearl Harbor had set off another war and this time his son, Ernie, would be in the fire. This knowledge itself was unbearable. It was the last straw of his suffering.

Ernie, eighteen years old, made the wooden cross that marked his daddy's grave. It was now mostly rotted but still readable.

Andrew Ernest Balbach, 1895—1941

Mary June held Ernie's head to her bosom while he cried. Jimmy laid his head on Mary June's shoulder.

Chapter 11

Maymie Balbach finished her prayers, stepped out of the pew, genuflected towards the altar, and hesitated. There was no one in the cathedral except her and Father Eric Faulkenburg, who moments before
had emerged from the sacristy to prepare the altar for that evening's
mass. Maymie caught Father Faulkenburg's eye and he motioned
her to join him at the altar. She did, and Father Faulkenburg shook
his head before speaking. "Maymie, several more parishioners have
come to me about Father Chris."

"Father," said Maymie, "Father Chris tells me they're rumors, and
that's all. I have no reason not to believe him."

"Chris has said as much to me since the talk started last summer. I
believed him then and tried to locate the source of the rumors. I failed.
Have you tried?"

"Yes, Father."

"Did you...?"

"No."

"I want to believe Father Chris now," said Father Faulkenburg,
"but too many people have come forward. Chris has made passes at
other men. Now, it appears he has a male lover."

"Father, no!"

"I'm afraid it's true. Maymie, I think I can trust you to keep this to
yourself. Not even Chris can know. Father Hagemeyer came to us from

St. Andrews Parish in Omaha about three years ago. So, on a hunch, last week I called Bishop Flannery in Nebraska. His diocese includes St. Andrews. Bishop Flannery told me that he is certain Father Chris Hagemeyer is a homosexual." Father Faulkenburg's voice broke, but he coughed and carried on. "Chris denied it then. That is, until several men in St. Andrews told Bishop Flannery that Chris made passes at them. Then one man came forward and told Bishop Flannery that he and Chris were lovers.

"It turns out Bishop Flannery and Bishop O'Grimmels are long-time friends. Bishop O'Grimmels agreed to take Chris from Omaha and bring him to our diocese."

"My God!" Maymie exclaimed, then she dropped Father Faulkenburg's gaze and looked down. "There is no doubt, then. Chris lied to me."

"Maymie," Father Faulkenburg's voice broke. "I am so sorry."

Maymie wiped her eyes. "What happens next?"

"I must report this to Bishop O'Grimmels."

"What will the bishop do?"

"Homosexuality is a severe mental illness that resists most treatments. The bishop will probably admit Chris to a hospital. We can only hope and pray that Chris can be cured and return to his ministry."

"Here?" Maymie asked.

"I doubt it. If Chris is cured, Bishop O'Grimmels will send him to another parish."

"Father, isn't there something else we can do?"

"I'm afraid not, Maymie."

"Father Chris is a good man and a good priest."

"I would say the same if I was to ignore his transgressions. Chris took a vow of celibacy when he joined the priesthood. Not only has he broken that vow, he is breaking it with another man. He is committing mortal sins that put his soul in danger of perpetual hellfire—adultery, breach of the vow of celibacy, homosexuality—just to name several. He compounds these sins with his lies. The bishop will take the position, consistent with Church doctrine, that Chris cannot carry on a ministry with these things on his soul."

"Father Falkenburg, shouldn't we focus on the good in a person, and not his sins? Father Chris may be living in sin, but look at the good he does! What do his sins have to do with his goodness?"

"Maymie, the soul before God is not a bank account. God does not accept deposits, allow withdrawals, and cover overdrafts. Likewise, the soul of a person tainted by mortal sin is not measured by the value of his good deeds subtracted by the liability of his bad. If only it was that simple."

"Didn't Jesus himself say judge not? And doesn't 'judge not' include the Catholic Church, which now condemns Father Chris to eternal hellfire because of doctrine?"

"No one is judging Chris, Maymie, but we live in a real world where there are real consequences for real actions. A priest is held to a higher standard in his personal conduct. Father Chris Hagemeyer does not meet that standard. I have to consider the St. Augustine flock. How does this affect their faith? They might leave the parish, take their children out of our school, and join another church. What would all this do to the church finances, especially when we have the school to support? How can we preach against sins of fornication if one of us freely engages in those sins, and, in this case, with another man?"

"Even still, Father, it is the Catholic faith, not the Catholic Church, that counts. The Church is a group of humans run by humans. It's never been perfect and never will. Why would anybody leave the faith or this parish because of the imperfections of the Church?"

"You and I understand the distinction between the faith and the Church," answered Father Faulkenburg, "but most others do not. We must face this reality."

"Did you give Father Chris a deadline?"

"A deadline?"

"For reporting this to the bishop."

"No, Maymie, I didn't. It just isn't in me to go that far. Yet. Chris is a lonely man in great pain. I know he loves ministering. Sometimes I think I'm the failure in all this."

"You mustn't blame yourself, Father. If there be sin, it is Father Chris's, not yours. Maybe Chris needs more time."

"Maybe. However, you're a nurse, Maymie, so you know there's another aspect to this. Homosexuality is a very dangerous mental illness. The next step for a male homosexual is children. How can I trust Chris alone with the altar boys and other children at St. Augustine School?"

"Has he done that?"

"Not that I know of. There have been no complaints, and I've seen no signs among the altar boys and the children in school. But I am quite worried."

"Was Father Chris accused of molesting children at St. Andrews?"

"I made it a point to ask Bishop Flannery about that. He said there had been no such thing, but only because he'd gotten rid of Father Hagemeyer before it happened. Chris is especially good at working with families who've suffered tragedy. He's only thirty-eight and has many good years left. He was well on his way to getting his own parish. But that is now impossible, I'm afraid. Maymie, I am torn between my love and compassion for Chris and my duties to my bishop, my Church, and my flock!" Father Faulkenburg's voice broke again.

"Father, this hell is not of your making. You mustn't forget the good you yourself bring to the world. You helped the desperate people in your German homeland after the surrender. Then you moved here and joined the Diocesan priesthood. You have great responsibility here, and you've done a wonderful job. The school is outstanding. Don't get down on yourself because you can't change Chris."

"Maymie, thank you. I pray that Chris will change and this will go away, but God doesn't answer, or He doesn't answer the way I want him to. I guess God has other plans." Father Faulkenburg gathered himself together. "Maymie, priests need prayer, too. I know that you pray for Chris. Will you...could you...also pray for me?"

"Father, I've always prayed for you."

"It's a special blessing to hear that from you, Maymie. Your family is going through hard times, too. It might be a comfort for you to know that Ernie faithfully attends my masses at Piankashaw, takes communion, and gives his confessions."

Maymie gazed at the crucifix on the altar. "Ernie left us about two years ago. Tim is with the Marines in Vietnam. He won't admit it in his letters, but I just know that he's in the fighting. I try to do what I can for Mary June, but she can't get over the loss of Gunny. Henry lives with us. He and Joey are the same age and are good friends, so it works out."

"I hear that Gunny moved to Mannheim in Germany. Is he still there, Maymie?"

Maymie looked up. "So far as I know, Father."

"Well, Mannheim is a good city. I hope he's doing well. Does anyone know why he left? Marital problems, maybe?"

"Gunny's and Mary June's marriage was strong. There were no problems that I saw. They haven't divorced, Father, and I take that as a sign that maybe Gunny will move back to Mary June."

"Could there be another reason why Gunny left? Has anything been said about this?"

"No, Father."

"Well, Maymie, I have to go back to the rectory in a few minutes."

"And I'm working the evening shift at the hospital," Maymie replied. "I'll see what I can do with Father Chris."

Maymie walked to the phalanx of candles in the back of the cathedral and lit five. Please, God, help Ernie, she prayed silently. Give Father Chris Hagemeyer the courage he needs to get back into your graces. Help Mary June and Gunny. Keep Tim safe. And forgive me for the little white lie I just told Father Faulkenburg about why Gunny left America and moved to Mannheim. Amen.

Maymie turned to leave but stopped when she saw a young woman enter the back of the cathedral. The lady genuflected, knelt in a pew, lowered her head, and clasped her hands together in prayer. Maymie recognized her as Maria Reller, the young lady who had moved to Dubain from Germany with her mother, Greta, about one year ago. Greta mostly kept to herself, but Maria had recently bought a house in Dubain.

Maria was beautiful, strikingly so. She had thick, black hair, which she wore neatly on her shoulders. Her large hazel eyes contrasted with her hair yet enhanced her looks. Maymie admired Maria's high cheekbones, large lips, firm chin, and long, thin neck. She was petite at about five-feet-six or seven inches. She had a larger than average bosom, a thin waist, nicely shaped hips, and long legs. Maria dressed nicely and modestly, but not expensively. Today she wore a pretty white blouse and a dark skirt that covered her knees and the tops of her calves. Not like all those other young women with skirts so short their rear ends practically hang out!

Maymie first spotted Maria working at First Dubain State Bank and had asked around about her. The bank had hired Maria to open its import-export division so local Dubain wood furniture manufacturers could sell their products overseas. Maria had grown up in Europe, spoke three languages, and was very personable. Maymie heard that some of the younger women at the bank had resented Maria at first because of her beauty and talent, but Maria had won them over with kindness and by helping them with their own jobs.

Maymie guessed that Maria was on a late lunch break from the bank and was using part of it to pray. A pretty woman, modest, and a devout Catholic. Maymie imagined introducing Maria to her Tim. She would be quite the catch, Maymie thought as she watched Maria pray. Could it happen? Probably not, but it's nice to think about, anyway.

Maymie watched Father Faulkenburg at the altar and saw Maria and Father Faulkenburg smile at each other. Maymie inwardly grinned and thought, There is always something to be thankful for! Father Faulkenburg makes it a point to meet and come to know new parishioners. Clearly he did so with Maria. God bless the man!

Maymie left the cathedral. She stepped down the stairs toward her car when Father Chris Hagemeyer pulled up next to her at the sidewalk in his Ford and rolled the window down. "Maymie, I have to talk to you."

"I have a little time before my shift at the hospital, and we have about forty-five minutes before the boys get home from school. Meet me at my house."

Father Chris sat at Maymie's kitchen table. They talked while Maymie prepared peanut butter and jelly sandwiches for Joey and Henry and an evening meal for herself for when she went on shift. Father Chris nervously sipped his coffee and avoided eye contact with Maymie.

While she worked at the kitchen sink, Maymie spoke over her shoulder. "Chris, you've lied to me about your homosexuality."

"Maymie, I have not lied!"

"Chris, Father Faulkenburg told me that many parishioners have come to him."

"All this is just talk. I am not a homosexual!"

"Then why all the rumors, Chris? Where there's smoke, there's fire. And in your case, the fire is flaming."

"Maymie, you have to believe me. Someone is falsely spreading these things."

"Who?" asked Maymie.

"I don't know. I can't think of anyone who has an axe to grind with me."

"Chris, who is your man lover?"

"Maymie, I have no lover, man or woman!"

Maymie dropped her knife in the sink and the clatter filled the room. She let it sit there and assembled the two sandwiches on dishes at the table. "Chris, I don't...I can't...believe you."

"You must, Maymie!"

She turned around. Maymie needed to look him in the eye for her next question. "Chris, do you ever have an urge to...well...to be with children? Boys?"

Father Chris stared into Maymie's face. Given her job as the head emergency room nurse at St. Mary's Hospital and her family tragedies, Maymie didn't scare easily. But Father Chris at this moment frightened her. She saw a piece of life drain from him. His blood-shot eyes explained the new lines and wrinkles on his face. Shades of gray criss-crossed his unkempt hair. His shoulders sagged. Maymie watched him rise from his seat, walk to the kitchen sink, and stare out the window above it. Father Chris, his back now to Maymie, lit a cigarette and puffed on it, gripping the sink with his other hand. Maymie noticed that he'd lost weight.

"Father Faulkenburg is going to the bishop," Father Chris said, facing the window.

"Of course he is. It's his job."

"I love being a priest. What can I do?"

"The only thing you can do, which is to get away from your lover, renounce your homosexuality, and get treatment."

"Ah, Maymie." Father Chris returned to his seat, picked up his cup, and stared at the coffee in it. "It's no good," he mumbled. "It's just no good. It's over for me."

Maymie felt a tremor inside. What's going on here? she thought. What is Chris telling me?

"Can I stay in touch with you?" Father Chris asked.

"Chris, this house is always open to you. You know that. You can call anytime, but we have to be careful. Others might listen in. Eleanor Wetzel just loves to eavesdrop when she's on switchboard duty at the phone company. If the matter is sensitive, which is likely, you can come see me."

Father Chris nodded at Maymie's words, though he didn't seem comforted by them. He looked up and tried smiling sympathetically at her. "Well, enough about me, Maymie. Has anything changed for your family?"

Maymie's mood lifted a bit with the change in subject. "I take food to Ernie and the others at Piankashaw Rock. That and praying are all that I can do. There's always hope, and I hold on to that. But if I ever uncover Hans Peiper's identity, I'd probably have to confess to murder."

"Do you have any leads?" asked Father Chris. He leaned in to their conversation, already engaged with the secret Maymie had confessed to him some time ago.

"No. Ernie and Gunny won't even talk about it."

"They're protecting their families, Maymie."

"I did tell an itsy-bitsy lie to Father Faulkenburg a little while ago in the cathedral. He asked about our family and wondered aloud why Gunny left Dubain and his family and moved to Germany. He asked about marital problems, and I told the truth. Gunny and Mary June had no marital problems. Then he asked if there was any other reason for Gunny's abandonment of his family, and I lied. I told Father Faulkenburg that there was no other reason I knew of."

"Father Faulkenburg is an intelligent man," said Father Chris. "It's too bad you can't confide in him about the real evil that lies in Dubain that no one else can see."

"Chris, I almost faint when I remember Peiper's threats to kill our families."

She would have shared more, but just then Joey and Henry entered the back door.

"Mom, we're starved!" cried Joey.

"Hi, Father Chris," said Henry.

"Well, I'd best be going." Father Chris rose and put on his coat. "Thanks for the coffee, Maymie. See you, boys. Don't forget that you serve the Sunday 8:30 mass."

After Father Chris left, Joey looked up at Maymie. "Mom, what was he doing here?"

"We had to chat about a few things, Joey."

"That's okay. I guess."

Chapter 12

Maria Reller turned the key in the safety deposit box while her customer, Herman Streicher, the president of St. Mary's Hospital, turned his.

"Take all the time you need, Mr. Streicher," said Maria. "I'll be at my desk. When you're done, call me so we can lock it."

"Maria, I'll only be a few minutes. You can stay. I don't mind," said Herman.

"It's against bank policy for me to be in the room when a customer opens his box. I could lose my job."

"That would be fine with me, Maria. Then I could hire you as my personal assistant at the hospital."

"Thank you for the compliment, Mr. Streicher."

Maria returned to her desk in the customer service area on the opposite side of the bank lobby from the tellers' cages. First Dubain State Bank had hired Maria to open and operate its import-export division. Normally, a person in Maria's position would work out of a private office behind the customer service area. However, the bank had stationed Maria's desk to the side of the service area and nearest to the door so Maria could also fill in as a customer service representative when she had time away from the import-export division. She took her seat and resumed the paperwork on savings and checking accounts for customers whom she'd waited on earlier that day. It amazed her that the people of Dubain, many of whom were skilled workers in Dubain's factories, saved so much of their money. She'd lived in other places where the workers saved almost nothing of what they earned. They spent their money as fast as they got it on anything that brought immediate pleasure—cigarettes, beer, whiskey, gambling, the latest fad in beauty products, and in those places where men go and women only whisper about. She admired that about the people she'd met in Dubain, but it saddened her how the one town, Dubain, couldn't make up for the destroyed German cities. They were filled with sad people, stung by the destruction and defeat. If only all the people could see the world the way it should be, like Mama and Papa and I do, she thought.

She put these things out of her mind when Mr. Streicher emerged from the deposit box room and motioned for her. They locked the box and Maria walked him through the lobby to the exit where he stopped. It was late afternoon and the bank would close in about thirty minutes. It was very important, Maria knew, that she handle the next matter gently and tactfully.

"Maria, would you care to join me for a drink at my house when you get off work?" asked Herman. "No one is home tonight. My wife is on a shopping trip to Chicago, and it gets lonely for an old man like me." Herman smiled at her with a hoping, wishing, almost begging light in his eyes.

Maria returned the smile. "I can't, Mr. Streicher. It's my evening to work at the St. Vincent de Paul Food Bank. I have to be there right after work."

"I just thought," said Herman, "that maybe this evening would be a good time. Can I call you?"

"Of course, Mr. Streicher. I'd love to learn more about the hospital. First Dubain is a long-standing and proud supporter of St. Mary's Hospital."

She stood at the bank doors and watched Herman walk away. When Herman reached his car, he looked back at Maria. She waved at him. Then, out of the corner of her eye, Maria saw Timmy Balbach, recently returned from Vietnam and the man she'd been waiting for since they met several days before. Maria forgot all about Herman Streicher as Tim met her by the bank doors.

"Well, hello." Maria held the door open for him to come inside. "Who have we got here? Could it be the handsome marine I met in the forest? Why, by gosh, it is him."

"Hi, Maria. It's nice to see you again," said Tim. "Can someone help me open my accounts?"

"Well, I can help you, but you could also go to any of the other girls in my section."

"You'll do, Maria."

"Where are your sunglasses today, Tim?"

"It's cloudy out. I don't need them."

Maria took Tim's arm and walked him into the lobby. She couldn't help but notice that the young ladies—and even most of the older ones—followed Tim with their eyes as she led him to her desk. She took her seat, but Tim remained standing, looking at her. For a few seconds, Maria's poise failed her and she didn't know what to do. Then she remembered. This man was a marine! He would stand all day if she didn't say something.

"Please take a seat, Timmy."

He did, and Maria handed Tim the applications. Most customers filled them out at the small tables interspersed in the customer service area, but Maria wanted this man close by. Careful, Maria, she thought. Don't be pushy.

"Tim, you can stay here and fill this out on my desk."

"Are you sure?"

"Of course. That way I can help you when you get stuck on a question."

"Do you think I'll need help?"

"Maybe. We close in about a half hour, so I'd best stay close so you don't waste time."

They'd met four days earlier in Hoosier National Forest on a sunny and sweet-smelling Southwestern Indiana spring day. Maria had sat against an elm tree for a short rest and let her mind wander in that half-asleep half-awake state she found so pleasurable. It was too soon for leaves, but some of the tree branches greened slightly with sap. The temperature was in the low sixties. There was no hint of a return of the rain showers that had moved through the forest the night before. The soaking had matted the leaves on the ground and made it easy to move through the woods without making noise. To Maria, the forest was a great cathedral and the trees stood as its spires against the deep blue sky. She loved forests, loved walking them, loved slipping through them unseen and unheard. She'd learned these skills as a little girl when she played hide and seek in forests with Papa. Sometimes Mama joined in. They always let her win, pretending fright when she popped out from behind a tree and said, "Boo!" Maria reminisced.

Tell me another story, Papa! Tell me a fairy tale, Mama! Okay, meine liebling, Papa said, do you see the sun up there? Maria closed her eyes. No, Papa, I can't see it. Well, then I can't tell you the story of the sun. She opened her eyes. I can see it! I can see it! Do you see the sun moving? Just a little, Papa. The sun is sad. Do you see its tears, liebling? Her child's imagination soared. I see them. Papa, why is the sun sad? Well, Maria, summer is over and the leaves are falling. The sun is going south for the winter and it's very sad because it has to leave you. Will it get happy again, Papa? Probably, but you can never be sure. The sun must get happy again! The sun must take a trip to the southern hemisphere every year, liebling. There, after a time, it hesitates, then stops. Why, Papa? Because it is tired, and sad, and confused, and does not know quite what to do next. Gosh, Papa, what happens? The sun makes the only decision left to it. It must move north, and it does. It comes back to you, liebling, moving faster and faster. Then it shines on the forest and warms it. The sun gets happy again, liebling!

She woke from her reverie when she sensed someone walking through the forest. She opened her eyes and spotted a young man wearing sunglasses coming towards her on the path. She fingered the Luger pistol she carried. He walked slowly, was below average height, and she noticed how handsome he was. He had short dark hair and wore military style pants and boots and a brightly colored, non-military sweatshirt. As he neared, she saw that he also carried a pistol. However, her intuition told her he was no threat.

Maria stood from her spot against the elm tree. "Hi."

He showed no surprise and didn't slow his gait until he stopped about ten feet in front of her. He said nothing, so Maria added, "I didn't think I'd see anyone in the woods today." Maria smiled at him. "I'm Maria Reller. I work at the bank."

Her introduction seemed to soften something in him. "Hi, Maria. I'm Timmy Balbach."

"What are you doing in the woods, Timmy?"

"I'm on my way to Piankashaw Rock and mushroom hunting between here and there." He removed his sunglasses. He looked sad, but then he fought his sour expression to smile warmly at her.

"Mushrooms? Aren't they poisonous?" asked Maria.

"Not the morels."

"Can I see them?"

"Sure."

Tim didn't move, so Maria walked the rest of the way to him. He didn't seem scared, just wary of her. When she stepped in close, Tim opened the small sack he was carrying.

"April is the season for mushrooms, but a few come up early when there's sunshine, like today."

"What do you do with them?" asked Maria.

"We eat them."

"Eat them? Good gosh! How do you fix them?"

"My mom makes them into soup or fries them. They're very rich and fill you up before you know it." He had sounded so comfortable before, but then he suddenly looked up at Maria and asked in a colder tone, "Why are you here?"

"Well, Timmy Balbach, I walked to the river, skipped rocks across it, then headed back this way. I was resting when you came along. Do you go there often?"

"Where?"

"Piankashaw Rock."

"Only occasionally."

"I love to hike in the woods. Do you?"

"I guess so."

"Well, do you or don't you?"

"We...my friends and I...when we were kids we spent so much time in the forest that some people in town said we might as well live here."

"You haven't answered my question, Timmy."

"I got out of the Marines about two weeks ago. I guess I can't get out of the habit of hiking. So, yes, ma'am, I like to walk in the forest."

"Don't call me ma'am, Timmy. It makes me feel like a mean old maid. Call me Maria."

"Okay, Maria."

"Did you want to?"

"Did I want to what?"

"Live in the forest."

"Some of my friends did."

"Did you?"

"Sometimes."

"Why?"

"We—some of my friends and me—well, at home....I mean... not so..." Tim trailed off. "Gosh, Maria, you sure ask a lot of questions."

"I'm sorry. Almost everyone tells me that. I just like to know about things, I guess."

"Nothing wrong with that, I guess."

They laughed.

"Were you in Vietnam?" asked Maria. She'd seen and talked to other young men, fresh back from their tours of duty in Vietnam, when she waited on them at the bank. Many carried a special sadness, a burden they'd picked up and could not put down. She could see that Tim bore an invisible weight, so she had to tread carefully with him.

"Yeah," Tim answered, confirming what she could already see.

"Where were you stationed? Saigon?"

"No, Da Nang. But I'd rather not talk about it now."

Maria had had similar experiences with former German soldiers. Her papa had said nothing about his war experiences until after her graduation from Heidelberg University three years before when she'd finally gotten the courage to ask him. He told her only that he served on both the eastern and western fronts and that it was very painful to lose a soldier under his command.

Other soldiers, she noticed, talked about their fighting days only with other veterans, and then only in low voices they assumed no one else could hear. But Maria heard and learned and absorbed. Eventually, a few confided in her, but only haltingly, and only a little at a time. How hard they had fought for Germany, for the friends they had lost. They raged against the futility of fighting the Russians on one side and the British, Canadians, French, and Americans on the other. Some admitted to killing. Maria never judged them. She wouldn't judge Timmy Balbach, either.

"It's okay with me, Tim. I'm sorry. Again."

"Don't be sorry. Many folks ask me about it. Even my mom. I'm just not ready is all."

Change the subject, Maria said to herself. This marine is interesting, smart, handsome, and clearly hurting. Can I help him feel better? I certainly want to try!

"I see we both carry guns," said Maria.

"Nothing wrong with that. Never know who or what you'll meet this deep in the forest."

"You met me. Are you going to shoot me?"

"Only if you try to shoot *me*."

They laughed again.

"Mine's a Luger," said Maria. "My papa carried it during the war. He gave it to me on my last birthday." She showed it to Tim, then handed it to him. Tim gripped the handle first in his right hand, then in his left, then with both hands. He sighted down the barrel and pulled out the ammunition clip, which was fully loaded.

"You take good care of your gun, Maria."

"What kind is yours?" Maria asked.

"Beretta."

"Italian?"

"Yeah. You can see it's small. Normally I just carry it in my jacket pocket."

"When was it made?"

"Don't really know. It was my dad's. He carried it in France in 1944."

"Can I see it?"

"Yeah, sure." He handed the gun to Maria.

"Wow. This is lighter than my Luger." She slipped out the clip. "You keep yours fully loaded too." She handed it back. "Do you live in Dubain?"

"Yeah. With my mom and brother. I've been here all my life. Except the Marines. Where are you from?"

"Ulm. Germany."

"I know the town. I drove through it around Christmas." The subject clearly made him uncomfortable. He shuffled between his feet before he said, "Well, I'd best be going, Maria. Maybe we'll meet again."

"Bye, Timmy."

He put on his sunglasses and walked past her on the path towards Piankashaw Rock. She watched his back, captivated by the way he walked, how his shoulders swayed with every step. He stopped about twenty feet away and turned around, as though he knew she still stood there and couldn't move until he gave her permission. Maria felt a tremor of annoyance at herself for allowing this man to have so much control over her.

"I closed all my bank accounts when I went into the Marines," Tim said. "Can I come around the bank next week sometime and open new ones?"

"Yes. Certainly," Maria said, trying not to let her excitement slip through her voice.

"See you then."

Maria wanted to say more. Much more. *Timmy, I spotted the Vietnam in you long before we talked. Your words confirmed it. You say you do not want to talk about Vietnam, yet inside you scream it.*

How do I know? It doesn't matter. I just do, and you can trust me, Maria wanted so much to say to him. I see the pain, the hurt, the sunglasses, the slow but tense walk of a man from war who'd killed and almost been killed. War is outside of the body, some say. It is in fields, trees, jungles, rivers, clearings in woods, mountains, and movies. Others say that it is only a job, and they did it, and now it's over. But you, Timmy, disagree, Maria thought. You might fathom the reasons for your disagreement, but you cannot put them into words. At first, Vietnam carried you. You went along for the ride because you had to. Then slowly, by a strange process of transference, Vietnam moved into you. Now you carry it. It lives inside you, a parasite that feeds on you and drains the life from you and wants to kill you. I know these things and you can trust me, Timmy. Trust me.

Tim finished the applications and handed them across the desk. Maria gave him a small savings passbook and some blank checks.

"You can use these checks until your new ones are printed. Do you want to make the deposits now?"

"Yes." Tim pulled ten separate hundred dollar bills from his pocket. She took the money and recorded the deposits.

"Mr. Balbach, you're almost a rich man!"

"I wouldn't say that."

"So, I just said it for you."

"Thank you for your help, Maria." Tim stood, took the passbook and checks, shook her hand, and started walking across the lobby. Maria felt herself deflating. Oh, for heaven's sake, Maria, she berated herself. He's just a guy. No need to get all school-girlish about it. Remember what Papa told you about finding a husband.

Then, almost sensing her thought, Tim stopped, turned around, and walked back to her.

"Is there something else, Tim?"

"Not really, but I was...well...just wondering. Would you care to go with me to my brother's seventh grade basketball game Saturday night? We wouldn't have to get there early. I mean, well, I sit with my mom and her friend, Mary June Smith. Mary June's son also plays on the team. They'll get there early and save two seats for us if I ask."

My God, thought Maria. He's asking me on a date to a basketball game? Don't be too eager! "Tim, I usually go to 7:00 mass on Saturday evenings. I'm afraid I'll make you late."

"I go to that mass too. There's no problem. Father Chris usually says it, and he's fast. We can make the game in plenty of time."

"Can you pick me up at, say, 6:30?"

"Do you mind riding in an old clunker? It's all I got to drive right now."

"I'd ride in any car with you, Tim." She realized what she'd said, and looked away from him. She could already feel her face turning red. On no! she thought. What did you just do, Maria? You blew it! You scared him away!

Tim laughed at her discomfort. "Give me your address and I'll be there at 6:30. Clunker and all."

This time, Tim did make it to the door. He left, and Maria went back to her work, but she couldn't concentrate on it. Her entire body flushed. You just accepted a date with a guy you met only twice, she thought. And not to a fancy restaurant, or a movie, or a museum like your dates at the university, but to a seventh grade basketball game with his mother as company!

Chapter 13

Maria ended her date with a kiss on Tim's cheek. She watched him drive away in his clunker car, and then climbed the five steps onto the small back porch of her house. She pulled open the screen door, turned the key in the lock of the main door, and felt the knob turn loosely. Maria acted without thinking and spun around and jumped off the porch with catlike reflexes.

Maria yanked the Luger out of her purse and chambered a round while she pushed her body against the front of the porch where it was darkest. She pointed the gun into her backyard and searched the darkness for movement, odd shadows, anything or anyone that wanted to harm her. She always locked her house, but the doorknob had turned freely. She noticed now that the interior of the house was dark. She always left a lamp on when she wasn't home, and she changed the bulb in the lamp monthly, so burnout was unlikely. Someone had picked the lock and switched off the lamp. He could be gone, but she had to assume otherwise, and besides, her instincts told her he wasn't.

Maria remembered her training: assess the threats, prioritize them, take them out. The threats were either inside the house, outside the house, or both. She needed to first protect her back by eliminating the threats outside the house. Outside, darkness was her friend, but streetlights lit up the roads around her house. The unattached garage stood about five meters from the porch. The opening faced the well-lit street. She was hidden in the shadow of the porch, but, she knew, still visible to a shooter. The light was her enemy, and her enemy had won. In spite of her dark skirt and dark maroon jacket, Maria was an easy target outside her house. Had the intruder drawn a bead on her? Would he squeeze the trigger?

Can't think of that now, she thought. Remember what Papa said. "You'll have no choice, Maria. It's me. My work. My enemies. I have put you and your mother in danger. We can protect her, but only you can protect you. One day they will come for you, Maria, and you must take them out that first time. They will come again, and then again, and you must take them out again, and then again. If you don't, you'll be dead or a prisoner. After enough times, they might leave you alone, but I doubt it. You must never let your guard down. Trust no one but yourself. Verify, verify, verify. All people and all things. Accept nothing as it seems. The day will come, Maria. The day will come."

Well, Maria mused, Papa was mostly right. The day did come, but at night.

The night? Maria's adrenaline pushed her to anger. You cowardly so-and-so! You lack the courage and decency to come at me in the daylight. You slither on your belly in the dark but you don't bother to cover your tracks. You announce yourself by turning off the light and leaving the door unlocked. Then you coil unseen, bide your time, and wait for the perfect moment to strike with your snaky body and suffocate the life out of a young woman whom you believe is helpless and naive. You are the snake and you believe I'm the mouse. Well, I am not a mouse!

But where is the snake? Maria asked herself. If he was outside— Maria assumed it was a man—he'd had a clear shot at her when she walked from Tim's car to the backdoor. But he hadn't taken the shot. This meant he was inside the house. Of that she was certain.

Maria crept on her elbows and knees back onto the porch, the gun pointed in front and her finger on the trigger. She moved to the door, turned the knob, and pulled it open just enough for her to crawl into the hallway. Once she was inside she locked the door, violating a basic rule for survival: Always leave yourself an escape route. Maria thought, To heck with that rule. The locked door also blocks his escape, if only for the few seconds it will take for him to unlock the door and flee. So you got it wrong, my snakely friend. I, Maria Reller, am now the hunter, and you the hunted.

Inside, light was her friend and darkness her enemy. She needed to work her way through the house room by room, turning on lights and eliminating hiding places. She reached up and flipped on the kitchen light. Nothing. Next the dining room. Light on. Nothing. Watch your back, she thought as she moved on. Then the summer kitchen, utility room, bedroom. Nothing. This left only the family room. Maria smiled to herself. I got you cornered! She stood and inched towards the door with her back pressed against the wall. She kept her Luger ready. She smelled cigarette smoke. The nerve of him!

It was speed that counted now. She remembered: Flip the light switch, hit the floor, roll behind the couch, and fire at anything that moves. On three, Maria, she told herself. One... Two...

"I see you learned your lessons well," a man said in English from inside the family room.

Maria stopped and crouched. Could it be him? she thought. Don't trust. Verify.

"What is your name?" asked Maria in English.

"Hans Peiper."

"Where were you born?"

"Munich."

"And your family?"

"There is my wife, Greta. And I have one child. Her name is Maria, she is a beautiful young woman, and she is talking to me now. I hope she does not shoot me."

Maria stood, turned on the light, and peered into the family room. The man who sat in the loveseat was middle-aged, handsome, over six feet tall, and trim. He smoked a cigarette, his only vice but for wine and an occasional scotch. His curly blond hair showed shades of gray, making him even more good-looking. His winter coat lay on the coffee table. He wore a navy blue sport jacket, white shirt, khaki pants, and wing-tipped shoes. There were his broad shoulders, large hands, manicured finger nails, high forehead, and perfect teeth. His deep blue eyes radiated the room, betraying his high intelligence, charisma, and charm. There was pain there, too, as though he bore some of the world's suffering even while he struggled to relieve it. He dominated every room he entered, just as he dominated this one.

"Papa!"

Hans Peiper stood, Maria ran to him, and they hugged. Maria stepped back and tried to put on a disapproving face. "Mein Gott, Papa! Du hast mich erschreckt!"

"I'm sorry I scared you, meine liebling. Forgive me?"

"You're forgiven, Papa." Maria sat beside her father.

"I worry about you so much, Maria."

"Oh, Papa, I'm not a little girl anymore."

"You'll always be my little girl, liebling. Even when you come close to shooting me!"

"I wouldn't shoot you, Papa."

"I have to leave on business for several days. I needed to see you before I left. Can we sit?" Hans gestured to the love seat and they both sat down.

"Where are you going, Papa?" asked Maria.

"You don't have to know, schatzie, and it's better that you don't."

"When are you going to take me with you on one of your trips? I want so much to see how you're building the new world—The Great Reich—and the people you're doing it with. Papa, I want to see you in action. I want to hear you talk. I want to see you take charge. I want to see others stand at attention and listen to you."

"You overestimate me, Maria."

"It's dangerous for you sometimes, isn't it, Papa?"

"Hardly ever. Actually, Maria, it's the danger that you have gotten yourself into that I want to talk about."

"What danger, Papa? Whatever it is, I can handle it."

"You have to listen to me. Can you do that?"

"Well sure, Papa."

"Maria, you must never again go into the forest alone."

"I can protect myself."

"Hush, Maria! Listen to me. The forest is not your friend. It is your enemy and quite dangerous to you. Remember when you were a child and we pretended there were good forest spirits and evil forest spirits?"

"Well, yes, Papa, but I am twenty-four and that was just pretending."

"Do not argue with me, Maria."

"Yes, Papa."

"You believed in them then. Do you still?"

"Well, maybe just a little, Papa."

Father and daughter laughed, but Hans grew serious once again. "There are times when life must be simplified and we must go back to these things. Why? Because of our enemies, Maria. Because our enemies believe we are evil and want to kill us. We must think like them to protect ourselves against them. To live. To survive, Maria. For without our survival there will be no new world, no Great Reich. Our enemies are the Hebrews and those they brainwash. Some of them know of us and want to destroy us. We take appropriate steps to counter these things. However, I digress.

"Maria, there are evil spirits in the forest. Evil spirits in the forms of evil people, like those I just mentioned, who will harm you, even kill you if they have a chance. Ach, meine liebling, the loss of you would destroy your mother and me! I can't bear to even think about it. So, Maria, if you go into the forest, you must go in the company of either me or another man chosen by me. Am I clear?"

"Yes, but—"

"There's another thing about the forest, Maria. You are not to go near Piankashaw Rock, with or without a protector."

"Why?"

"You don't need to know."

"Papa, I have a right to know."

"You have no such right! Maria, remember the reasons that your mother and I allow you to live in Dubain rather than our chateau and tree farm. First, we feel that you are entitled to some independence. Second, Mr. Kaetzel, your boss, told us that First Bank prefers that its employees live in Dubain for customer relation purposes. Third, while our chateau and tree farm are certainly not a secret, it is important that we attract as little attention to it as possible. Your home here helps to preserve and perhaps increase the privacy of the chateau."

Maria looked down. Her father never talked to her like this, his voice loud and tense, his head forward, his shoulders pushed out, his eyes narrowed. She had done nothing wrong. She didn't deserve to be treated this way.

"Maria, I'm not done. Raise your head and look at me."

"What else, Papa?"

"You must stay away from Tim Balbach."

"But Papa, he's a nice! He and I—"

"He is not! He is your enemy. The Great Reich's enemy. He was a marine counter-intelligence specialist in Vietnam. Do you know what this means?"

"He spied?"

"No. He didn't bother to spy. He destroyed Viet Cong who spied on the Americans. He went into the enemy's underground tunnels and killed the enemy inside, if not with a gun then with dynamite or grenades or his bare hands. Tim Balbach is not what he seems, Maria. He is a cold-blooded killer. Did he tell you that he was in Germany?"

"Yes."

"Did he tell you why?"

"Well…no."

"Well, I will. The American Marine Corps presumably sent him to teach other American soldiers the art and techniques of counter-intelligence. This is false. He spent time at the American Landstuhl hospital for treatment."

"Was he hurt?"

"No, Maria, he was there for the murderous insanity he'd taken from Vietnam."

"Well gosh, Papa."

"Maria, the treatment for these things is rarely successful. Tim Balbach is like a ticking bomb. That he will explode is certain. The time of the explosion is not. So you are not to go near him! We've talked about this many times, Maria. You will marry a man chosen by your mother and me. He will be attractive, strong, and intelligent. He will be a good husband who will give you beautiful babies."

"It's not done that way in America."

"Are you falling for America's foolish freedoms and its insistence on the equality of the sexes and all races?"

"Well, Papa ..."

"Are you?"

"No," Maria said, just as she thought, I'm being truthful, Papa. But it's no sin to live as Americans live!

"I hope not. America's silliness is there for all to see. I can't think of a greater race of untermenschen than the negroes. Yet America is too frightened to deal with the negroes who burn its cities. Look at the stupid war America is fighting and losing against the communists, sacrificing its young men in hopelessness. Yet America is afraid to use the weapons that would end the war and crush North Vietnam in a matter of a few days. Nuclear weapons, Maria. The war would end if the Americans dropped these weapons on Hanoi and about five or six other cities in North Vietnam.

"Would not the others shoot back with their nuclear weapons?"

"No."

"Why not?"

"They wouldn't dare. When it comes to nuclear bombs, hydrogen bombs, and missiles and advanced jets to deliver them, America is far ahead of the Russians and Chinese. When we rule America, Maria, we will use these weapons when we have to. Communists understand only the language of death and destruction. The Russians and Chinese will quake before us. The world will be a better place for it.

"I have raised you to be a leader in the Great Reich, Maria, but do not forget the duty of all Great Reich women. That duty is to give birth to the next generation. In this you will trust in my judgment and listen to what I say."

"Yes...Yes, sir."

"I have made arrangements with certain people to install an alarm system in your house and floodlights around it and the garage. You can control these devices with switches as well as a hand device, which you will carry with you at all times. Do you understand?"

"Yes, sir."

"Maria, remember that you are a soldier in the greatest army in the history of the world. You will follow my orders."

"Yes, sir."

Hans Peiper stood, took Maria's hand, and pulled her up and into his arms. Maria felt comforted, in a way.

"Ach, my Maria, meine liebling. There is a new world coming. It is our destiny, yours, your mother's, mine, all of us who believe in it, reach for it, see it in all its dazzling beauty. God is with us, Maria. We walk at His right hand. We are the tools of His will. His will is our will, our means to power. Not power for its own sake—we won't repeat Hitler's egomaniacal foolishness—but power as the means to the new world, Maria, peopled by men and women such as we who are truly in His image and likeness. This is the promised land of which God spoke three thousand years ago. He spoke of it then to Moses and his Jewish rabble, but they were corrupt, filthy, and sinful.

"They viewed God's promise as a land of milk and honey. They had it wrong then, and they have it wrong now. God saw their infidelity and treacherousness and has punished them again and again for it. But God also saw us, the truly Chosen Ones, and He brought about this time and this people—who are us—to work His plan and make it a reality, not just a fantasy. He also gave us the Jews—His enemy then and His and our enemy now—as a great obstacle to the new world. God is testing us. We are not worthy of His new world unless we crush the Hebrews. Crush them in spite of their power, their world domination, their wealth, their greed. We are but a few, and they are very many, but God is against them and for us. We shall overcome, as the negroes sing. Someday, we shall overcome, and then we shall live in glory before the throne of God."

Headlights flashed through the house. "I see that my chauffer has arrived. I must go, Maria. I will contact you when I return next week."

"Papa, I will walk you to the car."

"You can walk me to the door. Maria, I do not enjoy issuing these injunctions on your life."

Maria said nothing. She felt tired and defeated. Worse, she knew she was powerless against her father, the man she most respected and looked up to and who had just now taken away a large and valuable portion of her life. She couldn't say no to him no matter how hard she tried. She pushed the hair out of her face and fought against her tears.

"Goodnight, meine liebling."

"Goodnight, Papa. I'll pray for you."

Maria kissed him on the cheek. He opened the front door, walked through it, and closed it behind him. A moment later, a car door slammed and an engine accelerated. He was gone. Maria turned her back to the door, leaned on it, and slid down to the floor. She stared up at the ceiling and sobbed.

Chapter 14

Maria stood naked before the full-length mirror in her bathroom while she waited for the shower to warm. Since moving to America she shaved her legs, underarms, and part of her pubic hair. She had lost the ten pounds of fat that she carried in Germany and was lean, in shape, and clear skinned. She now wore her dark hair shoulder length and used mascara. Maria was pleased with her body but carried and dressed it modestly. She seldom dated even though she had many opportunities. When she did go on a date, she was easily bored and, more often than not, had to fend off her date's sexual advances. Tim Balbach was different. Maria sensed no threat from Tim despite her father's warnings. Quite the contrary. Tim treated her with dignity and respect. How many men would take a woman on a date to mass and then a grade school basketball game where you sat with his mother, who treated you like part of the family? Her father had shot her down before she could explain all this to him.

"Stay away from Tim Balbach," Papa had ordered.

But how can a man, so nice, so attractive, and so in need of her be denied to her? How did Papa know she was in the forest? That she met Tim there? That they went on a date that night? The only explanation was a spy, a stalker. Papa was spying on her, scrutinizing her life. Why? Because he feared for her safety? That was the most probable explanation. Was there another? Did Papa and Mama not trust her?

Didn't she have the right to live her own life, to choose her own husband, to plan her own family? She wanted to shout, I am Maria, Papa and Mama! I am Maria, Great Reich! I am a real person, with real feelings, with real wants and needs and aspirations. Why can't I serve the Great Reich in my own way? You will find me a handsome man, you say, but you've made no such attempt. She was twenty-four and, before she met Timmy, had asked her parents about the man they had promised her. After all, she had told them, she was not getting any younger, and she wanted to have her babies while still in her twenties. Besides, Mama and Papa, she so wanted to say to them, I am a healthy and vibrant young woman, and I have my own needs. How could they not know this?

Did they see her only as a baby factory? Was she a mere human tool for the propagation of the Great Reich? Her mama certainly wasn't. She'd had only one child.

How did Papa know Tim was in Germany? The only answer Maria could think of was that her papa spied on Tim also, and had been doing so for several months. Why did the Great Reich feel the need to do all this snooping? In Dubain and the forest, and on Timmy Balbach and her? That made Maria ask the real questions, the whys.

Why can't I roam the forest alone? Why is there danger, and what is it? Why is Tim Balbach off-limits? Papa, she imagined saying to him, why would Tim Balbach be anything more than he seems, a marine veteran sick from war and unable, as yet, to talk about it? Why has Papa bothered to search out Tim's past? There are hundreds of young men in Dubain. Do Papa and his people spy on them also? So what if Tim served in Vietnam? So what if he served in counter-intelligence? So what if he did his job, which was killing in the tunnels. Why is Tim so special and so much of a threat to Papa and the Great Reich? Papa says to stay away from Piankashaw Rock because it is a dangerous place. Why? How? Tim goes there and nothing happens to him. How is Tim connected to whatever it is at Piankashaw Rock that Papa wants me to stay away from? Papa, I have a right to know what you know!

And love! she thought. What about love? Real, true, romantic love between a woman and a man? My parents have this. How can they deny it to me, their only child and daughter? How can I marry a man chosen by other people if I do not love him? I have feelings for Tim Balbach, and I believe he has them for me. How on earth can Timmy and I be apart while I make babies with another man? Why do Papa and Mama want to pull me away from Timmy and happiness and put me with a man, a lusty baby-maker, I do not know or love? I will be miserable for the rest of my life!

Papa and Mama are wrong! I do have a right to know. If Papa won't tell me, I'll get the answers on my own. I have a right to my own life, Papa and Mama!

Maria admitted to herself that she didn't know everything about Tim, but she could not picture him as a cold-blooded killer and an enemy, as Papa claimed. He was too sensitive, in need of so much healing, and not a good actor. He does not fake his inner pain. Maria saw in Tim the signs of a war veteran and their contradictions. He carried an air of authority, yet a look of deep sadness. He knew he had a purpose, but not a destiny. He knew where he had been, but not where he was or to where he was going. Tim was compact, muscular, and in shape, yet his shoulders stooped at times, as though he carried a great weight. His face and brown eyes exuded hope and despair, sometimes pleasure but mostly pain, bravery and fear, control and rage. In a word, the man was damaged.

And there was another dimension to Tim, one she met and came to like that very evening at the ballgame. Maymie Balbach, Tim's mother, was a warm and friendly woman. Maria had seen Maymie lighting candles in the cathedral about a month before. She had no doubt that one of those candles had been for Tim.

There was a moment during the last quarter of the game when Maria and Maymie watched Tim at the same time, and then their eyes had met. They'd understood each other in that moment. *My son is damaged, Maria. I know, Maymie. Can you help him? Can we help him? We'll try, Maymie, and we have to win! Both of us love Timmy. There is nothing else to do.*

Maria stepped into the shower, and her heart jumped again. Timmy—Timmy Balbach. The thought of him thrilled her while the warm and steamy shower and body soap washed over her. She imagined Tim in the shower with her. Would he wash my hair? Massage my scalp? Soap and rub my body? Would he put his arms around me and kiss me deeply, unashamed of the swelling between his legs while I massage it with my belly and fingers? Would his mouth search out my breasts and maybe even go...down there?

Maria watched the beads of water drip from her nipples and from between her legs. Her nipples hardened, and she felt herself moisten and go wet in a way completely separate from the shower water. She could not stop her own hands. She tried, but no, she could not. Tim was there with her, doing those things to her. He knelt in the shower, parted her thighs, and buried his head between her legs. Timmy, oh my God, Timmy! Don't stop. Don't stop now! Tim went on and on until she peaked. Timmy! Oh sweet Jesus, I love you, Timmy! Her knees weakened, then buckled, but Tim held her up with his mouth, his tongue, his head. The passion subsided, slowed, and stopped. Her breathing calmed and Maria regained control over her body.

Then she looked down to see him, to tell him she loved him. But Tim wasn't there, and Papa said he never could be.

Well, Papa, we'll just see about that!

Maria finished her shower, toweled herself dry, and dressed in her pajamas. She locked her bedroom door, lay in bed, and placed the Luger on the night stand. Still trembling from her rapture in the shower, Maria opened *Grapes of Wrath* and started reading where she'd left off the night before. Grandpa Joad died and his sons and grandsons buried him. Tom Joad placed a note on Grandpa's body for the world to read. He died of a stroke. She fell asleep when she got to the part where the western states were getting nervous.

Maria startled when she heard the phone ringing. It reached its fourth, maybe its fifth ring before she could answer it. "Hello?"

"Hi, Maria. It's me, Tim. I know it's kinda late and all. I can call in the morning if you want."

"It's okay, Tim. I'm reading."

"Maria, um, I had a good time tonight, and I hope you did too. Did you?"

"Yes." Lord, Timmy Balbach, she thought. If only you knew what you did to me in the shower!

"Would you care to go on a hike with me to Raven Rock tomorrow? I'll pack some lunch. Mom will have supper ready when we get back."

Maria said it before she could even think, and her response shocked her. "Yes. Yes, Tim, I'd like that very much."

"Okay. I'll pick you up around noon," said Tim. "Now you can go back to your book, or go to sleep. Good night, Maria. Oh—what?"

"What?" Maria asked, confused.

"Yeah, what?"

"What...what?"

"What are you reading?" Tim laughed.

"Steinbeck. Grapes of Wrath."

"Good. We can talk about it in the woods tomorrow. I promise I won't ruin the ending for you. Good night, Maria."

"Good night, Tim."

"Oh, Maria, just one last thing."

"Yes?"

"Be sure to bring your Luger and several clips of ammunition."

"Why? Are we going to plink at logs?"

"Probably. Maybe we can target shoot. See who's the better shot."

"Don't get mad when I beat you, Tim."

"You won't beat me. Good night."

"Good night."

She hung up.

Maria's stomach fluttered at the thought of an afternoon and evening with Tim. But she imagined Papa standing between them. My gosh, Maria, what did you just do? Hardly two hours ago, Papa ordered you away from Tim Balbach and the forest. Now you accepted a date with him Tim to hike and target shoot in, of all places, the forest. Then she imagined Tim Balbach standing in her bedroom, and Papa slowly disappearing behind him. You are defying Papa for the first time your life! she thought to herself, and she felt both excited and fearful.

Her papa would, of course, learn of her disobedience. What will he do? What *could* he do? He would reprimand her. He may order her to sell her house and move back to the chateau. He may order her back to Germany. But she would defy him again. She'd made up her mind. This was the time to make it clear to Papa and Mama that she was not only taking control of her own life, but also building a piece of it separate and apart from the Great Reich.

Maria, now wide awake, read another chapter of *Grapes of Wrath*, then rolled over and fell back asleep. The next morning she awoke refreshed and even more defiant.

Chapter 15

Hans sat on the love seat left of the fireplace, and Kurt Getz on the chair to its right. The fire in the hearth gently warmed the room. Kurt poured wine and Greta entered with a tray of snacks. An assortment of Beethoven and Wagner symphonies floated from the stereo as Greta set the tray on the coffee table and resumed her position next to Hans. The Peipers' two German Shepherds, Schmeling and Leni, lay asleep near the hearth, preferring warmth over the unseasonably cold and blustery weather outside. From time to time, one or the other woke, sniffed, and went back to sleep.

Hans dealt the next hand of Skat around the coffee table. He looked forward to the Friday afternoon card game at the chateau. He enjoyed the nearness of Greta and the company of Kurt, his close friend and confidant since 1944. The chateau sat on a piece of the two hundred acre farm which Hans had bought at a low price when he came to Dubain in 1960. Although he paid with some of the gold he had put away in a Swiss bank account during the war, he'd placed the title in Greta's name. The farm was shaped in a rectangle, east to west. Its east boundary line abutted Hoosier National Forest. Greta leased the one hundred twenty tillable acres to neighboring farmers who appreciated the low rents. Good, hard-working Germans, Hans thought.

Today's game, however, offered Hans no respite from the crises that threatened to destroy the Great Reich. In the desperate years after

Germany's surrender, Hans, along with Otto Skorzeny and other SS leaders, formed the Great Reich and set up its governing structure. Hans recalled how hard he had fought for a simple governing structure and a Great Reich Oath as the means to bind together all Great Reich citizens, from the premier down to the lowliest foot soldier. He mostly succeeded at both. At the top of the governing structure was the premier. Immediately beneath the premier was the Assembly, composed of all deputies of the Great Reich. Each deputy presided over a gaus. A gaus was a territory of any size, shape, or political division, ranging from a small nation, like Holland, to one or more contiguous states, like in America. Each gaus was further divided into districts. The deputy for that gaus also served as the deputy of the districts. The premier appointed the deputies. The Assembly, over the opposition of Premier Skorzeny, adopted the Great Reich Oath as drafted by Deputy Hans Peiper:

"I do solemnly swear: I pledge my allegiance to the Great Reich of the World, above any that I owe to any other nation, territory, place, or entity. I place the Great Reich and future generations of Great Reich citizens above my personal interests and ambitions. I will maintain the secrets of the Great Reich and will preserve, protect, and defend the Great Reich against all enemies, external and internal. I pledge to give my life to these ends. So help me, God."

Otto Skorzeny, with Hans's support, was elected the Great Reich's first premier. In turn, Skorzeny appointed Hans as deputy of the Indiana gaus. Twenty-two years later, both Skorzeny and Hans continued in those positions and, twenty-two years later, their relationship, always strained, had reached—perhaps moved beyond—the breaking point.

Hans and the deputies who sided with him had been meeting clandestinely. The group had started with Hans and about twenty deputies from the United States and had grown to include most of the North American deputies, about half of the European, and a smattering from South America and Russia, about eighty in all. At the last meeting, the deputies agreed with Hans's opinion that Skorzeny had succumbed to the madness of megalomania and could no longer be trusted with the premiership.

Six months before, Skorzeny secretly resolved that the Great Reich would present itself to the world by the end of 1970 by seizing Argentina. When word of this decision along with rumors of Skorzeny's failing health and mental instability reached Hans, he and seventeen other deputies flew to Buenos Aires to confront Skorzeny and his vice premier, Wilhelm Hess. Skorzeny admitted his illness but used it as the impetus to move forward with his Argentine plans. Skorzeny told Hans and the others that the Great Reich was now the Fourth Reich, the logical successor to the Third Reich, and that he, Skorzeny, was the logical successor to Hitler.

It was Hans who had spoken up. "Premier Skorzeny, your actions violate your oath and will destroy the Great Reich."

"Deputy Peiper, you forget history—our history!" exclaimed Skorzeny. "Do you not recall that we were released from the Hitler Oath when the conditions under which we gave it no longer existed? This is 1968, Herr Peiper, not 1945, and world conditions now threaten our very existence. The Jews rise in their filthy Israel, and the communists spread everywhere. The Soviet horde will soon dominate all of Europe while China, under Mao Zedong, grows ever more powerful. The communists will soon conquer all of Southeast Asia and will move from there to subjugate Japan, the Philippines, Australia, and all islands and territories across the Pacific to the west coasts of the Americas. Our enemies will annihilate us unless I take action now."

"Premier Skorzeny," Hans replied. "I cannot disagree more. It has been understood from the beginning that world conditions are unpredictable and that the Great Reich cannot emerge until it builds the necessary support. We agreed that this required no less than its control of the United States, and we accepted the fact that this was unlikely in our lifetime. You yourself confirmed this when you swore the oath and 'placed future generations above' your 'personal interests.' The United States, though losing in Vietnam, will stop the communists there with its navy and air force."

"You dare challenge my authority, Herr Peiper?"

"Premier Skorzeny," Hans said, fighting to control his temper. "I challenge not your authority, but your miscalculation. You speak of a Fourth Reich and your personal succession to Hitler, and you conjure up this Argentine business to fulfill your ambitions. Yet you have no military forces and no prospects of any. You have not only forgotten the consequences of Hitler's mistakes—mountains of death and destruction, the vengeance of the victors, and soul-piercing dishonor— you propose to repeat them. You move in the deadly circle of history and cast away the oath for your doomed Argentine fantasy and your own farcical glory."

"It is you who miscalculates, Peiper," Skorzeny replied. "Military forces are unnecessary. Argentina's government is unstable and incompetent. I need but to appeal to the Argentine people and they will come to me like children! Besides, President Carballo is sympathetic to our cause."

"President Carballo's sympathy is one thing," said Hans, "but peacefully giving up power to you and your Fourth Reich is altogether another. When you move to seize his country, Carballo will certainly order his armed forces to resist. Do you possess the ten thousand or more loyal, armed, and trained soldiers with the courage to stand guard at the palace and protect your Fourth Reich from Carballo's counter-attack?"

Then Hans turned to Vice Premier Hess. "Do you support this lunacy, Wilhelm?"

"It is not lunacy, Deputy Peiper." said Hess. "So, of course I support it."

"You are weak and timid, Peiper," said Skorzeny, "where Hitler was strong and bold. Yet you dare criticize him and question me!"

"You must reconsi—"

"My decision is final!" shouted Skorzeny. "And you, Herr Peiper, border on treason."

"Against whom?" Hans asked. "The Great Reich? Your Fourth Reich? You? I think not. There is treason in this room, Herr Skorzeny, but it is not mine."

"I should arrest you at this moment, Peiper, but I will give you another chance to prove your loyalty."

"Do not insult our intelligence, Herr Skorzeny," Hans replied. "You give yourself, and not me, another chance. For you well know that my arrest will lead to a revolt against you in the Assembly."

"I will not brook this disrespect, Peiper," said Skorzeny, who then turned to Vice Premier Hess. "Wilhelm, please arrange the deputies' transportation to the airport." He wished the deputies safe returns to their gauses and then turned and walked out of the hall.

Greta laid down her cards and placed a small log on the fire. "Hans, you are distracted," she said.

"Yes, Greta, my mind is not on the game," said Hans. "I apologize."

"It is the Skorzeny business, again. Perhaps you would rather talk?"

"Yes, if that is agreeable to Kurt."

"As you wish, Colonel," Kurt replied.

Kurt was a large man, six foot two and two hundred fifty pounds. He was mostly bald and today wore old but comfortable clothes. He had spent the previous night in the Peiper home. It was Kurt's ambition to rise in the Great Reich. This was commendable but, as of now, Hans held mixed feelings about Kurt's hopes. However, he did nothing to dispel them.

"Kurt, Premier Skorzeny is aware of the Balbachs and has ordered me to eliminate them."

"How does Skorzeny know about the Balbachs?" asked Kurt.

"He has a spy somewhere in the Dubain vicinity," said Greta.

"We have been unable to uncover him. This spy provides detailed information to Skorzeny," said Hans, "so it must be someone close to me whose loyalty I believe to be above question."

Kurt scratched Leni's ears but said nothing. Greta and Hans exchanged looks.

Hans continued. "Skorzeny refuses to understand the workings of America. I have told him repeatedly that the disappearance of even one of the Balbachs will lead to investigations that could implicate us. We have controlled the Balbachs with threats to their families and to disclose the war crimes of Ernie and Gunny at Mortain, and now Timmy in Vietnam. I like the Balbachs where they are, cowardly, malleable, and alive."

"Hans," said Greta, "is there any chance that Skorzeny will back away from this Argentina foolishness?"

"No, schatzie. I have called him several times since our meeting in Buenos Aires. He is adamant to be the first Fuehrer of the Fourth Reich. He is drunk with power that he does not have. Yet it is possible to protect the Great Reich from Skorzeny's Fourth Reich."

"Colonel," asked Kurt, "are they not the same?"

"No," Hans replied, "except to Skorzeny and the sycophantic deputies who support him. Skorzeny committed a serious mistake when he cited the precedent of our releases from the Hitler Oath in support of his decision to release himself from the Great Reich Oath. When our Hitler Oaths ended, we severed our allegiance to Hitler and the Third Reich and pledged ourselves to the Great Reich. Skorzeny has turned this against us by breaking his allegiance to the Great Reich and pledging his loyalties to his Fourth Reich. In our view, there are now two groups, our Great Reich and Skorzeny's Fourth Reich. I and the deputies allied with me have met several times in secret to plan the Great Reich's break from Skorzeny's Fourth Reich."

"Have you made any decisions?" asked Greta.

"We will break with the Fourth Reich, schatzie, when Skorzeny can no longer coerce us. It is possible that this opportunity will arise when Skorzeny launches his insanity in Argentina."

"Do you know when?" asked Kurt.

"No," Hans replied. "However, the spy game goes both ways. We, too, have a well-placed source close to Skorzeny. I am not at liberty to say who. However, I can tell you that we have people placed in apartments around Skorzeny's residence on Florida Street in Buenos Aires. They report on the movements of Skorzeny and his people. Based on the information we have and the speed of the advancement of his cancer, Skorzeny will move soon, perhaps by the end of this year or the beginning of next year."

"Kurt," said Greta. "Skorzeny is cunning and cruel. I have begged Hans to hire personal guards to protect himself."

"Colonel, I must side with Fraulein Peiper. I offer my help."

"I have armed myself and am considering guards," Hans replied. "However, I refuse to become a prisoner to Skorzeny's animosity, which he hides well behind his deceitful smile. We will save the Great Reich from Skorzeny, but that is not enough. No, we must revolutionize our view of history and our role in it. History need not be a record of the past. History can be—indeed for the Great Reich it must be—a prediction of the future! All the world, including Skorzeny, view history as a circle, but the circle means exactly what it implies. It repeats the mistakes of past empires. The Third Reich is a clear example. It succeeded spectacularly but then fell ignominiously because of Hitler's megalomania and military missteps. All this could have been avoided had Hitler and the fools around him read and applied the lessons of past empires that committed similar mistakes and fell in similar fashions.

"The history of the Great Reich must not be a circle, but a spiral! We can create the spiral if we have the daring to will it by means of courageous, rational, and wise decisions. If we do this, we and we alone will forge our destinies. We will bury the errors of the past and move forward with the best of the future. We will infuse every aspiration we have, every idea we conceive, every action we take, into the great things of the universe—art, literature, mathematics, astronomy, architecture, music, philosophy. These things will drive our splendid race, of which we are both heirs and progenitors, ever upward until the day, that most fantastic of days, when we reach the topmost point of the spiral and touch God's face with the living flesh of our hands!

"The spiral must start now so that it is well on its way upward when we formally introduce ourselves to the world. However, if either our timing or place of introduction is wrong, the spiral will change direction, rapidly move downward, and take the Great Reich with it."

"Colonel, when and where should we present ourselves?"

"The right place is the United States, and the right time is when the Great Reich controls the government and the governments of a majority of the states, particularly those of New York, Texas, and California. The path to these governments lies with the Great Reich's fusion with one of the American political parties, Democrat or Republican."

"Which one, Colonel?"

"The Democratic Party is riddled with Jews and communists. It is chaotic, fractious, and corrupt, as Daley and his Chicago mob attest. It calls itself the 'people's party,' and proves it by stealing tax dollars from the bright and productive and giving them to lazy negroes, which only encourages them to make more negroes. It is stupid. It warred against Germany instead of joining our cause against the Bolsheviks. Kennedy's weakness emboldened Khrushchev to place nuclear missiles in Cuba. Truman bumbled into Korea and Johnson into Vietnam. Its policies—civil rights laws, no prayer in schools, the 'great society' goal of eliminating poverty, school desegregation, and equality of all races—have unleashed dangerous forces that it cannot control. The backlash against the Democrats is well underway as more and more Americans see the Democrat Party for what it is: An anti-capitalist socialist club of snobbish elitists that rewards sloth, punishes hard work and thriftiness, and buys the votes of untermenschen Americans with gifts of other's tax dollars.

"On the other hand, the Republican Party grows stronger. Even now, its ranks swell with former Democrats who openly admit that the party of their fathers has sold out to the Africans. These Democrat defectors, once a trickle, are growing into a flood because of Kennedy's and Johnson's Civil Rights Laws. At the same time, there is developing in the Republican Party a stronger and stronger core of what are called 'conservatives.' These call themselves 'Conservative Republicans,' and their goal is a conservative Republican Party to rule an ever more conservative America. I am certain that Conservative Republicans will dominate America and rule for decades, perhaps beyond decades. I have met and talked to them at length. The Conservatives are organized, stable, and disciplined. They have clear goals and not the slightest fear of what it will take to attain them. They are careful planners, adroit administrators, skilled propagandists, and talented in the art of timing. They strengthen their party daily with sympathetic recruits and by purging it of what they call the 'liberal Rockefeller Eastern Establishment Republicans.' Americans are desperate for new leadership and they will turn to the Conservatives for it. Why? Four words: Fear, Enemy, Morality, and Patriotism.

"I predict that conservatives will elect the no-nonsense and sworn anti-communist, Richard Nixon, as president. By the time Nixon leaves office, conservatives will have in place the basic mechanisms for achieving dominance: propaganda machines, dependable sources of money, the best election specialists available, secret intelligence groups, and the tacit support of those who profit from military contracts. Conservatives will push ever more wealth and power up to the already and soon-to-be wealthy and powerful, and away from the untermenschen Americans on whom such things are wasted."

"Where does the Great Reich fit in, Colonel?" Kurt asked.

"The conservatives will fuse with the Great Reich under the umbrella of the Republican Party. This is not as difficult as some might think. Many conservative Republicans are Aryan, or at least believe they are, and so they instinctively understand that God has shed his grace on them, and them alone, and that America is theirs, and theirs alone. To them—as well as to us—America is simply a means to more wealth and more power. I have met with the more influential conservatives in the Republican Party. They not only agree with and share our aims, they respect us because we have already elected Great Reich citizens as sheriffs, mayors, members of town and county councils, even state legislators. They are even more impressed that the Great Reich holds ministerial positions in several state governments, including Indiana's."

"Hans, when do you predict the Great Reich will gain control of the Republican Party?" asked Greta.

"In thirty to thirty-five years, maybe less, Greta. The conservatives must strike a delicate balance here. The subjugation of Americans must be fast enough to deny the liberals time and means to ruin the conservative strategy, but slow enough to lull the rest of Americans into a slow descent to economic stupor, submission, and servility."

"Your talk is thrilling," said Greta. "However, I worry for you. You carry much responsibility. Sometimes, I am afraid it is too much."

"Ach, Greta, mein schatzie, I, you, Kurt—all Germans—share the majesty of the German soul. It is the German soul that sees and feels and loves too much. We shed tears for Germany, our comrades, the Great Reich we are building, our families, the splendor that once was Berlin. But who can change the soul? Who can deny the love? Who can swallow the tears? None of us can, and none of us wants to. These set us apart from the rest of the world. Do you wonder why forests are irresistible to us Germans, and why, right now, you and Kurt and I are sitting snug and warm in the middle of the woods? It is because of our souls, Greta. Germans love forests because they, too, have souls. Souls that embody and reflect the German soul, so wide, so deep, so melancholic, so simple, so complicated, so hard, so soft, so alive. This same spirit abides in some of the people of Dubain, appropriately descended from the Fatherland. The separation of generations and the Atlantic Ocean does not sever this spiritual tie."

Hans stopped and stared into the fire for a few moments. The room was silent except for the snapping of the flames. He glanced at Kurt, then he turned to Greta.

"Perhaps I have bored my wife and best friend," said Hans.

"Hans," said Greta. "You have not bored. You have inspired."

Kurt sat up in his chair. "Colonel, you have spoken many times in my presence. Always I am impressed. But this—today, just now— might have been the best. It was my good fate to hear it."

Greta rose. "Hans, you must be hungry after that sermon." They all laughed. "I will prepare a supper for you."

Kurt rose to get another bottle of wine from the cellar. Schmeling and Leni woke, shook their fur, and walked to the door. Hans let the dogs out and fed them, then checked the small culvert under the patio. The culvert drained water from the higher ground south of the patio to the lower ground north of it, but it sometimes clogged with the detritus of the woods. Water trickled out the north end of the culvert, which meant it was unclogged. Hans returned to his seat, emptied his wine glass, and stared into the flames. Kurt opened a new bottle, filled fresh glasses, and waited. In a few minutes, Leni and Schmeling yipped at the door and Hans let them inside. They curled up near the fire and closed their eyes.

Hans looked at Kurt. "See Leni and Schmeling? I never question their loyalty to me. But I do wonder about the loyalty of others. Do you have any suspicions as to the identity of the spy in our midst?"

"I do not, Colonel."

Hans stirred the fire with the poker.

"Kurt," Hans lowered his voice, "you have been a close comrade all these years. Now you watch over my family and protect us from the Balbachs. I thank you for all this."

"It is my duty, Colonel."

"Do...do you remember that night in Switzerland?"

"Yes, Colonel."

"You told me the truth of my family in Dresden. I turned to you in my grief that night. You were so kind and gentle. You charmed my good friend, Klo. You walked me to the hospital to see Maria. Then you helped me find Greta. I owe you more than you can know."

"Colonel, you owe me nothing. You honored me when you named me your adjutant after Ernie Balbach killed Stresseman at Mortain. Always you are my colonel, and I your adjutant."

"And now," Hans said, "Maria is a beautiful young woman. She is precious to me, and yet she hurts me."

"It is good that you ordered Maria away from the forest and Tim Balbach," said Kurt. "I have no children, so she is like a niece to me. It pains me to watch her without her knowledge, and more so to have to report to you that I saw her and Tim Balbach together in the forest twice in the last three weeks."

"Maria is young, headstrong, and accustomed to having her way. Perhaps Greta and I have spoiled her. To spare her feelings, we have kept from her the truth of her parentage as well as many of the realities of the Great Reich, which she might find unpleasant. Perhaps we have waited too long to find her a husband, but there is a reason for that also. Now she has become attracted to Tim Balbach and will want something more with him. I do not have it in me to upbraid her for disobeying my orders. So Greta will talk to Maria. Do you think that will help?"

Kurt rose, put on his coat, and looked over the family photos on the ledge above the fireplace. "I must get back to my station, Colonel."

"You have not answered my question."

Kurt faced his colonel. "Maria might listen to her mother. However, I believe you must deal with Tim Balbach. It can be done cleanly and in such a way as to not risk you or the Indiana gaus. It is unlikely that Maria can free herself from him. It must be done for her."

"Thank you, Kurt."

Kurt petted both dogs, wrapped his windbreaker around his neck, finished his glass of wine, and walked to the door where he stopped, then turned around. "Good evening, Colonel."

"Good evening, Kurt."

Greta entered the great room from the kitchen alcove just as Kurt shut the front door behind him. She examined the door for a moment before turning to face Hans. "Well?" she asked.

"It is not Kurt."

"How can you be certain?"

"I've known Kurt for twenty-five years, schatzie. He is not stupid, but he is incapable of hiding something like this. I watched his eyes when I spoke of loyalty. He showed not the slightest comprehension of my hints."

"If Kurt is not Skorzeny's spy, then who is?"

"We will uncover him soon, schatzie."

Hans poured another glass of wine and considered Kurt's advice. Is Kurt right? he thought. Yes. You must call your man in Germany. There can be no mistakes on this mission.

Hans looked around the chateau. Eighty of the two hundred acres were rough and wooded. Hans, with Greta's help, designed the chateau and chose its location near the eastern end of the tree farm near Hoosier National Forest. The patio and the parking lot lay to the chateau's west. A gravel lane, the only ingress and egress, started at the parking lot's west side and ended one-half mile west where it intersected a north-south paved county road. This and another county road bounded the entire farm on both the west and southern sides.

The chateau was his place of rest and peace. It was a warm fire, a lovely and lively wife, nourishing and tasteful food, obedient dogs, quality wine and scotch, interesting company, and memories. Kurt, Greta, and Maria had helped with the construction of the chateau. Hans recalled the aura of Greta as she hammered and sawed. Her sweat and determination and her blond hair hanging to her shoulders and flowing across her face created about her a sensuality that, even now, stirred Hans. She'd not lost this passion. There, in the home they built together, he raised his hand for her to join him by his side.

Chapter 16

Premier Otto Skorzeny and Vice Premier Wilhelm Hess sat on the terrace of Skorzeny's apartment on the top floor of the Kavanaugh building, one hundred twenty meters above Florida Street. A garden of plants surrounded them but did not hinder, Otto saw, the spectacular view of Florida Street, much of Buenos Aires itself, and the Rio de la Plata River. Lately, as Otto slowly lost weight and fought against fatigue and a growing pain in his back, he spent more time in the warmth and sunshine of the Buenos Aires subtropical climate. The heat warmed his body and eased the pain that until recently he attributed to normal aging. He would turn sixty in two months, but ever the fatalist, he doubted he would see many birthdays after that. When the Court of Death issued a summons, there was no staying its writ. Even still, he smiled as he considered the good fortunes of his life. For while destiny had decreed his earthly death, and maybe soon, it had also filled his earthly life with daring, success, and joy, and promised more. The premiership leavened fulfillment, a constant thrill born of his belief that his entire life had been but a preparation for just this position at just this time and in just this place.

"Premier Skorzeny," Hess said, starting his report. "We now have over five hundred soldiers. This does not include the latest recruits from the Argentine army or by the deputies in all the other Argentine gauses. Our friends in the Argentine army continue to smuggle weapons to us. Our man in the government reports that Carballo exhibits no signs of alarm. Also, as you ordered, I have finished the preparations for the Assembly meeting tomorrow. The agenda includes your timetable for the seizure of Carballo's government. I deleted the subject of Deputy Hans Peiper."

Skorzeny had appointed Wilhelm Hess as vice premier just two years earlier because of his youth, intelligence, and loyalty. Hess, thirty-seven years of age, stood at five feet and eleven inches and wore his blond hair short. He dressed tastefully, like a Buenos Aires businessman, but not ostentatiously so as to draw attention to himself. Hess had grown up in the Hitler Youth and served bravely at the age of fourteen in a volkssturm unit against the British.

"When I decide on Peiper's fate," said Skorzeny, "I want it to be a surprise to everyone, and this includes the deputies who remain loyal to me."

Over the years, Hess had proven his loyalties. Skorzeny decreed the strategy and tactics of the Fourth Reich, and delegated the details to Hess. Hess carried out his duties efficiently and competently. He was totally loyal to Skorzeny. However, Skorzeny more than sensed that Hess coveted the premiership for himself. Hess was one of a number of possible candidates for it. While Skorzeny was certain Hess would continue the work of the Fourth Reich, he was not yet certain that he possessed the ruthlessness necessary to fend off challengers and successfully carry out the Fourth Reich's policies.

"Wilhelm, you do well for the Fourth Reich. Your efforts are appreciated."

"Thank you, Premier Skorzeny."

Skorzeny, still in his reflective mood, continued, "When I was a boy, my father taught me a valuable lesson, which I have carried since. My native Austria was all but destroyed from its defeat in the Great War. My family went without many things. I once complained to my father that I had never tasted butter and wanted to. My father was a wise man who saw my future. He said that there was no harm in doing without because such circumstances prevented one from falling into a soft life. I have tasted butter many times since then, but I have never forgotten my father's real lesson: The most crucial parts of life are those that teach, and the best teacher in life is denial. Put another way, Wilhelm, many of the best events in life are those that deny you something you wanted at the time, or force on you something you did not want at the time.

"I stood at the gates of Moscow and glimpsed the spires of the Kremlin but went no further because the Soviet armies drove us back. This was quite painful, but I remembered my father's words and got through it. I was wounded in battle—you see the scars on my arm—but battle brought me the Iron Cross and then the Oak Leaves to the Knight's Cross, awarded by the Fuehrer himself. These raised me to the attention of my superiors, which resulted in promotions."

"Mr. Premier," said Wilhelm, "as a boy it thrilled me when you rescued Benito Mussolini from his own countrymen. They said you were the most dangerous man in Europe."

"Yes." Skorzeny laughed. "Goebbels proclaimed it on radio. But do you know that I failed at the first attempt?"

"No."

"I certainly did, Wilhelm, but my father's lesson sustained me. I got another chance and succeeded."

One of Skorzeny's guards interrupted to report a call from a person in America identified as a "friend." Otto motioned Wilhelm inside where Otto picked up the phone and Wilhelm listened in on an extension to take notes. It turned out to be a short but very informative conversation with Skorzeny's spy in Deputy Hans Peiper's inner circle. Skorzeny thanked the spy, and he and Wilhelm returned to the terrace.

"Just as we suspected, Wilhelm. Peiper is plotting against me. It started twenty-two years ago when we formed the Great Reich. Peiper is a talented and resourceful man, but he is also ambitious and covets the premiership. In earlier years, I saw to it that he moved up in the organization. Now he refuses my vision of a Fourth Reich and substitutes his own vision of the Great Reich."

"At our last meeting," said Wilhelm, "Peiper was obsessed with the fanciful romanticism of the Great Reich. 'Why,' I wanted to ask him, 'do you continue with the Great Reich, which we now know is impractical and unreachable? Do not you see that Premier Skorzeny's Fourth Reich will conquer first Argentina, and eventually all of South America, probably within the next several years?'"

"Ah, Wilhelm, you see and think clearly where Peiper does not."

"Mr. Premier, perhaps Peiper has spent too much time in his Jewified and Negrified America. How do you propose to move against him?"

"I have given that much thought, Wilhelm. But I would like your opinion."

"Peiper must be eliminated. However, the time, place, and method are critical. The goal is not only to remove him, but to send a warning to other real or would-be traitors. It must be done before the Fourth Reich seizes Argentina. It should occur on Peiper's home territory before many witnesses, and the method must be as humiliating as possible."

"You show ruthlessness, Wilhelm," said Skorzeny. "I like that in you. It is essential if you are to succeed me."

"Thank you, sir." Wilhelm smiled. "Sometimes, your best friends turn into your worst enemies, and you have no choice but to remove them. There is no room for sentimentality in these cases. The Fuehrer himself set the precedent thirty-four years ago in his Night of the Long Knives when he purged Ernst Roehm and his rabble of street brawlers. They were among the Fuehrer's earliest supporters, then they turned on him. They left him with no choice."

"I remember it well, Wilhelm. I myself arrested several of the provocateurs."

"Sir, Peiper leaves you no choice. However, I warn you that Hans Peiper is not Ernst Roehm. Where Roehm was a homosexual, grossly insubordinate, the leader of an undisciplined faction that Hitler no longer needed, and stupid, Hans Peiper is charming, a qualified leader, a family man, wealthy, smart, and resourceful. If you move against Peiper without sufficient provocation, you could face a revolt in the Assembly. So there must be a powerful and undisputable basis for removing him."

"What do you consider a 'powerful and undisputable basis'?" asked Skorzeny.

"In my opinion, Peiper's insubordination in refusing your orders to put the Balbach families out of the way do not justify his removal. His treason against the Fourth Reich does."

"I agree with you, Wilhelm," said Skorzeny. "Do you see that it is my papa's lesson once again? Hans Peiper was once a valuable asset. Now, he is a powerful threat, one I certainly neither wanted nor asked for. But I, with your help, can turn this unpleasantness into opportunity. One, to get rid of Peiper, and two, to gain the fear and obedience of all the Assembly and their acquiescence in my designs on Argentina and all of South America."

Deputy Hess excused himself to prepare Skorzeny's remarks for the next day's meeting. Otto Skorzeny smiled. After he conquered South America, he would choose a worthy successor—and Hess looked more and more like the proper man—and endow him with the springboard of an entire continent. Once he knew his legacy was secured, he could lay down his earthly burdens and peacefully pass into the next life.

Chapter 17

Father Chris Hagemeyer made his way through the forest to the top of a hill. He sat on the forest floor facing west, leaned back against a beech tree, took the rosary from his top pocket, and laid it aside. He pulled a pint of whiskey from his jacket, unscrewed the cap, and drank about one-third of the liquor. He placed the cap with his rosary, rested his head against the tree, and closed his eyes. He spent the next few minutes swallowing the remainder of the pint. Then he placed the empty bottle next to the rosary and brought out a second pint. The hot liquid sloshed in his stomach, then calmed it, then spread its numbness throughout his body.

This particular spot in the forest was his alone for quiet contemplation. Chris had discovered his place of peace and solitude shortly after he arrived in Dubain from Omaha. It was here that he caressed beauty. It was here that he eavesdropped on God's creatures going about their lives. He heard the rustling of squirrels and chipmunks in last year's leaves on the ground and the new ones in the hardwoods. He heard the singing, crooning, and cawing of creatures blessed with flight and voice. It was here that he whiffed the singular yet indefinable aroma of the woodland. In this place he existed in child-like wonderment at the certainty of the presence of God in all these things. And it was here that he prayed for others.

But now he prayed mostly for himself, asking God and His mother for the courage to stand up to and face down the false charges of homosexuality and pedophilia. His superior and mentor Eric Faulkenburg believed the rumors—or most of them—because he said credible witnesses had come forward. Even Maymie Balbach doubted his protestations of innocence. Many of the parish shunned him and his masses. At the Schnitzelbank bar, people distanced themselves from him in the belief that physical proximity equaled common guilt.

There was no priest to comfort a priest. There were only the balms of alcohol and prayer and, Chris discovered, more and more of the former and less and less of the latter. Chris picked up the rosary beads with his right hand, held the pint in his left, faced the dark clouds that began to blot the sun, and started the Rosary of the Sorrowful Mysteries. He prayed to the Blessed Virgin, sometimes in silence, occasionally out loud, and mostly mumbling. "Hail Mary, full of grace, the Lord is with thee…Glory be to the Father, and to the Son, and to the Holy Spirit… The First Sorrowful Mystery, the Agony in the Garden…"

Chris recited the decade of Holy Mary's then stopped. He lowered his head and cried, sobbing and hiccupping beneath the tree. He quaffed small drafts from the pint when he could. He skipped over the Mother and beseeched God directly. "My friends have deserted me. My enemies bear false witness against me. Is it your will that I accept this cup and drink of its bitterness? Must I carry the cross to Golgotha and there be crucified?"

A thunderstorm gathered in the west and bolted lightning. The woods quieted, then dimmed and then turned a greenish hue. Chris's tears slowed, stopped, and dried. He pocketed his rosary, emptied the second pint, and laid it aside with the other.

"What are you doing, Chris?"

Chris looked up at an apparition against the darkening forest, one dressed in jeans and a Boston College sweatshirt. Slung over his shoulder was a little satchel full of accruements for masses and oils for anointing. Father Faulkenburg, Chris's antagonist, an Old Testament prophet reeking of hellfire and brimstone, stood over Chris with his hands on his hips.

"I'm praying, Eric," Chris replied.

"What are you praying for?"

"That's between God and me," said Chris.

"But you are drunk. I see the empty pints," said Father Faulkenburg. "You cannot pray in a state of intoxication."

"I'm content to let God be the judge a that."

Father Faulkenburg sat on the ground opposite from Chris and leaned against a log. "Chris, we are friends. Together we have built upon St. Augustine's reputation as a paragon of faith and goodness. But I am afraid you cannot go on."

"I'm fully capable of carrying on. Why do you think otherwise?"

"We have talked about these things many times, Chris," said Father Faulkenburg. "Your soul is darkened with the sins of homosexuality and pedophilia. You are mentally ill and you need help. Mumbling prayers in between shots of whiskey are not the acts of a stable man." Father Faulkenburg lowered his voice. "Moreover, I watch you with the children on the playground at recesses. You are becoming all too familiar with them."

"Familiar? What the hell's that mean?"

"You touch them in improper ways."

"That isn't true, Eric, and you know it. I'm not a homosexual. I have no urges with children. I hug 'em. I've always hugged 'em. 'Specially those whose homes reek with alcohol and violence. I'm a priest who stands falsely accused."

"Chris, you are, I'm afraid, a drunken priest and are rightly accused," said Eric. "I have no choice. I must report this to the bishop. I am very sorry, Chris. The bishop will see that you go to a hospital for treatment."

"Eric, no sinner likes his judge. 'Specially when the sinner is no sinner but is wrongfully accused by the judge. So fuck you, Father Faulkenburg!"

"Chris, you are insane!"

"Am I? All this started last summer when I saw you driving with a blond woman in the seat beside you. Is this why you persecute me?"

"What on earth do you speak of?" asked Father Faulkenburg.

"Oh, I think you know, Eric. I've been watching you. Seen you driving with this woman several more times."

"Chris, she is a communicant and I am her confessor!"

"Like hell you are. I saw you and her together in the woods 'bout three weeks ago. I saw no communion and heard no confession. But I saw smiles and heard laughter. You're breaking your celibacy vows, Eric. Don't have to speculate on the bishop's reaction to that, do we?"

"You are making a serious mistake, Chris. You must accept your responsibility in all this and not try to victimize others."

"Victimize? What 'bout those you left behind in Germany, Father Eric Faulkenburg? I've looked into that, too. Are you really who you say you are? Buncha Nazis hid out after the war. Undercover. Some faked being priests so they could get the hell out of Germany. How can we be sure you're not one a those bastards?"

"I pray for you, Chris."

"Pray for me? You'd best pray for yourself, because I won't stop. If you're a priest, you were attached as chaplain to a German unit. Which unit, Eric? You go on many trips. Never say where you're going and why. If the trips're for the faith, then I'd know. What'll the bishop say 'bout these trips? Or mebbe he's a part of it all. Yeah, That's it. Eric and the bishop!"

"Father Hagemeyer, your drunken lies only add to your burden of sins. Stop it. Stop it now!"

"Lies, Eric? Other parishioners're curious 'bout these things."

"Who?"

"Won't say. It's the confessor thing. But you...you know 'bout that, don't you?"

"You will not say, Chris, because you are lying. Shame on you."

"You will not destroy me without a fight!"

"You are committing the sin of blackmail, and false blackmail at that. I pray for you, Chris."

"Don't bother. Blackmail shmakmail, pissmail, fugmail."

"May God bless you in your suffering and insanity."

"I suffer, but I'm sane. So may God damn you!"

Father Faulkenburg rose and walked away. Chris didn't see where he went, but fifteen minutes later the storm broke. Chris rose, pocketed the empty bottles, and walked—stumbling some—in the rain to his car. He surprised himself. Even after the confrontation with Father Faulkenburg, for the first time in weeks, peace drove away the anguish and filled his mind and body.

Through the rain, Chris looked up into the sky and shouted for his God to hear, "It's not my will, but yours be done. Amen."

Chapter 18

Radius crouched in the muddy German trench and faced another Boche trench about a hundred feet farther up the hill. He held his pistol in his right hand and his trench knife in the other. Radius was alone except for dead Boches and Doughboys, and maybe some Tommies, all muddled together in untidy heaps. Black, greasy smoke fumed over the trench and coiled around him. This time he felt the water's cold. So cold, he thought. Where's Brute? Did Brute get killed? Where's my rifle? Probably behind in one of the fields we crossed to assault this goddamn hill. Or maybe it's lyin' in the woods where we tried to hide from the German machine guns.

Radius remembered that the American commanders said the bombardment of the German positions before the attack knocked out the Boche's machine guns. After the attack began, the commanders sent word to the doughboys that they had miscalculated and to be careful of the German guns. That stupid British Field Marshal Doug Haig proclaimed that the machine gun was a much overrated weapon. But no one had ever ordered Haig to jump out of his trench and wear one out with his chest.

Radius, who spoke German, listened to the Boche plan their counterattack on Radius's trench. The German NCOs told their men that only a few Americans manned the trench and taking it should be easy. "Don't jump into the trench at the intervals where the Americans can easily shoot you," they said. "Zigzag until you get within fifteen meters of the trench, then lay flat on your stomach and crawl. We'll shoot tracers over your heads at any enemy who reveals his position. Follow the tracers nearest to you and throw a grenade into the trench at that point."

There was a short low whistle. The German soldiers jumped out of their trench and raced towards Radius. Radius hear them yelling, "We want our trench back, you Amerikaner bastards!" Radius raised his pistol above his head and fired, moved ten feet to his right and fired again, and then ran in the muck to avoid the grenades landing in the trench. He'd gotten about twenty feet to the left of his original position when one Boche jumped on him, one attacked from the left, and two more attacked from behind. Radius slashed with his knife and shot his pistol point-blank into the Germans, but no wounds appeared on the Germans, and they didn't fall.

Then Radius heard muffled voices. "Careful," they said. "He's crazy. Don't hurt him!"

Radius tried to talk back but could only manage little more than a whisper. "No! You can't have me as your prisoner and you can't make me talk!"

Then the scene changed. Radius lay on his back, chest deep in the water. Someone took the wooden pistol and wooden knife from his hands. He saw Brute beside him and was overjoyed. Good ol' Brute! Brute! Thought you got killed! I knew you'd make it, Brute! Hotdamn! Brute, they...they killed everybody but you and me. We gotta kill 'em, Brute!

Then the scene changed again. The smoke went away, and Radius heard American voices, one excited, others soothing.

"We got 'em, Radius," said Brute. "They skedaddled. Radius, we gotta move up to the next trench. You're cold. Can you make it?"

"Hell yeah, Brute!" Then Radius saw the other three Boche turn into Americans. Now they were five.

Brute said on three. One, two, three.

Brute, Ernie, Tim, and Gabe pulled Radius out of the Patoka River and carried him up the hill as far as Piankashaw Cemetery. Radius shivered in Brute's arms while Ernie built a fire. Ernie sent Tim and Gabe to get more firewood and blankets. Brute and Ernie stripped off Radius' wet clothes and moved him closer to the flames. Ernie walked to the other side of the cemetery to find more twigs and small brush.

"Radius, it's okay. Everything's okay. We're alive and goddammit did we give hell to the Boche! We took the hill, Radius. Just rest now and get warm."

"I'm so cold. So cold, Brute."

"Shh. Shhh," Brute soothed. "There, you're getting warmer. God bless you, Radius. Goddamn the Meuse-Argonne! Goddamn the gas! Goddamn the Boche and goddamn their machine guns!"

"Brute, it's Black Jack Pershing what got us through, right?" Radius asked.

"Yeah, Black Jack got us through," replied Brute.

"Brute, are those some of our guys buried over there, where the crosses are?"

"No, Radius, they're dead Boche."

"Brute, my leg hurts. Was I hit?"

"No, Radius. I checked. You're just cold from the water in the trench."

"Brute, somebody said the war's over. Is it?"

"Yeah. We won."

"We did?"

"Yeah. Radius, can you keep that in your head?"

"When?"

"November eleventh, it was."

"I musta missed it."

"Yeah. A lot...a lot of our guys did."

"When can we go home, Brute?"

"We are home. Remember the parade around the courthouse?"

"We're not home. You're sayin' that, Brute, cuz I'm dyin'."

"You're not dyin'."

"When're we goin' home, Brute?"

"Ah, Radius."

"When?"

"When the treaty's done."

"When'll that be?"

"Soon."

"How soon?"

"Don't know."

"Where're they doin' it?"

"Vur-sales."

"Vur-sales?"

"Yeah. Some pissant town in France."

"Why aren't you there, Brute?"

"They didn't invite me."

"Who did they invite?"

"The top guys. Wilson and the Brits. The Frogs and Wops too."

"What about the Germans?"

"Don't know for sure. Probably not."

"Brute, what're they gonna do in Vur-sales?"

"Make it so there's no more war."

"Do you believe that?"

"Yeah."

"You're lyin', Brute."

"About what?"

"You don't believe 'em about no more war."

"Shh. Shh, Radius. Save your strength."

"I gotta know the truth, Brute. Do you believe 'em?"

"Yeah. Now be quiet."

"Brute—"

"No!"

"We gotta stop 'em, Brute."

"Stop 'em from what?"

"Makin' more war."

"We can't, Radius. There'll always be more war."

"No!"

"Shh."

"Why're you cryin', Brute?"

"Ain't cryin'. Just some smoke in my eyes."

"You're cryin', Brute. Smoke's blowin' the other way."

"Shhh. Rest now, Radius."

"Do you know the way, Brute?"

"The way where?"

"Home."

"Yeah. I've been there, but I came back."

"Why?"

"To get you, Radius, and to take you home."

"I wanna go home."

"You're almost there, Radius."

Chapter 19

The forest floor sloped gently from Radius's fire to the Patoka River.
Tim Balbach sat on a log uphill from the fire. Ernie sat to his right and
Mary June to his left. Tim had brought the food, two hotdogs and two
buns apiece, all Maymie could afford. He'd been surprised his mother
had packed so much food, but then, there were five more bums living
at Piankashaw than before Tim had left for Vietnam. His father had
offered a quick greeting before he warned the others not to burn the
hotdogs or let them fall into the fire.

Radius, wrapped in blankets, slept beside Brute. Trocksley,
Bernstein, and two new faces, Hal and Gus, arranged themselves in
an arc on the left side of the fire and roasted their hotdogs on sticks.
The fire gave enough light for Tim to watch Frenchie and the new-
comers, Wop, Gabe, and Peanut, sit in a square to the right of the fire
and play bum poker while eating their hotdogs cold. Georgie, strumming his guitar, sat cross-legged to the right of the poker game but
farther up the hill and closer to the cemetery. Georgie wasn't hungry
and didn't like hotdogs, he'd told Tim. All except Trocksley drank
sloocum. Tim hid a jug of Ferdinand Dew hooch behind him and
held it back for later in the night. Peanut "borrowed" the hooch, not
aged and still green, from the still of a farmer who had graciously
and unknowingly lent it. Green or not, aged or not, the Piankashaws
drank it.

"Frenchie, we ain't got all night," said Wop. "Call or drop. Shit or get off the pot."

Frenchie dropped.

Gabe raised three cigarettes. Peanut raised three more cigarettes. Wop folded and Gabe called. Peanut laid out four aces. Gabe laid out a heart straight flush and raked in the pot. "You goddamn cheatin' nigger," Peanut slurred.

Tim noticed that Peanut was always the first to accuse. Gabe just said nothing.

"Calm down, boys," said Trocksley. "It's just a friendly little game of poker."

"Peanut, you cheat too," said Wop. "It's just harder to see because your back's to the fire and you keep leanin' over to block out the moon."

"You oughta know cheatin' when you see it, Wop!" Peanut rejoined. "You were a crooked double-crossin' bookie. They said you cheated everybody on the ponies. The guys you cheated got tired of it and brought in the cops to shut you down."

"Damn cops found my books. Shut me down and put me out of business," muttered Wop as he started dealing the next game. "Five card draw. Ante a nickel or three cigarettes."

Tim chewed a hotdog while he looked over at the poker game. He only came up to Piankashaw Rock to spend time with his dad, and because sometimes it felt like the only place he belonged. He'd spent many a night with the Piankashaw bums. He was used to hard times like Radius acting up, but then there were the times when they played bum poker.

The basic cannons of bum poker were the same as those for country club poker. A pair beats a high card, two pair beat one pair, trips beat two pair, and so on. The similarities ended there because there was no regular deck to count on when playing bum poker. The deck they used came with a wild assortment of cards. Bum poker hands defied the odds. A pair, two pairs, and triples weren't worth betting on. A straight might be, a flush could be, and a full house probably was. You always bet with four-of-a-kind and you bet like hell with a straight-flush. Country club cheating was rare. Bum poker cheating was common because you had to cheat to win. If you won, you were happy. If you lost, you might not eat the next day, or you owned only twenty cigarettes for the next week, or you lost all your hooch and sloocum, which is the very worst that could happen to a bum, thought Tim. A poker bum who got caught cheating might get smacked once or twice, maybe more, but he was never seriously hurt. Then the other players almost always allowed the cheater back in the game.

At first, Tim had asked himself, Why would you let a cheater back in the game, and even the same game in which he got caught cheating? The answer had come to Tim after he spent several weeks in and out of Piankashaw. It was basic economics, a science in which bums were experts. The wealth in the game went up with the number of players. A caught-at-cheating bum kicked out of the game meant less wealth in the game. Welcoming the cheater back mean more wealth in the pot: dimes, quarters, dollar bills, food, cigarettes, aspirin, al-ka-seltzer, hooch, sloocum, more of Maymie Balbach's stew, better clothes, and anything else a poker playing bum had that at least one other poker playing bum wanted.

Tim put another log on the fire, sat, and stared at the game. But this time he saw more than bum poker. He saw real gambling, the highest form of it. He'd played it himself. The games were played in paddies, jungles, tunnels, maybe a helicopter, and sometimes—one time—a village. The stakes were the players' lives. The losers never lament their losses or accuse anyone of cheating. It's the winners you have to worry about, Tim thought as he watched the game and fin-gered the Beretta in his pocket. Even if the winner is you.

Tim looked over at Ernie, who also stared at the bum poker game. Tim imagined a connection with his father in that moment, and he felt something move inside himself, or maybe outside him, sort of like a facade breaking away. But then a cold tingling covered him all over, a bit of something akin to an electro-magnetic field that surrounded and suffused him. The fire, the place, the people all changed for him, as though he had become the central actor in a play from which he couldn't escape.

It was the only explanation that, later, made sense to him.

"Dad?" Tim knew Ernie heard him, but he wasn't listening. He was still focused on the poker game.

"Dad? Daddy?"

This time, Ernie turned his head to face him.

"Dad, the best cheating in gambling is when the other players don't know they're in the game." Tim looked him in the eye and hoped his father understood what he meant.

"I know, son." It was the first time in years Ernie had called him son.

"I cheated. In 'Nam."

"I figured that, Tim."

"I cheated, too," said Gus.

"Well, I didn't cheat," cried Brute.

"Heard that, Brute." Radius sat up, just woken from his sleep. "I cheated. And so did you. We were there. Together."

"No, Radius! No cheatin' for us! Shut your mouth!"

"I can but I won't, Brute. The German prisoners, remember? The brass told us to take 'em to the rear. But they never made it. We hated 'em. Gunned 'em down, we did."

"They were in the game, Radius, and they knew it."

"Their game ended when we took 'em prisoner and disarmed 'em, Brute."

"But our game didn't end. So why should theirs?"

"Black Jack didn't say nothin' 'bout that," said Radius.

"Hey Bernstein—and you, yeah you, nigger," Brute called to the poker players, trying to change the subject. "I don't like niggers and Jews and queers. Why don't you get the hell out of here?"

"Abomination and hellfire!" Bernstein shouted back.

"More a us than you, Brute," said Gabe. "Why don't you hit the road?"

"This place's for whites only!" Brute said.

"It ain't no more," Gabe threw back at Brute.

"Get off 'em, Brute," said Ernie. "They ain't doin' nothin' to you."

Brute hung his head and cussed under his breath.

The gambling and cheating at war thing had gone much further than Tim had wanted. He'd only brought it up as a chance to talk to his father. "Dad, I gotta ask you something."

"Yeah?"

"You might get mad."

"Maybe."

"Leave it alone, Tim," said Mary June.

"No. Go ahead, Timmy."

"Dad, you don't fight anymore. When you drink."

"So?"

"Why?"

Ernie didn't answer right off, and his silence hung over the group like a thunderstorm just before it cracked.

"Because there's nothing to fight about here. I don't gotta live a lie with Maymie and Joey. I don't gotta fight the lie out here. Everybody here has secrets, things they don't want anybody else to know about. I got secrets, Timmy. Brute and Radius have 'em. Even Gus."

"Yeah," Gus agreed.

"Except here, the secrets don't mean much. We all know the truth about Brute, whether he admits it or not. Radius. Gus. Me. At home, we guarded our secrets with lies. Here, we don't gotta. No one judges us. I can't do this at home with your mother, with Joey. By just being within my sight, they remind me of what I did in France. I gotta hide this monster from them. So I hurt, and drink."

Tim couldn't respond right off, nor could he stop the avalanche of emotions cascading down on him.

"You come back from war, but you never make it home," said Gus. "I didn't. I'm filled with hate and fear. So full a these there ain't no room for nothin' that's good, like hope, like love, like forgiveness, and like girls and babies. You love your mom. You love your dad. Your sisters. You scream inside yourself. 'I love 'em! I love 'em!' And you might for a little while. Then the war comes back, and you remember and know what you're capable of. You know how easy it is to kill other humans. How easy it was for you yourself to kill other humans. Hell's fire, they ain't real people. They're just gooks, animals. No one can ever know your true thoughts. Sometimes even you don't know 'em. You can't tell your mom about Vietnam because you can't keep yourself out of the story. Ernie's right. It's better here. You can drink and smoke and forget. You don't have to hide yourself."

The poker players ended their game and left for the caves under the rock. Bernstein and Hal followed. Timmy opened the Ferdinand hooch, took a long drink, and passed it around to the others. Even Trocksley drank. Georgie stopped the guitar and moved beside the fire. He lit a joint and gave tokes to Gus and Tim.

"Fire," said Brute. He pushed a log farther into the flames with his stick. "It's fire, too. Here, it's okay. There, it was dead people. Lots of 'em."

"What's the difference?" asked Trocksley, who everyone there knew had never been in the military. Flunked the physical, he told them.

"The fuckin' smell. It's the Goddamn fuckin' smell!"

"What sme—"

"Trocksley, shut up!" Gus shouted.

Trocksley gave the group a look, then said goodnight and walked up the hill.

Tim's stomach churned and the green whiskey rose to his throat. The last time he'd felt this way was when he met Gunny in Mannheim and they'd talked about sleeping dogs, and about his father.

"Dad?"

"Yeah?"

"I know about Mortain."

Tim expected his father to react in some way, but without batting an eye or looking away from the fire he said, "Gunny?"

"Yeah. How did you know I talked to him?"

"I have ways, Timmy."

"Mom?"

"Yeah."

"Ernie, what about Mortain?" Brute jumped in.

"French collaborators. There was a mother and her son. The son... it was the boy who turned me and Jimmy and another guy over to the

SS the day before. They murdered everybody but me. I got away. Gunny and I helped each other. The mother was a prisoner of the French partisans. The boy was along. I guess to protect his mama."

"Did he?" Brute asked.

"No."

"Why not?"

"Because he couldn't."

"Why not?"

"Because I'd shot him. I murdered both of them, right there in the woods. And so help me God, if there had been a hundred of them I woulda killed all hundred. Pass me that hooch."

Tim lifted the bottle but he didn't feel his father take it from his hands. His head swam, and for a moment he felt he would fall over. His father's stories and his own played over and over again in his head. Everything was slowly coming unglued.

Gus stirred the hot coals with his stick. The fire flared then damped down, but it put out less smoke. He took a draw on Georgie's joint, then he handed it back to Georgie. "Georgie, you were right to run away from the draft," said Gus. "We're losin' the war. Sure as shit we're losin' it. The South Vietnam government is corrupt and it can't care less about its people. They hate their government. They hate us because we support it. We can't win. Johnson and McNamara know it. They kill Americans and gooks every minute of every day and they lie about it. The dirty rotten no good bastards! We should get the hell out. Now."

"Wait just there, Gus." Timmy could not escape his part in the scene around the fire. "You went. I went. Hundreds a thousands of others went. Many of 'em'll never come back. Me and you still fight in those jungles. Why should Georgie get a free pass?"

"He don't get no free pass."

"The hell he don't!"

Gus looked at Georgie. "Georgie, when do you plan to go back home?"

"Can't go home, Gus. You know that."

"I do, but Tim don't. Tell him."

"Because I'd be arrested and jailed. The whole town hates me. My family hates me. They say I'm chickenshit. I'm not! If there were enough like me, we'd end the war in two weeks."

Tim said nothing, but Gus went on. "Timmy, we've all been around Piankashaw long enough to know why we're all here. It's time for your confession."

"My confession, Gus?" Tim asked. "Don't you have one to make?"

"Yeah," said Gus. "But yours will cover mine."

"That don't make sense," said Tim.

"It does, Timmy. There's hope for you, but not for me."

Tim tried to tell Gus he wouldn't say anything, but Gus looked at him so hard through his drunken haze that all Tim could think to say to get out of it was, "Gotta piss."

Tim stood and stumbled into the woods to piss. He finished, zipped up, turned towards the fire, and stopped. All he could think was, Goddamn you, Gus! You sicced the devils on me. My own little private hell. They love fire. When it burns out, they come after me. They find me. They always do. I can't go back there. I can't confess. It'll only encourage the devils. And Dad...

Tim watched his father lean in close to the fire. What about him? he thought. You don't owe him a confession. After all, you didn't get his about Mortain until tonight, and only after he learned that you already had it from Gunny. I ain't goin' back. I'm just gonna walk into the woods and sleep on some leaves in a swale. Maybe the devils won't find me there.

Tim turned around to walk deeper into the forest, but then his head swirled, and not from the hooch and sloocum. He remembered talking to Gunny in Germany: *"What can I do for you, Tim?"*

"I need help to save my family."

"From what?"

"Wars, Uncle Gunny."

Tim had been unsure of his motives then, but now they were clear to him. Now he couldn't help thinking, Is the Balbach family doomed? First Grandpa in Flanders, then Dad at Mortain, then me at Bon Duoi. Are Joey and Henry next? Then their sons after that? Is this our fate? Is there no escape? Can't I break the circle? Is Gus right? Can I be saved?

The answers were all maybes, the worst type of answers. And at this Tim vomited some of the hotdogs and some of the hooch. He didn't feel much better afterward.

Tim walked back to the fire. He put another log on it, then took his seat. They might get my confession, he thought, but they'll have to fight for it.

"Now, Tim," Gus commanded.

"Now what?"

"Your confession."

"You're not my priest, Gus."

"Confession don't need a priest. It only needs a sinner and confessors. You're the sinner. Your confessors are me, your dad, Brute, Georgie, and Mary June. And Radius, if he wakes up again."

"You're not interested in my little sins."

"You're right. We're interested in your big sins."

"Gus, you shut your mouth or goddammit I'll shut it for you."

"Go ahead, Tim. Come at me. I ain't afraid a you."

Gus stood. Brute got between them and ordered both to sit. They did.

"You sinned, Tim, at Bon Duoi. It's tearin' your soul apart. I know because I was there. I saw you. I was there beside you. I sinned too. I tried to talk to you about it the first time you came up here to the rock after you got home, but you said you didn't remember me at Bon Duoi. You wouldn't say another word about it."

"You weren't there, you fucking liar!"

"Yeah. I was there. You know I was Army in 'Nam. You were Marine. We sacked the village together."

"I don't wanna talk about it."

"Tell us, son," Ernie said from the other side of the fire.

"You're not my commander, Dad. Besides, you never told me about Mortain. I had to get it from Gunny."

"And that, Tim, explains why I'm here. I can't talk about it, can't cope, but you still have a chance."

"Pass me the hooch."

Tim took a short drink and fought to keep it down. No one spoke. Tim managed another pull from the jug, then placed it between his knees and looked down at it. The fire popped and crackled. A coyote howled in the distance. Another coyote, much farther away, answered. Tim raised his head and looked at Gus, who nodded.

"Do it, Tim. I started it. Now you gotta finish it."

Tim put his head down. His mind jumbled, not with sentences, but with bits and pieces of flashback. He started in a whisper.

"I joined the Marines. There was basic training, then 'Nam. 'You, Balbach,' they said. 'You're smart. You're small and strong. You're counter-intelligence. You be a tunnel-rat. Go down and kill 'em. Kill the VC guard. Blow in the tunnels. Watch out for the booby traps.'

"We took prisoners. Found a helicopter. 'Pilot, you keep your head forward and this flight never happened.' Up and up and up. Now talk, you slant eyed bastards! No talk. Okay. Throw one out, the other would talk. Always. Sang like a fuckin' canary. Destroy the enemy's intelligence with your side's intelligence, which just increased. Burn this village. Burn 'em all. Napalm sticks on kids. Good. They got my buddies killed. Move to a different place. Say no to hope and fear. Say yes to hate and rage. The killing hate. The killing rage. One village. Two villages. Many villages. See the tunnel holes that the little yellow people hide in their huts? Burn the fucking place!

"Da Nang. Orders. We got orders. Search-and-destroy missions for ten days. Take Highway 14B. Turn north. Go north, then go north. Bon Duoi. I see flashes. I hear pop-popping all over. Begging. Wailing. No mercy cuz you're all VC and you've been-a killin' us. Marines cryin'. Marines screamin'. Marines laughin.' Marines killin'. Shoot! Shoot 'em! Mother Mary, make it stop. Make me stop. She didn't, and I couldn't. Flashing. Pop-popping. My M-16 on automatic. Short bursts into the gook-eyed screamers. I'm shooting the screaming fuckers! Rats. Old men. Women. Kids. All enemy rats. See them go down?

"These things happened. Maybe not. No, they never happened."

"Yeah, they did," said Gus.

"Yeah they did!" Tim echoed. "You'll burn, Balbach. Sure as shit and on-fire flesh stink. It helps not to talk. So stop talking. Get sent to Germany. God bless America and we'll heal you, Marine. Make you all better. Buck up like a man! Bullshit! Whiskey. Pills. Steal 'em from Landstuhl. Bribe the nurses. Hide the gun."

Tim lifted his head and eyed them. Dad, Mary June. Brute staring into space. Georgie strumming, again, but I don't hear nothing. Goddamn you, Gus, you started this.

"Why don't I shoot myself? Why don't we all shoot ourselves?" Tim looked around at the others. "'It's painless,' said a brave man in Mannheim. 'Do it. Right here.' But I couldn't do it. I know I'm gonna lose this game anyway, but I just couldn't do it. I would have, though, back in Bon Duoi."

"How many you kill, Timmy?" Gunny had asked back in Mannheim.

"Why ask me,? Go ask somebody else! Bon Duoi. Duoi Bon. Forwards. Backwards. Means the same damn gook place. I just wanted out, so I lifted my M-16. Then somebody's grabbin' me, hittin' me, holding' me down. You sonofabitch. They're the enemy. Tunnels all over their hooches. Or hutches. Or huts. Get off me!

"'Calm down. Calm down, Timmy,' he said. "It—this—ain't right. Stop. We gotta stop! It's ok, now. It's ok. I looked at 'im. The sun. Hard to see his face. 'Calm down. It's okay.' I looked again. 'Gus,' he said. 'My name is Gus, from Dubain. You know me. Calm down, Timmy Balbach.'"

"It was you, Gus."

"Yeah, Timmy, it was me," said Gus. "I had to bring myself back. I'd already killed. Five, maybe ten. I lost count. I couldn't stop myself until I stopped someone else. Don't know why. Never will. I looked and saw you, Tim."

"Then it was you, Gus, who stopped me."

"Yeah, Timmy, it was me. But I can't cry. Can you?"

Tim dropped his head. There was a pause. He started crying, then looked up.

"Gee, Gus. Thanks. Thanks for refillin' my cup with the blood of 'em that died and makin' me drink it. I never ever wanted to think about Bon Duoi again. You're a great guy for bringin' it back. See the demons flyin'? They'll get me later when I try to sleep. You brought 'em, Gus. Can you make 'em go away? Hell no. You can turn 'em loose, but you can't take 'em back. Nevermind, Gus. They won't haunt you. Just me. Me, Gus. Dad? Do you see 'em? Brute? Mary June? Georgie, can you help? Oh, I forgot. You ran away. Your family and town hate you. Boy, do you ever have it tough, Georgie. Can you fight one of 'em for me? Just for a little while? Oh, look, now I'm cryin' even harder. I'll never stop. Never! Great life, ain't it, Gus? How can I ever repay you?"

"It ain't their fault, Timmy." The group turned and looked at Radius. "Go on and cry as long and as hard as you have to. Don't stop. If me and Brute had cried, we mighta made it all the way home. Maybe Ernie, too. Maybe Gus, who can't cry but has the guts to make you.

"How many times must this scene play out? How many places? How many Timmy's? How many Boche, Tommies, Poilus, Ivans, Japs, Aussies, Miks? Thousands. Hundreds of thousands. Millions. We have—let me count—six right here: me, Brute, Ernie, Gus, Tim, and Mary June. Yeah, that's right. Mary June. She didn't fight on a battlefield. She didn't kill. She never left home, but she carries it as much—maybe more—as any of us. Why? Because she loves someone who did these things. There're others. My kids, Brute's grandkids. I know what they say. 'Don't say nothing to Dad. Don't talk to Grandpa. They're mean. Stay away from 'em.' Then Maymie, Joey, Henry. Ernie carries a double dose. Tim carries a double dose, maybe even a triple when you count his grandpa over there in the cemetery. Georgie's family and town and draft board tried to fly him to Saigon, but they'll never fly him back home.

"Timmy, cry, goddammit, and don't stop until I say so. Do it for yourself, for the others, for us, for those who can't cry. There, Mary June, there. That's right. Hold his head on your shoulder. If he stops bawling, tell me.

"All of you look at Timmy's pocket. See it? See the bulge? It's his gun. He never talks about it. He don't gotta. The gun's his insurance. It's his peace, his death. There're other ways. Look over at those crosses in the cemetery. Almost all of 'em are vets. A few shot themselves, maybe with a gun they carried, maybe with one they found. Don't matter. They're just as dead. Me and Brute planted plenty of our buddies there. Liver disease, cancer, natural causes. Natural causes my ass! I'd like to shoot the next fucking doctor who says a vet died of natural causes.

"But the real grind of it is this: You can't be a little dead, but you can be a little alive, which is worse. You, Timmy, are a little alive now, but you still got a choice. You don't gotta end up like us. What choice, you ask? It's a question as old as Abraham and as new as that hooch there. The choice is one of three: death, a little life, or a full life. The first two are easy for us vets. The last is the hardest. It's a hard thing to be a man, a veteran. It's a sad thing, but it's a proud thing, too, and that's all that is left to most of us.

"You, Timmy," Radius said, pointing at him. "You find the courage to choose a full life, and the strength to get there and stay there. Cuz if you don't, you'll never make it home. You'll go back to the tunnels again, and again, and again. Timmy, you can stop anytime you want. You can stop cryin' now."

Together, they drank the rest of the hooch, put their arms around each other's shoulders, and stumbled up the hill toward the caves and Piankashaw Rock. Tim fell three times, but the others picked him up.

They abandoned the fire to burn to its coals. The coals burned away, and the fire left, taking the demons with it.

The next morning, Trocksley shook Tim awake. He found himself in a bed of rags inside the Piankashaw caves. "Tim. Timmy. Wake up."

"What is it, Jack? Goddamn, my head hurts."

"You got visitors. Outside."

"Who?"

"Your brother, Joey, and Henry."

"What do they want, for crying out loud? I gotta sleep this thing off."

"They won't say, but I think it's important, Timmy. You better get out there right away."

"Where's Dad?"

"Asleep. The boys said not to wake him, but I rousted Mary June. She's out there now."

Tim dragged himself to his feet and walked to the entrance. He saw Joey, Henry, and Mary June standing in a close circle toward the northern end of Piankashaw Rock. As Tim neared, he saw from their faces that their news was serious.

"Joey, what is it? Is it Mom?"

"Mom said for you and Mary June to get home right away," said Joey.

"Is Mom okay?"

"Yeah. She's fine."

"Joey, what the hell's going on? What happened?"

Joey lost his voice.

Tim grabbed him by the shoulders and shook him. "Goddammit, Joey, what is it?"

It was Henry who answered. "Tim, Father Chris hung himself in the cathedral last night. He's dead."

Chapter 20

"Maymie, there's been an accident at St. Augustine's," shouted the police dispatcher over the phone.

"Easy, Freddy. What is it?" Maymie asked in a calm voice honed from years as the head emergency room nurse at St. Mary's Hospital.

"Serious, Maymie. Possible life or death. You're the emergency medical technician on call, right? They said for you and Dr. Friesaman to get there with the ambulance as soon as possible. That's all I know."

Maymie frowned. She was an emergency room nurse. Sure she dealt with trauma victims on a daily basis, but that didn't make her a paramedic. Still, Dubain was a small enough town for Sheriff Beckam to know she was certified to answer emergency calls. He probably knew she was on shift that night.

"We're on our way. Notify them if you can, Freddy. You can call the rectory or the phone that's in the small office behind the sacristy."

"Yes, ma'am."

Maymie hung up the emergency line and quickly called Stuart Friesaman, the doctor on call that night. "Stuart, it's Maymie Balbach. Sheriff Beckam asked that an ambulance go to St. Augustine Cathedral. We'll pick you up at Newton and Third." Maymie quickly hung up the phone then motioned for Carl, the ambulance driver waiting on call with her, to head for the door. "Siren on, immediately."

As the ambulance ran red lights and stop signs and passed vehicles that had pulled over, Maymie focused her mind on her job, which was saving a life, or failing that, comforting the next of kin. Carl pulled over just long enough for Dr. Friesaman to jump in the ambulance with his emergency bag, then they were off again.

"Maymie, do you know what the emergency is?"

"Freddy didn't say. Since it's at the cathedral someone must have fallen or suffered a stroke. We'll be lucky if we get there in time for the latter, but maybe someone has already started CPR."

"You've really thought this through. I'm glad it's you on emergency call tonight."

"We're short-handed, Stuart. One nurse called in sick and another is out on maternity leave. Someday, St. Mary's will grow large enough to hire sufficient staff. C'mon, Carl. Step on it!"

Maymie, Dr. Friesaman, and Carl hastened into the cathedral with the gurney. They found four men behind the altar in the sacristy. Father Faulkenburg knelt with his hands folded beside someone who lay on his back. Maymie recognized Sheriff Wilfred Beckam and his chief deputy, Alphonse Huff, standing beside Father Faulkenburg, their hands also folded. Off to the side stood Melvin Eichert, the county coroner. It didn't bode well that the county coroner had made it on the scene before the ambulance.

Maymie saw Father Faulkenburg anoint the person's head with oil and heard him intone the words of the last rites of the Catholic Church. "Through this holy anointing, may the Lord in His infinite love and mercy take you into heaven with the grace of the Holy Spirit." Father Faulkenburg then anointed the hands and the lips. "May the Lord who frees you from sin save you and raise you up."

Maymie and Dr. Friesaman reached the group and looked down. Maymie gasped. It was Father Chris Hagemeyer. There were cord-like burns around his neck. A noose hung at the end of a rope tied to a rafter above. Father Chris lay almost directly under the noose. The top of the janitor's aluminum ladder leaned on the rafter about one foot to the left of the rope's tie-off point. The sacristy floor secured the ladder's rubber soles. A chair rested on its side beside Father Chris, and a rosary lay under the chair. Father Chris's eyes, partially closed, bugged slightly from their sockets, and his mouth, open and twisted, revealed a swollen tongue that lay on his lower gums. His hands were folded as if in prayer.

Maymie saw Doctor Friesaman and Melvin Eichert exchange looks. Stuart checked Father Chris's neck. He caught Maymie's eye and shook his head. Father Chris Hagemeyer was beyond the help of earthly medicine.

Father Faulkenburg gazed up at Maymie. His face displayed a mishmash of anguish, sorrow, and guilt, and his eyes glowed through a sheen of tears.

"Maymie and Stuart? Sheriff? Al and Mel? Will you please pray with me?"

Maymie knelt by Father Chris's head. Dr. Friesaman took the side of Father Chris opposite Father Faulkenburg. Sheriff Beckam crouched beside Dr. Friesaman and next to Father Chris's feet. Huff and Eichert folded their hands and bowed their heads but stood back several feet from the body. "Our Father, who art in heaven, hallowed be Thy name…Thy will be done on earth as it is in heaven…forgive us our trespasses, as we forgive those…and lead us not into temptation, but deliver us from evil…For Thine is the kingdom, the power, and the glory, now and forever, Amen. Eternal rest grant unto him, Oh Lord, and let perpetual light shine upon him. May he rest in peace. Amen."

Dr. Friesaman closed Father Chris's eyes, and the group stood silently for a moment over their deceased friend.

When the moment ended, Sheriff Beckam took charge. "Well, it looks like a clear-cut case of suicide, Mel. I don't think an autopsy is required, do you?"

"No," said the coroner. "But the law requires me to investigate cases of death by apparent suicide."

"I'm terribly sorrowed by this tragedy," said Dr. Friesaman. "If you don't mind, I'll wait outside until you need help transporting the body to the hospital morgue. Maymie, would you care to wait with me? Allow the police to conduct their investigation."

It made sense for her to leave, but Maymie shook her head no. She couldn't bear the thought of leaving Father Chris alone. Sheriff

Beckam waved Dr. Friesaman off. Everyone in town knew how close she and Father Chris had been. Dr. Friesaman stepped outside of the cathedral while Maymie remained inside to listen to the police and coroner talk around her.

"Well then," Eichert continued. "This all seems very self-explanatory. Father Chris Hagemeyer died of asphyxiation secondary to strangulation by hanging from a rope that supported his full body weight."

"Then we can finish the investigation before anyone else comes into the cathedral," said Sheriff Beckam. "Did you read the note, Mel?"

"Yeah."

"Note? What note, Sheriff?" Maymie demanded.

"If you want, I can let you read it, Maymie. I know you and Father Chris were close, and it's only right that you read his last words." Sheriff Beckam then turned to Father Faulkenburg. "Father, we must seal the cathedral before the media and the curious get here."

"I have the keys to the sacristy outside entrance," said Father Faulkenburg. "You can lock all the other doors from the inside."

"Al, see to it. You," Sheriff Beckam pointed to Carl. "Go outside to the ambulance, turn off its flashers, and park it behind the rectory. Move it as close to the back wall as you can. Turn off all its lights. Stay in the driver's seat until I come get you. Do not talk to anyone other than to say that you don't know what's going on inside. Do not exit the ambulance or turn on any of its lights until I personally authorize it. Are you clear on this?"

"Yeah," Carl said. He hurried out the door.

"Sheriff, what's the rush?" Maymie asked. "Why the precautions? I want to see the note."

"Maymie, we're a small force. You know that. We don't have the tools for a full forensic investigation. We can only work with what we got here." The sheriff waved at the noose. "It's obvious what happened. We gotta wrap this up. You'll see the note. Can you bear with me, Maymie?"

"I guess so."

Sheriff Beckam moved the group to the pews in front of the altar. There, he ordered, "Mel, get out your notepad and pencil." The sheriff then turned to Father Faulkenburg. "Father, you were the first on the scene. Can you tell us what happened?"

"At the scene or before?"

"Start when you last saw Father Hagemeyer alive."

Yesterday, Maymie thought, but no one had asked her and knowing that wouldn't help uncover how Father Chris had died. Still, Maymie couldn't help thinking, It was only yesterday I saw Chris alive.

"Chris left the rectory about 9:00 p.m. to prepare for tomorrow's early mass," said Father Faulkenburg. "I was in my room at the time but I heard him go out the door."

"Had he done this before?"

"Many times. Chris liked the altar prepared beforehand so he would not have to rush in the morning."

"How long did it normally take him to do this?"

"Thirty minutes. Forty-five minutes at the most."

"What happened next?"

"I read until about 10:30. I realized that Chris had not returned. Many times, he would go to the Schnitzelbank for a Saturday night beer. Sometimes I would go along, so I was not concerned."

"Did he have a beer tonight?"

"Probably not, Sheriff. At 11:00 p.m. I became worried. I looked outside and saw his car parked in the driveway, so I knew he either had not left or had returned from the Schnitzelbank."

"Did you call anyone?"

"Not yet. There was no reason to. I walked over to the cathedral and entered the south side door. I called for Chris several times, but there was no answer. I saw light coming from the sacristy and I found him there, hanging in the noose." Father Faulkenburg wiped his eyes.

"Did you see or hear anyone else?"

"No."

"What did you see?"

"My God! It was Chris hanging in the noose. I tried to get him down. I held his legs and pushed up, but he was limp, and his head only dropped forward. The noose—it was too tight."

"Did you see anything else?"

"Nothing, Sheriff. However, you must understand that my immediate thoughts were with Chris. I called the Sheriff's Department. Freddy said you and Al were patrolling. I told Freddy there was an emergency in the cathedral—I think I said 'life or death'—and to call you and an ambulance."

"I've since talked to Freddy, who confirmed your call, Father, at about 11:10," the sheriff said. "Freddy radioed me and Al. Then he called the emergency room. Maymie, Freddy said you took the call. Did you note the time?"

"No, Sheriff, but I had just finished my half-hour lunch break, which I take at 10:45. So the call came in around 11:15 or so."

"Mel, you getting all this down?"

"Yeah."

"Father, what did you do next?"

"I rushed back to the sacristy where I again tried to free Chris from the noose. I could not."

"Were there any signs that Father Hagemeyer tried to free himself?"

"No. His hands were clasped in front of him as though he had been praying while...while he hung himself."

"What else did you see?"

"Everything that you saw. The aluminum ladder propped on the rafter, the chair turned over, and the rosary lying under the chair. There was also the note."

"Al and I can confirm that we reached the cathedral about 11:20," said the sheriff. "Al, Father Faulkenburg, and I freed Father Hagemeyer from the noose and laid him on the floor. We used the chair, then placed it in its present position. Father, can you confirm that the chair was situated in about the same position as it was when you entered the sacristy after you called Freddy?"

"Yes."

"Were Al and I the next to arrive on the scene?"

"Yes."

"Who was next?"

"Melvin."

"I called Melvin on our radio band immediately after we received Freddy's call," said the sheriff. "Al and Melvin can confirm this." Melvin nodded.

"And Dr. Stuart, Maymie, and the ambulance arrived next. Correct?"

"Yes."

"Other than the ambulance driver, Dr. Stuart, and the rest of us here, has anyone else entered this the cathedral since you first found Father Hagemeyer?"

"No."

"Father, to the best of your knowledge, had anyone else been in the cathedral, other than Father Hagemeyer, between the time he left the rectory and when you found him?"

"To the best of my knowledge, no."

"Let's go back to the items that Chris used. Father, did you move any of those items other than the chair that I've already explained?"

"Yes, but only the note. It lay several feet in front of the body. I picked it up, read it, and gave it to Al when you found us behind the altar."

"Al?"

Deputy Huff reached into his shirt pocket, pulled out a folded piece of paper, and handed it to Beckam, who unfolded it and gave it to Father Faulkenburg.

"Father, is this the note you found in front of the body?"

"Yes."

"Have you read it?"

"Yes."

"For the record, Mel, Al, and I have also read it." Sheriff Beckam looked down for a moment. "Father Hagemeyer's homosexuality wasn't exactly a secret in this town. Most of us looked the other way but, as it turns out, we shouldn't have."

Sheriff Beckam looked over at Maymie, whose fingers itched to grab the note. The sheriff paused, as though weighing his options for a moment. Then he handed the note to Maymie.

"Here, Maymie. I know you and Father Hagemeyer were close. He woulda wanted you to know his dying thoughts. I warn you, it's straightforward and shocking."

Maymie examined the note. It was typed on standard letter-size paper. She read:

To my parishioners, family, and friends:

I am tortured beyond endurance. I can no longer live with the guilt that rends my body and soul. I am a homosexual and have engaged in sins of the flesh with other men. My homosexuality is an abomination to God, the Church, and you. However, my sins far exceed the bounds of pleasure with other men. I speak of the children. I love children and always considered myself strong enough to restrain my unnatural desires for them born of homosexuality. However, beginning about one year ago, I lost control. Since then, I have lured young innocents into private places where I gave in to my cravings and betrayed their trust. I've tried and tried to change my ways. I beg you to believe this. I prayed to God for His strength, help, and guidance, but for some reason He has not answered my prayers. Perhaps he has another design. Maybe he has willed this, my earthly ending. I can only hope so. I have prayed for the young innocents who found themselves in the clutches of my unspeakable crimes. May the Lord God restore their childhood purity and return to them their trust in the ultimate goodness of this life. I have also prayed for the men I've touched. May they find their way out of the homosexual sickness and into the Grace of our Heavenly Father. I ask all of you to pray for me, though I understand if you do not.

Chris Hagemeyer

"It's my fault," Father Faulkenburg started, "all my fault. I should have seen this coming. I told him I'd decided to see the bishop about his homosexuality and liberties with children. He begged me not to, to give him another chance. I told him no." Then he glanced at Maymie.

"Father Faulkenburg, I too have some blame in this." Maymie pulled out her handkerchief and blew her nose. She knew it was a sin to lie, but an instinct, an intuition, compelled her to fib by withholding the whole truth. "Father Chris and I were close friends," she said. "We discussed his homosexuality, which he denied. We never talked about indecencies with children."

"Father Faulkenburg, Maymie, the rest of you," Mel began, "I've seen a number of suicides during my years as a coroner. Always, some people blame themselves for the suicide. I tell them they are blameless. Father Faulkenburg, you're a priest. Maymie, you're an emergency room nurse. Both of you have witnessed the darkness of suicide before, but I am certain that neither of you had anything to do with Father Hagemeyer's hanging. These things happen. Nobody knows why, but they do. Father Hagemeyer was an educated man of God. He, and he alone, decided to take his own life. May he rest in peace."

"But we have to get to the real point right now," said Maymie. "The media and other people will arrive with questions."

"What point, Maymie?" asked Sheriff Beckam.

"Father Chris typed the note in a moment of anguish and impending death. If this note becomes public, it will smear him." Maymie turned to Father Faulkenburg. "Father, could we consider Father Chris's note to be in the nature of a confession to you or another priest? It would then fall under the confessional seal."

Father Faulkenburg thought for a few moments. "Well, Maymie, it's the penitent's intention that mostly counts. In other words, did Chris intend this note to be a confession to another priest? I think not because the note is addressed 'To my parishioners, family, and friends.' Also, the note lay in clear view. Chris couldn't be certain that I, a priest, would be the first on the scene. A lay person could have found him and the note. Finally, Chris himself was well versed in the Church's rules governing the Sacrament of Penance and the application of the confessional seal. All this makes it clear, I'm afraid, that Chris under no circumstances intended the note to be an act of Catholic confession. In fact, his actions and the words of the note strongly show that he desired the opposite, its publication."

"Come on, Father," replied Maymie. "How do we know that Father Chris wasn't under the influence of drugs or alcohol when he wrote the note and then killed himself?"

"Maymie," said the sheriff, "it's likely that Chris typed the note shortly before he died. To me, the note and the way he rigged up the stuff on the altar says it all. A man under the influence of alcohol or drugs could not have done a better job of killing himself than Father Hagemeyer."

"Did you look for bot—"

"Maymie," Sheriff Beckam cut in. "Father Hagemeyer drank a lot of whiskey in the past year. So, yeah, we searched for bottles, but we didn't find any. There's no smell of alcohol around his body. Father Faulkenburg, have you known Father Hagemeyer to use other drugs?"

"No, Sheriff. Chris drank, but I saw no signs of other drug use."

"But he couldn't have been in his right mind!" Maymie exclaimed. "Father Faulkenburg, surely there is something in Catholic doctrine that covers this. As Sheriff Beckam said, Father Chris's homosexuality is no secret. But the molestation is. Father Chris is dead. Why should we destroy what remaining reputation he has by letting this note out? Why can't it remain a secret among this group? Why must we trample on his grave?" Maymie waived her hand at the others.

"Maymie, think about what you're saying," said Sheriff Beckam. "The molestation is not a secret to Father Hagemeyer's victims. They're out there somewhere, and I'm pretty sure some of them will step forward with the truth. Quite frankly, I believe it's best to disclose Father Hagemeyer's suicide note now. Besides, the public has a right to know."

"Sheriff Beckam," Maymie thought, "I've seen you cover up worse than this."

"I agree with Sheriff Beckam," said Father Faulkenburg. "No

doubt the note will reflect badly on Chris, as well as the Church and me. We failed in our ministries. I failed in my ministry. But I can't worry about the Church and me now. We have a responsibility to the victims. Those young, innocent children." Father stopped to wipe tears from his eyes and face. "If the note is published, the children and their parents might come to us. Then we can help them with the Church's rites of love, healing, and reconciliation."

If the men were so set against preserving Father Chris's reputation, Maymie would have no further part in it. She cast one last menacing scowl at the sheriff and Father Faulkenburg before she walked behind the altar to the death scene. She bent down, lowered her head, and kissed Father Chris on the cheek. She also noted the exact locations of the ladder, chair, rosary, and rope.

Chapter 21

Maymie stood near All Souls Point in Kundek Cemetery. St. Augustine Cathedral was to her back. In front of her and a ways downhill was Father Chris's grave. She stood uphill from the densest part of the mourners. She watched her son, Tim, his friend Gus, and the four other pallbearers lift Father Chris Hagemeyer's casket onto the funeral bier, then step back. Five of them folded their hands and bowed their heads. Tim, the rebel pallbearer, crossed his arms and glared at the coffin, then nudged Gus to do the same. The casket pressed in towards Bishop O'Grimmels, Father Faulkenburg, and the new priest, Father Paul Kessler.

It had been strange meeting Father Paul. He didn't look like other priests Maymie knew with his shaggy hair and large bifocals, but Tim had taken a liking to him when they met to discuss Father Chris' funeral arrangements. Where Father Faulkenburg looked penitent and mournful, and Bishop O'Grimmels looked down his nose at Father Chris' coffin, Father Paul looked around at the people gathered, taking them in as though wondering how best to heal their loss and pain.

The three priests stood on one side of the bier and the pallbearers on the other side. Bishop O'Grimmels stuck to the script written for just this occasion and honed into the bosom of the Church over the centuries. Then Tim Balbach stopped the proceedings.

"Hey you!" Tim pointed a finger towards the sky. "Yeah, you—you goddamn God of Abraham, Bishop O'Grimmels, and Father Chris. You should do better than this! Who—or what—really counts here? Is it the soul who supplicates, the bishop who prays, or you laughing, over-praised and under-performing? Tell me! Tell us!"

The celebrants and mourners gawked. Maymie stood straighter.

"I know about your laws—catechism and Father Chris's religion classes in eighth grade. No one'll say it, but I will. Chris Hagemeyer, the sinner with the rope burns and the typed message on your altar, might this very minute be in the clutches of Lucifer! Know anything about that? Wanna tell us about it? No. No, you won't. You don't care about a man who's hurting. You don't give a good goddamn."

Father Paul moved around the bier and took Tim's hand. Tim yanked it back.

"Where were you when Father Chris needed you? Where were you when me and Gus here lost our lives in that shit-smellin' pissant gook-crawlin' hellhole on the other side of the world? Your world! Where were you when my grandpa marched home a hero and then killed himself? Where were you when my dad's life fell to pieces in Normandy and at Mortain? Where are you now, right this minute, while evil roams this town and holds innocents hostage?"

Maymie saw Father Faulkenburg motion Father Paul Kessler to stop Tim's sacrilege. She held back a smile when Father Paul shrugged his shoulders. No one could stop Tim from releasing what had been building inside of him for so long.

"You don't even have the decency to expose these bastards!" Tim looked up into the sky. "You do nothing for we, the desperate ones. You say your son Jesus died for our sins. Bullshit! It's the other way around. Good men die for your sins. In Flanders, France, Korea. Good men a half a world away right now die for your sins. You sit up there in Heaven, dispensing nothing of value to the people you swear are made in your image and likeness."

Bishop O'Grimmels turned and looked at Maymie. His eyes begged, Can't you stop your son? Maymie smiled and fluttered her right index finger at him.

"See my mom there?" Tim pointed to Maymie. "See her standing by All Souls' Point? What have you done, oh dear one, to lessen her burdens? Like Wop says, you gotta shit or get off the pot. I'd say this to your face if you had enough guts to show it to me. You can get off your throne, kiss my ass, and go straight to hell!"

Tim had finished his tirade. Maymie watched Father Paul Kessler step in and hug Tim. They conversed and Maymie heard only one word, "Sorry." When Tim disengaged, he raised his head and focused his eyes on something behind her. Maymie turned and beheld another pair of eyes locked onto Tim's, dancing with tears, looking out from another young soul laid bare. Maria. Maymie saw that Maria's eyes held no judgment, fear, or desperation, but strength, hope, and love.

Timmy took his place with the other pallbearers and this time he folded his hands, and nudged Gus to do the same.

Tim's fierceness didn't embarrass Maymie. She caught Tim's eye and winked. Good for you, Timmy, she thought. Heal yourself, because your pain is one no doctor can cure. At best, he can facilitate healing. The sick person is ultimately—indeed must be—alone, for he alone is the healer. A combat veteran sick from combat must heal himself or spend the rest of his life at Piankashaw Rock. Patient, Maymie prayed for Tim, heal thyself.

There was another dimension at play. Stubbornness and bullheadedness ran high in the Balbach side of the family, and Tim inherited large portions of both. Most people lumped stubborn and bullhead together. Not Maymie, who had thought all this through years before. A person was stubborn if he refused to change his mind. He was bullheaded if he refused to change his mind and direction. He was exasperating when he turned these traits outward in rejection of commonly accepted wisdom and behavior. He was in trouble when he turned them inward on himself, maybe to hide dark secrets or to punish himself, whom he loathed.

Maymie also considered another facet to her philosophy: conscience. Conscience, whether good or evil, was a prerequisite to these traits. No one could have the latter without the former. Conscience existed in most people, although its forms and degrees varied considerably among them. Timmy, my damaged son, Maymie wanted to cry out, you are possessed of a strong conscience of goodness and decency, but you exist in sickness and pain because you turn the stubbornness and bullheadedness on yourself. Now I see the hope! Your defiance at this dark rite is the beginning of the outward turn of your stubbornness and bullheadedness.

Tim, Maymie hoped and prayed, had maybe begun to heal himself.

But Maymie's attention at this rite involved more than Timmy, and more than her dear friend, Father Chris. It spanned certain of the living. She opened her missal and pretended to follow the prayers commending Father Chris's soul to God and everlasting life with Him. In reality, she studied some of the people who were inside the Cathedral at Father Chris's death scene during the time Sheriff Beckam locked the cathedral and conducted his little investigation. Maymie scrutinized their dress, their faces, their behaviors, and took a bit of comfort at the memory of her sandbagging during the investigation. At the time, it was the faintest of inklings, the tiniest pangs of unease, the smallest of gut feelings that told Maymie something might not be quite right.

The twenty-one gun salute reverberated over the cemetery. Then Taps, a sweet, mournful, haunting homage to Father Chris Hagemeyer for his service to his country. Maymie watched them lower Father Chris into the earth, which welcomed him, covered him, and guarded him. Guard from what? Maymie asked herself. There are so many answers here, but none of them fit. Chris, I hear you calling me on the wind from your bit of dust. You must rest, Chris. You must give it up. Chris, stop it! Leave justice to God. No one and nothing can hurt you anymore. Crawl into the womb of the sweet earth, roll onto your side, curl up, rest your head on your hands, and sleep! I must look after the journeys of others whom I love, who dwell on this side of life, and who, God help them, are hostages to evil. I must shield them from the storm, Chris, and I cannot fail.

Tim walked between his mother and Maria from Kundek Cemetery to the cathedral cafeteria for the after-funeral meal. He took their arms in his but his eyes drooped towards the ground. When they entered the cathedral, Tim blurted, "Did...did I embarrass you?" It took a moment for Maymie to see that Tim had asked the question to both her and Maria.

"No, Timmy," said Maymie. "You're healing. To hell with the others."

"Timmy, I am so proud of your courage!" Maria exclaimed. "You said more in a minute than the bishop and priests did in hours."

"Maria, do you still want to go—"

"Tim." Maria stopped him. "Pick me up Sunday at noon, just like we planned."

Tim awkwardly kissed Maria on the cheek, then tripped on her foot. Maymie saw from the corner of her eye how he smiled a little.

Chapter 22

He followed them through the woods, relying on his training, keen senses, and military issue camouflage uniform to move quietly and avoid detection. He did so while carrying a telephoto lens camera leashed around his neck and his favorite sniper rifle outfitted with a scope strapped tightly across his back. He stayed out of sight, but never out of hearing. They stopped and talked at intervals. He stopped too, lay down on the forest floor, and listened. His superior had ordered the hit but also wanted information. So he snapped a number of photos, beginning when Tim Balbach arrived at Maria's house in his old beat up car. He followed them across town to the small picnic area by the forest where they donned their backpacks, belted their pistols, and started their hike.

He learned at an early age to never underestimate an enemy. His father had made that mistake and it cost him his life. He had learned to plan the mission in detail and obtain as much intelligence on a target as possible. What are his habits? Where does he work? What hours? What is his family like? Is he nearsighted? Farsighted? Does he drink? Where is the best position for the shot and which weapon should you use? What ammunition? Both must be untraceable. What if this happens? Or that happens? And, distasteful but quite necessary, how do you abort? To abort meant failure of the mission, and he seldom aborted his missions.

Tim handed his canteen to Maria, who drank and passed it back. They sat at the top of Raven Rock and looked out at the forest below. A cliff formation set in a broad arc facing east, Raven Rock spanned about one hundred fifty yards north-to-south and interrupted the forest growth anywhere from seventy-five to one hundred yards east-to-west. Scattered boulders and smaller rocks lay both on top and around the base of the cliff.

Tim lit a cigarette and inhaled.

"May I have a puff?" Maria asked.

"What?"

"You heard me."

Tim handed her the cigarette. He brought out the whisky flask, drank from it, and was surprised when Maria reached for it and took a swig.

"Those boulders were put there by glaciers about thirty thousand years ago," said Tim.

"How do you know?" Maria smirked. "Were you alive then?"

"Yeah. Freezing my butt off somewhere in Europe," said Tim, "probably chasing you."

"Did my butt freeze off, Timmy?"

"No. I remember that you always backed it up near the fires in the caves we lived in."

They laughed then moved closer to each other. It was overcast but warm. Occasionally, a southwest wind picked up and swayed the trees, now heavy with new leaves. The wind also brought that peculiar but not unpleasant Southern Indiana April-in-the-woods aroma: a jumble of muskiness from last year's leaves, freshly tilled earth mixed with manure, and the bitter-sweetness of forest wildflowers and fast growing May-apples.

"If my rear gets cold today, Tim, will you start a fire to warm it?"

"You betcha I will," said Tim. He lit two cigarettes and handed one to Maria.

"Um...Maria, do...do you mind if I put my arm around you?"

"No."

Tim pulled Maria to him until their thighs and knees touched. They gazed into the woods east of the cliff. He liked this girl. A lot. It started that day he'd come across her in the woods. At first, 'like' was the best he could do, and he grieved over a potential love that he could not have. It was him, not her. The Berretta stalked him. Tim trusted no human being, not even himself. How could he risk a chance at love, a chance at more pain in his life?

His mother had told him he had to heal himself. "I can help you. Maybe a doctor can. Maybe even Maria, who, in case you haven't noticed, is in love with you. But you, and only you, can fix whatever it is deep inside you that is broken. Whiskey and living under Piankashaw Rock will only make you sicker."

Ah, Mom, he thought. Oh, Maria.

But Tim felt better than he had in months. It started that night around Radius's campfire beside the Piankashaw Cemetery. Radius and his dad and Brute and Gus dug a hole deep inside him, forced him to find the poisonous rock and confront it. Look, he thought. See? It's kryptonite, but you're not Superman, so it won't hurt you. Dig it out. Sink your fingers around it, beat it with another rock, dissolve it with your tears. Anything. Just get rid of it.

"Kry—Krypto what?" asked Maria. "What did you just whisper, Timmy?"

"It's nothing. I was daydreaming, I guess."

"I'm sorry, Timmy."

"About what?"

"I shouldn't have brought it up." Maria lowered her eyes to Tim's knee.

"That's okay, Maria. Really, it's okay."

Tim looked at her. He remembered how after he carried Father Hagemeyer to his part of the earth both Maria and his mother helped to support him. He remembered Maria's strength. She was witty, beautiful, and easy to be with. She had…what? Life. That was it. That was what drew him to her.

Maria is alive, Tim thought, in a way I'm not. She is thrilled with life. You, Tim, have been one bullet away from death. The bullet is now in the distance, but it's still in sight and might come back. Why did you ask this girl out? Could it be that the kryptonite inside you that denied love has gone away? But these thoughts brought new burdens on his conscience. Was it fair to intermingle his life with hers? Was it fair to take life from Maria and use it to heal his own? Was it fair to gamble her gift of love and its healing touch on a Wop poker game?

"Tim, we—your mother and I and later Father Paul—we were not embarrassed. We meant what we said after the gravesite rites."

"Yeah?"

"Really," Maria replied. "I...I mean we are happy about it. Even proud. You are brave, Timmy. You may not feel it just yet, but you will. You have a right to be angry at God, so you yelled at him. God's big enough to take it."

"Bishop O'Grimmels didn't think so," Tim replied. "He tried to chew me out at the after-funeral lunch, but Mom heard him and told him to shut up."

"Sometimes," said Maria, "people must question God. Not for His sake, but for theirs."

"I've felt better since then, Maria."

"I do have one question," she said. "You said something about evil and holding people hostage. What did you mean by that?"

"Well...nothing really, Maria." Tim remembered his promise to Gunny about Hans Peiper. "I didn't mean it like it sounded. It was just...sorta something I felt at the time."

"It's a shame about Father Chris, Tim, but his death brought you back from Piankashaw Rock. I'm happy about that. Really happy."

At this, Tim's thoughts moved away from kryptonite and anger and guilt to those of a man who looked at a woman with love and desire. He felt the growing sensation in his groin, the first in many months. Maria turned her head and looked into Tim's eyes, not with surprise or prudishness or surrender, but with a tenderness and wish that matched his own. They dropped their cigarettes and crushed them into the dirt. Tim placed his hands on her shoulders while she moved hers to the small of his back. Each gently, slowly, pulled the other closer. Maria's lips parted, and Tim moved forward to taste them with his.

At that moment, Tim glimpsed a man in camouflage standing behind a chest-high rock on the other end of the cliff snapping pictures of Maria and him with a telephoto lens.

"Maria, look! Behind you. See him? He's in camouflage."

Maria turned, but the man had ducked out of sight. "I don't see anything."

"Stay here, keep low, and pull out that Luger. I'm going after him."

Tim ran in a crouch towards the man's position, saw him peek over the edge, then escape northwestward into the woods. Tim saw the left side of his face, a rifle with a scope in his right hand, a camera around his neck, and a pistol strapped on his rear side.

"Get back here, you bastard!"

No answer. Tim stopped at the rock. He saw military grade boot prints and the imprint of the bottom of a rifle stock behind a boulder, studied them a minute, then walked back to Maria.

"I caught a glimpse of him, Timmy. What's going on?"

"He's carrying a rifle and pistol. Let's get into the woods."

Tim pulled out his Beretta. He and Maria chambered rounds.

"It seems he headed northwest," she said.

"I agree. So we move southwest."

"Let's do it."

He'd guessed correctly. A young couple attracted to each other and who courted by means of hiking would likely visit Raven Rock. Preparation, reconnoitering, intelligence. The marine, who wasted his life in guilt and self-pity over dead slant-eyed untermenschen in Asia, would under no circumstances take his lady to the other cliff-like formation, Piankashaw Rock. Piankashaw, a three mile hike from Raven Rock but worlds away from it and her experience of living, hid more of the marine's sordid secrets: the easier company of drunken bums, including his own father, and the maudlin releases of alcohol and marijuana.

The couple perched on the cliff facing south. He watched their head and eye movements through the camera lens from the safety of the woods northwest of Raven Rock and snapped a few photos. When they turned to talk, he moved into position behind a boulder on the north end of the cliff. Everything was going according to plan. He set the rifle stock on the ground and leaned the barrel in an indentation on the side of the rock. Then he raised the camera, adjusted the telephoto lens, and began snapping pictures. Dozens of them. Some of the lady, more of the marine, and many more of both. Every so often he stopped to reload film. He smiled when the marine, obviously desirous of the woman—and she of him—placed his arm around her. He stopped smiling when the marine spotted him and moved towards his position. He dropped the camera to his chest and took up the rifle. He had only a few seconds to decide. He saw the lady go down out of sight and the marine sneaking towards him in a crouch. Should he take the shot? No! Abort! He turned and sprinted into the woods.

Maria and Tim traveled southwest. They stopped about every fifty yards to get their bearings and listen for movement.

"Tim, there may be more than one."

"I doubt it, but we have to assume it."

They'd gone about two miles when they heard someone, or something, rustling in the woods to their south. Not from the north, the likely direction of any attack. They waited as the rustling got nearer. Then an unarmed and barefoot elderly man appeared about twenty feet in front of them and stopped. He was medium height with thin scraggly gray hair that, in the back, hung almost to his shoulders. He wore a ragged shirt and equally ragged pants held up with twine. The man was thin, close to emaciated even. His pallid face supported sunken cheeks caused mostly by loss of all but a few of his teeth. He scrunched his pinched face and darted his swimming eyes around him, searching. He held a stick but carried it like a rifle and gasped for breath even though he'd been walking, not running.

Eventually, he spotted Tim. Tim lowered his gun and motioned Maria to do the same.

"Brute!" the man shouted. "Goddammit all, Brute. The Kaiser bastards're attackin' again. You got ammo? I ran out. Gotta kill 'em, Brute." He stumbled to Tim but stopped, swaying and gasping about five feet away. Then he raised the stick and pointed it at Tim's chest.

"You ain't Brute."

"No, Radius, I'm Timmy."

"You're lyin'! You're a damn Boche, and I'm gonna shoot you!"

"Radius, calm down. I'm Timmy Balbach. You remember me, don't you?" Tim gently pushed the stick downward.

"You Andy's grand-boy?"

"Yeah."

"Ernie's boy?"

"Yeah."

"Well, then, you're okay." Radius tottered until Tim moved behind him and rested him on the ground.

"Take a breather, Radius. The Germans can't move very fast since you and Brute shot the shit out of 'em last time they attacked."

"By God..." Radius went into a fit of coughing. "By God, we did, Timmy. Then the bastards gassed us." Another fit of coughing. "Some...sometimes...I can't hardly breathe. Brute all...allaze... pull me through. Gotta find him."

"Radius, I saw Brute a few minutes ago. Talked to him, I did."

"Wha...what'd he say?"

"Brute says he's looking for you. Said he's going back to Piankashaw to wait for you. That's where you'll find him, Radius. Do you know the way there?"

"Course I do, you dumb sumbitch! Been livin' and fightin' there for years."

"Radius, get back there now. There're Boche up that-a-ways." Tim pointed to the northwest. "Heard 'em talkin', sayin' they're gonna attack Piankashaw Rock. You gotta get back there and set up the perimeter in the trench. Here." Tim pulled two bullets from his pants pocket. "Here's some ammo for the machine gun. Get going, Radius. Me and my friend here'll hold 'em off as long as we can. Okay?"

Radius saw Maria for the first time. "God...dammit...Tim, it's a dame! Trenches're no place for a woman! How many...times me and Brute gotta say it?"

"Shhh. Shhh, Radius. Her name's Maria and she's very brave. French spy. For us. She gives us info on the Boche."

Radius rose, and Maria stepped towards him. He looked into her face. "Looks like a goddamn Boche to me, but I trust you Timmy."

Then he placed his gnarled and filthy hand around Maria's and shook it. "Brave. Brave girl. Thank you, madam."

Tim handed the stick to Radius, then put his arm on Radius' shoulder. "G'bye, Radius. And good luck."

Radius ran back through the forest in the direction of Piankashaw Rock. Tim saw the curiosity in Maria's eyes, but he said nothing. He motioned for her to follow, and they continued searching for the gunman.

They reached the edge of the woods, then moved north to the picnic area and Tim's car. Through all their searching, there had been no sign of anyone. They both agreed that they needed to leave the open forest for safer surroundings. Tim drove while Maria crouched in the back seat to cover their rear and sides.

"Tim, go to my house."

"Why?"

"It's wired with alarms."

Chapter 23

Maria locked the doors of her house and pulled the blinds, then she and Tim sat on the floor in front of the couch. They laid their guns on the floor within easy reach. She looked over at Tim and asked him what she had wanted to know about since leaving the forest.

"Tell me about Radius, Tim. He looked so...pathetic."

"What's there to say? You saw and heard him yourself, Maria. He's a sick old man."

"Where does the poor man live?"

"Piankashaw Rock."

Maria remembered what Papa had said about Piankashaw Rock. Was this the big secret? She needed to know more. "He talked about another guy—Brute. Who's Brute?"

"Brute's his buddy."

"Tim. Radius...he believes he's in the trenches fighting the 'Boche.' Does Brute?"

"No."

"Why are they buddies?"

"They fought together in the American Expeditionary Force in World War I. With my grandpa, Andy. Radius and my grandpa never came back. Brute made it most of the way."

"When you say never came back, do you mean, in their heads?"

"Yeah. Brute was wounded slightly. So was my grandpa. They were all gassed. They came home shell-shocked, as they called it then, he and Brute and my grandpa and tens of thousands of others. Radius is sane only part of the time, Brute most of the time."

"Your grandpa?"

"Never knew him. He killed himself at Piankashaw Rock in 1941."

"When did your dad die?"

"He didn't. He's shell-shocked also. World War II in France."

"Where is he?"

"He's...he's at Piankashaw, too. It's hard on Mom and Joey."

"Is it hard on you?"

"Yeah."

"Is there anyone at Piankashaw who cares for Radius and Brute?"

"There are a few. Dad helps them."

Is this the big secret about Piankashaw Rock Papa doesn't want me to know about? Maria thought. He thinks it's dangerous for me to be there, but I have been around many veterans. Does he not want me to help these wounded veterans? Oh, Papa. How could I turn away from anyone in so much pain? Radius, Brute...Tim.

"I want to do something for them," said Maria. "It is not right that old men like that have to live in the woods. They need food, fresh clothes, probably a doctor, and definitely a dentist. I can carry food and clothing to Piankashaw Rock."

"Maria, please. Don't go near Piankashaw Rock. It's not healthy... for you."

"What is so bad about Piankashaw Rock?"

"Nothing is bad about it, I guess. But it's where lost souls go to live with their pain. They live bum lives because it's the only way they can deal with what they've done. What I've..."

"Tim, are you afraid that you will become like these men, Radius and Brute?"

"No."

Tim looked Maria in the eye and then turned away. They both knew what he said was a lie.

"You have to talk about it, Timmy. You can trust me."

"I've talked to others, Maria. It's not nice stuff. It's hateful. You can't understand, not in a million years."

"I've conversed many times with my father and his friends, his comrades who fought in the war."

"And what did you 'converse' about? You weren't there, Maria. It's okay to talk about training and marching and learning how to shoot and getting bawled out by an instructor. Sneaking off base at night and getting caught and doing KP for two weeks. Making sure you can take your M-16 apart and put it back together blindfolded. Drinking in bars. Some gal would wiggle her ass, ten drunk marines would fist-fight over her, and no one would get her. Getting a letter from your mom telling you all about your Uncle Floyd's hemorrhoids. Sending snapshots of you and your buddies home."

"Soldiers love photographs and letters from home," said Maria.

"Sure," Tim replied. "And the home people like them from the soldiers, too, don't they? 'Hey, Mom and Dad. Everybody's happier'n hell out here on the front lines. War's just a big party. Having a great fucking time. Wish you were here.'"

"Timmy…" Maria tried to find words to comfort him, but this was the first time Tim had really opened up to her. The better she knew him, how he thought and felt, the better she could help him. She so wanted to be the one to heal his soul. "Go on."

"Yeah. And oh. PS. Remember little Ricky? You know, the kid from that poor family who lived on the other side of town across the tracks and whose old man got drunk and beat the piss out of him every night? Well, the funniest thing happened. Last week, his head was blown off. Shoulda seen it, little bro. Clean off his shoulders, and his head rolled down the hill. The graves registration guys had to go hunt it up. Big grin on his face. Ain't this funny? Yeah, little Ricky, funniest goddamn thing we ever saw! Love, Tim."

Tim leaned back, laid his head on the couch, and closed his eyes. Maria put her arm around him. Tim's eyes watered, then tears left the corners of his eyes and rolled down the sides of his head. Tim sniffled and tried to stifle a sob. Maria reached behind his head and pulled his forehead to touch hers. Then she pulled his head to rest against her shoulder. She wrapped her arms around him and rocked him back and forth.

"It's okay, Timmy. Everything's okay. I'm right here with you. You're safe. Shhh. Shhh. It's just you and me in this little spot in the universe. Let it out, Timmy. Let it go."

"It's...it's the ba...bastards. The no good rot...rotten bastards who start wars, Maria."

Maria squeezed Tim to her body, pushed his face into her neck, and as he cried, she felt a passionate joy, an elation born of oneness with the soul of the man she loved, and the certainty that he loved her. Tim's sobs in her neck and her reception of his tears set them free from earthly restraints. They became weightless, massless, floating, not in air, but in the ether of the ancients' universe, among planets and stars and galaxies. Time neither slowed nor speeded nor stopped, but left altogether. Darkness receded into shadow, and shadow into oblivion, leaving only light and warmth.

Maria's arms surrounded Tim, and his her. It was easy for him to turn his face and kiss her neck, her ear, her hair. Then he moved in front of her and held her against the couch to better kiss her lips. She opened her mouth and he his, and they tasted each other slowly, gently. Then Tim moved against her with more intensity and fervency.

Tim left her lips and moved downward on her body, unbuttoning her blouse as he went. Maria reached and pulled his shirt off his back. They undressed each other on the floor beside the couch until they lay naked. Tim's tears had dried. His erection swelled. He kissed Maria's breasts, her nipples, her belly button, then down, farther down. He kissed the insides of Maria's thighs, then her knees, then slowly back up her thighs. She wasn't about to let him get away, not after all this time wanting. Maria grabbed Tim's head and pulled his face down between her legs. The touch of his tongue and lips at first was light and tentative, but then he filled her deeper and explored.

Maria's moans and cries followed Tim's motions, then urged him on, then followed him again. Timmy, Oh my God, Timmy. Oh Sweet Jesus, don't stop. Don't stop, she pleaded. She arched her back and curled her fingers into Tim's hair, bringing him closer to her as she climaxed, then climaxed again.

She crested at the edge and her fingers went slack. Tim took the opportunity to rise from Maria. He tugged on her ankle and pulled her away from the couch until she lay flat on her back. No interlude, no wait, Maria raised her knees and he guided his hard penis into her. At first they went slow. Then they moved faster, then faster. They moaned, writhing in a lovers' agony. Maria accepted his thrusts, which grew stronger, moved deeper, until she felt hot spurts inside her and heard Tim's cry. This fueled another peak for her. They slowed, and slowed, then rested in each other's arms.

After some time when the floor became too hard for them, Maria pulled Tim to his feet and led him to her bedroom. She pulled back the covers and lay down first with her legs slightly parted in an invitation. Tim fell upon her and she received him again. This time, their lovemaking lacked urgency. It was sweetness without vulgarity, wonderment without recrimination, God's command and not sin.

Chapter 24

Maymie had often observed an interesting phenomenon in the St. Mary's emergency room. Many patients arrived at the emergency room under shock from the trauma they'd undergone. Sometimes these patients could not immediately recall the incident that caused the trauma. Many times they remembered the incident, but could not summon its details. Maymie surmised that the patient's ordeal temporarily overloaded his mind with information the brain then stored in a remote place not amenable to easy recollection. Later, as the mind calmed and the patient's health returned, the brain retrieved and processed the overload. In some cases, the process took years, and some patients never recalled a thing. Many times, the brain unloaded the excess in strange ways. This happened to Maymie nine days after Father Chris's funeral.

For Maymie, the excess from the night Father Chris died surfaced in a bizarre dream during an almost sleepless night. The setting was Maymie's high school graduation. The band marched onto the football field, not with trombones, tubas, or any other musical instruments, but with typewriters. Only typewriters. Yet the band never played so beautifully. The school choir, standing on tops of risers and facing to the right, never sang the Battle Hymn of the Republic so movingly. The valedictorian and salutatorian read their speeches backwards, yet the crowd gave them standing ovations. The keynote speaker, a hero aviator and admirer of Nazi Germany, Charles A. Lindbergh, proclaimed that President Roosevelt lied about the Japanese attacking Pearl Harbor because he was a Jew, and did anybody know a Jew who didn't lie? All the crowd except Maymie and her family belted, in unison, "Nein!"

The candidates for graduation held rosaries made of rope with wooden beads. As each received a diploma, he or she dropped the rosary on the grass in front of the principal, where they formed a pile. Then the band director, a homosexual, it was rumored, fell over dead, and was buried on the fifty yard line in the middle of the football field. All present—the graduates, their families and friends, the band and choir members—stood and clasped their hands and bowed their heads in prayer as the homosexual band director was safely buried.

Maymie woke, went to the kitchen, made coffee, and started on yesterday's crossword puzzle to distract herself from the disturbing dream. She filled her mind with clues, but not all of them fit into the crossword. Three across: Which Jews lie? Answer: Allofthem. Oh, that answer fits but it's wrong. Erase. Rethink. Eight down: How big is Piankashaw Rock? Answer…well, the number keeps changing depending on who knows the secret. Five down: If a rosary drops in a church, who is there to cover up the sound?

Oh. My. God.

Maymie backed her chair away from the table and spilled her coffee across the crossword puzzle. The scratches on the newspaper looked chaotic, but the process of scribbling them down had helped to organize her thoughts into a picture of clarity. She remembered the day before Father Chris died when he sat at that same table.

Father Chris had rested his arms on the kitchen table. He'd come stumbling onto her back porch, slightly hung-over from the whiskey he drank the day before, and very upset. He nursed a coffee in his hands that Maymie had offered to help him with his hangover. "Maymie, Father Faulkenburg told me he's going to the bishop."

"He won't believe you?"

"No. If I could only find the source of the rumors, I might have a chance. Maymie, have you any idea where they're coming from?"

"No."

"He's more adamant than ever, Maymie," Father Chris had said. "We…we had an argument in the forest. I'd walked to my favorite spot to pray. He found me there. I guess I drank more than I could handle and things probably went further than they should have."

"What happened?"

"He called me a homosexual and accused me of touching children improperly. That he'd seen me do it. None of it's true, Maymie! I told Father Faulkenburg that I have no such desires and I've never touched a child improperly and never will. He said he didn't believe me. That's when I got angry, I guess, and I let him have it."

"How?"

"I told Eric that if he went to the bishop about me, I'd go to the bishop about him."

"What?"

"Maymie, I've seen Father Faulkenburg driving around with an attractive lady in the front seat with him."

"You spied on him?"

"Not really. I was driving the other way. Then later I saw him walking in the forest with the same woman."

"You threatened Father Faulkenburg with this?"

"Yeah, Maymie. But it's true! Faulkenburg admitted it but said it was a penitent…confessor thing. Maymie, they were laughing. Do you know anyone who goes to confession and laughs about it?"

"Sometimes, Chris. Did you argue about anything else?"

"Well, yeah. I guess you could say I bluffed. I told him I was re-searching his war record."

"Good gosh, Chris."

"I have to stop him, Maymie! Surely you can see that?"

"What did Father Faulkenburg say?"

"He said I was committing a sin by bearing false witness against my neighbor and that he'd pray for me."

"Were you trying to blackmail him?"

"Yeah. I have no other choice."

Maymie waited two hours after she spilled her coffee on the cross-word puzzle to really think things through. Once she was sure of the idea forming in her mind, she picked up the phone and dialed the connection switchboard.

"Number, please."

"Eleanor? Eleanor Wetzel? Is that you?"

"It certainly is, Maymie. May I connect your call?"

"No, Eleanor. Do you have a few minutes? It's about what happened with Father Chris."

"Oh, Maymie, isn't that just terrible? Father Chris was such a good man. And to think he molested kids! I just can't believe it. But it's all there in the note he left."

"Eleanor, did you work the switchboard that night?"

"Yes. I connected those calls. Poor Father Faulkenburg. He hardly made sense when he phoned for the sheriff."

"Well, that's that reason I'm calling, Eleanor. Father Faulkenburg feels guilty something awful. He says he could have done more to save Father Chris. He couldn't have, of course, and the sheriff, Melvin, and even the bishop have told him so, but he can't find peace with it. I'm tying up some loose ends to try to help him. I'd like some information from you, if that's okay."

"Sure."

"There's some confusion about the call and the timing—when, to whom, that sort of thing."

"How can I help?"

"What time did Father Faulkenburg place the call?"

"Which one?"

"He only made one. To Freddy. After he found Father Chris in the sacristy."

"No, Maymie. As I recall, Father's first call was to the sheriff's office."

"When?"

"About nine, maybe a little after. I'd say about two hours before his second call—the one about Father Chris."

"I guess Father was worried about the parish kids, or maybe even Father Chris."

"Well..."

The whole town knew that Eleanor sometimes listened in on their calls. Maymie would let this one pass.

"Go ahead, Eleanor."

"Father Faulkenburg could have been concerned. I forgot to switch off my connection so I sorta overheard a little bit. Father asked Freddy where the sheriff and Al were. Freddy said they were patrolling on the other side of the county. Freddy connected Father Faulkenburg to Sheriff Beckam on the sheriff's radio. They talked, but it was all jumbled. I couldn't make out the words. I didn't think anything of it because Father Faulkenburg and the sheriff call each other, oh, I'd say two to three times a week, usually late in the evening during my shift."

"Well, Eleanor, those calls are probably about keeping parish kids out of trouble. Father Faulkenburg cares about them so much, you know."

"The man is a saint, Maymie."

"I agree. Can you connect me to Freddy?"

"Sure. Home or jail?"

"Home. He's probably off duty."

Maymie waited several seconds for Eleanor to put her through. The phone line rang four times before it picked up on the other end. "Hello?"

"Hello, Freddy. This is Maymie."

"Maymie. What can I do for you?"

"I'm trying to help Father Faulkenburg, poor man. He feels responsible for Father Chris's suicide. Maybe you can help."

"I doubt it, but I'll try."

"Freddy, Eleanor told me that Father Faulkenburg made two calls. The first about 9:00 p.m. The second was about 11:15, after he'd found Father Chris. Where were Sheriff Beckam and Al Huff when Father's first call came through?"

"They were clear on the northeast side of the county. There're moonshiners up there. I remember that Father Faulkenburg asked the sheriff to come back to Dubain."

"Father Faulkenburg asked the sheriff to return to Dubain in the 9:00 p.m. call?"

"Yeah. Actually, it was about 9:10. I remember loggin' it. It might have been about some kids causing a ruckus somewhere. Didn't pay much attention. I do know that Beckam and Huff made it back to Dubain about—I'd say—9:45, because they radioed in."

"Did they leave Dubain after that?" Maymie asked.

"No," said Freddy. "Otherwise they would have called and told me."

"So they were in Dubain when Father Faulkenburg's second call came through, the one about Father Chris?"

"Yeah, Maymie," Freddy answered.

"Poor Father Faulkenburg," said Maymie. "He'll drive himself to the grave worrying about all the parish kids."

"Yep. He will, Maymie. I wish he'd relax more."

"Thanks, Freddy."

Maymie hung up on Freddy. She quickly placed another call, this time to Bishop Flannery in Nebraska. A receptionist answered.

"May I help you?" she asked.

"Yes." said Maymie. "May I speak to Bishop Flannery?"

"Bishop Flannery?" responded the receptionist. "There's no Bishop Flannery here. Ma'am, maybe you have the wrong number."

"I don't think so," said Maymie. "A friend of mine said he talked to Bishop Flannery in Nebraska about a week ago."

"Ma'am, there's never been a Bishop Flannery here during the thirty years I've worked here. I've never heard of him. I'm sorry."

"Thank you," Maymie said.

Maymie hung up, walked to her kitchen table, and sat down. The calls confirmed her suspicions, but she hadn't wanted them to be true. They all pointed to the same thing as her dream, as Father Chris had unknowingly hinted at. He'd never thought to consider it himself. Maymie put her face in her hands. She prayed for courage and direction.

Chapter 25

Tim downshifted the clunker at a stop light on his drive to Maria's house for a date of hamburgers and a TV movie. His mind was on Raven Rock Man. He had glimpsed the side of the man's face and saw his build as he ran into the woods. Tim had recognized something about his stalker in the woods that he'd pondered for a few days until he remembered what it was. In Hoosier National Forest, he was Raven Rock Man. In the Palatinate in Germany, he was Porsche Man. Once he made the connection, Gunny's words in Mannheim played back in Tim's head: "I'm certain he watches you even now… This person no doubt is very good at his job and watches you intimately, but from a distance, and reports your activities to Peiper."

Gunny was right then, and he was right now. Raven Rock Man almost certainly worked for Hans Peiper. He was a photographer and watched from afar, but he was also a highly trained professional killer. He'd prepared for the hit on Tim with chilling thoroughness. Tim played out the scenario in his mind. Raven Rock Man spied on Maria and Tim weeks before their date on Sunday and deduced their destination. He guessed correctly the general route Tim and Maria would take through the woods. He followed Maria and Tim so expertly that Tim, an ex-marine extensively trained and experienced in counter-intelligence, failed to detect him. He surmised that Tim and Maria would sit at the top of the cliff, giving him the chance to move into position behind the boulder a ways from them. He probably snapped a number of photographs. At some point, he would have picked up his rifle and killed Tim. But Tim saw Raven Rock Man, which caused him to abort the mission. However, Tim was certain Raven Rock Man or a new assassin was out there, right now, stalking him and setting up for another attempt.

But why the photographs? Why would the assassin snap pictures after moving into position for the kill and increase several times over the chances he'd be spotted by his target or his target's date? Was it to later prove the kill? No, that didn't make sense.

Tim knew his disappearance or death would be plastered all over the local news, and Hans Peiper certainly knew this. Did Raven Rock Man snap photos before the kill to satisfy a ghoulish fetish? Tim asked himself. It's very unlikely if he is an expert hit man. The assassin's handlers? Nah, they would have more simple goals: Tim Balbach is a threat, so we need to remove him. They would hire their best killer, make sure his weapon and ammunition were untraceable, and instruct him to make the kill and then get the hell out. So why the photographs?

Tim couldn't imagine why Hans Peiper would want to photograph him before killing him, so there was only one other option: Maria. Raven Rock Man's handlers had also instructed him to spy on Maria, and both Maria and Tim when they were together. The photographs were about Maria, not Tim.

As he pulled into Maria's driveway he wondered what that meant about Maria and what role she had to play in all this.

Maria cooked the hamburgers, served them on plates in the living room, and then sat on the couch against Tim.

"We have time to watch the news before the movie. Is that okay?" Maria asked.

"Fine by me."

Walter Cronkite opened the broadcast with a ten minute report on the Vietnam War then closed with a commentary on it. "The war drags on with no end in sight," he said. "The President has broken too many promises. The American commanders have proclaimed victory at the end of the tunnel too many times. The bombings have failed to weaken the enemy's resolve. The war becomes more and more futile against a mostly unseen enemy who hide in tunnels and among the population and kill American boys from these hideouts." Cronkite closed with a quote from an American army officer to drive home his point. "We had to destroy the village in order to save it."

Maria got up to turn down the volume and then returned to sit next to Tim. "Timmy, do you think Mr. Cronkite is right? That the war is a lost cause?"

"Hell no," Tim said, taking a big bite out of his hamburger.

"Why not?"

"We could win the war, Maria, if they'd just turn us loose."

"How do you mean?"

"They hold us back. They hold back our weapons. They order us to treat villagers as innocent civilians when they are clearly on the other side, cooperating with the VC and feeding and hiding them. The North Vietnamese Army has sanctuaries in Cambodia, right across the border. We could take them out, but we're not allowed to set foot in Cambodia because, they say, it's neutral. They all wanted this war, but now no one wants to face the realities of having to fight it. What a crock of shit!"

"Timmy, calm down," said Maria. "It was a simple question. I didn't mean to rile you up like that."

Tim took another bite from his hamburger. If she didn't want his answer, why had she asked the question in the first place? He didn't get where Maria was coming from, but he loved her anyway.

"I'm sorry, Maria. I try. You know that. I've been moving away from the war, but then ol' sanctimonious Walter had to bring it up again. He thinks he knows what's going on, but he hasn't been in the tunnels. He hasn't seen Americans killed by the 'innocent' villagers. He's never had to push his buddy's guts back into his body only to watch him slowly die in agonizing pain because there is no morphine available. We need to win this thing so all those deaths weren't in vain.

All he's doing is making it harder for good soldiers to do their jobs and get the recognition they deserve. I hate the know-it-all bastard."

"He's just doing his job, Tim. He's letting people know how terrible war is so they can stop it."

"His job, Maria, does not include encouraging those spoiled-ass chickenshit college bastards to burn their draft cards and stab us in the back."

"But they're protesting the war," said Maria. "Isn't that a good thing?"

"They're not protesting. What they're really doing is encouraging the enemy. They know nothing of the war. Nothing of fighting. Nothing of the enemy, the filth, the blood, the death. Maria, no one has the right to judge the guys who're doing the fighting and dying."

"I'm not judging you, Timmy."

"Never said you were, Maria, but Walter and his friends certainly do. After our tours, the military flew us into New York. Know what happened when we entered the concourse? A bunch of these college bastards were there. They screamed at us, called us names like 'baby killers' and spit on us. Most of us headed to the rest rooms and changed from our uniforms into any civilian clothing we had so they couldn't identify us anymore."

In his anger, Tim bit into his hamburger and chewed quickly before he tried to swallow. The food stuck in his throat and he coughed it out onto his plate. He turned away from Maria.

"Damn it all, Maria, I was looking forward to being here with you and watching the movie and maybe spending the night with you. That would have been nice."

"Tim, I want you to spend the night here, with me. Nothing's changed."

"Yes, it has," Tim replied. He needed to move. He felt the need building and worked his hands open and closed to keep from jumping off the walls. "Cronkite ruined everything, the hamburgers, the movie, the night. He just marched me back to 'Nam and won't ever let me leave."

"Shhh, Tim."

"None of this, 'Shhh, Tim' bullshit, Maria. I'm not in the mood for the movie anymore. Can't even watch it. All I'll see are the yellow slant-eyed cockroaches crawling through the jungles and the tunnels, and the turncoat peasants living in their shitty villages."

"Is that how you see them? Cockroaches?"

"You're goddamn right I do!"

"Tim, stop it! You can't mean such things."

"I do, Maria, and I'd expect you, of all people, to understand. You're German."

Maria suddenly went very stiff on the couch. "Yes, I am. But what does that have to do with Vietnam?"

"Plenty."

"How?"

She doesn't get it, Tim thought. She's German and she really doesn't get it! He couldn't sit still any longer. He stood up and started to pace away from the couch.

"Germany. Your country, Maria. Look what it did in World War II, in World War I, the war with France in 1870. Why do you think Radius, my grandpa, Brute, my dad, and all the tens of thousands of others like them are nuts? I can tell you why. They fought the bastard Germans. They saw the crimes your country committed. They saw them every day. They still see them. You grew up there after World War II. You've read the books. You've seen the photos and newsreels. You know of Hitler's crimes. You know of the Nuremburg trials. You know of the concentration camps, the death camps, the final solution. Millions of innocents killed, Maria!"

The look she gave him was so cold, but it was the honest truth. Tim tried to control himself but he couldn't back away.

"Most of it was made up," Maria replied. "That's what Papa says. The Allies concocted the photos and made up the stories about the camps. Then they prosecuted the Germans when our only crime was to fight for our country against the Russians, the British, and you Americans. Even now, you subjugate Germany. You keep it divided and torment its people. Now you hold it hostage with your damn nuclear bombs. The world has always been against Germany, and this will continue because the world is afraid of Germany. Afraid of what Germany could accomplish if given a chance. Afraid of Germany's might and the talents of its people. Afraid that Germany may someday find its way into the sun."

"Maria, do you really believe that shit?"

"Don't you, Tim Balbach? Are you really that ignorant?"

"I'm a lot of things, Maria, but I'm not ignorant." Tim paused in his pacing and looked at Maria for a moment. Raven Rock Man, also known as Porsche Man, had been taking pictures of Maria in the forest. He was spying on Tim, but keeping tabs on Maria. She was from Germany. She was the right age. In a lower, sharper voice, Tim asked, "What did your father do in the war?"

"What does my father have to do with anything?"

"Answer me."

"He fought for Germany, just like every other German man his age."

"He did more than fight, didn't he?" asked Tim. "Your father was an SS officer, wasn't he?"

"What does it matter what my fa—"

"Answer me."

"No."

"What?"

"No, I'm not answering you. What's gotten into—"

"The Luger, Maria."

"My Luger? The one I carry? Papa gave it to me."

"Exactly."

"Exactly what?"

"The Luger was the sidearm for many SS officers and you know it. Everything is clear now. You can't hide the truth forever."

"Tim Balbach, what's happened to you? We were having a nice evening. A few nights ago you sobbed in my arms and we made love. What's changed?"

"Raven Rock Man."

"The man who spied on us?"

"Yeah."

"What about him?" Maria asked.

"He's brought it all into focus. I've seen him before. In Germany. The Palatinate. He drove a Porsche. He was following me there and he was at Raven Rock trying to kill me."

"He was taking photos, Tim. He had a gun but didn't use it."

"He didn't use it because I spotted him before he had a chance to. Why was he snapping pictures? Was he shooting me or you or both of us? Or was he out on an innocent little nature hike, hoping to win a Pulitzer Prize for photography? What's his name, Maria? Is he a friend? A lover?"

"How dare you—"

"He could be a friend of your father's. Where did your father serve? The eastern or western front? He committed war crimes, you know. All the SS did. Atrocities. He murdered Jews, Russians, Americans, prisoners in cold blood. Didn't he?"

Maria stood from the couch and thrust her finger toward the door. "Get out of my house. I won't let you make these wild accusations about my father in my own home."

"Oh, my dear, they are not accusations. They are the truth and you goddamn well know it. Or do you merely pretend ignorance of the crimes of your father and his SS?"

"Get out of my house."

"Fuck you. The master race, Maria. The SS—your dear papa and his fellow bastards—said they were the master race. They swore allegiance to Hitler, and he ordered them to kill untermenschen, Jews and Russians and Poles and a whole bunch of others, whether they appeared as enemy soldiers or not. He so ordered your father, and he and his band of criminals carried out these orders."

"Get out or I'll call the police."

"You'll do nothing of the sort, Maria, and you know it. The last thing you want is attention from the police."

"You talk of atrocities, Tim Balbach, you sanctimonious hypocritical American. You have personal experience with them yourself, don't you? Timmy Balbach, the marine, the poor damaged war hero. How many men did you kill? How many women and children did you slaughter? How many prisoners have you shot in cold blood? This is why you grieve, isn't it? This is why you scream at funerals, drink whiskey until you drop, and cry."

"You know nothing about these things. You weren't there."

"And you weren't in World War II. You accuse my father of committing war crimes, Timmy Balbach, but what is it you Americans say? 'If you live in a glass house you'd best not throw stones?' Well, stand in front of the mirror in your glass house, Mr. Balbach, before you cast your stones, because you can't have it both ways. You Americans were the real monsters."

"I'll have it as many ways as I want."

"No, Tim, you will not because you cannot. The winners of the war get to write its history. The Americans and the British and the Russians won the war and they wrote its history. A pack of lies! Someday the truth will come out, Tim. You are right about Walter Cronkite. He is wrong. He obviously wants America to withdraw from Vietnam. But America can't. Know why? Because then it can't write the history. It won't be able to cover up its crimes—your crimes—against the Asians."

"Maria, you speak of lies and truth, but you live a lie and you say to hell with the truth. What are your lies? What is your truth?"

"Do you really want the truth," Maria replied, "about what the Americans did in France and then in Germany? You aren't the innocents of the war like they show in those sickening Hollywood movies. Quite the contrary. Papa's told me the stories. Do you want to hear one? It's about what you Americans did at Mortain."

Tim's blood ran cold when she said the name.

"Papa and his men were at Mortain. That's in France, in case you don't know. The Americans took Papa and his men prisoners at the base of a hill—Hill 314 you Americans called it—outside the city. You Americans lined up Papa and his men, all disarmed and helpless, and shot them down with machine guns."

"That's a lie, Maria. Stop it. I'm warning you."

"Warn away, Tim Balbach. But I will not stop. Papa and his adjutant fled into the nearby woods where they hid until the Americans gave up looking for them. There were more shots, only this time it was the American officers killing their own soldiers so there would be no witnesses to the massacre of my father's men. They saw the fire and heard the popping. That's right, Tim. Popping. Your American 'heroes,' as you love to call them, soaked the German soldiers' bodies with gasoline and set them afire. The fat in a human body pops when the body is burned. But you already know that, don't you?"

"That's not how it happened!"

"Papa's adjutant was later killed, but Papa survived to tell the truth. Is this too much for you, Timmy? Does the truth hurt? Have you burned bodies, Timmy? The bodies of the little 'yellow slant-eyed cockroaches' who got in your way? How many people have you murdered? Well, goddammit, how many?"

A redness clouded the room and everything in it when she called him a murderer. Tim lashed out. He smashed the lamps, threw the furniture against the walls, and tossed the television through a window. Maria tried to stop him, but he backhanded her across her face and she went down. He busted every piece of glass and every memento. When nothing remained in the living room he moved on to the kitchen. He opened the cabinets, shattered plates and glasses, and dumped the refrigerator on its side. He reached for the pots and pans when a shot whizzed over his head.

Tim turned, and there stood Maria with the Luger. He moved to disarm her, but Maria placed another shot inches from his toes. Tim stopped. He breathed hard as the red cloud drained from his eyes until nothing remained but his simmering anger and Maria threatening him with her gun.

"Tim Balbach, you leave this house and don't you ever come back."

"Don't concern yourself, Maria. *Maria Peiper*."

He back-stepped toward the door. He was on the porch when he turned and stormed off to his car. Tim started his car and backed out of the driveway. He didn't hear the gun report, but he heard the bullet when it entered his car through the side of the back window facing east. He felt the sting as it hit his right shoulder and spent itself in the speedometer. Tim caught a glimpse of Maria standing on the porch, the Luger at her side, her head looking eastward. He backed out of the drive, hit low, and floored the accelerator.

Chapter 26

Maymie arrived home from Saturday evening confession and walked into the living room where Joey and Henry were watching a war movie.

"Where are Tim and Mary June?"

"Don't know," said Joey.

"I—said—where—are—Tim—and—Mary—June?"

This got the boys' attention. "I think they're at the Schnitzelbank, Maymie," responded Henry. "Tim's there. He called Mom to join him."

"Did they say when they were coming home?"

"No."

"Mary June has no car or license. How did she get there?"

"Walked. She left in sort of a rush."

Tim and Mary June would have to take care of themselves for the time being. Maymie went to task securing the house. She locked the front and back doors. Then she moved around the house, basement, main floor, and upstairs and locked every window.

"Mom, what's going on?" Joey asked as he watched her from the living room.

"Joey, Henry, you are not to step outside this house unless you first ask me and I give you permission."

"Why, Mom?"

"It doesn't matter why. You will obey me. Both of you. Do you understand?"

"Yeah, Mom."

"Henry?"

"Yes, ma'am."

Maymie moved to the kitchen and picked up the phone. She kept her back to the boys as the operator connected her to the bartender at the Schnitzelbank. When he answered, she didn't bother with pleasantries. "Put Tim Balbach on the phone. It's urgent."

The phone muffled for about a half minute as the bartender asked around for Tim. Maymie tapped her foot while she waited. Then the bartender returned. "He left about ten minutes ago."

"By himself?"

More muffling came from the phone.

You idiot bartender, Maymie thought. It's a simple question.

"They say he left with Mary June Balbach. Who is this asking?"

"Never mind who this is. Do you know where they went?"

More muffling. The bartender got back on the line. "A guy here tells me they didn't say. There's more, but I gotta know who this is."

"I'm Maymie Balbach, Tim's mom."

"Well, Mrs. Balbach, Tim was throwing back whiskeys to kill the pain."

"Pain?"

"From his shoulder. Blood all over the front and back of his shirt. If anybody asked about it, he'd say he was shot and kept on drinking."

"He was shot? Did any of you fools think to call an ambulance?"

"I'm not a fool, ma'am. Two customers offered to drive Tim to the hospital but he refused. He was pretty drunk when he left. Ain't natural for a man to get drunk after taking a bullet and still bleeding like hell. I called the sheriff then had to go back to the kitchen for something. That's when they say the lady dragged him outta here."

Maymie slammed the phone on the receiver. She thought over her options for a moment and then walked to the living room where the boys no longer watched their movie. She had their full attention.

"Boys, I'm going out to look for them. Lock the back door behind me. I have the key. Under no circumstances are you to allow anyone in this house other than Tim, Mary June, or me."

She only waited long enough for the boys to acknowledge her order before she left the house and went to the garage. Maymie started her car, but just then Tim's clunker pulled into the driveway, Mary June behind the wheel and Tim slumped on the passenger side. Maymie turned off her ignition and hurried to Tim's passenger door.

"Maymie, I pulled Tim out of the Schnitzelbank as soon as I got there," said Mary June. She opened the driver door and slammed it shut before rushing to Tim's side. "That's when they called the cops."

Mary June opened the passenger door and Maymie leaned in to examine her son. Tim lay hunched over and unconscious, like he had fainted on the drive home. Maymie checked the wound and how fast he was bleeding out. "We have to stop the bleeding. Mary June, are you okay?" Their eyes met. There was no mistaking the question. It spanned years of anguish, dozens of broken promises, and several dryouts from the snakes. Mary June looked away from Maymie, ashamed. "Mary June, you're either on or off, and I have to know right now if I can count on you."

"I drank nothing. I'm okay."

"Then help me with him."

Maymie and Mary June shouldered Tim between them and carried him into the house. Joey must have been watching from the window because he had the door open for them before Maymie needed to holler for his help. She and Mary June laid Tim on the kitchen floor. In that moment Maymie stopped thinking like a scared mother and started thinking like an emergency room nurse. He's barely coherent, Maymie thought, going through her options. Is it the booze, loss of blood, or both? Probably both, but it doesn't matter. Get the bleeding stopped.

The others crowded around her in the kitchen. Maymie ordered the boys to bring towels, washrags, and blankets from upstairs. She and Mary June stripped Tim naked and found no wounds other than the crease on his shoulder.

"Hi, Mum...god shod. Ow! Ow!"

"When?"

"Maria...Peiper...bisch...bitch."

"Did Maria shoot you?"

"Was backin' out. Then a bullet hit my sho—sho—der. Didn't hear no shot. Jes' the bullet."

"You damn fool! You got shot, you're bleeding like hell, then you get drunk!"

"Fool, at's me all right. Jes' bullet and fool."

"Maymie," said Mary June, "the sheriff'll be here any minute. What are you gonna tell him?"

"I'll think of that when he gets here. Beckam can see in the kitchen through the backdoor window. Let's get you and Tim upstairs. Joey and Henry, help us carry Tim. Joey, dammit, stop gagging!"

They worked to get Tim upstairs and then laid him in his bed.

"What's hap—penin'? Hurt's like a b-bitch."

"Timmy, your shoulder will hurt a helluva lot more before we're done. Now be quiet. Boys, watch for the sheriff." Tim hollered when Maymie applied rubbing alcohol. "Hush, Timmy."

Maymie bandaged the wound and stopped the bleeding. Then she wrapped Tim's lower arm across his stomach.

"Mom, they're here," Joey reported from his watch post at the window. "Lights are flashing outside. It's the sheriff's car. They're getting out. Looks like Sheriff Beckam and a deputy, that Huff guy."

A few seconds later, Maymie heard banging from downstairs.

"Mary June, I'll try to hold them off. You stay with Tim. Whatever you do, keep Tim quiet. Clamp your hand over his mouth if he even whimpers. Lock that bedroom door and don't unlock it for anyone but me. Henry and Joey, you stay here with Mary June. And stay away from the window. I don't want the sheriff to see you."

"You're not telling me everything, are you, Maymie?" Mary June asked.

"Just do as I say."

Mamie ran downstairs to her bedroom, grabbed the loaded Smith & Wesson .38 from under her bed, and stuffed it in the back side of her waistband. There was more banging, then someone tried the doorknob. Maymie, she told herself, you don't have to be nice, but you have to be calm and you have to bluff. She breathed in deeply and then out before she walked slowly to the backdoor. The window framed the face of Sheriff Beckam. Deputy Huff peered over his shoulder.

"Open this door," Sheriff Beckam ordered.

Maymie did so and stepped into the doorway. She looked up at the sky and then at Sheriff Beckam. "Gosh, Sheriff, it's such a beautiful night. What can I do for you?"

"You know why we're here, Maymie. Move out of the doorway."

"You don't have to get all huffy. Just tell me what this is about and maybe I can help."

"Maymie," started Sheriff Beckam in that overbearing, no-inflection cop voice Maymie found so irritating when she heard it in the hospital emergency room, "your son, Tim, was shot. We got called to the Schnitzelbank but missed him and Mary June. His car's out here, so we know they're inside. Tim's the victim of a crime and we need access to him immediately."

"Ah, Sheriff. You're—what do you call it—investigating. How nice. Oh—hi there, Al."

"Step aside, Maymie."

"Gee, Sheriff, where's your warrant?"

"We don't need a warrant. We have probable cause that a crime's been committed."

"My, my, Sheriff. What crime?"

"He—well, Tim or Mary June drove home from the Schnitzelbank. Both of 'em were drunk, so the driver is guilty of drunk drivin'."

"Did you actually see either of them drive?"

"Al here says he glimpsed 'em. Others saw 'em. Now get out of our way, Maymie. That's an official order from an officer of the law in the course of performin' his duties."

"Oh, my. Official? That sounds important." Maymie tried to close the door, but Deputy Huff put his shoe against the frame.

"I'm warnin' you for the last time, Maymie. If you don't move in the next three seconds, I'll arrest you."

Maymie stepped through the doorway onto the porch. Beckam and Huff shuffled backwards. She closed and latched the door behind her.

"Warn away, Sheriff, but you and your lackey there—sorry, Al—will not enter this house. You will not see Tim. You will not arrest him or Mary June. Know why? First, you have no proof that either drove while drunk, and really, Sheriff, you wouldn't arrest a person for driving to get help for a gunshot wound, now, would you? Second, your job is not here. It's out there looking for the shooter—you know, the person who committed the real crime here. Third, you're not out there because you already know the real shooter. Even I got it narrowed down to two. It's either a guy that you hired or Maria Peiper—oh, excuse me—Maria Reller. She's great with that .45, as I'm sure you know. And fourth, this makes both of you—oh, gosh, what do the lawyers call it—accessories! That's it. You're accessories to attempted murder."

"Maymie, you're askin' for big time trouble," said the cop voice.

"Am I? Here, Sheriff. Here are my arms. Arrest me and handcuff me. I ask you to. I beg you to. Know why? Because then I'll have an audience. The media will love this story, Sheriff. I have witnesses behind me, so I'm safe in your hands, which is more than I can say for others. No suicide for me, Sheriff. You're not that good at it. I'm just a sweet little woman who put it all together. Figured it out on my own, I did. Aren't you proud of me?"

Maymie's smile disappeared. She narrowed her eyes, pushed out her chin, and lowered her voice. "So, Sheriff Beckam, unless you're looking for a world of hurt, you can take your investigation and shove it you know where. We're done here."

Chapter 27

Hans placed his arm around Greta as they rested together on the sofa. Gustav Stresseman sat upright in the overstuffed chair facing Hans and Greta Peiper. Gustav held Leni's head in his lap and scratched her ears. The uneasiness that always visited Hans when in Gustav's company welled up inside him. Gustav's forced sincerity could not hide the air of suspicion, furtiveness, and danger that emanated from him. So unlike his father, Fritz Stresseman, Hans had told Greta. But these qualities and Gustav's build and handsomeness made him attractive to some women, and Greta was one such woman. Today, Hans noted, she could not hide her admiration of Gustav Stresseman.

Hans had stayed in touch with the Stresseman family after his adjutant was killed fighting the Americans at Mortain. He had watched as Stresseman's son, Gustav, grew into a handsome man, filled with hatred for all Americans and a desire to seek his revenge upon them. It was why Hans had recruited Gustav when he came of age. Hans trusted Gustav to get the job done, which was why he sent Gustav on important missions like spying on Gunny Balbach in Mannheim and assassinating Tim Balbach in Dubain.

"Gustav, I commend you for your courage in bringing the news to us personally."

"As do I," joined Greta.

"Thank you, Colonel and Fraulein Peiper."

"We especially appreciate the photos," said Hans. "Tell us about the rest."

"I failed twice, sir. First in the forest at what is called Raven Rock. I followed Tim Balbach and Maria from the picnic area to Raven Rock. I am certain that neither detected me when I followed them through the woods. I hid behind a boulder and shot almost two rolls of film. Then, without warning, Tim Balbach turned his head in my direction and spotted me with the camera. They...well...they were on the verge of kissing. You see that the photos end at that point."

"Did Balbach get close enough to identify you?"

"No, sir. Of that I am certain. The distance was at least one hundred meters, and the foliage in the woods covered me completely."

"What happened on Saturday?"

"I followed Balbach to Maria's home. I moved into position on the south side of the backyard of the house directly across from Maria's house. I had inspected the position a number of times in the previous two days and concluded that it was ideal. There had been no mail—not even junk mail—a sign that it was all being sent to another address. The occupants probably were on a trip. Although Balbach normally parked in Maria's driveway, he occasionally parked on the street. The position I chose was surrounded by foliage and provided a clear view of Maria's driveway as well as the street in front of her house. About an hour elapsed. Then, apparently, Maria and Balbach got into a fight."

"How do you know this?"

"Well, sir, I heard loud voices. Then, it got violent."

"How so?"

"It was Balbach, sir. He smashed things and broke windows. Then I heard two shots fire from inside the house. A moment later, Balbach emerged from the house, went to his car, and backed out the driveway. I had a direct bead on him through the back window of his car. It was a shot I have made before, but this time I missed. I believe I wounded him, however."

"Where was Maria when you took the shot?"

"She was standing on the porch with the pistol in her hand."

"Did she shoot from there?"

"No." Gustav drank from the glass of water Greta had given him. "At that point, I aborted."

"Good judgment."

"Colonel Peiper, you stood beside your adjutant and my father, Fritz Stresseman, when Ernie Balbach killed him at Mortain in 1944. Then Balbach almost killed you. I can tell you that my failures with Tim Balbach burn deep inside of me. I am disappointed in myself, and I feel bad for failing you and the Great Reich."

"Gustav, do not punish yourself. I am sure you did your best. After all, you are up against a United States Marine with extensive experience in combat and counter-intelligence. You are more talented than he, but misses happen, and aborts are often necessary. We shall leave Timmy Balbach alone for now. He is no doubt living in fear of a second attack, and that is precisely where I want him. You, Gustav, shall go back to your hotel in Dubain and await further instructions from me. When you are done here, you will return to Germany and await further orders."

"Thank you, Colonel. And thank you, Fraulein Peiper."

Chapter 28

Tim drove Henry and Joey home from school. His shoulder ached when he turned corners, but at least his mother's anger towards him had cooled. Tim imagined that she'd gotten some of her anger out when she cleaned the wound and poured the rubbing alcohol on it. He was drunk at the time, but that pain sobered him considerably.

The shooting and Tim's actions in the Schnitzelbank had gotten all over town. People now looked at him strangely when he drove past. Most of his friends and acquaintances avoided him. The school teachers had even given him fearful looks when he picked the boys up outside the school, like they might not have allowed Joey and Henry in the same car as him. He tried not to think about the looks and about being shunned. And he tried to not think of Maria Peiper. Of course, that only made him think of her more.

The day after the shooting, Maymie decreed without explanation that Henry and Joey would no longer walk to and from school, or anywhere else. She or Tim would drive them to and from school and they could go nowhere else. The boys complained that it was Tim who'd gotten shot and they had nothing to worry about, but one look from Maymie shut them up real fast. Tim didn't dare question her reasons for the change, although Tim was certain Hans Peiper underlay them.

When they made it home, they entered Maymie's house and found their mothers in the living room, Maymie sobbing on Mary June's shoulder.

"What happened?" Tim asked. "Is it Dad? Gunny?"

"No." Mary June replied. "Here. The Dubain Curier Journal arrived a few minutes ago. Your mother read it and broke down."

"Mom, sit down for a few minutes," said Tim.

Maymie moved to the couch and Mary June sat beside her.

Tim and the boys saw the front page. "Two Tragedies. Two Families Grieve." One of the smaller headlines said, "Eleanor Wetzel Killed in Car Wreck, Husband Disputes Police," and the other said, "Fred Caldmeyer Drowns in Fishing Accident." Tim handed the paper to Henry and knelt next to his mother. He lifted her head. Tears rolled down her face and smeared the little makeup she used. Her shoulders sagged between heaves, and she moved her hands around her lap, opening and closing them as though searching for a safety handle to grab hold of. Maymie rarely cried. She'd dropped a few tears for Father Chris, but she hadn't broken down like this since Tim moved Ernie to Piankashaw Rock before he left for the Marines. She looked older, shrunken, vulnerable, defeated.

"Mom, what's the matter?" Tim asked. Maymie tried to talk but couldn't. "Henry, what does the Daily say about Wetzel and Caldmeyer?"

"Looks like Mrs. Wetzel died last night and Mr. Caldmeyer died this morning. Let me see...says here that Mrs. Wetzel left the switchboard at the end of her shift at midnight. She lives on the east side of town, but they found her west of Dubain on a country road. Sheriff Beckam said she fell asleep at the wheel. No skid marks. They smelled alcohol. Mrs. Wetzel was thrown from the car and died instantly when it rolled on top of her. Art Wetzel—that's her husband—says there's something fishy. Says his wife always comes home right after her shift. He said she never drank except for a beer or two on weekends.

"Mr. Caldmeyer went fishing at his favorite spot on the Patoka River. Mrs. Caldmeyer got suspicious when he didn't come home at 9:00 a.m. She went to find him and saw slip marks on the riverbank but no rod and reel. Sheriff Beckam and Mr. Huff investigated this case also. Sheriff Beckam says Mr. Caldmeyer was a good friend. Always careful around the river. Mel Eichert—that's the coroner—

said that Mr. Caldmeyer may have suffered a stroke or heart attack and fell in the river, but they won't know until they find the body. State Police are dragging the river. That's all."

"Mom," said Tim, "I don't want to sound cold or nothing, but Eleanor and Freddy weren't exactly close family friends. Why are you bawling like this?"

"The Courier's wrong."

"How, Mom?"

"Eleanor and Freddy were murdered."

"Mom," Tim cried, "have you lost your—"

The front doorbell rang.

"Goddammit, what's that!"

There was rapping on the door.

Tim ran to Maymie's bedroom, retrieved the Smith & Wesson, and then motioned the boys to stand by the couch so they would stay out of sight of the front door. Tim unlocked the latch, crouched, opened the door outward, and pointed the gun at the man standing there. Once he saw who it was, Tim lowered the gun and stood up.

The man's glasses fit crookedly on his face, and scotch tape bound the left temple to the frame. The strong bifocals enlarged his deep blue eyes, making them owl-like. His long hair, uncombed and messy, and his several days' beard spoke to the modern hippie movement. His thin belt, protruding at least six inches from the buckle and bunching up the waistline of his trousers in several places, added to his borderline emaciated appearance. He'd eaten recently, however, because some of the meal's remnants stuck to the front of his shirt.

The man gazed at Tim. Then, embarrassed, he looked down at his feet where he—and Tim—saw unmatched socks and an untied shoe. He tried to straighten his glasses but gave up. He glanced at the gun, but showed little comprehension of it, as though facing a gun was a common daily event for him. The man looked up into Tim's eyes, rubbed his forehead, then closed and opened his eyes. Tim watched him as one in prison for murder watched another in the same prison for another murder. However, Tim felt a strange connection to this man. He showed no emotion other than a thin, embarrassed smile. His eyes left Tim's and turned downward in a peculiar slant, as though there was a burden, a weight, attached to them. His meekness bordered on docility, but this only added to the aura of mystery about him. This man is damaged, Tim thought. What is it? Alcohol? Maybe. A bad childhood? Could be. Queer? Probably not. Women? No. Beaten by life? Maybe, maybe not. Then Tim saw his own haunted reflection in the man. War, and its satanic companions.

"Oh, uh, hi, Tim," said Father Paul Kessler. "I want to ask Maymie and Mary June to help in the quilting stand at the church picnic next Sunday. Are they home?"

"Yeah, Father Paul. Come in."

Tim stepped aside to make room for Father Paul. He walked into the living room, turning his head about to see where everyone was. Tim watched him stop and stare at Maymie, still sobbing on the couch.

"Perhaps this is a bad time, Maymie. I'll come back tomorrow."

"Yes, Father Paul, this is a bad time, but you must stay. You have been so kind to this family already. I'm sure we can trust you. Please, take a seat."

"Mom, what's all this about trust?" asked Tim. "You've been on edge for weeks. You put restrictions on Joey and Henry. You keep a loaded Smith & Wesson in your nightstand. You deliver a sermon to me on being careful and watching out for dangerous-looking people every time I leave the house. I can understand some of this because of the shooting, but now, you say that someone murdered Freddy and Eleanor. Mom, we can't have you losing your mind."

"No, Tim, I'm quite sane, and I intend to remain that way." Maymie sniffed back some tears and then accepted tissues Mary June handed her and blew her nose. "I carry secrets that I've shared with no one…well, except for one person, but I'll get to that. They've already murdered three people and tried to kill you, Tim. They've threatened me, Joey, Henry, Mary June, Ernie, and Gunny. Paul, you, too, may be in danger just by being here. I've kept all this to myself out of fear for the safety of all of you. But, Father Chris, Eleanor, and Freddy are dead, and secrecy is no longer possible. All of you must learn the truth.

"Joey and Henry, when I'm done, you'll understand why I grounded you the way I did, why I won't let you go anywhere alone without my permission. You complain that I treat you like children. You're right, but I want you alive and safe.

"All of you have to know who they are and what they represent. These people are extremely dangerous and will not hesitate to murder again if they feel threatened. So you must hide what you are about to learn. You cannot speak of it to anyone. Do each of you understand this?" There were murmured assents. "Joey and Henry?"

"Yeah, Mom."

"Yes, ma'am."

Tim offered Father Paul a chair and moved to lean against the far wall of the living room to hear Maymie's explanation. "It centers around a man named Hans Peiper. He lives a double life. He spends most of his time undercover here in Dubain, but his real residence is a secluded place outside Dubain. Mary June and Tim are aware of Hans Peiper's existence but don't know his alias. Ernie and Gunny know both him and his false identity but, for reasons which I now appreciate, have refused to disclose it to us. Tim, I'm pretty sure you have something to add here."

Tim repeated Gunny's story of Mortain and his explanation of Hans Peiper and the Great Reich. He said how his friendship with Maria ended when she, out of the blue, told Tim another story of Mortain. "Maria heard about it from her dad, only his story is ass-backwards. She said it was the Americans who murdered the Germans. Maria gave away her cover when she told me the story. Maria's true last name is Peiper, not Reller, and I'm pretty sure she's Hans Peiper's daughter. Gunny also said that the Great Reich watches me because I'm a threat." Tim related his Jeep race with Porsche Man in Germany, and then his confrontation with the same man at Raven Rock in the forest. "The man is connected to Peiper and the Great Reich, and I'm sure he's the one who shot me in Maria's driveway."

"Mary June, can you add anything?" Maymie asked.

"Nothing that you haven't already said," Mary June replied. "Maymie, to be honest, I've had no desire to discover Hans Peiper's disguise. 'Ignorance is bliss,' I told myself. But all that's changed. I want to know."

Maymie continued. "Gunny spoke the truth about Mortain. Ernie told me the story shortly before we married. And Tim is correct about Maria. She is Hans Peiper's daughter. Hans Peiper has blackmailed both Gunny and Ernie for the past eight years with these lies and threats to our families. Peiper forced Gunny to move to Germany and Ernie to remain at Piankashaw Rock.

"Yes." Maymie looked at her family and Father Paul. "This is the cold hard truth of our families. The Great Reich is real. Gunny uncovered it in 1944, but no one other than Ernie believed him. The Great Reich is a worldwide conspiracy of former Nazis—and new ones—who want to gradually seize leadership of the world and rule it as Hitler did Germany. These people work deep undercover and have already made inroads in this country and, I am certain, many others. We are their hostages. Hundreds, thousands of others are also hostages but don't know it. We are trapped in Dubain, Indiana, the Great Reich's modern version of the concentration camp, and there are certainly others out there. I don't know how the Great Reich is organized, but there is no doubt in my mind that Hans Peiper is one of its leaders in this country. In the case of the Great Reich and Hans Peiper, ignorance among the Balbachs is no longer bliss. It's deadly."

"I can attest to that," said Tim, thinking back to the bullet that clipped his shoulder.

"Hans Peiper," said Maymie, "is supported by his World War II SS comrades and some Americans, including some local Dubain people who've joined the Great Reich. They murder some of their enemies and use blackmail and terror to control others who are too visible to kill. So far, the Balbachs are in the too visible to kill category. I will keep it that way at all costs.

"Peiper murdered Chris Hagemeyer but disguised it as a suicide. Chris was neither a homosexual nor a pedophile. Peiper was the source of the rumors about Chris. Why? Chris unwittingly got too close to the truth of Peiper and the Great Reich and threw it in Peiper's face. Peiper removed Chris as a threat. Then Peiper murdered Eleanor and

Freddy. Why? Because they were links between Hans Peiper and
Chris's murder. Peiper removed them."

"Maymie," said Father Paul, "all this is quite a stretch. How do
you know these things?"

"It started with Chris's death in the cathedral," Maymie continued. "The evidence at the scene and the quick investigation by Sheriff
Beckam rang false to me. About two weeks after Chris's funeral, I had
an epiphany of sorts and I acted on it. Both Eleanor and Freddy were on
duty the night Chris died. Both had relayed calls between Hans Peiper
and Sheriff Beckam during the time leading up to Chris's death.

"I called Eleanor and Freddy to get information but hid from them
the real purpose for my questions. Their information confirmed to me
that Chris was murdered."

"Mom," said Tim. "How did you figure this out?"

"I'll get to that, Timmy."

"Fine, Mom. But make sure you get there."

Maymie continued. "Peiper's spies at the phone company must
have reported my calls to Eleanor and Freddy. Peiper had them murdered to keep them quiet. They were innocent and I was not. Peiper
should have killed me, not them."

"Maymie, don't talk that way!" cried Mary June.

"Dammit, Mom," said Tim, "What's gotten—"

"Tim!" Maymie flashed him a look of anger. "None of this,
'Dammit, Mom' stuff."

Tim couldn't think of a response, so he was relieved when Father
Paul stepped in.

"Maymie, have they threatened you?" asked Father Paul.

"Of course. Hans Peiper himself. If I step out of line, if I go to the
authorities or fight the Great Reich in any way, they'll kill you, Tim.
Or you, Mary June. Or you, Joey and Henry. Maybe Gunny and Ernie.
Anybody close to me. Maybe even you, Father Paul. They've already
stalked and shot Timmy, but he was lucky.

"Peiper owns a very nice chateau deep in the woods of the farm
that abuts Hoosier National Forest about three miles south of the picnic area. When he's not in Dubain, he lives there with his wife, Greta.

Maria, of course, is a member of the Great Reich and is aware of her father's position. I assume that she knows of her father's murderous activities, especially after Tim's shooting at her house."

Maymie looked at her son, this time with sympathy. "Tim, it's possible Maria dated you at the direction of her father, first, to see how much you know about the Great Reich and the names of people you may have told, and second, to set you up for assassination."

"Could be, Mom," said Tim. "But we'd had a number of dates and she never raised anything about her father until our fight at her house."

"Who started the fight?" asked Father Paul.

"I..." Tim looked at the ceiling. "I guess I did. Walter Cronkite reported from Vietnam, said the war was futile and practically condemned the soldiers who fought it. Maria defended Cronkite and told me the false story of Mortain, and I went into a rage. Busted up her place. I stopped when she confronted me with her .45 and placed a few shots, one near my foot, and the other over my head.

"I was backing out of her driveway when the bullet hit my shoulder. I saw her standing on her porch after the bullet grazed my shoulder. She...she was looking the other way, towards the place where the bullet came from. The shooter used a silencer, so she must have heard the crack when it came through my back window."

"Are you sure about this?" Father Paul asked.

"Yeah, I'm sure."

"Maymie, who are the Dubain Great Reich people?" Father Paul asked.

"I know that Sheriff Beckam, Al Huff, and Mel Eichert are members. I am certain there are others, but I don't know who. They are probably people you see every day. They appear to be nice, smiling, and helpful. In reality, they are evil, fanatical, and murderous. We can never be sure who is listening, watching, and reporting. They tap phones and open mail. They've been opening the mail between me and Gunny for years. They go to church, pray, confess, and get communion. They have steady jobs, pay taxes, take walks, and go to church picnics and little league games. They—"

"Mom," Tim cut in, "Who is Hans Peiper?"

"Hans Peiper is a well-educated, charming, and charismatic leader. He's a great actor, very popular in Dubain, and a deadly threat to anyone who stands in the way of the Great Reich or him. You know him as Father Eric Faulkenburg."

Chapter 29

"Maymie, are you sure of this?" Father Paul moved to the edge of his chair.

"I'm certain, Paul."

"How?"

"I went to confession once I put all this together. I know now it wasn't the smartest thing to do."

"Well what did he say? What kind of threats did he make?"

Maymie sighed and took a sip of water offered by Mary June before she recounted her confrontation with Hans Peiper, just before she learned about Tim being shot.

The confessional in St. Augustine was a wooden structure with three small rooms. It was built against the cathedral wall to the left of the altar as you entered from the back of the cathedral. The priest would sit on a swivel chair in the middle room enclosed on its open side by a curtain. The other two rooms, also enclosed by a curtain, were for the penitents. The penitents stood in line outside the confessional and awaited their turns. When a forgiven sinner emerged from one of the rooms, a soon-to-be-forgiven sinner entered the other room. The priest swiveled to hear a confession on one side and then swiveled one hundred eighty degrees to hear a confession on the other side.

And so on. All the while confessions and absolutions were traded in low volume murmurs within the rooms.

Maymie stood in line and waited until she could speak privately with her confessor. She entered the confessional and knelt on the kneepad. A perforated window separated the priest's box from her own as a way to keep her confession private with God. However, tonight, Maymie knew who was on the other side, and God would have nothing to do with her "confession."

"Bless me, Father, for I have sinned. But this confession is about your sins, not mine."

"What? Maymie?"

The window slid open, and Maymie and Father Faulkenburg came face-to-face. Maymie looked directly into the blue eyes of her false confessor. He was a handsome man in his early fifties. His blond hair showed smudges of gray around the temples. His slightly lined face smiled with friendliness, empathy, and charm. Certainly he was attractive to women, even men, and the air of his priestly celibacy made him more so. His broad forehead hinted at his high intelligence, and his leadership, sermons, prayers, and his acting proved it. To his parishioners, he was a man of the highest integrity, honesty, humility, and Godliness. Even she had fallen for his act.

"Maymie, what's wrong?"

"Don't insult my intelligence with your little act. It won't work with me anymore. You..."

"You...what?"

"You are what's wrong, you false priest, you lying prophet, you blackmailer and murderer."

Maymie felt the tumblers of his mind running over the possibilities.

"Let me save you the trouble. Don't deny it. Come clean, because I know. Finally. No one told me, not Ernie, not Gunny. I uncovered you. Me, myself, and I. With a little help from the man who hung on the rope over there behind the altar just three weeks ago tonight. So there's no need to lie and stink up this the cathedral even more."

"Ah, Maymie, you walk in a minefield and you know not where you tread."

"Don't I? You gave yourself away—you and your murdering compatriots who stood around your victim in that Sacristy. Chris got too close, didn't he? He unleashed you and your cabal of conspirators when you argued in the forest. Yeah, I know about that because Chris told me the day before you killed him. You had to get him out of the way with either blackmail or murder, and Chris came up on the murder side. Did you really believe I'd fall for that typed suicide note? The quickie investigation? The ladder? That I wouldn't figure out the rosary on the floor and Chris's clasped hands at his death?

"The note was typed perfectly with no misspellings. You forgot that Chris could neither type nor spell. Chris was left-handed, but a right-hander tied the rope to the rafter. Was it you? Beckam? Huff? Somehow your henchmen drugged him so that he couldn't resist when they put him in the noose and sucked the life out of him. But you and they made a crucial mistake, and Chris made you pay. You under-dosed him. Chris's hands were held in prayer even after his body was lowered, yet his rosary lay on the floor. I put it together. As he strangled, Chris held the rosary in his hands, which were clasped together. Then something caused Chris to open his hands, drop the rosary, and reclasp them before he lost consciousness. Chris wasn't praying. He was sending a signal. You missed it. I didn't. He folded his hands to tell us that his murderer was another 'holy man.' You were standing in front of him. What did he look like as he slowly died in the noose?"

"Maymie, be quiet and listen to me."

"No. It is you who silences Gunny in Germany. It is you who holds my husband hostage at Piankashaw Rock. It is you who murdered the innocents at Mortain. It is you who murdered poor Eleanor and poor Freddy. You are the Nazi, the war criminal, Hans Peiper.

"You asked me to pray for you and I did. I will continue to do so, except this time I will pray against you. God is not on your side no matter your arrogance and fanaticism. He destroyed your psychopathic hero, Hitler. He will destroy you in time. Count on it."

Maymie watched him lower his head for a few moments, and then raise it. He held his smile, but now it seemed more menacing.

"Are you done?" asked Hans Peiper.

"For now."

"No, Maymie. You are done forever. You see, I know where you live, where Ernie lives. I know that Mary June has sobered up and now resides with you. She lives in your basement. We—I and my 'compatriots,' as you call them—know the streets Joey and Henry like to walk to and from school. Gunny lives in an apartment in Mannheim. Do you want his address and phone number? Oh, I forgot. You know them because you and Mary June have been sending him letters for years. Has Tim confessed to his murders at Bon Duoi in Vietnam yet? Did he tell you he was in Germany for psychiatric treatment? Do not look so shocked, Maymie. We know all about Timmy."

"You bastard!"

"Watch your mouth, Maymie. You're in confession and talking to a priest, you know."

"You're no priest. You're not even human. I swear to God, Hans Peiper, I—I'll take you down!"

"You'll do nothing of the sort, Maymie. You will leave this confessional. You will say and do nothing about me or the Great Reich. Because if you do, you will lose a son, or a husband, or a close friend. It will be an accident, of course. Drowning, an auto wreck, an errant bullet while hunting, drinking bad 'hooch' as your husband and the Piankashaws call it. Or maybe another suicide. Those can be so much fun!"

"If touch anyone close to me, I swear I'll—"

"Do nothing. Because then you will risk another reprisal, another loved one on the executioner's block... Oh! I almost forgot." Hans Peiper made the sign of the cross in front of Maymie while wearing his most solemn face. "Maymie, your sins are forgiven, if you ever had any in the first place. You have to leave before the others outside think you are confessing mortal sins. Imagine, Maymie Balbach with mortal sins! Oh, I apologize for the little joke. Well, anyway, for your penance, nothing will change. You will go home this evening and fix supper. You will smile and comfort and give cheer. You will continue to participate in St. Augustine as you have with the bazaars, picnics, fundraisers, and the PTA. You will work your shifts at the hospital and continue to heal those who pass through your care. You will attend my masses, receive communion from me, nod at my sermons, and accept my blessings. These are the rules, Maymie. If you violate any of them in the least, well, you'll just go to another funeral."

Maymie worked her mouth, but there was nothing more she could say. She was powerless and Peiper knew it. And he was a man unafraid to follow through with his threats. She needed to get home quickly. She needed to make sure her family was safe. Maymie reached for the confessional latch.

"Oh, by the way, Maymie. My daughter, Maria, is a member of the Great Reich as well. So please tell your son, Timmy, to stay away from her. That is something I'm sure you can manage. Can you do that for me, please?"

Chapter 30

Father Paul got two more beers from Maymie's refrigerator and popped off the caps with the bottle opener attached to his keychain. It was a warm overcast night, and the street light on the other side of the house reflected slightly off the empty beer bottles pushed to the edge of the porch. He felt his way into his lawn chair on the back porch and sat down, then lifted one of the beers to Tim, who rested in a chair beside his. Paul released the bottle only when he was certain Tim had taken hold of it.

Surprisingly, he was invigorated by Maymie's confessions of the truth. He too had detected another, darker, dimension to Dubain, one especially manifested in the Balbach family. To Paul, awareness, many times messy but most of the time clear, was always better than avoidance, mostly weighty and depressing. Maymie had chased away the latter with the former. However, the Balbach's were in various stages of shock at the grim news of the deaths of Eleanor Wetzel and Freddy Caldmeyer and Maymie's connection to them.

Paul had volunteered to cook supper. They'd only had canned beans, salad, and hot dogs, but the Balbachs enjoyed it well enough. Cooking gave Paul time to think and take everything in. He had inherited this flock from a good man, Father Chris Hagemeyer, and the thought that such evil as that of Eric Faulkenburg / Hans Peiper could blanket a town like this appalled him. He was trained to calm and heal souls, not fight the evil that stalked those souls. Or was he? At another time and place he'd dropped his duties to souls in order to fight evil. Why not now and here? Had God guided him to the Balbach house this afternoon? Had He bid Paul to see the struggles this one family had endured for years? Paul decided all this didn't matter. He would support the Balbach's any way he could. He, himself, would fight.

He thought about the young man sitting next to him and the courage he would need to face and confront even more struggle. Tim reminded him so much of his younger self. He'd felt a connection right away. The women and children remained in the house, giving Paul the perfect opportunity to continue his discussion with Tim, which was long overdue.

"Tim, you've told me in confession that you have thought of suicide, that at times you felt it was the only way to escape the trauma of your past. Do you still feel that way?"

"Not really," said Tim. "The feeling comes and goes. I don't know why, but since Mom unloaded on us about the real Hans Peiper and his murders and threats, I feel freed, and I feel better."

"Funny. So do I."

"Knowing about who Peiper really is makes me feel…I don't know, back in control? At least I can see where the danger is and where it's coming from. But now I have another fight, another war on my hands. I don't want it.

"Somebody's gotta get my family through this Hans Peiper and Great Reich shit. Who else is there? Dad and Gunny can't. The boys can't. Mary June is just as lost as Dad, and Mom is just about to lose it with all the pressure Peiper's put her under. So it's up to me. I'm the one who has to defend the homestead. Again. Damn it all. And damn God for doing this to me!"

"Don't know if that can happen. Only God can damn. Why would He damn Himself?"

They laughed.

"But there's the next question," said Tim. "What can I do that won't get everyone killed? None of us are safe. Not even Gunny in Germany. I know something about the enemy. What I don't know is their order of battle. What are their assets? How many soldiers do they have here in Dubain? What are their weapons? How many will stand as soldiers for them if we decide to start something? You can't fight an enemy you can't see. Tried that. Doesn't work."

Tim got up and walked into the house. Paul didn't look behind him, but he heard Tim open two more beers. When he returned, Paul bummed a cigarette and they lit up. Paul let Tim's last comment hang between them in the time it took to puff his first breath of smoke. Then he broke the silence.

"Bon Duoi?"

Tim exhaled and hunched over in his chair. "Yeah. Can't seem to lay it down."

"Why not?"

"If I had the answer we wouldn't be talking about it. So why ask me?"

"Who else is there to ask? It's your burden."

Then Tim turned to looked at Paul in the dim light. "There's you."

"Me?"

"Korea. Right?"

"Yeah," Paul replied, but at the same time wondered how Tim found out.

"We all look the same, don't we? I noticed it before. I look like my Dad, Gus looks like me, I see my reflection in you. Which outfit?"

"First Marine Division," Paul answered.

"Were you with the First when it was surrounded by the Chinese at the Chosin Reservoir?"

Paul looked away as the memories came back. They weren't as sharp for him as such memories were for Tim, but they still stung if he thought about them long enough. "Yeah."

"Some of the instructors at boot camp were with the First at the Chosin," Tim said, leaning back. "Heard them talk about it. The fighting retreat. Outnumbered fifty, maybe a hundred to one. Thirty below zero weather. Pissing on the machine guns to keep them from freezing, then pissing on the barrels to keep them from overheating."

"Yeah."

"How long were you a chaplain for the First?"

"For a while," said Paul. "Then I stopped."

"You can't just stop being a chaplain. It doesn't work that way in the Marines."

"No, it doesn't. But I did."

"When?"

"Two days after the Chinese attacked us at Chosin."

"Then you know about the fire."

Paul exhaled. The cigarette smoke was nothing like what he saw at Chosin. To help the American troops escape, the air force flew planes over the Chinese and dropped napalm on them. He remembered the screaming Chinese soldiers, the stench of their burning bodies, and the welcome heat from the firestorm.

"Yeah," he said, "I know about the fire."

The answer seemed to satisfy Tim.

"Who told you about Bon Duoi?"

"Your dad."

"When?"

"Yesterday. I said mass at Piankashaw."

"How can I fix Bon Duoi, Paul? Can't bring all those people I killed back to life."

"No, you can't. But you'll get a chance to make it right."

"When?"

"Can't say. But when it comes, you'll know it."

"Dad hasn't gotten his chance."

"He will."

"How do you know?"

"Can't really say, Tim."

"Can God forgive Dad? Me? Gus? Brute and Radius?"

"Hell, Tim. I don't even know if He can forgive me, but I believe it'll all come out right in the end. I have faith that it will. Don't know how or why I believe it, so don't ask."

"I gotta take a leak."

"So do I."

They crushed their cigarettes and moved off the porch into the backyard to do their business. They found bushes near each other and stared straight ahead into the trees beyond the yard.

"So I'm back to the same question," said Tim while he flowed. "What's my next step against Peiper? How do I keep the people I love safe?"

"You have to make choices."

"What choices?"

"The right ones, Tim. And no one's going to do it for you. Not me. Not Maymie. Not Ernie. It's you, and you alone."

"But I've made choices, Paul, and they're always the wrong ones. I feel like I'm traveling in circles, doomed forever to repeat the same mistakes over and over, and not just mine but my dad's and his dad's. How is this gonna change?"

"I can't say, Tim."

"Goddammit, Paul! You're just like all the chaplains in 'Nam. All they did was talk in riddles, and none of them had any answers at all!"

Paul said nothing as they each finished. They zipped up and moved back to the porch. Tim threw himself into his chair and hunched his shoulders.

"Sorry about the outburst, Father Paul."

"No apology needed. I feel the same way sometimes. There're no easy answers here. Hell, in most cases there're no answers at all."

They lit new cigarettes.

"Tim, you say you are stuck on a circle. Tell me about this circle."

"Where do I start?"

"Start with your grandpa, Andy."

"Yeah. Grandpa Andy—with Radius and Brute—fought the Boche in World War I. They killed their German cousins, and their German cousins killed them. We won. Then, twenty-three years later, my dad sailed over and fought his German cousins, and his German cousins fought him."

"Why do you raise the cousin thing?"

"For some reason, I think it's important. Why does no one else talk about it? I know this is unrealistic, but I like to think neither war would have been fought if the cousins on both sides had gotten together and said we won't kill each other but we will drink Schnapps and Vodka and beer together."

"Timmy, your sensitivity has hit the nail on the head. I agree with you."

"Why do you agree with me, Paul?"

"A circle, Tim."

"Yeah. So what?"

"Keep going," said Paul. "We might be on to something here."

Paul waited for Tim to think through his last comment. Tim had to go to a place he didn't want to, but Paul knew he had no other choice. It was important that Tim come to this conclusion on his own.

"Then Peiper and his Great Reich," Tim resumed, "moved from Germany to here, and blackmailed Gunny back to Germany. Two more parts of the circle, right?"

"Yeah."

"Now, Paul, you say that I, Tim Balbach, a member of the next generation of German-Americans, have to wage war against that bastard German Nazi Peiper and his Great Reich. Certainly many of them are around my age and we're related. Just another run on the treadmill, huh?"

"Tim you're thinking in a narrow tunnel. Think wider. Look out into the universe."

"And see what?"

"All of nature's actions are cyclic. The earth revolves around the sun. The moon around the earth. Right now, the earth is in exactly the same place in relation to the sun as it was exactly one year ago. Look at the forest. New life grows in the springtime, then there's summer and fall, then winter when life hides, then life flows again into the new spring. Humans are born, grow old, and die. But along the way they make new humans. The first generation gives life to the second. The second buries the first and gives birth to the third, and so on. Kingdoms are born, they rise, and then fall, and new kingdoms replace them. You see? Cycles aren't evil, they're just another part of the universe we find ourselves in."

"That's all very nice, Paul. But then we're doomed."

"How?"

"You say that kingdoms rise and fall in a cycle. I agree. History is full of examples: the Babylonians, the Roman Empire, the rises and falls of England, France, Germany, China, Russia, Spain. The cycles are the same. Only the weapons change. Now it's the United States' turn. The USA started, has risen and maybe still is rising, but pretty soon it's gonna fall. And when—not if—America falls, it'll take the whole world with it! My God, Paul. All-out war with thermonuclear weapons. A world where the living will envy the dead. Why would we want to bring children—the new generation, as you say—into it? Just so they can be part of a natural and endless cycle that is certain to bring them or some generation after them to a hellish end?"

"Probably not."

"See. You agree. So tell me, where in the hell is this God of ours when we need Him? I yelled this question at Father Chris's funeral. Got no answer but got a helluva lot of dirty looks. I ask it again."

"Maybe God is waiting for you to help yourself. He created the circle, and now He's waiting to see what choices you make within it."

"Now you're talking in circles, Paul."

"Tim, you miss the best parts of your circles!" Paul exclaimed. "Your Dad and Gunny were deadly enemies but found they were cousins. What did they do? They came together and saved each other's lives. They are close friends now, with families in America. They drank beer together, like in your fantasy except it's not a fantasy. It's real."

"They're the good parts of a circle? Is that what you're telling me?"

"Yeah, but there's more to it. The circle is made up of both good and evil in equal parts. There are times when we see great evil. This happened with Hitler, Stalin, the Black Death, the Crusades, Mortain, Korea, Bon Duoi. But then there are times when we can see the good. It comes in the form of good people who choose to fight the evil. This is never easy. The good are confused, manipulated, mostly not in control, forced to take actions against their wills. It happened with people like Solomon, Job, Jesus, St. Paul, Joan of Arc, Winston Churchill, President Lincoln, even your dad. It's happening to us now. It's happening to Maria Peiper. But especially to you, Timmy."

"Maria? I gotta think about that one, Paul."

Paul just smiled. Tim wasn't ready yet to recover from his anger at Maria and again see all the good that she had to offer. Tim had tasted some of Maria's love, but not all of it.

"Another beer?" Paul asked.

"We're not cousins!" They laughed. "Your turn, Paul."

Paul entered the house and walked into the kitchen where he got two more beers. He saw the boys turning off the TV and making their way upstairs. He imagined Maymie was in her room resting after the ordeal she'd faced that day. Paul turned to rejoin Tim outside, but he noticed a shadow duck back farther in the house. He hesitated a moment, then stepped outside. He opened the beers and handed Tim one before he sat down.

Tim tilted his head back and downed several large swallows. He gasped when he came up for air and wiped his mouth and chin. "Paul, I don't know what to do. All I got are my gut and instincts. Hell, even my combat training isn't enough to stop Peiper. He has trained assassins on his side. He made everyone believe Father Chris was a homosexual and a pedophile. How can I possibly stand up against that much power?"

"Gut and instinct are all those other people had. But you, Tim, can have something more than just gut and instinct."

"What?"

"Faith."

"In what?" asked Tim.

"In God," said Paul. "In the goodness of His creation, His universe."

Tim's mood darkened. "Well, that's just dandy, Paul! Sure, I'll have faith. And in the meantime, my family and the world can all go to hell. Joey and Henry will get shot somewhere, and I'll say, 'Oh well,' to Mom and Mary June. 'Too bad, but it's okay because I got faith in the goodness of God. Go see Father Paul. He'll clear it all up for you.'"

"Timmy, nobody asks you to be Job."

"Good. Because I'd make a damn poor Job. If I were Job, I woulda told God to go to hell like I did at Chris's funeral."

They laughed a bit and Tim's mood lifted. Paul especially remembered the look on Bishop O'Grimmels' face when Tim shouted to high heaven. Paul hadn't been upset with Tim. He knew it was part of the healing process.

"Did that help, Timmy?"

"Sure as hell did. Told him off. Made me feel better."

Vehicles with powerful engines whined in the distance. These were familiar sounds, part of the rhythm of life in Dubain. Paul found them comforting and knew, without looking at Tim, that he did also.

"Paul, how do I escape my circle?"

"By turning it into a spiral."

"How?"

"Move forward, Tim. Use your free will. Go with your gut, your instincts. You're a good person. Your suffering means that you have a strong conscience, that you detect good and evil, and that you know the difference between them. Throw a piece of the burden you carry."

"What piece?"

"The piece where you obsess over the obvious: how cannot the enemies see the difference?"

"Yeah. How did you know?"

"Because I've done the same," said Paul. "Now follow me here. Just because you were forced into certain situations in the past doesn't mean you'll be trapped by them again. Keep moving forward, learn from your mistakes, and make better choices. Therein lies your redemption and the redemption of many others. If you learn from the mistakes of the past and make the right choices for the future, the circle will spiral upward. The wrong choices will move the spiral down back into the history you're so afraid of repeating. Sometimes the spiral will stop completely and do circles. Fat ones. These things will happen because you'll make mistakes. But if you keep fighting, if you don't give up, the spiral will move upward."

Tim smiled hesitantly at Paul, then his smile grew, like Paul had given him permission to let go of his painful past. Paul saw the weight begin to lift from Tim's shoulders, and it gave him hope. They smoked a few more puffs on their cigarettes before Paul dared to broach another subject with Tim.

"Tim, are you in love with Maria Peiper?"

"Yeah. I threw her away when Walter Cronkite spoke the truth. So I can't exactly ask her to marry me, now can I?"

"No. Not yet."

"Do you know something about her that I don't, Paul?"

"I only see her when she attends my masses and I give her communion, but these are enough."

Paul allowed Tim to ponder this for a few minutes. Tim's profession of love for Maria confirmed his instinct. Moreover, Paul was certain that Maria was in love with Tim. Just like with Tim, Paul had only to look into her eyes to see she was a genuinely caring person. And he had seen the way she and Tim walked off together after Father Chris' funeral. She had genuinely cared for Tim in that moment. A chasm— the Great Reich and Hans Peiper and his minions—had opened between them. Paul sensed that Tim and Maria could reach each other again, but both would have to suffer to get there.

"Paul, I didn't trust myself around people when I left 'Nam. I knew how easy it'd been for me to kill all those people. I was scared to really open myself up and let someone get close to me because of what I might do, like I might react the way my dad did when people got too close to him. But I allowed myself to trust again when I met her. Maria…well, she was there for me all the way, and she sorta gave me permission to trust her. She was so strong and had so much life. It seemed like she had plenty to share, and she wanted to share it with me. She loved her way to my core, the one I'd hidden from everyone.

"I was almost in shock when I heard myself unburdening to her. Then, well, the conversation turned into something special. We - well, I don't think it's a sin – we made love. It wasn't sex, Paul. It was love. Spectacular and innocent.

"Then I got stupid. Best way to describe it. I reverted back to 'Nam, and I forced her to fight me. I hurt her, and I had no right. I broke the trust she had in me and threw her love back in her face. I'll probably never get it back."

"Maybe you can."

"How, Paul? She's one of them. She's the enemy! Her father kills innocent people, and she evidently condones it."

"I don't believe any of that."

"How the hell can you not, Paul?"

"Tim, you know Maria as well as anybody outside her family can. Trust your instincts. How good of an actress do you think she is? If she knows about the murders, if she was setting you up for your murder, do you think she could hide these from you?"

"My gut tells me no. Maria is too open to hide her innermost thoughts. I'm certain she can play a character in a play on stage, but day-to-day lying is beyond her. She's too genuine, too kind."

"So," Paul replied, "Maria cannot be a total enemy. This gives you another chance with her, Tim."

"I don't see how."

"Keep your eyes open. It'll happen. And remember, have faith."

Their conversation dropped while they smoked and sipped their beers. When his cigarette reached the nub, Tim crushed it into the ground with the others.

He broke the silence. "Paul, I'll take on these bastards, but I'll need your help."

"You know you got it."

"Even if I have a hard time finding my faith?"

"Tim, faith is just another word for what keeps the universe's circle turning."

"There's something else, Paul."

"What?"

"Ever since 'Nam, I've hated sunny and warm days. I like cloudy and gray and cold weather. Maria pushed this away for awhile, but it came back after I lost her. Depressing weather makes me feel better, somehow."

"Timmy, my experiences of the fire in Korea are then, now, and always. They come every day. They happen every day. They never end and they never will. I prayed for the strength and wisdom to heal myself. And I did. I made amends as I could. I love each and every day, no matter the weather. I think, the Lord made this day, and I give thanks and rejoice. Timmy, I look into the sky, be it blue, gray, sunny, or black, as it is tonight. I look up, and there—right there—I see my God. You can do this also."

Mary June heard the men say goodnight to each other from where she was hiding in the kitchen. She'd crept there after she dosed Maymie with something to help her sleep. Father Paul might have noticed her, but he never showed any sign as he continued his conversation with Tim.

She felt drawn to Father Paul. Not a romantic tug, but more like a moon in gravitational peace with its host. When Father Paul entered the living room, earlier, she sensed more than just a parish priest. This man held a marvelous aura that flowed like living energy around and through him. There were contrasts, but these only made him more alluring. He was magnetism and confusion, purpose and insecurity, strength and weakness, kinship and distance, basic humanness and transfiguration, certainty and doubt. He stood on a line between two worlds, but feared neither. Mary June knew the line between the worlds all too well, and she feared both.

She rushed and hid in the living room when she heard the clank of the empty beer bottles as Tim gathered them from the porch. She heard Father Paul start his car and rev the engine. Then she heard Tim enter, lock the door, and throw the bottles into the trash. Mary June listened as he walked up the stairs to his bedroom and shut the door. This was her cue to exit the house through the backdoor. She walked on the lawn to the basement door and quietly opened it. She was about to step down inside when a hand clapped her on the shoulder.

"Mary June?"

She jumped back, opened her mouth to scream, then stopped when she saw who it was.

"I'm sorry for scaring you, Mary June," said Father Paul.

"How…how did you know I was in the kitchen?" asked Mary June. "Did you see me?"

"No."

"Then—"

"I take it you overheard us." Paul said.

"Yeah."

"I hoped you would."

"Why're you here, Paul?"

"Because I knew you were listening, and I knew you needed to hear what I said too. And because I know you can help."

"Help? Help with what?"

"Tim lost his life once to the violence and tragedy of war. I think you know something about that. You know well the wars that rage inside people's hearts. Tim is struggling with the wars inside him. Now there wages outside him another battle."

"Peiper?"

"Yeah, and they're connected. So you can't crawl back into a bottle, Mary June."

"Why not?"

"Tim needs you. He's on the Great Reich's death list. He can't stay here with his family where he'll put them in danger. He doesn't know it yet—I think it would hurt him too much to realize it's another one of his circles—but for his own protection, for the time being, he must hide out with men at Piankashaw Rock. They can protect him."

"You want me to move to Piankashaw and stay with him? Is that it?"

"I'm not asking you to live there. I'm asking you to spend time there with Tim and watch over him. And make sure the others do the same."

"I've been there, you know, to Piankashaw."

"I'm aware of your past, Mary June."

"That's wonderful! So you know all about me. You think I can go back there all willy-nilly as if nothing's changed? Oh, it's Mary June Balbach. Poor drunken bitch. Abandoned her family. Went off to screw bums in the forest."

She didn't tell Paul that the last several weeks had been the best for her in years. She woke up sober the morning after Tim had been shot. In the emergency, Maymie commanded her away from alcohol. She'd craved the hooch and sloocum something fierce. But on one of those days when Tim drove Henry and Joey home from school, Henry, her son, had walked through the front door and shouted, "Mom, I'm home!" Not even being the bum mama of Piankashaw made her feel as good as she had then.

However, she had to flush Paul out. "What makes you think I can help Tim fight his war when I can't fight and win my own?"

"They're the same fight, Mary June."

Mary June looked away from Father Paul. "I'll just drag them down."

"No you won't."

"How can you doubt it? I've always fallen off the wagon."

"Because you've suffered the pangs of alcoholism and the guilt, anger, and fear it carries. You've been there and back. These have deepened your soul and a deep soul will make you tougher and braver than any soldier. And now you know what you're fighting for."

Chapter 31

Maria Peiper believed that time healed all wounds and answered most questions, so she expected the passage of time to ease her disquietude over the deaths of Father Chris, Eleanor Wetzel, and Freddy Caldmeyer. These things happened, she thought, because such things have always happened. But Tim's reproach the last time she saw him made her question things she took for granted. Then there was the singular event of the attempted murder of Tim in her backyard by someone safely hidden across the street. What should I do next? she'd asked herself. You can either do nothing or go to the source. Go to Mama and Papa.

Once she gathered up the courage to face her parents, Maria drove to the chateau. However, in the far reaches of her mind, in places outside her control, the sorry events of the past three weeks kaleidoscoped into a cacophony of doubts, hesitations, and misgivings. Why can't you drive these things away, Maria? she asked herself. Is someone or something forcing you to think what you dare not say aloud, even to yourself? Can you, or any human, through no fault of their own be presented with facts and realities that are so painful yet so unassailable that they turn convictions and change the memory of a happy life into lies?

When she pulled up to the chateau, Maria closed the door of her car, greeted Leni and Schmeling, who were chained near their shelter on the edge of the patio above the culvert, and entered the chateau. She saw her mother baking in the kitchen alcove at the far side of the great room. Her father sat at an antique oak table near the kitchen writing on a pad of paper. A large black binder lay on the table. He looked up from his pad and laid down the pencil.

"Well, hello there, meine liebling."

"Hello, Maria," Greta called from the kitchen.

"What brings you to visit us older folk on such a beautiful afternoon?" asked Hans.

"I must speak to you, Papa und Mama."

Greta wiped her hands clean on the apron she wore and moved to sit beside her husband at the table. "What is on my daughter's mind?"

"Sheriff Beckam, Deputy Al Huff, and Coroner Mel Eichert."

"Have they mistreated you, Maria?" Hans asked.

"No, Papa."

"Then what is it, schatzie?"

"It is impossible, Papa, that three people from Dubain could have died under such strange circumstances in a three week period: Father Chris supposedly by suicide, Eleanor Wetzel in an auto accident, and Freddy Caldmeyer by accidental drowning. There are no witnesses to any of these events, but the common threads are Sheriff Beckam, Deputy Huff, and Coroner Eichert."

"Go on," said Hans.

"Eichert ruled Father Chris's death a suicide, but is it not possible that someone killed Father Chris and disguised it as a suicide? Some at the bank who knew Father Chris told me that he was a poor typist and even worse speller. However, the suicide note was neatly typed without even one misspelling. Father Chris spoke of his sins with children in the note, but not one person has come forward and accused him of such things. Is this because there is no such victim and the composer of the note made up those things?

"Could someone have forced Mrs. Wetzel to that road, drugged her, and then rigged the accelerator on her car to cause the crash? Beckam and Huff arrived first on the wreck scene. The sheriff said that Eleanor had been drinking, but the Wetzel family emphatically denies it. Her family and my friends at the bank tell me Eleanor rarely drank alcohol. Several hours later, Freddy Caldmeyer died, supposedly in the Patoka River. Beckam and Huff were the first people on the scene, after Mrs. Caldmeyer, where Freddy had been fishing. The sheriff, deputy, and coroner ruled his death as an accidental drowning. However, the police failed to recover Freddy's body after dragging the river for several days, so we may never know what happened to him."

"What is your point, Maria?" Greta interjected.

"Has the Great Reich any complicity in their deaths?"

"Maria!" exclaimed Greta. "Your fantasies run wild like a child's and cause you to accuse your father!"

"Mama, please! I do not accuse Papa. I question his soft heart! I know Sheriff Wilfred Beckam, Deputy Al Huff, and Coroner Mel Eichert are Great Reich citizens, and, so far as I have known them, decent men. But is it not possible for them to disguise a murder as a suicide, a car accident, or a drowning?"

"Maria, you make very serious accusations," Greta responded.

"I charge no one, Mama. I came to you and Papa today for peace of mind. Am I not entitled to that?"

"Yes, liebling," said Hans. "Maria, we are law-abiders, not law-breakers. We do not engage in cold-blooded murder. I have made these things clear to all Great Reich citizens in my gaus."

"I am aware of your orders, Papa."

"But still you are troubled, schatzie."

"Yes. Papa, I know you are incapable of Hitlerian tactics. However, it only makes sense that not all Great Reich citizens feel the same as you. It only makes sense that Eichert, Huff, or Beckam might be among these. If this is so, then any one, two, or all three could easily disobey you and violate all manner of laws, even commit murder, in the false belief that they are advancing the Great Reich."

"Maria," said Greta, "this is a side of you that is quite disturbing."

"Disturbing or not, Mama, I must have the truth."

"Then you will have the truth, Maria," said Hans. "I personally recruited Beckam, Huff, and Eichert. They are good men with families.

I trust them to follow my orders. Why? Because they understand, as we do, that the Great Reich cannot exist and cannot advance unless there is both a chain of command and unquestioned obedience to orders from those in that chain."

"I accept your word on this, Papa."

"They are valuable in another sense, Maria. They report to me the goings-on in and around Dubain, those that I am not privy to as the Pastor of St. Augustine Parish."

"Papa, that makes them spies."

"A harsh term," said Hans Peiper. "The Great Reich has enemies, Maria. If possible, it operates in the background, out of sight, and in secret. Nevertheless, our enemies want to make certain that the existence of the Great Reich itself is not a secret. Our greatest challenges many times are not the enemies we see, like the Hebrews, but those we do not. Not the enemies who are disciplined and predictable, like the Israeli Mossad, but those who are not. Dubain is full of enemies for us, and a magnet for more—seen and unseen, known and unknown—simply because they suspect my presence here. Thus the need for greater surveillance in Dubain."

"Papa, were Freddy, Chris Hagemeyer, and Mrs. Wetzel enemies of the Great Reich?"

"Of course not, Maria!" exclaimed Greta.

"Maria, your mother and I can neither explain their deaths nor the fact that they occurred within a three week time span. These are as much mysteries to us as to you. We pray to our Father in heaven for the peaceful repose of their souls. It is the best we, and you, can do."

"Does this ease your mind, Maria?" asked Greta.

"Yes, Mama, as to Father Chris, Eleanor, and Freddy."

"But you are not finished," said Greta.

"No, Mama. Is Ernie Balbach an enemy of the Great Reich?"

"Yes, Maria."

"How is Ernie an enemy? He is just a lost war veteran living in the forest. What are you withholding from me, Papa?"

"Maria," said Greta, "it has to do with Mortain, a subject that is very painful for your father."

"I know the story, Mama."

"Not all of it, Maria," said Greta. "You have a right to the full story. Your father withheld it from you at my insistence. I felt like I was protecting you. Now I see that I was wrong."

"Then tell me the truth, Mama. What really happened at Mortain?"

"It is Tim's father, Ernie Balbach, who killed most of your papa's command. This is the reason your papa ordered you away from Tim Balbach."

"Does Tim Balbach know this?"

"Yes." said Hans. "Ernie Balbach lives at Piankashaw Rock. I have it on good authority that Tim Balbach moved back to Piankashaw several days ago. There are a number of other louts who also live there who are sympathetic to the Balbachs and would not listen to reason if I or anyone else tried to explain things to them. Ernie and Tim are well-armed and violent enemies of the Great Reich and me."

"Why?" Maria asked. "After all, it is Ernie who committed atrocities against you and your men, not the other way around. If the truth got out, you would have nothing to fear from him."

"Ernie Balbach cannot forgive himself for the killings he committed at Mortain," Hans replied, leaning back in his chair. "This explains his insanity and the reason he lives at Piankashaw Rock on green whiskey and his wife's soup. Perversely, he and his family, particularly Timothy, are driven by Ernie's guilty conscience and blame us, their victims, and especially me, for what happened. This twisted reasoning of 'blame the victim' is common among our lessers, particularly Americans."

"I see. This is awful for you, Papa, but I feel a little better with the truth."

"But I see that you have more questions, Maria," said Greta.

"Yes."

"Go on."

"It started when a man spied on Tim and me at Raven Rock," said Maria. "He snapped photos of us but also carried a rifle. Tim spotted the man and chased him into the woods. Tim later said that the same man had followed him while he was in Germany, through the Palatinate. Tim confronted the man in a bierstube in Bad Durkheim. They had words but nothing else happened. One week after the Raven Rock incident, someone shot at Tim as he backed his car out of my driveway. The gunman used a silencer because I heard no gun report. However, the shot came from the east side of the street because the bullet entered Tim's rear window as he backed eastward from my driveway. Later, I traced the shooter's position into the backyard of the house located on the east side of the street directly across from my place. I discovered military boot prints in and around a small patch of foliage in the family's backyard. The bullet missed Tim's head but, I later learned, grazed his shoulder."

"Maria, there are more hard truths which, in retrospect, we should have disclosed to you."

"Disclose them now, Papa."

"You were never the object of Tim's romantic intentions," said Hans, "though he capably led you, a highly intelligent and sensitive person, to believe otherwise. To Tim, you were simply the means to his end. He made up the story about the man in Germany. However, the man at Raven Rock and the gunman with the silencer across the street from your house are the same person."

"How can you know this, Papa?"

"Because Tim Balbach hired the man."

"To shoot him?"

"Quite the contrary, Maria. Tim set up the gunman to snap photos of both of you and to shoot at him in your presence. The gunman's bullet was supposed to get close to Tim but not hit him." Hans smiled. "So it is fair to ponder whether Tim paid the man."

"Why would Tim do these things?" asked Maria.

"He staged them to obtain your sympathy and to eventually turn you against the Great Reich."

"Maria," said Greta, "Timothy Balbach is a disgruntled ex-marine who spends his time drinking rotgut whiskey, smoking marijuana, injecting heroin, and chasing young women for sexual favors. He can be unstable, as you learned. However, he is a fanatical enemy of the Great Reich. Now, some fanatics, even though they are mentally unbalanced, are highly functional when dealing with the object of their fanaticism. Tim Balbach is one of these. He is a single-minded extremist and so uncompromisingly militant against the Great Reich that he deludes himself into the belief that he is a god-like hero whose mission in life is to save the world by taking down the Great Reich. We see this sort of twisted mentality in many assassins of leaders throughout history. The men who killed John Kennedy and, recently, his brother, Robert Kennedy, are very good examples of these."

"Assassins?"

"Yes, Maria," said Greta. "Tim Balbach used you in an attempt to get close enough to kill your father."

"My God, Papa, I almost got you killed!"

"You could not have known, and in any event, the threat is contained," said Hans. Then he added with a rueful grin, "Tim Balbach is neither the first nor will he be the last person who desires me dead."

"Does all this ease your mind, Maria?" asked Greta.

"Yes, Mama."

"Maria," said Hans, "our monthly meeting begins in about an hour. Our guest speaker is a Great Reich citizen from Chicago who is a major functionary in the Richard Nixon presidential campaign. We desire to contribute to Mr. Nixon's campaign fund, but anonymously. Our speaker will explain how we can do so. The guests will start arriving soon. Will you stay for the meeting?"

"I will greet the guests, Papa, and attend part of the meeting, but not all of it. I have other things I need to take care of. Is that okay?"

"Yes, schatzie. That will be fine."

Chapter 32

Maria shook hands with her boss, George Kaetzel, president of First Dubain State Bank. In turn, she greeted Kevin Denham, Dubain's State Senator, Firmus Langerman, Dubain Postmaster, and William "Bill" Miller, Vice President of the Dubain Phone Company. Her father took up the first order of business, which was the administration of the Great Reich Oath to Joe Briggeman, the longtime maintenance man at St. Mary's Hospital.

"Congratulations, Joseph." Hans shook his hand as the others applauded.

Maria slipped out the chateau's back entrance when the ceremony concluded. The heat and sultriness swathed her when she stepped through the door. Nothing moved outside, no leaves, no saplings, no forest critters. Leni and Schmeling lay on their stomachs, their heads on their paws. It was much darker than usual for this time of the evening, and there were no sun rays in the trees. The woods hid the western sky from Maria, so she pictured a cauldron of dark bubbling clouds building up, the precursors of a violent thunderstorm.

She walked out to her car, pulled the handle on the driver's side door, then stopped. There came something else in the air, wholly detached from atmospheric violence. It was a palpable feeling of foreboding, not only of the future, but of times gone by. These compelled her to see and then look deeply into the shadows that crept around her when she was a little girl, then an adolescent, then an adult. They'd been there all along, she now comprehended, but the cocoon of Mama and Papa shielded her from them and kept the truth they whispered at bay.

The cocoon had fallen away when she went to university, moved to Dubain, and started her career at First Dubain. Without the protection of Mama and Papa, she had seen things that were new and learned things that were different. Despite the assurances from her parents that very afternoon, she had her doubts. This astounded her and she felt a wall rising between her and her parents.

Then she was torn from her thoughts and thrown back to her senses as she stood beside the car. There came a ghostly, spine-chilling harshness, a sinister fusion of evil with space and time, here and now. A thousand needles pricked her. Then a deep swooshing sound rushed from the sky above and reverberated through the woods. Was it the thunder of the approaching storm or something else? She wheeled around and scrutinized the blackening forest. Stillness. No movement. She spun and scanned the scene over the top of her car and the chateau behind it. There came a kind of shriek, maybe, over the chateau. Then Schmeling and Leni were on their feet and facing her, their heads down, the fur shackling on their curled backs, their growls so low as to be almost inaudible.

"You are Maria Peiper, yes?"

Maria whirled around and leaned back on her car. He stood in the gloom at the edge of the woods, maybe three, four meters away. She stiffened for a moment, then recalled that this man, chosen by her father, stood security outside the chateau during the meeting. He wore blue jeans and a navy blue polo shirt. He carried a pistol on his hip and a scoped rifle in his hands. Maria noticed the lower pants-legs of his jeans stuffed into heavy boots.

"Yes. Can I help you?"

"No, ma'am."

"Who are you?"

"Gustav. Gustav Stresseman. Nice to meet you, Maria."

The man spoke English with a heavy German accent. A sinister air, something like his own private, violent atmosphere, surrounded him. Maria felt certain of his power to seize her, pull her into himself, and force her to breathe only the air that he wished to provide. The man looked vaguely familiar to Maria and she thought, Where have I seen him?

"Nice to meet you, Gustav."

"I apologize for startling you so. You seemed deep in thought."

"Just daydreaming."

"Sometimes daydreams are pleasant, sometimes not."

"Well, Gustav, I must be going."

"Goodbye, Maria. Maybe we will meet again when next I have business in America. No?"

"Perhaps."

The man walked back into the woods and disappeared. Maria entered her car, started the engine, and rolled the window down. She hung her head out, peered at the ground, and shuddered. Gustav's boot prints matched the pattern and size of those behind her neighbor's house.

The windstorm, which preceded the rain, knocked out Dubain's electricity. The town lay dark but for the headlights of a few vehicles and lightening flashes. As she drove home, Maria watched tree branches, old newspapers, leaves, and crumpled hamburger wrappers race by in the wind, their lines of travel parallel to the ground. During lightening flashes, Maria saw the wall of rain move like a billowing curtain northeastward across the town. She turned on the radio, tuned in to the Dubain station, and heard snippets in between the static: "... emergency flash...reports...severe thunderstorm...tornado warning... Dubain area...seek shelter immediately..." The station went dead.

Two blocks from her house, the rain hit hard, reducing visibility to a few feet. She turned into her driveway, parked her car in the garage, grabbed the flashlight from the glove box, and pulled the Luger from her purse. She switched on the flashlight and turned off the car's lights and motor. Before she could exit, the right back door opened and a man entered her car.

Maria swung her arm and the Luger towards the man, but his strong arms and hands pinned her wrist and arm to the top of the front seat. Maria struggled to turn the gun, but the best she could do was aim it slightly upward. She fired twice, putting two holes in the roof of her car. Then, over the temporary deafness caused by .45 caliber reports in a closed space, she picked up soothing words coming from a soothing voice.

"…'re safe…It's okay…nothing to fear…No need to be afraid, Maria."

"Who are you?"

"It's me, Maria, Father Paul Kessler."

"Let me see your face."

"First put that gun down before someone gets hurt."

She removed her finger from the trigger but kept the gun in her hand. Father Paul leaned into the front seat so she could get a clear view of him.

"What do you want, Father Paul?"

"I want you to drive to St. Augustine Cathedral. We can hide your car under that big catalpa tree outside the sacristy and talk behind the altar.

"And why should I do that? You sneak into my garage, attack me in my car, and then invite me to the cathedral?"

"Because I have answers for you, Maria, to questions I'm sure you've begun asking yourself."

Maria considered Father Paul's words for a long moment. The sense of foreboding hadn't left her, and she felt she didn't have the strength to confront the shadows that surrounded her and her family. Yet, she'd known Father Paul since he'd arrived at St. Augustine's. She liked his masses, and his sermons poured not from his head, but from his heart. She'd seen his humility and grace when Tim yelled at God during Father Hagemeyer's burial ceremony. In that moment, she felt she could trust him.

They entered St. Augustine Cathedral behind the sacristy. Father Paul lit a candle with help from Maria and her flashlight, retrieved a bottle of altar wine, opened it, and handed it to Maria, who took a long drink. Then Father Paul lifted the bottle.

"Not the best stuff, Maria. But it'll have to do."

"Who sent you, Father Paul? Was it Tim? Maymie? Are you working for them?"

"No one sent me, Maria. I just wanted the chance to talk to you away from listening ears. Calm down."

"Calm down? Calm down? You practically kidnap me from my garage in the middle of one of the worst thunderstorms to ever hit Dubain, I shoot holes through the roof of my car, and you want me to calm down!"

"You can leave any time, Maria."

"Fine. I am going home. Goodbye." Maria stood and walked towards the door.

Father Paul lowered his head to his chest. "It might be kidnapping, I suppose," he ruminated aloud, "but probably not, because there was no force or coercion." He stood up, and said to Maria's back, "'Course, Maria, you can call Sheriff Beckam and ask him to arrest me. The phone is in the corner."

Maria's hand froze on the doorknob.

"I know the truth, Maria," said Father Paul.

"The truth of what?"

"Freddy Caldmeyer, Eleanor Wetzel, and Father Chris."

Maria turned. "I went over all that with Mama and Papa today. It was a suicide and two unfortunate accidents. That is all."

"No, Maria."

"Eleanor died in a car wreck. Freddy drowned. Father Chris hung himself."

"No, Maria. I have more truth to tell. About Tim and Ernie Balbach, Mortain, the Great Reich, and Sheriff Beckam, Al Huff, Melvin Eichert, Gustav Stresseman."

"If you know your 'truth' then you must know who my father is. But you're wrong. It was Ernie Balbach who killed Papa's men at Mortain. Tim Balbach used me to try to get to Papa and murder him."

"No, Maria."

"Mama and Papa do not lie to me!"

"Quite the contrary, Maria. Your father ordered his men to line up the Americans for execution, then killed one of them with the Luger you carry. He was about to execute Ernie when Ernie pulled a gun – it's the Beretta that Tim Balbach now carries - killed your father's adjutant, Fritz Stresseman, and wounded your father."

"I don't believe you."

"Belief might matter. Truth certainly does. I learned the truth from the confession of a penitent who gave me permission to break the confessional seal and tell the truth to others. Did you know one German regular survived the attack at Mortain? He was a German soldier who searched Ernie Balbach after his patrol had been captured by the SS, and he purposely missed the Beretta Ernie carried in his pocket. That man's name is Gunther Balbach."

"Why should it matter who he was?" asked Maria. She walked back to where Father Paul stood, staring deep into his eyes.

"Because Gunther Balbach is Ernie's fourth cousin, Mary June Balbach's husband, and Henry Balbach's father. He is the proof for you of the events that took place at Mortain, so much so that your father coerced him to leave his family and Dubain to protect his secrets. He moved to Germany and lives in Mannheim because your father threatened the lives of his family if he did not."

"I do not want to hear this inanity, Father Paul."

"Ah, Maria. The truth is inside you. You must have some understanding of it by now. You run from it, you dodge it, you try to kick it away, but nothing works. You have one last defense. 'Maria,' you tell yourself, 'the truth is not true so long as it is not spoken.' But you must say it, Maria! Blurt it out, yell it, scream it!"

"No! That is my choice."

"A false choice, Maria. You are too smart and too decent to wallow in such childish nonsense."

"Stop it, Father Paul."

He grabbed her shoulders. "Listen to me, Maria! No, don't look down. Lift your head and look into my eyes. I've looked into other matters around Dubain. I've contacted friends of mine in Germany. I discovered that Gustav Stresseman is a highly paid and skilled assassin for the Great Reich. Your father uses his talents often. He orders Beckam, Huff, and Eichert to aide and abet Stresseman."

"No! My papa does no such things. The Great Reich is peaceful! It presents a wonderful future if only its enemies would leave it alone!"

"Maria, the Great Reich is monstrous! It aims to enslave the world! So it blackmails. It murders. It tortures."

"You lie!"

"No, Maria. It is you who lie. You lie to yourself. It is your father, Maria, who hired Gustav to murder Chris Hagemeyer. Why? Because Chris had gotten too close to the truth and your father could no longer control him."

"Stop it!"

"It is your father who hired Gustav to murder Eleanor and Freddy."

"Papa—No! They died in accidents!"

"No, Maria. Gustav, aided by Beckam and Huff, murdered them on your father's orders. Why? Because they were links—innocent links—in a chain that led from Father Chris's murder to the Reich and your father. Maymie Balbach completed the chain with their help. She confronted your father with the truth. They died for it."

"Papa—No!"

"It is your father who hired Gustav to murder Tim Balbach in your backyard. It is your father who will not stop until Tim Balbach is dead."

"Papa—No! Papa—No! Papa—No!"

"Maria, I can't protect you," said Father Paul, holding her head on his shoulder, his black shirt and Roman collar absorbing her tears. "No one can. But I know this: You must lose the life you have. You must walk through the valley of the shadow of death and face the evil and defeat it. Alone. There is no rod and no staff to comfort you. You must make it to the other side. Then, and only then, will you gain the life that is meant for you."

Chapter 33

They came together in the Hoosier National Forest at the place where Tim and Maria encountered Radius on their last date at Raven Rock. Maymie, Ernie, Mary June, and the boys assembled on a log in front of Tim. Father Paul and Hal sat on the forest floor to Tim's right, and Gus and Georgie to Tim's left. Tim stood a little ways inside the semi-circle.

It's a family reunion, right here in the woods, thought Tim. Here are Mom and Dad, my brother, my aunt and cousin, and me. Here's the family priest, Father Paul, and here are three new family friends, Gus, Georgie, and Hal, invited to share in the celebration of the family's good fortune.

Tim scoffed at his own thoughts. Fortune? Celebration? The fortune at hand is not a wedding, a baptism, a first communion, or a graduation. These are easy because they're good fortunes, and the celebrations for them are simple and fun. Aunts, uncles, cousins, any remaining grandmas and grandpas, family friends. Fried chicken and German potato salad. Beer straight out of the tap of a sixteen gallon keg set in a washtub full of ice, but you gotta pump first and then pour down the side of the cup or you'll get too much foam. The old folks talking in German. There are politics and poker games, and maybe a quick fist fight between uncles. Kids and soft drinks and bruises and cuts and broken arms, then a trip to the emergency room, or worse, to your ancient country doctor, low on sympathy and lower on Novocain. Teens sneaking beers and drinking them in the garage or hayloft. Then after dark, sometimes in the middle of the night, piling everything, including kids, into the back of a pickup truck, and going home.

But here and now, the fortune, taking on and defeating the Dubain Great Reich, was perilous, and the celebration was not in sight. Tim's job was tough, maybe impossible, because the crux was his mother. He needed to convince her of the fortune's righteousness and make her see a celebration. If she said hell no, the fortune would die and there would be no celebration.

Can't dance around it, Tim, he told himself. You have to convince her that the weapon of courage is not only in our hands, but is powerful enough to defeat the weapons of the Great Reich. Today, Timmy, it's your stubbornness against Mom's.

"Well, Tim, we're here. What do you want?" Maymie asked, her stern monotone voice leaving no doubt that she'd already gone for Tim's jugular.

Meet it head on, Timmy, he thought. "Mom, we're taking on the Great Reich, and we're going to defeat it."

"How?"

"Don't know yet."

"Then why're we here?" Maymie asked. "The only thing that matters is survival. I will not allow you, Timmy, to get your dad and Mary June and the boys killed."

"What about you, Mom? And Gunny and me?" asked Tim.

"They might go after Gunny, but not me. Maybe even not you, Timmy."

"I doubt it, Mom. I'm a marked man. You were the one who patched my shoulder. Remember?"

"Yeah, Timmy, I remember. But there's a difference between life and death, and that's what we're talking about here." Maymie turned to Father Paul. "Is this the crap you dragged us out here for?"

"Yeah," Father Paul replied.

"Mom," said Tim, "Peiper and the Great Reich make us captives in our own lives. This isn't life. It's living death. We—you—have to decide between accepting lives as permanent prisoners versus peace and normal lives.''

"Tim's right," Ernie said, fully sober for the first time in months.

"Mary June?"

"I'm with Tim, Maymie."

"Paul? You helped them set me up for this meeting, didn't you?"

Father Paul nodded. "Yeah."

Maymie looked around for anyone else to support her position. "I know Gus is a fighter and he's with you, Tim. I don't know Hal right off. He's not from around here, but he's your choice, Timmy, so I assume he can fight." Maymie turned to Georgie. "But what about you, Georgie? You can't shut off pacifism like a light switch. Now you say you can shoot, that you can kill. I don't believe it for one minute."

"Haven't shut it off, Mrs. Balbach. Can't and won't. Thought a lot about it. Peace has to work both ways. Peaceful people die at the hands of enemies who aren't. A dead peace-and-love-at-all-costs guy can't do nothin' for nobody unless he's a martyr. And I ain't no martyr. I can shoot and kill."

"Paul," she said, turning to the priest, "Can you kill?"

"Mom," Tim interjected, "a shooting war is pointless unless we're forced to defend ourselves against their guns. Our strategy is to compile as much information on the Great Reich as possible, and then expose them with it."

"Expose? Where? How?"

"Don't know yet. Newspaper. FBI. Public event, like at one of Father Paul's masses."

"Who's going to write it all down?"

"Mary June."

"What'll you do for protection?"

"Gus, Georgie, and Hal. They'll work in shifts at the house and act as bodyguards for anyone who leaves it. Dad, Paul, and me will take care of ourselves."

"Have they sobered up?" asked Maymie, motioning towards Gus, Hal, and Georgie.

Hal responded. "Ma'am, we've promised Tim no drinking or drunkenness and no hangovers while on duty. Mostly, we're just glad to be of service to someone again."

"How long will this take?" asked Maymie, ignoring Hal's promise.

"Don't know."

"I don't like this, Tim. Not one bit. I see nothing but funerals in our future."

"I doubt there will be funerals," said Father Paul.

"Gee, Paul. Has God Himself come down and assured you of this?"

"No."

"You have some nerve, said Maymie. "Timmy himself belted it out at Chris's funeral. Just where in the hell is God in all this? Where was He when they murdered Chris? Where was He when I got Eleanor and Freddy killed? Tell me, how many candles should I light?"

"Look around you, Maymie," said Father Paul. "You must trust Ernie, the only person here who's already defeated Hans Peiper once. Feel the hope in Mary June, who's sobered up. Imagine what Henry and Joey see in their futures and try to tell yourself that they won't store an ocean of hatred that will boil over before they even graduate from high school. Admire Timmy, who's fighting to keep his family safe. And remember, Maymie, it was you who uncovered the truth, carried it into the confessional, and flung it in the face of an unsuspecting and astounded evil man, with whom you then went eyeball-to-eyeball. By the way, I pity the guy who finds himself staring down the barrel of that .38 you keep in your bedroom."

Maymie said nothing. Tim's instincts told him to keep his mouth shut, and he hoped the others had the good sense to do the same.

Maymie sighed and hunched over. "Well, Father Paul Kessler," she said slowly and grimly, "then you'd best hope that none of you find yourselves in that position."

The others' laughter drove away the tension that had been building, and Tim knew that with a strong person like his mother on board, their family would finally be able to move forward together.

"Mom," said Tim, "Hal'll escort you, Mary June, and the boys back to the house and stay with you until tomorrow morning, when Georgie'll relieve him. Father Paul, if you would like to give mass at Piankashaw, we'd all appreciate it. It'd be nice to have a little help in all this from the Old Man Above."

Chapter 34

Father Paul started the mass. Kurt Getz made the sign of the cross and bowed his head along with his fellow Piankashaws. They knew him only by his alias, Jack Trocksley. Kurt noted the disappearance of Tim and Ernie Balbach—and Hal, Gus, and Georgie—for several hours that afternoon, then their return to Piankashaw Rock in the company of Father Paul. It was his job to notice these things. Peiper regularly chose Kurt for such special missions. This explained Kurt's latest assignment, that of living the life of a bum at Piankashaw Rock and passing back to Colonel Peiper such information as could be gotten on the Balbach family. Lately, Kurt's mission had expanded to include the Balbachs' newest friend, Father Paul Kessler, and those Piankashaws who might ally themselves with the Balbachs. It was not the most pleasant of missions, but Kurt devoted himself to Peiper's cause and would follow wherever his Colonel led him.

In 1941, SS Private Kurt Getz found himself in Major Hans Peiper's unit on the eastern front fighting the Russians. Major Peiper cared deeply for his men. During the Russian winters, most of the German Army lacked fuel and winter clothing and consumed low rations, a deadly combination amidst twenty below Celsius temperatures, blizzard after blizzard, mountains of snow, and Russian attacks. Major Peiper's men, on the other hand, stayed warm in insulated uniforms and boots, ate well on full rations, and never lacked fuel for

their armored vehicles or to start small fires. Private Getz told no one
of his suspicion that Peiper bribed the quartermasters with his own
money.

There were other things that endeared the man to him. Peiper's
unit measured one of the lowest casualty rates in the SS, although it
saw action in some of the worst fighting on both the eastern and western fronts. Peiper took care of his men and found every way possible
to ensure not only their victory, but their survival.

Kurt was thrilled when Colonel Hans Peiper asked him to become
his adjutant to replace the dead Stresseman. It was then that their personal friendship started, though Kurt was careful to show due respect
to Hans. Even after all these years, he refrained from informality in
the presence of the Colonel or Fraulein Peiper, and even though there
was no military rank in Hans Peiper's gaus, he never forgot his status
as Colonel Peiper's subordinate. In return, Hans took on Kurt as a
close personal companion and confidant, and treated him as family.

Kurt learned that nothing more strongly cemented the bonds of
friendship than family. His own family life had not prepared Kurt for
the camaraderie Peiper offered him. Kurt was the oldest of five children born of Heinrich and Lydia Getz, and his neighbors had often
commented on Heinrich's drunken, abusive, and cruel nature. Kurt
had grown up acting as a shield, protecting his mother and siblings
from his father's beatings by taking their places under his father's
fists.

One night, when everyone was in bed, Heinrich made the mistake of walking into the woods and not watching behind him. Kurt
sneaked out of the house, grabbed a shovel he had hidden near the
outhouse just for this purpose, and followed Heinrich. The next morning, Kurt awoke in his bed, refreshed and happy, but he dared not
show it. Heinrich did not awaken in his bed because he was not in
it. In fact, he was not in the house or anywhere on the farm where he
could be found.

Kurt took part in the neighborhood manhunt for his father and
cried when it became clear that his papa had deserted his family.
Several days later, however, Kurt whispered to Lydia that Papa had

not deserted them. He told her she need not worry because Papa would never return home to hurt them again. Lydia and Kurt never spoke of it, but from such a young age, Kurt made it clear how far he would go to protect his family.

Kurt divulged the story of his father's disappearance only to one other person, Colonel Hans Peiper. It was during the time near the end of the war when Hans Peiper's Werewolves—Colonel Peiper, Adjutant Getz, and their unit—hid out at a secluded place in the Black Forest near the Swiss border. Colonel Peiper told Kurt he'd done the right thing. Several weeks later, it was Kurt who delivered to Colonel Peiper the news about the colonel's wife and children, and he learned then what family meant to his colonel.

Adjutant Kurt Getz and the six men under his command were the last of Colonel Peiper's men to leave the Black Forest hideout. Colonel Peiper had smuggled all his other men into Switzerland and safety. On the afternoon of May 8, 1945, they reached the rendezvous point, a small clearing on the edge of the woods near the town of Steinen, Germany, located along the Swiss border. They concealed themselves in the woods to await Colonel Peiper.

Of Colonel Peiper's loyalty, bravery, and daring, Kurt and his men held no doubts. However, they wondered if those things would be enough to guarantee their success. Could their colonel evade the American and French patrols operating from Steinen? They waited in the dark.

At 2300 hours, they picked up the low hum of a truck moving very slowly in low gear over rough terrain. The truck reached the clearing and its motor shut down. Then, someone by the truck gave the prearranged flashlight signal: SOS in Morse code. Kurt returned the signal immediately. He motioned his men to stay put, then walked out of the woods, into the clearing, and up to the truck. There, two men with flashlights greeted him and shook his hand. A man opened the driver's side door and walked to the back of the truck. It was Colonel Peiper.

"Kurt," said the colonel, "it is over for Germany. Today, the high command surrendered unconditionally to the Allies. Please tell the men."

"Yes, sir."

There was no more time to chat, and Kurt knew that Colonel Peiper would not inquire about his family until his men reached safety. Two hours later they entered the colonel's flat in Berne. Hans had prepared cots and blankets for the men, but none bedded down in spite of the fatigue that hung on their faces and bodies. They seated themselves on chairs around the kitchen table with Hans and Kurt.

"You men are tired. Why aren't you in bed?" asked Hans.

"The men insisted on being here when I told you, Colonel," answered Kurt. He put his hand on his colonel's shoulder.

"My family? Yes?"

"Colonel," said Kurt, "we received word two days ago from our source in Dresden. Your family died in the bombings. The source searched the area of the apartment, but the fire and high winds left nothing but ashes and blackened debris. He said there was no doubt of their deaths. I am sorry to bring you this news, Colonel."

Their colonel looked down for a few moments, then he raised his head. "I moved them to Dresden for its safety. Dresden has no war industries and therefore could not have been a target for American and British bombers. I was wrong. I should have known, somehow. My God! They died because of my bad judgment."

Kurt put his arm around Peiper's shoulders and held him close. The men bowed their heads in respect. They'd never seen their colonel cry, never thought it possible. It was unnerving, yet touching. The men had families, too.

"It is not your fault, Colonel," said Kurt. "It is not you who targeted such a beautiful and harmless city as Dresden. It is not you who dropped the bombs. It is not you who started the fires. It is the British and the Americans. They are animals. Monsters!"

Colonel Peiper stood up, shook hands with each of the men, and asked Kurt to join him outside. "I must show you something, Kurt."

They walked towards the Lorrainebrucke Bridge, which spanned the Aar River.

"Kurt, my wife was so beautiful and smart. I met Kirsa at Heidelberg University. She studied music and finished first in her class. Our children were so young. Rose was only four years old. Little Hansel only two. Rose…she loved to play the piano. She was so talented, and I was so proud of her."

"Colonel, they have found peace and joy in the arms of God."

Peiper said nothing more, and Kurt had nothing more he could offer.

They stopped short of the bridge at what looked to Kurt like an abandoned warehouse. Colonel Peiper knocked. An older man opened the door and smiled when he saw the colonel.

"Please come in, Colonel, and introduce your companion."

"Klo, this is my adjutant, Kurt Getz. Kurt, this man is Klo Himseling, my friend. He and his group here," Hans waved his arm around at the sleeping people, many of which looked to be civilians, "are courageous in their mission, like you. Klo heads the group. He is a wise and caring leader."

Klo and Kurt shook hands. The men took chairs around a small table near the door and several meters away from the rows of cots.

Klo explained to Kurt, "Our group numbers about thirty. We escaped the allied armies in Germany, crossed the border into Switzerland, and found shelter in this old warehouse about four weeks ago. We had very little food and no medicine, clean water, sanitation, or clothing other than what we wore in our journey here. We are women, children, and older men. Herr Getz, we were in a sorry condition. Our food was the puny fish we pulled out of the river and edibles from garbage containers. Colds, influenza, and diarrhea infected over half the adults and most of the children. Two of the women are pregnant.

"Then, your colonel became our friend. He brought food, blankets, cots, clean clothes, and drinking water. He shamed two German doctors in Berne to provide medical care to our group. All of us have gained weight and most of the illness cases are gone. The ladies started a school, and the children are learning again thanks to the books the colonel supplied us. Colonel Peiper even teaches fractions to some of the younger students. But the best, Herr Getz, are the children themselves. They run and play and get into mischief. Their mothers even spank them again! I sometimes feel like we're back in the Fatherland just before the war. We can never repay your Colonel Peiper."

"Herr Himseling," said Kurt, "tonight Colonel Peiper grieves. A short while ago, the colonel learned that his wife and two children died in the Dresden bombings."

"Colonel, I...I am terribly sorry," said Klo. "Is there anything we can do for you?"

"Would you have a drink we can share, Klo?" Hans asked. "That would be most welcome."

Klo produced a bottle of French Cognac. "I saved this for a special occasion. This is the occasion, even though it is sad. The colonel's loss is the loss of all Germans. There's been so much of it. So let us drink to dull our grief, and that of the colonel's, if only for a short time." They passed the bottle until it was empty. Then they stood.

"Klo, we are on our way to the hospital to visit Maria. I hope you don't mind our quick departure."

"Not at all. Please, look in on the dear girl."

Colonel Peiper led Kurt into the city to the hospital. The admitting nurse recognized Peiper and motioned him and Kurt through the doors. They reached the children's ward on the third floor. The night nurse, a stout woman around fifty, Kurt guessed, smiled and told him the good news. "The medicine lowered the baby's fever," said the nurse. "Her appetite is up and she no longer gasps for breath. The doctor predicts a full recovery. Colonel, she would have died had not you brought her to us when you did."

"Can I hold her? Just for a few minutes? Please?" asked Peiper.

"Of course. It's best that she hear the beating of your heart."

Peiper reached into the crib, gathered Maria in his hands, and held her to his chest. Then he kissed the child, laid her in the cradle, and pulled the blankets around her.

"Kurt, I must visit Klo again this night, but I needed to see this child. After everything that has happened, the news about my family, visiting Maria is now the only joy I have in life. I could tell you about Maria on the way back to the warehouse if that is all right."

"Of course."

Colonel Peiper thanked the nurses, and quietly the men left the hospital. They started on the road back toward the warehouse.

"About a week ago, as I delivered food to Klo and the refugees, I heard the crying of an infant and asked Klo if either of the pregnant women had delivered. Neither had. Klo said that a German girl—about twenty-three, he guessed—had come to them with a baby girl the previous night. The mother said she'd given birth to the child about two weeks before, but she couldn't care for it."

"Why not?"

"Because, she said, she and the baby were in danger. She left shortly after, and left the child with Klo. When he told me about the child I asked to see her and I held her in my arms. She was hot with fever and very weak. Klo and his people were helpless to treat the child, so they allowed me to take her to the hospital. It had been over a year since I held my own children, Kurt. I felt drawn to this infant, as though I was her father and blood of her blood. By caring for Maria I felt I was helping my own family.

"You said they were in danger, Colonel."

"Yes, Kurt. It involves her husband, an SS soldier. She said he beats her with his belt and fists. He told her he would kill her and take their baby if she left their home in Ravensburg. Nevertheless, she escaped from Ravensburg and made it to Berne. No one knows how. Klo saw the bruises on her face and arms and believes she is telling the truth."

"Where is the husband?" Kurt asked.

"He followed her here and is somewhere in the city. She refused Klo's protection because her husband has searched out German refugee groups who were likely to take her in. The man is heavily armed and, she says, will kill anyone who interferes with his wife and child. She said the man wants the child so he can raise her as a true Nazi in Germany. He is not only a nasty brute, he is a fool. The Allies will kill Nazism in the Fatherland and anywhere else they find it."

"I agree, Colonel. Where is the woman now?"

"No one knows. He might have taken her captive or killed her. She said she would return for the baby but could not say when. Klo said the young lady was frightened and distressed, but brave."

"Did she give names?"

"Her name is Greta and the child's name, as you know, is Maria. She refused to disclose further information about herself."

When they reached the warehouse and knocked, Klo answered again, this time with a smile on his face. "Colonel, I know you are in mourning and there are things we must discuss, but you must come with me first. We've found her!"

Peiper glanced quickly at Kurt before both men entered the warehouse. Klo led them to a far corner where many women sat chatting in a circle. Klo told them to move and the women did, revealing a woman sitting on an old crate in their center. Although she was tired, dirty, and disheveled, Kurt took in the blond hair, the blue eyes, the high cheekbones. He noted the pride in the way she held her head, and the bravery with which she hid most, but not all, of her fear. Kurt knew the look of someone who had endured much from seeing his reflection in a mirror, and he recognized it in this woman.

Kurt looked to Peiper, who had eyes only for the fierce and determined woman. He stepped forward and offered his hand. "Hello, Greta. My name is Hans. Hans Peiper. This is Kurt Getz, my friend. Your daughter Maria is safe and in good health, as I'm sure Klo has told you. You need fear nothing. For you, too, are now safe."

Chapter 35

Kurt knelt and received communion from Father Paul, then he stood. The mass ended and Father Paul said to go in peace to love and serve the Lord. Kurt made the sign of the cross. A few minutes later, he saw Father Paul motion to Tim and Ernie and point downhill towards the river. Kurt watched them leave, then he muttered to Frenchie that he felt like a night in the woods and that he'd be back in camp sometime the next day. Kurt walked from the camp, then he moved quickly in a southern arc towards the river. He stopped when he spotted the three men sitting on logs about five meters north of the Piankashaw Cemetery. Kurt hid and listened.

"...Gunny," Kurt heard Father Paul say.

"It'll be dangerous for him, Paul," said Tim.

"Clearly. But do you understand why Gunny is important?"

"Yeah, I do," Tim replied. "Only Gunny can identify all the German SS in Peiper's unit who immigrated to this area with Peiper. But how do we convince Gunny to come here and help? He'll resist like all hell because of Peiper's threats to Mary June and Henry."

"I have a plan that might work," said Paul. "We call Gunny from a phone booth, preferably in a neighboring town. There are several people who can ask him. Mary June, Maymie, and you too. If he's anything like the man you've described him to be, I believe Gunny will consider this more of a combat mission than anything else. He'll feel hard pressed not to come."

"Paul," said Ernie, "when you chew it all down, it *is* a combat mission."

"Which is why it is you, Ernie, who will have the best chance of convincing him."

"What if I can't get him here?"

"You must get him here."

Their conversation continued, but they discussed nothing of more importance than the return of Gunther Balbach to Dubain. Kurt knew he needed to share this information with his colonel immediately.

Hans Peiper stared across his living room coffee table at Kurt. He thought over all the information Kurt had just reported to him as Greta filled Kurt's wine glass then sat beside her husband on the sofa.

"This news is quite disturbing, Kurt," said Hans. "Are you certain of Tim Balbach's statement that Gunther Balbach's purpose is to identify those of our war unit who have immigrated to this area, and that Ernie Balbach might not have been frivolous when he talked of a 'combat mission'?"

"I am certain I heard correctly, Colonel. They conversed in the way of conspirators who believe that no one overhears them."

"Gunther Balbach is aware of our identities and the events at Mortain," said Hans. "This almost certainly means that they desire to convince him to ignore my orders, come to America, and expose all of us, and probably by extension the Great Reich in the Indiana gaus."

"Expose to whom?" asked Greta.

"The American media. This will galvanize the American authorities into action against us."

"Then," said Greta, "Gunther Balbach cannot come to America."

"Cannot Gunther Balbach do the same damage in Germany?" Kurt asked.

"Yes, he can," said Greta. "Hans, I will go further than Kurt. So long as he is alive, Gunther Balbach can go to any media and any national authority and ruin us. Of course, we have known this for years. However, while the call he receives from the Balbach's may not motivate him to come to America, it might encourage him to take such action in Germany, or elsewhere."

"I agree with Mrs. Peiper. Colonel, if I may be so bold, you cannot take the chance."

"And I will not," said Hans. He stood and left the room to make a phone call.

Several minutes later, the overseas operator connected Hans Peiper's urgent call to Klo Himseling in Bad Durkheim, Germany. Gustav Stresseman lived only a short distance from Klo's bierstube, and it was easiest to instruct Gustav, recently returned to Germany, by sending a message through their mutual friend.

"Klo, there is extremely important business to conduct in Germany."

"Yes, Colonel," said Klo Himseling. "What is it?""

"You must follow my instructions carefully and to the letter. There is little time. The subject may leave Germany in a matter of hours. Under no circumstances can this be allowed to happen. Do you understand, Klo?"

"Yes."

"Summon Gustav when our conversation ends. Instruct him to deliver a message of extreme prejudice to Gunther Balbach in Mannheim immediately. Tell Gustav this is double the normal fee."

"Yes, Colonel."

"Thank you, Klo."

Chapter 36

First State Bank was closed on Wednesday afternoons. Normally, Maria Peiper spent this time working around her house or hiking in the forest. This Wednesday afternoon, however, found her driving to her parents' chateau in the woods. Maria's parents spent Wednesdays together, often driving away from Dubain and from prying eyes. In nearby Louisville, they shopped, idled in cafes, saw the latest movie in a cinema, and talked. Later they would check into one of several downtown hotels and stay the night. They often told Maria of their destinations and the name and phone number of their hotel in case something ever came up while they were away.

If only, Maria thought, I could drive away and not deal with all this...this, pain. That's it. Call it anxiety, nerves, doubts, falsehoods, lies, anger, betrayal, a sickness in the pit of your stomach, but sum it up as pain. Just drive and drive until you reach the ocean. Then board a ship and sail and sail until you reach another land. Then...then what?

The next steps in her escape fantasy eluded Maria, pushed away her very own personal hell of the no-man's land between the Who I Am and the elusive Who Am I.

Damn you, Germany, and your past, which traps me because I dare not question it, she thought. But I do!

Damn you, Great Reich and your future, which traps me because I dare not doubt it, but *do*!

Damn you, Mama and Papa, and your love and lives full of purpose!

Damn you, Father Paul Kessler, and your answers to questions I dare not ask!

Damn you, Fate, for giving me the illusion of a charmed life only to stand me naked against my reality!

Damn you, Timmy Balbach, for jump-starting my heart and forcing me on this dark journey!

And damn you, Maria, for daring this mission of disloyalty!

Maria ignored Leni and Schmeling where they guarded the door, entered the chateau with the key her parents had given her, and walked to her father's office. Maria had been in it only a handful of times. The desk was locked. Maria thought through the possibilities. The desk key was either away in Louisville on Papa's keychain or close by somewhere in the house. Where would her papa hide the key?

Maria searched around the desk, behind Papa's Heidelberg diploma on the wall, the classics on his bookshelf, the chandelier. No key. Maria pondered what resonated with her papa and where he would likely hide the key. Mama! she thought. Papa would hide the key around Mama and in a place that only they frequent. Their bedroom!

Maria found the key under Greta's side of her parents' mattress. She returned to the office to unlock it and looked around. Father Paul hadn't fully convinced her of any misdeeds her papa had done, but there was now doubt where there once was none. She hoped her snooping, free of anyone's interpretations, would shed some light and prove her father's innocence or guilt once and for all.

She sat in her father's chair and pulled out the large black binder she had seen on the table next to him when she questioned her parents about the Great Reich and the deaths of Eleanor, Freddy, and Father Chris. The book contained a collection of her papa's sermons. Maria read several of them and was comforted. They were kind, gentle, and straight from Papa's to his parishioners' hearts.

But then she saw, in her father's handwriting, a number of Greek Cyrillic writings. They appeared on pages, loose-leaf insertions, and odd-shaped pieces of paper scattered throughout the binder. Both

Hans and Maria had learned Greek at Heidelberg University. Maria found lists of Great Reich citizens, contacts, phone numbers, and Great Reich organizational charts. She found another list of names with the words "Extreme Prejudice" written at the top. Most of them meant nothing to her. Six did: Chris Hagemeyer, Eleanor Wetzel, Freddy Caldmeyer, Tim Balbach, Ernie Balbach, and Gunny Balbach. The names of Gunny Balbach, Hagemeyer, Wetzel, and Caldmeyer were crossed out, but not those of Tim and Ernie. The backside of the list contained the names, addresses, and phone numbers of Gustav Stresseman and a man unfamiliar to Maria, Klo Himseling. Both lived in Bad Durkheim, a small town in the German Palatinate.

Maria pulled out a file of photographs from one of the drawers. There were pictures of her father and his men during the war. Hans had shown these to Maria when she was a teenager and he started relating his war experiences to her. In one, Papa and his then adjutant, Fritz Stresseman, were shaking hands. In another stood Papa and his new adjutant, Kurt Getz. Then there were photographs she'd never seen and, as she learned, was never meant to see.

One was a photo of Papa with another woman and two small children in front of a Christmas tree. The writing read, "Hans, Kirsa, Hansel, and Rose, Christmas, Dresden, 1944." There was another of Papa and the woman, Kirsa, and "Wedding Day, July 8, 1939, Best Wishes." Others: "Klo & His People, 1945." "Colonel Peiper & Adjutant Getz, Black Forest, April 27, 1945." Maria saw crude bunkers in the background. Another wedding photo with an infant: "Colonel Hans & Greta Peiper with Maria, Wedding Day, September 9, 1945, Berne, Switzerland." There they all were, Mama, so beautiful in her wedding dress, Papa, so handsome in his uniform. And...she, Maria.

There were photographs of Maria and Tim at Raven Rock, all dated April 21, 1968, and signed by Gustav Stresseman. Another picture was of Maria's house, dated April 25, 1968, also signed by Gustav Stresseman and taken from the backyard of her neighbor's house across the street. Another file contained a lockbox agreement, dated 1944, between Hans Peiper and a Swiss bank. Attached to the agreement was a receipt from the bank to Peiper. The receipt read:

Received of Major Hans Peiper, via postal Aus-
chwitz-Birkenau, Poland, of 90 (ninety) kilograms of gold in
8 (eight) bags, gold consisting of small pieces.

Maria saw another file with "Peiper, Maria" on the tab. There
was a birth certificate for Maria, born Berne, Switzerland, April 8,
1945. Mother, Greta. The father's name and the last name of all
three meant nothing to Maria. Then she found a Swiss Court Decree
of Adoption. The form documented the adoption of Maria by Hans
Peiper on October 18, 1945. There was also an odd-looking letter dated February 16, 1965, written in German to Hans and Greta
Peiper from a doctor in Buenos Aires, Argentina. Subject: Peiper,
Maria, Ancestry.

Dear Colonel and Fraulein Peiper:

I have examined the records, photographs, and physical
descriptions you submitted to me surrounding the paternal
ancestry of your daughter, Maria. Her natural father was in
the SS and his photo shows that he was tall and blond with
blue eyes. Unfortunately, he disappeared in 1945 and it is
assumed he was killed in the last days of the war. Those of
his family who survive are hostile and refuse contact with me.

In any event, the Nazi government screened SS candidates to ensure their Aryan ancestry. This was done in
various ways, such as searching family records back up to
two hundred years. However, due to the German military
exigencies during the period 1943-1945, the German government relaxed this screening. Maria's natural father was
inducted into the SS in April, 1944. Apparently, his physical
appearance with some family records satisfied the government's Aryanism standards for SS soldiers.

While his and Greta's physical features are clearly Aryan, Maria's physical traits and lack of proof of her natural

father's ancestry cause concern. That Maria is a beautiful woman, there is no doubt. She has very dark hair, bordering on black. Normally, this is no proof of inferior genes. However, the dark hair combined with her hazel eyes and meager proof of her natural father's ancestry raises certain questions that cannot be answered to any reasonable degree of mathematical certainty. The eye color of hazel is common not only in Europe, but also the Middle East, the Americas, and Central and South Asia.

It is my conclusion that Maria's genetic makeup, solely from her natural father, is such that there is a statistically significant probability that she has one or any mixture of Jewish, Slav, Arab, and perhaps Oriental, Greek, or Italian ancestry, and that such ancestry transpired in her bloodline one or more times in the past two hundred years. You may contact me for follow-up questions and analyses of any additional evidence you may uncover.

There were three more documents in the file. The first, dated April 25, 1968, and postmarked in the United States on May 2, 1968, was a confirmation from a doctor associated with a hospital located in Stockholm, Sweden. "Patient: Reller, Maria, a/k/a Peiper, Maria. Age 24. DOB: April 8, 1945. Indication: Tubal Ligation (sterilization) Procedure August 2, 1968. Without patient's knowledge or consent." The other two documents were plane tickets for Maria Reller and Greta Peiper to Stockholm. "Arrival: August 1, 1968. Return: August 5, 1968." Maria traced her contact with her parents over the past two weeks. They received the hospital confirmation more than one week before Maria went to them for assurance of the Great Reich's benign intentions and its non-involvement in the deaths of Chris Hagemeyer, Freddy Caldmeyer, and Eleanor Wetzel.

Maria gathered the Extreme Prejudice list, the lockbox agreement, the South American doctor's letter, and the Stockholm hospital confirmation. She folded them as one and placed the packet, the plane tickets, and the photos she had not seen until that day under her blouse and inside the waistband of her slacks. Maria locked the desk and re-placed the desk key under the mattress. She left a note for her parents:

I am no longer bound by the Great Reich Oath and no longer consider you my family. Goodbye, Maria.

She opened the door, locked it behind her, and placed her chateau key under the welcome mat with part of it exposed. She stopped on the patio to pet Leni and Schmeling, then entered her car and drove away. Fifteen minutes later, she parked on the curb beside the St. Augustine rectory and knocked on the door. Father Paul answered.

"Father Paul, I must speak with Timmy. Will you take me to Piankashaw Rock?"

"Yes, I can do that. When do you want to leave?"

"Now."

"I have a meeting in a few minutes with a young couple who are to be married next week."

"It is extremely urgent."

Father Paul looked into her eyes and nodded. "I'll cancel. Give me a few minutes. You can wait inside."

"No, Father Paul, I will not enter this rectory. Too much evil has occurred here. I don't think I could face any more."

"Maria, what's happened?"

"I will explain on the way to Piankashaw."

Chapter 37

Ernie and Jimmy looked up from their seats in front of Piankashaw Rock and saw Maymie hiking towards them. Father Paul, Joey, and Henry walked with her.

Jimmy: Gee, Ernie, Maymie's a nice lookin' chick.

Ernie gazed at his lady. There was her stride, girlish figure, and solid bosom. Her auburn hair, although short, fluttered in the breeze.

Jimmy: Careful there, Ernie. This ain't the time or the place for what you're thinkin'.

Ernie: Jimmy, how do you know what I'm thinking?

Jimmy: How can I not know?

Ernie eyed Maymie and stirred inside. How long had it been? Was it two, three years ago, that hot and sultry Saturday afternoon when he couldn't get enough of her and she him? Flashes of that afternoon, a fan, their sweat soaking the bed. Her cries of pleasure, louder, louder, then faster, then her peak, then his. That glimpse of Maymie days ago in the forest hadn't been enough for him. Seeing her reminded Ernie of all their good times, and he thought about holding her in his arms again.

Jimmy: Ernie, it ain't Maymie.

Tim strode up from the river with buckets of fish he'd caught on tro-tlines. Frenchie, Trocksley, Wop, Brute, and Georgie played rum on their makeshift plywood table with their worn and crumply cards. Ernie sat apart from them, his head turned left towards the north side of Piankashaw Rock.

Tim's gaze shifted in the direction of his father's when he got close enough. He stopped, placed the buckets on the ground, and watched Father Paul lead Joey, Henry, and Maria Peiper into the campsite. Tim didn't greet them. Ernie didn't blame him. Father Paul led them past the rum players where Maria stopped. She hadn't noticed Tim yet. Instead, she pointed at Trocksley, whose back was towards her.

"Du bist ein Spion, Kurt Getz!" Maria cried.

Ernie nearly jumped at the words of German. It'd been so many years since he'd needed the language it took him a moment to understand what she'd said. He wasn't sure what was going on, but Jack Trocksley seemed to know. He turned around and saw Maria. "Mein Gott, Maria!"

"Don't 'mein Gott' me!" Maria retorted. Then she calmly told the others, "That man is Kurt Getz. He works for the Great Reich and is a spy."

At that, Kurt jumped out of his chair, overturned the table, and ran out of the camp towards the south. Frenchie and Georgie chased him, but they gave up and returned a few minutes later.

Tim stared at Maria as she stood alongside Father Paul. He looked like he would take a step toward her, then he balled his hands into fists and stood his ground. Ernie didn't know what to do other than watch the scene play out for Tim and Maria.

"Maria must talk to you, Timmy," said Father Paul, "and you must listen."

"Listen for what? She's a goddamn Nazi. How do you know she and Trocksley—or Getz, or whoever the hell he is—aren't in cahoots on this?"

"Tim," said Maria, "I asked Father Paul to accompany me here."

"I got fish to clean," Tim replied.

"The fish can wait, Tim," said Father Paul.

"Timmy," said Maria, "you and your dad and Gunny are on the list."

"What list?"

"The assassination list of my fa—I mean Hans Peiper. Gunny Balbach is dead. Gustav Stresseman killed him in Mannheim."

The men stared at her without saying anything.

They sent Joey and Henry to the river to catch a few more fish. Father Paul said he and Maria had met the boys in the woods. They had defied their mothers, slipped out of the house, and were on their way to Piankashaw Rock. And they had defied Father Paul when he'd ordered them to turn around. They did, however, listen to Ernie when he sent them out of the way. It was good to see his boy, but the things that were going to be said weren't for a child to hear.

They sat around the campfire while Maria told them her story. She brought out the photographs she'd taken from Hans Peiper's desk, and passed them around. Ernie listened quietly as Maria shared her story with the others. Ernie swigged from the hooch bottle, then handed it to Maria on his left, who tipped it to her lips and passed it to Tim. Without drinking, Tim handed the bottle to Brute. Ernie shuffled through the photographs, but bore in on those of Colonel Peiper and Kurt Getz and the Black Forest. He handed the others one-by-one to Father Paul.

Jimmy: Gunny was right about the bastards hidin' out in the Black Forest. Guess it don't matter much now.

"It don't, Jimmy."

Maria studied the others for a few seconds then asked, "Who of you is Jimmy?"

"None of them is. All of them might be," replied Tim. "Dad's the only one who sees him." Tim pointed to Ernie's left shoulder.

Maria swung her eyes to Ernie. Ernie made it a point not to look back at her.

"You can't see him, Maria, because he's dead," Tim said. "His name is Jimmy Franken. He was a nice Jewish boy that your father murdered at Mortain in cold blood below the tree Dad was hiding in."

Ernie saw Tim's rebuff add to the hurt Maria carried into the camp with her.

Maria slouched and lowered her head to her breasts. Maria's hair suddenly straggled, and the wind flung it around her face. She pulled her knees to her body, wrapped her arms around them and gently rocked. At the same time, like all bums around all fires built against all late spring cold fronts, she stared into this fire and edged closer to it, hoping, Ernie knew, that the warming flames might save her.

"Brute, pass me the hooch," she said.

Brute grinned wickedly, half stood, and handed the bottle across Radius and Tim to Maria. She gulped it down, then coughed and spit some up. She wiped her mouth with her sleeve. She handed the bottle back to Ernie.

Brute snickered. "Hey there, Deutschland bitch, you be a bum now, just like us." Brute went into a spasm of cackling laughter, then a fit of coughing. He grabbed Radius's shoulder. "The f-f-fun-f-funny-funniest thing," Brute cackled and coughed, "is it's your own people who done it to you. The same b-b-bastards who done it to us! The f-fu-fuckin' Kaiser, the Boche in the trenches, Hitler, the SS. All of 'em." Radius wiped Brute's hands away, but Brute went on. "How's it feel? Take another drink. Puke again."

Maria said nothing at Brute's onslaught. She was well beyond discouragement.

Jimmy: Mortain again, Ernie.

"Goddamn Mortain, Jimmy. Goddam the SS! Goddamn scar-face and his whore of a mama! They say Mortain is in France. Bullshit. The real Mortain is anywhere and everywhere. Bon Duoi, Dubain, a lonely stretch of Indiana highway in the middle of the night, Mannheim, the Black Forest there, the Hoosier National Forest here, an altar and the confessional off to the side in a Church of the False God, a chateau in the middle of a woods, the Chosin Reservoir, Piankashaw Rock, the Patoka River. Death by Mortain turns up in foul forms, Jimmy, and at any time."

Ernie turned from Jimmy to the others. "Sometimes the Mortain death is a murder, other times a suicide, still others a slow death by hooch, sloocum, cigarettes, and to hell with my lungs and liver and heart and brain. And then the worse Mortain Death. Loss of hope.

Then the will to live, leaving only existence, and then that too disappears until there's nothing left but you lying cold and dead in the dirt at the bottom of Piankashaw Rock.

"Now Mortain's killing you, Maria."

Maria glared at him for a moment. But then Ernie saw something else in Maria. No, not a retransformation, but a plea and a hope in Maria's eyes. Ernie watched Maria lift her head, unfold her legs, reach inside her blouse, and bring out a pack of documents. "I found these in the chateau this afternoon along with those photographs." Maria said. "Timmy, please read them, will you?" She placed them in Tim's hands.

As Tim read them, his face went blank, loosened into incredulity, reddened towards anger, and tightened into rage, which he kept under control. Tim finished with the documents and looked to Maria. She nodded that it was okay, and he handed them to Father Paul, who sat between Brute and Hal.

"Tim," said Maria, "Father Paul read them in the car on our way here. Father Paul, would you give them to Ernie?"

Ernie took the documents and gave them a once over, saving the Extreme Prejudice list for last.

Jimmy: You, Timmy, and Gunny're on that list.

"This is 1968, Jimmy, and Peiper and his breed a bastards're at us again. And I'm the one who helped him find Dubain. Standing in that line, pissing in my pants, waiting for the bullet. Shoulda shot the bastard before I opened my mouth!"

Jimmy: So you gotta help stop the circle.

"What circle?"

Jimmy: Timmy and Paul might know. Go ahead, Ernie. Ask 'em.

"Jimmy, you talk like you got a paper asshole."

Jimmy: Ain't got no paper asshole. Ain't got no asshole at all. Lost it at Mortain.

"Pissed myself at Vimy Ridge," Brute said, picking up on Ernie's one-sided conversation. "Then I started in on Boche. They pissed like geysers. Shit like they had paper assholes. Hotdamn!"

"Dad, Jimmy, Brute, there's a lady here," said Tim, his wall torn down. "Watch your language."

"Then get that German bitch outta here, Tim," said Brute. "She don't belong. Take her back to Adolf Peiper—I mean Hans Hitler—no, goddammit, Peiper Kaiser. Hans Willy Kaiser. Hitler Kai...Aw, to hell with it."

They ignored Brute.

"Dad, let the others read the papers. That okay, Maria?"

Maria nodded and Ernie handed the papers around. In the meantime, Father Paul and Tim pulled Maria off to the side several yards behind Brute. There, the three sat and huddled in their own private conversation.

"Hey, me and Radius can't read this shit," said Brute as he handed the packet to Gabe. "Here, ni—I mean Gabe—read this for us. When Gabe finished, Brute turned around and stared at Maria. "Reckon I was wrong about her."

"Be a man, Brute," Radius said, "and apologize."

Maria and Father Paul returned to the fire. Tim entered the cave and emerged a few moments later with a small pouch. He didn't bother to close the cave door. The others handed the photos and documents to Tim, who placed them in the pouch.

The cold wind increased. Everyone moved closer to the fire: Ernie, Jimmy, Brute, Radius, Father Paul, Tim, Gabe, Maria. The others at the rock joined them: Hal, Peanut, Gus, Georgie, Wop, and Bernstein, who for once held back his Old Testament. At first, Ernie didn't understand why they were all coming together like that around the fire, so he asked Jimmy, who sometimes was better at reading people.

Jimmy: Sit up, Ernie, just like the rest of 'em.

Ernie: I don't get it.

Jimmy: They're turnin' into somethin' bigger 'an just them, Ernie.

"Maria has left the Great Reich and cut away her family," said Paul. "All of you know why from those papers."

Ernie didn't remember voting for the man to be in charge, but he sensed a sermon coming to catch the rest up to speed. Father Paul looked at each man in turn as he spoke to them. "Hans Peiper is her adoptive father, something she did not learn until today. A 'tubal ligation' means sterilization. Peiper and Maria's mother were planning on duping Maria into the operation because some crackpot doctor in South America says she has bad blood. Hans Peiper is a rich man. From these documents, it seems he still has two hundred pounds of gold in the Swiss lockbox, gold he got from fillings pried from the mouths of gassed and dead Jews at Auschwitz. Do I have to explain Auschwitz to anybody?"

There was a murmured chorus of no's and one, "Abomination!" from Bernstein, which set the group laughing.

"Hans Peiper is a powerful man in the Great Reich and can call on many powerful friends. This includes Gustav Stresseman, the son of the man that Ernie killed at Mortain. Daddy Balbach didn't miss Daddy Stresseman, but, so far, Sonny Stresseman has missed Sonny Balbach."

They laughed again.

"Hans Peiper murdered Father Chris and the others," said Father Paul. "He lives undercover in Dubain. However, his actual home is a chateau in the woods. He is married to Maria's mother, Greta, who, of course, lives with him. Peiper, thanks to Kurt Getz, is, by now, certainly aware that Maria has turned against the Great Reich and her family. And because of his spying on all of you here, no doubt at least some of you will now join Tim and Ernie on the 'Extreme Prejudice' list."

"Congratulations!" exclaimed Tim.

There was nervous laughter.

"Maria has placed us in the greatest of danger, but also in the strongest of positions," said Father Paul, "both because we know too much of the Great Reich and Hans Peiper and their plans. The Great Reich has to assume we're going to take some action, like go to the FBI. They cannot under any circumstances let that happen or even take that chance, so they know they must move before we do.

"They will try to stop us from spreading the word about their existence and what they have done. They may kidnap some of us and hold us hostage against the rest, or kill some of us, or both. That means they'll attack us here, at Piankashaw, and at Maymie's house, and anywhere between these two. We're now at war." Father Paul paused to let that sink in.

"So we gotta turn this place into an armed fortress," Tim chimed in. "Likewise at Mom's house. Gus's family and Maria will join Mom, Mary June, Henry, and Joey there."

"Where're we gonna get the weapons?" Wop asked.

"Hal, Gabe, and Peanut," Tim said, pointing to them. "Gus and Georgie, can you help?"

While the others waited around the campfire, Ernie watched Brute struggle with his chance to make amends with Maria. Apologies didn't come easily to Brute, and his impulse to offer one quickly passed. He said nothing and lowered his head.

Jimmy: Brute's a coward. Can't even say sorry to Maria.

Ernie: Brute's many things, Jimmy. But he isn't a coward. He's ashamed of himself.

Tim and his helpers returned, carrying large and heavy wooden boxes covered by dried dirt and some mud into the camp. They set the boxes on the ground and pried them open. Ernie peered inside and saw an assortment of automatic weapons, military rifles, grenades, and ammunition.

"Some years ago," Tim explained, "Gabe buried these on the north end of Piankashaw Rock. Don't ask where he got them. Just be glad he did."

"We have two sources of information," Father Paul said. "Maria can give us most of the names of the local people who have joined the Great Reich. Then she and Gunny Balbach can name Peiper's war comrades, like Kurt Getz, who now live in this area."

"Father Paul," said Maria, "Gunny is dead. Stresseman killed him in Mannheim."

Father Paul smiled at Maria. He left the campfire and walked to the far end of Piankashaw Rock. While still in sight, he raised his voice and shouted, "It's safe."

Ernie and Tim eyed each other and smiled. Father Paul had another talent: drama.

Ernie saw Maria gaze in puzzlement as they waited for Father Paul's big reveal. A man stepped out from around Piankashaw Rock and made his way down to greet them. The man and Ernie hugged each other. Except for Tim and Ernie, the others, particularly Maria, gazed at the man in bewilderment. He walked directly to Maria, took her hand, and raised her to a standing position.

"Maria Peiper, my name is Gunny Balbach. I am the German soldier who, with Ernie there, made it through the hell of Mortain. Mary June is my wife and Henry is my son. Ernie and I are fourth cousins. They say you are a very brave young woman. I am pleased to meet you."

"Gunny Balbach?" said Brute. "Well I'll be a monkey's uncle!" Brute rose and shook Gunny's hand. Ernie and Tim, who'd helped smuggle Gunny from Germany to Piankashaw Rock, lay back. All the others lined up to shake Gunny's hand.

Ernie waited until Gunny and the others were seated around the fire before the revelation of the next shocking secret. "Paul," said Ernie, "will you tell these men Peiper's real cover in Dubain? They're entitled to know."

"You're right, Ernie," said Father Paul. "Hans Peiper's cover is St. Augustine Parish. You know him very well. He has been to Piankashaw to meet with you many times. Gentlemen, Hans Peiper is 'Father' Eric Faulkenburg."

Chapter 38

Ernie and Gunny, now alone, stretched by the fire. The others, except for Tim and Maria, had gone into the cave for the night. The young couple, toting several blankets, walked towards the river and disappeared.

Ernie and Gunny munched on Mary June's hamburgers. "Good to have you back, Gunny."

"At first, Ernie, I wouldn't return to America. Scared for my family, as you know. Then I spotted that bastard Stresseman tailing me around Mannheim—at my job, the grocery store, church. I had two choices: death in Germany, where I can do no good, or death in Dubain, where I can help. I chose Dubain."

"Don't count yourself out just yet, Gunny."

"Never try to fool a native German about death, Ernie."

"Germany is over there, where you aren't. Dubain is here, where you are."

Gunny had no reply to this. He put another small log on the fire. "Henry surprised me," he said. "I thought for certain he'd resent me for abandoning the family. But it was the exact opposite. When I met him and your Joey at the river where they were fishing, we hugged and bawled like babies. When he left this afternoon, I gave him a note for Mary June, told him not to read it and to hand it to her as soon as he walked into the house."

"What'd it say?"

"Dear Mary June: I'll see you in the next several days. Please don't you and Maymie be hard on Henry and Joey. It isn't necessary because their papas and Tim have already kicked their asses. Love, Gunny."

"I almost laughed out loud when Tim grabbed their throats and stood them at tiptoe against the rock, then made Peanut march them back home," said Ernie. "Too bad you didn't see it, Gunny. It was funnier than hell. Do you think their mothers tanned their asses?"

"No," Gunny replied. "Might have tried to, but those boys're too old to be spanked and they know it. They took the tongue-lashings but escaped the ass-tannings. I didn't get to see Tim put them against the rock, but I would have given a million bucks to be there when Mary June and Maymie grabbed their ears and hauled them into the house."

"Me, too," said Ernie. "A coupla young guys getting into trouble, Gunny. Sound familiar?"

"Yeah. Except the only risks for Henry and Joey are ass-kickings. Not bullets and fire."

"Think we'll beat them?"

"No," said Gunny. "But we must try. I just wish our families weren't on the front lines."

"I think we can hold them off, Gunny. They've made mistakes—Chris Hagemeyer and the others—and they'll make more. Gunny, you ever go back to Mortain? To the clearing, if it's still there, and the woods?"

"No, and I don't intend to."

"Me neither."

"But I did something else, Ernie, which I've told to no one. Several years ago, on my own, I found the place in the Black Forest where Peiper and his men holed up at the end of the war. There were bits of wood that, I believe, marked their bunkers. I'd taken a shovel with me."

"Shovel?"

"Yeah. Suspected something else. Found something else."

"What?"

"Dead people. About thirty meters from the bunker area, some of the ground looked unnatural, like it'd been moved. I would never have seen it if I wasn't looking for it. I shoveled into part of it. About one meter down, I uncovered bones and found bits of clothing. The clothing had stripes and I could make out the Star of David on one piece. I found a skull with two bullet holes in the back."

"Peiper's slaves, siphoned from a death camp?"

"Yeah. The poor bastards built Peiper's bunkers, probably washed and cooked for him and his men. When Peiper was done with the place, he was done with them and they with life."

Ernie and Gunny fell silent and listened to the night. Ernie thought about Maymie alone at her house. He thought about Tim and Maria alone in the woods. "I don't know how safe we are, Gunny. Tim has a plan, but Peiper knows where we are. How do we know he's not out in the woods right now, getting ready to pick us off?"

"We don't. We just have to be vigilant."

Ernie nodded. "So long as I'm alive, the Hoosier National Forest in America will not become the Black Forest in 1945 Germany."

A man with an M-16 strapped to his shoulder slid into Piankashaw Cemetery and knelt behind a gravestone. The overcast skies allowed no light, so it was very dark in the woods and in the cemetery, even for a man trained to move soundlessly and into position in such conditions. The young couple murmured nearby, but the man could not make out any of the words. He thought he heard a sniffle or two, but he wasn't sure. The only other indication of their presence in the cemetery was the glow of a cigarette.

It moved like a firefly. First, there was a tiny flash of fire followed by a long glow. Then it dimmed and moved down where it rested for about a minute. Then it moved back to the place it was lit, and the glow doubled in brightness for a few seconds. It moved to the right, stopped, and again lit up brightly but for only a few seconds. Sometimes it rested. Other times it revolved in circles, moved up and down, and zigzagged. But always it stopped, and brightened. In a while, it disappeared altogether, only to be followed, several minutes later, by another flash to another cigarette. Then the same dance.

A good shooter could hit his target in the head when the target lit the cigarette or puffed on it, but there would be no such shot tonight. There'll be time enough for that, he thought. After a while, the couple's smoking and murmurs ended. Then other sounds came from the cemetery: sharp cries, low moans, then a stop. Then came more murmurs and another cigarette, only this one glowed much closer—the gunman guessed in the pitch black—to the ground. He heard a few snickers, then the sounds went back to kisses and moans. The man with the gun smiled. This couple was giving him another chance. He waited. Eventually, there came silence punctuated only by the deep contented sighs of a young man and woman in love and on their way to sleep. The gunman neither moved nor slept. He kept watch for the rest of the night.

At dawn, Tim and Maria woke, then donned their clothing, gathered their blankets, and walked up the hill towards Piankashaw. Ernie Balbach averted his eyes as they dressed. He waited until they were out of sight and sound, shouldered the M-16, and walked out of the cemetery, making his way back to Piankashaw in a semicircle to the south.

Chapter 39

Otto Skorzeny balanced the phone between his head and shoulder and scribbled notes on a pad on the desk in his study. Occasionally, he interrupted the American informant with a question or a comment. The subject was the American Indiana gaus and its deputy, Hans Peiper. The informant had no good news. The American Balbachs, helped by a mentally unstable priest, were, it seemed, emboldened to the point of taking action against the Indiana gaus. The informant said that armed guards protected the Balbach home around the clock. Because the guards were shabbily dressed, the informant opined that they were hobos who lived in the woods at the place called Piankashaw Rock, also the residence of Ernie Balbach and sometimes Tim Balbach. The guards stayed mostly out of sight under trees and behind bushes, but they carried what the informant thought were modern military-style rifles.

"Is there any intelligence on the events at this place, Piankashaw Rock, since Kurt Getz left?" asked Skorzeny.

"Very little, Herr Premier. The Balbachs have turned the Piankashaw area into a military compound. They have dug trenches, built gun emplacements, and placed lookout platforms in the trees. It is possible they have automatic weapons. They post guards around the compound and send out patrols at random times."

"How have they come into possession of the weapons?"

"That is a mystery," replied the spy.

"Do these hobos pose a threat?" Skorzeny asked.

"Yes, but it is believed to be very small."

"Even though they possess, or might possess, automatic weapons?"

"Yes. Kurt Getz, before he was discovered, consistently counted the number of hobos at around twelve, depending on the time of the year. He said that several are elderly, and all are in deficient health due to poor nutrition and heavy consumption of alcohol. Some also smoke marijuana. Several are insane. For example, one believes he still fights from the trenches in the Great War. Ernie Balbach himself talks to an invisible person called Jimmy. Still another, an elderly homosexual Jew, harangues the others with preachments from the Old Testament.

"But there is quite discouraging news, Premier Skorzeny. Maria Peiper defected to join the Balbachs. She did so after discovering Hans Peiper's secret documents in a binder and other documents he stored in his desk. More alarming, she stole a number of the papers as well as photographs, all of which incriminate Peiper and others in various crimes, including several recent 'extreme prejudice' events. If the American authorities obtain these documents, they will certainly take action."

Skorzeny thanked his informant for the update and ended the call. That evening, Skorzeny picked up the phone and asked for the overseas operator.

Chapter 40

Hans, Greta, and Kurt Getz sat in a semicircle in the Peiper great room.

"Kurt," Hans asked, "can Greta and I ever regain Maria's trust? Do you think she will ever come home?"

"Colonel, it will take time."

"How much time?" asked Greta.

The phone interrupted them. Greta answered it, listened for a few moments, then told Hans, "It is the overseas operator. She is placing a person-to-person call from the premier to Hans Peiper."

"I will take it in my office." Hans excused himself from his wife and adjutant. He closed his office door and picked up the phone. The operator completed the connection.

"Herr Premier Skorzeny," Hans started, "this is Deputy Peiper. Good evening."

"Good evening, Hans," replied Skorzeny. "This is a most important call. You are not to take notes, so you must listen very carefully."

"Yes, Premier," Hans replied as he gathered a pen and notepad.

"You have performed quite poorly, Hans. You substituted your own judgment for mine and disobeyed my orders to take action against the Balbach family. You disobeyed my order to sterilize Maria, your adopted daughter, at a younger age, when she would have been unaware of the purpose of the procedure. You failed to disengage her from the amorous advances of the wily Tim Balbach and the platitudes of the failed and pathetic priest, Paul Kessler. You ignored the signs of doubt in Maria and carelessly exposed highly classified documents to her. She found and stole the most incriminating of them, and no doubt has delivered them to the Balbach family. Our enemies, Hans, now have these documents in their possession. They can either hold them and blackmail you, or deliver them into the hands of the authorities and destroy you and the Indiana gaus. What do you propose to do about all this?"

"Premier Skorzeny, I must first respond to your allegations."

"Go on."

"America is neither Argentina nor the Third Reich. Indiscriminate killing in America will lead to massive investigations—"

"We have discussed this ad nauseum, Hans. I point out, however, that you successfully put out of the way the priest, Chris Hagemeyer, and the links to that action, a Mrs. Eleanor Wetzel, and a Mr. Fred Caldmeyer. There were no investigations. Why can you not repeat these successes?"

"They were not entirely successful, Herr Premier," replied Hans. "Mrs. Balbach used the Hagemeyer incident to uncover my identity."

"Mrs. Balbach evidently capitalized on clues that you, Hans, in your irresponsibility, left for her. I do not desire another of your tales of ingenuity by an untermenschen American."

"Sir, I have never told you tales."

"It is pointless for us to rehash the past, Hans. So again I ask you to state your solutions to the problems you yourself have created."

"I need time to persuade Maria of the errors of her ways and to return herself and the documents to us."

"There is no time, you fool! It is certain that the Balbach's will strike with Maria and the papers, and soon."

"I do not have to abide these insults, Herr Premier."

"You will bear them and much more, Peiper. Clearly, you have no remedy, so I, the Premier of the Fourth Reich, must do my duty.

"I will arrive at your chateau in seven days. You may inform your wife of my visit, but no one else. Please make arrangements to put me up in one of your guest rooms and to accommodate my normal contingent of ten bodyguards. In the meantime, the Fourth Reich will take your daughter prisoner and hold her in your cellar. You and Greta will have no contact with her until I expressly allow it. She must either bring the documents with her, which is unlikely, or disclose their location and the names of the persons who possess them. You will not release her until I so expressly order. I will issue additional orders during my stay in America."

"What orders?"

"I will deliver them when I arrive. Except for one."

"Which is?"

"In the event your daughter fails to voluntarily deliver the documents or disclose their location and possessors within twenty-four hours of her captivity, I will order that the information be taken from her involuntarily."

"This is ghastly! You expect me to cooperate in the torture of my daughter?"

"There is no argument. That is all."

The call ended. Hans replaced the phone, laid his head in his hands on the desk, and, for the first time since Kurt told him of the deaths of his family, he sobbed. After some time, he composed himself and joined Kurt and Greta in the great room.

"What did the exalted Otto Skorzeny have to say this time?" asked Greta.

"He will visit us in seven days. He asked that we make arrangements to receive him and his bodyguards as guests here in our home."

"Hans!" exclaimed Greta. "You have been crying!"

"Greta, the premier has ordered that Maria be taken and held as a captive in our cellar. If she does not turn over the documents, he will torture her!"

"My God!" Greta cried.

"Colonel," said Kurt, "he cannot in good conscience order such a thing. He…he is mad!"

"There is more. Skorzeny's spy in the Indiana gaus has given him very precise and highly accurate information. It is now urgent that we find this person so we can find some way to make him a double agent and force him to give Skorzeny false information, to tell Skorzeny that Maria has returned the documents and admitted the error of her ways. There is then no reason for Skorzeny to visit America."

Chapter 41

Maria and Herman Streicher turned their keys to open Streicher's safety deposit box. Maria left the room, walked back to her desk, and started working. A minute later, George Kaetzel, President of First Dubain State Bank, buzzed Marie's phone and asked her to meet him in his office, which was secluded in the back of the first floor. Maria knocked on Kaetzel's door and entered.

"Maria, please close the door and take a seat."

Maria did so. Kaetzel frowned at her for an awkward few moments.

Maria broke the silence. "What is on your mind, Mr. Kaetzel?"

"Maria, this is painful for me," said Kaetzel. "Your performance here has been outstanding. Or, more correctly, 'was' outstanding. Recently, it has regressed."

"I don't understand, sir," said Maria. "I work hard and the import-export department is gaining new customers every week. No one has complained to me."

"But they've complained to me, Maria."

"Who?" she shot back.

"I am not at liberty to say. But I must take action. Effective immediately, you are demoted to customer service. You will work behind the counter as one of the cash girls. I will also be reducing your salary by one thousand dollars."

"Sir, you can't do this. You hired me to manage the import-export department at your bank. There is no one else qualified to manage it, and quite frankly, I am overqualified to merely take payments from customers and handle their deposits and withdrawals."

"Regardless, that is my decision and it is final."

"Who will take over at import-export?"

"That doesn't concern you, Maria," said Kaetzel. "You are to immediately clean out your desk and move into the booth that is being prepared for you."

"But—"

"That is all, Maria."

Maria, dazed, walked to her desk and started to remove her personal effects. None of the other girls would make eye contact with her.

Herman Streicher emerged from the safety deposit box room and motioned for Maria. She picked up her key and walked to him.

"I'm finished, Maria."

Maria entered the room with her head down and followed Mr. Streicher to his box. As she looked up to insert the key, she saw Sheriff Beckam and Kaetzel standing in front of her. Their faces were blank, and Maria could only gaze at them in confusion. Then, from behind, someone clamped a small wet towel over her mouth and nose, then pulled her backwards to his chest. She struggled against the powerful arms that held her and gasped for breath through the towel, which had a peculiar taste and smell. Then Maria watched the room swirl, felt her knees giving out, and sensed her body lowering to the floor. The last thing she saw was the hideous face of Gustav Stresseman looming over her.

PART 3

Chapter 42

Radius lay in the trench and waited for the Boche attack. He smiled to himself. The Great War was won and he'd arrived home in Dubain, Indiana, and he knew these things. There was the welcome home parade and Brute, marching beside him, so proud, so hurt, and he remembered these things. Wilson had struck out with the fool senators on the Vur-Sales Treaty, and so there came another war, and more wars after that, and he hated these things. Radius found a home after most of a lifetime of searching for it, but this was his last fight against the Boche, his last of anything in this life.

He had no fear of the dying part. "Bless me, for I have sinned," he'd intoned to Father Paul the afternoon before. "Bernstein, remember the plan," he'd gently warned the evening before. "See you one more time, then goodbye, buddy," he'd said to Brute late the night before. "Please bury me in Piankashaw Cemetery," he'd said to everyone else in a crudely written note. Then he sneaked away from Piankashaw for his last stand against the Germans. Radius would do his duty and help save the life of a very brave young woman, Maria Peiper, in the certainty that she would go forth and do good in the world.

Radius's smile widened, for he imagined himself in a trench, and only because a trench was familiar. In reality, he lay snugly in the culvert under Peiper's chateau patio, his head two feet from the outflow end of the culvert.

Gunny sat about sixty feet south of the chateau parking lot. Ernie sat several meters behind and to his right. The woods sloped upward from the parking lot, and this gave the Piankashaws the advantage of high ground. Gunny occasionally scanned through the foliage to the patio, parking lot, and backside of the chateau. He counted four of Skorzeny's bodyguards patrolling the parking lot and the clearing around the chateau. They sweated through heavy uniforms and swiped at mosquitoes, swarming and blood-lusting in the heat and humidity of the Southern Indiana afternoon. Occasionally, a guard ventured close to the edge of the woods and peered into them, but never entered. The drawn window shades and the windowless back entrance door thwarted any view into the chateau.

Skorzeny's two late model Cadillacs sat on the driveway nearest to where the rock-road lane joined the parking lot. The vehicles of local Great Reich citizens, who arrived later that morning, filled up the rest of the lot. Sheriff Beckam and Deputy Huff parked their patrol car immediately behind the Cadillacs. Then there arrived, in order, Melvin Eichert and his wife, George Kaetzel, Firmus Langerman, Herman Streicher and his wife, and several other Dubainites: a lawyer, two accountants, some factory bosses, some factory owners, several bankers, and one clergyman. Dr. Stuart and Gerdy Friesaman arrived last. Maria's car and the two owned by her parents were bunched together south of the patio, farthest from the rock-road lane entrance into the parking lot, and were blocked in by the other vehicles. The patio lay flush against the chateau's west wall, and the parking lot abutted the north, west, and south sides of the patio. In turn, the parking lot itself extended to the edges of the woods on its north, west, and south sides.

Three evenings before, Father Paul arrived at Piankashaw with the news that the Great Reich had kidnapped Maria. Late the next morning, Peanut and Frenchie returned from reconnaissance at the chateau to report the arrival of Otto Skorzeny, the Great Reich Premier, along with numerous bodyguards, at the chateau. Gunny explained to the others that Maria's kidnapping and Skorzeny's arrival meant that

Hans Peiper probably no longer controlled his home and the treatment of his daughter.

Gunny said that Skorzeny undoubtedly had two goals: retrieval of the documents Maria had stolen from her father's office, and Maria's permanent silence. Maria's guarantied stubbornness against returning the documents meant her torture, and her permanent silence meant her death. Tim Balbach, frantic for Maria's safety, insisted on a lone and almost-certain suicide mission to deliver the documents to the chateau in return for Maria. Gunny responded that the return of the documents to the Great Reich would save no one, particularly Tim, their arch-enemy, and Maria, their traitor.

Instead, he told the Piankashaws, "We have the firepower either to crash the chateau and attempt Maria's rescue, or we can wait until Skorzeny exposes his intentions and then act accordingly. I know about Skorzeny. Many in Germany still talk about his exploits in the war and they secretly cheer him. Some have even traveled to Argentina just to catch a glimpse of him. He is demanding, cruel, and ruthless. Therefore, I believe that it is more likely than not that Skorzeny will stage Maria's execution outside the chateau in front of all the local Great Reich citizens. He might also execute Hans Peiper, and even Greta Peiper. The citizens will draw the obvious conclusion: the penalty for traitors and anyone who defies Premier Skorzeny is death."

Then, the afternoon before, Gus and Hal returned from scouting Peiper's chateau and reported that Skorzeny's guards moved the two German Shepherds from their normal home on the chateau patio to a temporary tie-up clear on the other side of the chateau.

"Moving the dogs means that Skorzeny will act soon," said Gunny. "Probably tomorrow."

Gunny and Ernie organized the Piankashaws in teams of two. Each team was armed with at least one automatic weapon and two pistols. Gunny placed the teams in an arc somewhat less than a half-circle. The outside of the arc pointed southwest and uphill. The inside faced northeast and downhill. Gunny and Ernie—with Jimmy—were positioned on the top of the arc. Brute and Gabe, hidden under a patch of briars, lay behind the chateau near the patio and only several feet from the edge of the woods and clearing. Hal and Wop hid down-hill from the parking lot and patio. Tim with Father Paul, Bernstein with Peanut, and Frenchie with Gus and Georgie waited in gun nests around the rest of the arc. All had clear views to the patio and parking lot.

Gunny issued strict orders. "Do not move until you hear me give the order. Then fire at will. Do not charge in a straight line at them. That will get you killed. Shoot and maneuver, shoot and maneuver. The primary targets are Stresseman, Skorzeny's bodyguards, Hans Peiper, and whoever is close to Maria. Don't fire across the arc and risk hitting a fellow Piankashaw, and, for God's sake, do not hit Maria."

Doubt stabbed upward from Ernie's stomach. One of the guard dogs yipped from time-to-time. An air conditioning unit hummed on and off. Otherwise, there was silence—eerie, spine-tingling—building in pressure against the eardrum, against the spirit, against faith in the mission.

Jimmy: Ernie, what if Gunny's wrong? What if they're executin' Maria right now, in the chateau? What if she's already dead?

Ernie: Who here knows the most about Skorzeny and Peiper and the rest of those bastard Nazis?

Jimmy: Guess it's Gunny. Can't know for sure.

Ernie: Can't know anything for sure. But Gunny grew up and fought with them, then against them, then lost, and then won.

Jimmy: Won? When?

Ernie: He's here and alive, isn't he?

Jimmy: Yeah. But it means nothing if they carry Maria's body out that patio door.

Ernie: Can't argue with that. But look at Gunny. Cool as ice. There's no doubt there.

Ernie squirmed, then felt Jimmy doing the same.

Ernie: The waiting's killing me. Feels like Normandy. St. Lo. Mortain up in that damn tree.

Jimmy: Know how you feel. Hey! Ernie?

Ernie: What?

Jimmy: Thought I heard somethin' behind us. Twig snapped. Back there up the hill.

Ernie turned and scanned the woods behind them.

Ernie: Don't see anything. You're spooked, Jimmy.

Jimmy: Coulda swore I heard somethin' movin'.

There was silence for a couple of minutes.

Jimmy: Say, Ernie, where do you think Radius went last night?

Ernie: Gone loco. Nothing new. It's best he isn't here.

Jimmy: Kinda wish he was. Another crazy man on our side wouldn't hurt.

Ernie: Well he isn't here, so stop talking about him.

Jimmy: Ernie, if we make it through this, I gotta talk to you about somethin'. It's important.

"Goddammit, Jimmy," Ernie whispered, "you always got something to gab about. Shut up!"

Gunny looked over to Ernie and put a finger to his lips.

Jimmy: Yeah. First, we gotta save Maria.

Brute and Gabe lay under the briar patch.

"Dammit, ni—I mean Gabe—lay still," Brute whispered. "Don't want those goddamn Skorzeny guard bastards walkin' in on top of us."

"It's the mosquitoes and bugs, Brute," Gabe replied. "They're drivin' me crazy."

"Forget that. Listen up. Me and Bernstein and Radius rigged a little plan of our own."

"Radius ain't here, Brute."

"Yeah he is. Just can't see him yet."

"What's the plan? Is it different from Gunny's?"

"No. Well, maybe just a little."

"You're goin' against Gunny's plan, Brute."

"Ain't so," Brute said. "Just jumpin' it ahead a few seconds, is all. Gotta catch the bastards off-guard. Get 'em to hesitate, that's the thing. Then kill 'em."

"Gunny said no one moves until the first shot," Gabe insisted.

"I know all that. Shut up and listen," replied Brute. "I'm gonna start the attack. When I do, you run to those cars and start blastin' with that rifle. Hear?"

"Ain't goin' against Gunny. That's that."

"Look, you goddamn prison bait. You're under my orders now. If you don't obey 'em, I'll call Idaho and tell 'em to come get your black ass."

Gabe thought about this a few moments. "How're you gonna start it?"

"See that vine hangin' from that pin oak a few feet in from the edge of the woods?"

Gabe picked it out. "Yeah. But what does the vine have to do with—" Gabe turned to Brute. "You're nuts, Brute. Crazier than a bastard cat."

Death appeared to Gunny.

Gunny: Been waiting for you.

Death: There's going to be a harvest in a little while.

Gunny: No doubt.

Death: Gunny, why do the Piankashaws risk their lives for Maria, someone they hardly know?

Gunny: Because of you.

Death: Me?

Gunny: The Piankashaws know better than anyone that you exist. It may have taken them a while to figure out how to deal with you, but knowing you're out there has compelled them to lives of purpose and redemption. Maria gives them purpose. They'll find their redemptions in a little while.

Death: I don't get it.

Gunny: You don't have to. Just remember your promise in January—when Tim and I ate breakfast at the cafe—to leave the others alone until after you take me. Now go. I am busy.

Death disappeared.

Chapter 43

Hans and Greta followed Stresseman as he led Skorzeny and the citizens from the great room onto the patio. At Skorzeny's nod, Stresseman and one of the bodyguards reentered the chateau. Several minutes later, the door opened and the crowd hushed as Stresseman and the guard exited with Maria between them. They half-carried her across the patio to the light post. Hans last saw his daughter three days before, immediately after her kidnapping and before Stresseman secured her in the basement. Stresseman had been at her for three days under orders from Skorzeny. The left side of her face was a purplish mass, and her left eye was swollen shut. The right side of her face was darkened, but that eye remained partially open.

Maria had been tied up and immobile for three days and had been denied food, water, and bathroom privileges. Her distended tongue pushed forward and propped open her mouth while her bloody and swelled lips tried to shut it. She'd lost three teeth, one from the top, and two from the bottom. Dried blood matted parts of Maria's hair, which looked tangled and hag-like. Blood caked on the lower front of her white blouse, which was torn open, revealing her brassiere, also bloody, and her navel. Her left breast was puffed up under the brassiere cup, indicating Stresseman's use of his favorite torture, electrical shock treatment with ground wires clipped onto the victim's most sensitive areas. In the case of a female victim, those were the nipples and clitoris. Maria had wetted and soiled herself until her slacks, once light blue, darkened in splotches from above her crotch to below her ankles. The stench caused several people to cough and cover their noses as she passed. She limped on her left leg because it had received Stresseman's baseball bat treatment. The knee joint was so enlarged that it split open the front crease of her slacks.

When they reached the post, Stresseman leaned her against it and untied her wrists. Hans, standing beside Greta and Skorzeny several feet from Maria, saw her one good eye stare defiantly first at Stresseman, and then at Skorzeny.

"Maria Peiper," Skorzeny started, "you are charged with commission of high treason against the Fourth Reich. You violated your oath of loyalty to it. You stole crucial documents and passed them on to the eager and clutching hands of our enemies. Despite Mr. Stresseman's blandishments, you refuse to disclose their location or the names of the persons who possess them or take any action to effect their return. Before I pass sentence, do you wish to reconsider your refusal?"

Maria mumbled.

"Ach, Fraulein, you must speak up," Skorzeny ordered.

Maria mumbled again.

"What?"

Then Maria gathered her breath and in a voice loud enough for the citizens to hear said, "Fuck you."

Greta stepped forward and slapped Maria's bruised face. "You do not dare talk to the premier in such a fashion!"

"Greta!" exclaimed Hans. "What are you do—"

"Shut up, Hans!" Greta cut him off.

Hans saw Greta's eyes meet Skorzeny's.

"Maria Peiper," said the premier, "you refuse to cooperate, you disrespect the high office that I represent, and you insult me personally. In doing so, you shame yourself and your family, and you intolerably defy the Fourth Reich. You leave me with no choice. I hereby sentence you to death, sentence to be carried out immediately."

Then Skorzeny turned to the citizens.

"Before I give the next order, I must tell you that this is a most unusual case. For it was Deputy Hans Peiper himself who failed to adequately secure the records from the eyes and prying hands of his traitorous daughter. I have personally reprimanded Deputy Peiper for this. However, I deem the reprimand insufficient punishment given his position of high trust and responsibility and his glaring misjudgment."

Then Skorzeny turned to Hans. "So I order you, Deputy Peiper, to execute the prisoner. If you refuse my order, I will immediately relieve you of your position and imprison you in Argentina. If, on the other hand, you carry out the order, you will keep your high office, whether in this gaus so long as it is not destroyed by the authorities, or another gaus to be created especially for you. The choice is yours. Deputy Peiper?"

Hans lowered his pounding head. It had come to this? He then looked at his wife. In a barely audible voice, he asked, "Greta, what would you have me do?"

"She has collaborated with our enemies!" Greta exclaimed. "She is a deserter and traitor!"

"My God! Greta, you are her mother! Is that all you can say?"

"No, Hans. She deserves no mercy from the Fourth Reich. My only regret is that I brought her into this world."

"Fourth Reich, Greta? Is it not the Great Reich to you?" Hans asked. Then a sickening revelation came to him. "It is you, Greta!"

"Hans?"

"You are the premier's spy! You passed him the information about the Indiana gaus, me, your own husband, and Maria, your own daughter!"

"Yes, Hans," replied Greta as she moved to Skorzeny's side, "and I am proud to have performed the service for Premier Skorzeny. Now you must be a man and obey the premier, or face eternal condemnation. Shoot her!"

Hans looked to Kurt Getz, who lowered his tear-filled eyes. Then he turned to his daughter, whose good eye stared through him to somewhere else, as though she had already moved to another world. He hesitated, then saw Skorzeny nod to Stresseman. Stresseman walked to Maria with rope and a blindfold.

"Gustav Stresseman, give those to me," said Hans. "This is my duty, not yours."

Hans asked Maria if she wanted the blindfold. She shook her head. Then he moved behind her with the rope. He tied a loose knot behind the post and whispered one word, "Woods."

Hans stepped in front of her. Greta handed Hans the Luger that Hans carried in the war and then gave to Maria. He saw the symmetry. Maria would be executed by his, then her own weapon, handed over by his wife and her mother. It was his and Maria's final humiliation.

Hans raised the Luger and aimed it at Maria's forehead, standing about one meter away. "I will shoot on the count of three. One. Two."

"Hiiiii-Yeeeee-Hooooow-Dee-Doooooo-Yuuu-Bassss-Tuuuuuuurds! Raaaa-Deee-Ussss, take the treeeee-ench!"

Skorzeny, Greta, Hans, Stresseman, and the rest turned around and saw an apparition swing towards them on a vine. He passed over them. When he and the vine swung back, he let go and fell among them. Then another voice, that of another old man, sounded as a second figure squirmed his way out of the culvert. "Kill the Boche, Brute! C'mon, Bernstein! Take the trench and kill the bastards!"

The group looked down at the old man, then up to see a charging wild-eyed man with long gray hair and a thick, tangled beard, a phantom from the Old Testament. He brandished what looked to be a Bible over his head while he shrieked, "Abomination! Abomination! Murder! Spy on your own blood! Innocence tortured! Burn in hellfire, all of you!"

Hans turned to the two nearest Skorzeny guards and shot them in the heads. Then he wounded Stresseman as the man ducked down. Hans dropped his Luger and made his way to Maria. He pulled free a knife he'd hidden in his belt and cut Maria free.

It took only a moment for the other guards to organize themselves. They fired at the wild old men, and they shot at Hans. As Hans fell under their bullets, he turned and saw Maria limping into the woods, Stresseman, bleeding from his left shoulder and running after her, and

Greta, after picking up Hans' Luger, running after both of them. Hans lay on the patio, conscious and bleeding.

"Open fire!" came an order from a strong voice in the woods somewhere up the hill. Then sheets of bullets poured in from all sides.

Chapter 44

Ernie watched Brute play Tarzan on the vine, scream for what sounded like Radius, land amidst the crowd, and open fire on Skorzeny's guards with a pistol. Radius, pistols in both hands, ran uphill and fired into the crowd. Ernie turned slightly to the left and saw Bernstein, now among the cars in the parking lot, go down with his bible and rise with two spitting pistols. Brute, Radius, and Bernstein screamed like banshees. Gabe stood up behind Maria's car and shot into the crowd with short bursts from his automatic weapon. Peanut bobbed and weaved among the vehicles, popped up to shoot, then repeated the process.

Ernie watched Hans Peiper put down two guards and shoot at Stresseman. Then Hans himself went down. Maria half-crawled into the woods near Gus with the killer-torturer Stresseman right behind her. Gus shot and missed Stresseman but avoided Stresseman's return fire. Georgie stood to get a better shot, but Stresseman didn't miss him. Georgie fell backwards and gave Ernie an open view of Greta picking up her daughter's .45, which lay near her husband's hand, and dashing after Stresseman and Maria.

When he saw Maria, Tim abandoned his position with Father Paul and ran toward the southwest in the direction of Maria's line of escape.

The three old Piankashaws fired wildly into the crowd when they reached the patio, and Skorzeny's guards fired back at them. The other Great Reich citizens scattered in a panic.

Ernie, along with Gunny to his left, aimed low and shot at the Great Reich citizens. From his position he heard Frenchie and Gus do the same. Several bodyguards surrounded Skorzeny and led him into the first Cadillac. Wop and Hal had clearer shots than Ernie and Gunny. They fired at Skorzeny and Skorzeny's men fired back. The bodyguard at the steering wheel took a headshot from Gus. A live bodyguard pushed out the dead one, slammed the vehicle into gear, turned onto the lane, and threw rocks as far back as the chateau.

Ernie saw Huff escape to the east. Some of Skorzeny's left-behind bodyguards surrendered as Gabe and Peanut came in close. Two did not. They fired their pistols at Gabe who ducked and Peanut who didn't. Gus and Frenchie helped with cover fire and gunned the bodyguards down. Once the Great Reich men stopped firing and their survivors lost what fight they had in them, Ernie, Gunny, Gus, Frenchie, and Father Paul moved to the edge of the woods, then eased carefully out toward the chateau.

This battle was over.

Ernie closed in on the patio. Brute, Radius, and Bernstein lay dead there. Georgie, shot through the head, and Peanut, through the throat, lay on the rocks in the parking lot. Hal and Wop didn't appear. They, too, hadn't made it.

George Kaetzel, Stuart and Gerdy Friesaman, Sheriff Beckam, Firmus Langerman, and Herman Streicher's wife lay dead on the patio. The remaining Great Reich citizens were either wounded or running for their lives through the woods, no doubt, thought Ernie, pissing and shitting down their legs.

Father Paul opened his priestly bag, reached in for oils, water, crosses, and rosaries, and started his job of offering last rites. First, he prayed over the dead Piankashaws. He moved on to the Great Reich citizens, and then he noticed Hans Peiper gasping for breath and bleeding from his mouth.

Ernie walked to where Father Paul bent over Peiper. At first, he wanted to shoot Peiper. Then, after seeing Peiper struggle, thought, Why put the bastard out of his misery? Let him suffer.

Father Paul anointed Peiper and made the sign of the cross over him. As Father Paul intoned the last rites, Ernie crouched beside Peiper and placed the muzzle of his Beretta against Peiper's head. "You did this to Hightower at Mortain. How does it feel?"

Father Paul pushed the gun away and continued with his prayers.

Ernie whispered in Peiper's ear. "Remember Chambers, O'Reilly, Jimmy Franken? Remember your German soldiers? They're dead too. Remember? They were helpless and you killed 'em. See this Beretta? It's the same gun that killed Fritz Stresseman and wounded you. And guess what? I was up in that tree all the time. The bullets missed me because I laid down on a large limb. Gunny found me in the tree and lied to you. I wanted you to know this before you burn in hell."

Then Peiper found words. "Ma-ree... ah... wh... where... he?... ali... ve?"

"Dead," Ernie lied. "You got her killed. Take that into hell with you too."

"Ernie, that's enough," said Father Paul.

Father Paul moved on to others in need of his ministry. Ernie watched Peiper heave for another five minutes, then cease breathing. Ernie didn't bother to close Peiper's eyes.

A few moments later, Ernie heard, from the southeast, the direction in which Tim had run after Maria, one shot, then two more, then another, then two more, and then no more. Ernie motioned to Gunny and they ran towards the six-shot war.

Mary June had purchased the .22 revolver from a former drinking buddy at the Schnitzelbank. She'd tucked it in her slacks and secretly followed her man and his Army of the Piankashaws to Peiper's chateau. There, she hid behind trees uphill from Gunny and Ernie and away from the action. Once, while getting into position, she stepped on some dried twigs. They cracked and she ducked. She peeked up to see Ernie turn and inspect the woods behind him, but he turned back. She remained undetected and that was good.

Time split into distinct seconds, then tenths of seconds, then maybe hundredths of seconds. She watched Stresseman march Maria out to the patio, and she watched Skorzeny hand the gun to Hans Peiper. Then Brute—old, crazy, mean, I-don't-like-lady-bums, soft-hearted Brute—swung in on his vine to start his, Radius, and Bernstein's suicide mission. She gazed down, mesmerized by the spectacle—and then the reality—of battle. She watched as men she'd shared hooch with were gunned down, and she spotted Maria half crawling, half limping into the woods, and Stresseman and Greta Peiper running after her. Then she saw Timmy speeding to head them off.

In the sequence of these events, Mary June discovered her mission. She flashed back to Tim and Father Paul talking on Maymie's back porch, then Father Paul asking for her help. *"These have deepened your soul and a deep soul will make you tougher and braver than any soldier."* Mary June had thought hard on Paul's words, and, now, she'd discovered her mission. Mary June turned west and struggled her way through the dense growth so she could catch up to Timmy.

Chapter 45

Maria made it into the woods. She staggered when she put weight on her left knee and fell by a small sycamore. Pain coursed through her, but she pushed through and used the sycamore to pull herself to a standing position. She took several more steps and fell again. Weak from hunger, thirst, and loss of blood, her body a mass of pain, she fought off the blackness that threatened to consume her.

She crawled with her arms and good leg until she found a stick, which she used to push herself to a standing position. She heard heavy steps thrashing in the woods behind her but lacked the strength to turn around. Then a blow struck the back of her head—from a fist or forearm, maybe—and sent her down again. She rolled on her back, opened her good eye, and beheld her torturer, Gustav Stresseman, standing over her. Then there stood her mother, Greta Peiper, beside him.

Greta pointed the Luger at Maria.

"No, Greta," said Stresseman. "Not here and not now."

"She is a stain on me so long as she lives."

"We must escape the country. She will make a good hostage against the Balbachs and their allies, at least until we leave the country. There is little time. She cannot walk so I'll have to carry her. We'll follow the creek bed to where it meets the road. Then we'll hijack a vehicle and go into hiding until we can escape."

"Your shoulder?"

"Just a flesh wound. It hurts, but that's all."

Maria began to fade out then. She felt arms lift her and then she moved forward. Pain from the sudden movement made her cry out, and blackness faded her vision. She felt a sensation of bouncing uphill. She saw banks of a creek and heard water splashing. Water! Then more blackness, and when her vision occasionally cleared she saw her mama behind her. There was a sense of floating in the air, of weightlessness and being lost in emptiness. Then Maria heard voices, angry and threatening. Her feet touched the ground and something hard and cruel pressed against her temple. She heard a familiar voice shout her name. "Maria!"

Tim? Timmy, she tried to yell, I'm already dead. Shoot Stresseman.

There was a shot, and she fell to the ground. Then two more shots. Suddenly, her mama assumed gargantuan proportions. There was a shot and a hard slap on her rib cage. Two more shots fired, and then Maria heard another woman's voice, someone familiar. Then, Oh Sweet Jesus, the darkness.

The wide Maple tree stood in the woods close to the creek and about fifty feet north of the county road that bounded the south side of Peiper's tree farm. A large man carried a young woman up the creek. When they got within fifteen feet of the Maple, Tim Balbach stepped out from behind the tree and pointed his M-16 at the man.

"Stresseman," said Tim, "drop your gun, place Maria on the ground, and raise your hands."

Stresseman turned towards Tim. He shifted Maria so that her feet touched the ground. He crouched behind her, using her as a human shield. He pushed the muzzle of his gun against her head.

"I cannot do that, my crazy Jeep-driving marine," replied Stresseman. "You drop your gun, face the tree, and put your hands on your head."

"No, you torturing murderous bastard."

"Do it or I'll kill her!"

"Haven't you already killed her?"

"Ah, not quite." Stresseman squeezed Maria enough to make her cry out in pain. "You see? She still lives, but that can easily change."

"You need her as a hostage."

"Yes. But as you can fully understand, her usefulness to me can end at any time. Even now. Ach, Timmy. I'll say it one more time. Drop your gun or she dies right here."

Maria tried to talk. Her lips moved but there was no sound. She shook her head. Tim caught her message: No. Don't drop your gun. Shoot this man, even if you have to kill me.

"Can't do that, Honey."

"On the count of three," said Stresseman. "One...two..."

Tim dropped the rifle, but he did not face the tree or raise his hands.

Stresseman grinned. He pushed Maria to the ground and shot Tim in the abdomen. Pain exploded in Tim's stomach. He fell on his back, placed his hands over the wound, and lay there, helpless. Stresseman walked up to Tim.

"Timmy Balbach, you are a foolish American who lives in a make-believe world. You trust too much, and you believe your stupid American movies where the boy always gets the girl. Well, my friend, you should not have trusted me, this is not a movie, and you shall not get the girl. There is no happy ending for either you or her." Stresseman positioned the barrel of his gun within several inches of Tim's face.

Tim thought it was the end of both him and Maria. Then he heard two shots. He saw blood spurt from Stresseman's neck and a hole open in the man's left temple. Then Stresseman fell over. Tim rotated his head to see Mary June Balbach pointing a revolver with both hands.

Mary June moved to Stresseman and rolled him with her foot. His eyes stared into space. She stared down at the man she'd killed. Then she looked at Tim. Before she could ask how he was, Tim spotted another woman run up behind Mary June. The woman looked at Mary June and Stresseman, then glared down at Maria on the ground where

Stresseman had left her.

"You bitch!" the woman hissed. "Look at what you have done to us!"

Tim tried to shout for the woman to stop, but he could hardly move because of the pain in his gut. He could only watch as the woman pointed her gun at Maria and shot her in the chest.

"No!" he wheezed.

The woman then pointed the weapon at Mary June.

Two more shots.

But Mary June did not fall. Instead, the woman who had shot Maria collapsed onto the ground.

Tim watched his mother, holding a .38, run up to the woman she had just shot and kick away her weapon.

Maymie knelt by Tim's side. "Mary June, the ambulance is behind us on the road. There was no one else to come like you asked, so I brought the boys. We need to get him out of here."

Maymie pressed a gentle hand to Tim's stomach and probed the gun wound. Tim tried to relax and let her motherly touch wash over him. He thought he heard her shout for Joey and Henry to bring three stretchers. Then he cried, but not from the pain of his wound. Maria was dead.

He prayed for his own death.

Chapter 46

Mary June had told Maymie where the men would attack Peiper's chateau, and Maymie had been right to follow. She had stayed back on the road with the boys, ready to care for anyone who needed help after the bullets started flying. She just never thought her first patient would be her own son.

Maymie, Mary June, and the boys carried Maria, then Tim, then Greta Peiper to the ambulance and loaded them in.

"Mary June, you drive. Hit the siren switch under the dash next to the steering wheel and get to the hospital, stat. We don't have much time."

Maymie did a quick triage on her patients. Tim was conscious and would make it. Greta might live. Maria would not. She cleaned her hands as best she could before getting to work and calling the boys over to help her.

"Joey and Henry, we gotta stop the bleeding. Joey! Dammit! This isn't the time to get sick. Here, hold this compress on Tim's wound. If you gotta throw up, do it out the window, but don't let go of that wound!"

Maymie ordered Henry to compress Greta Peiper's wounds, then she took charge of Maria. The bullet had entered Maria's lower left torso. There was no exit wound, so the bullet was lodged somewhere inside her chest. Her breath came in gasps and blood foamed from her mouth. Maymie laid Maria on her side to keep her from drowning in her own blood.

"Henry, crawl to the front seat and unhook the radio transmitter. Flip the switch on the side. Yeah, like that. Push the button on the right. Yeah. Now three times, Extreme Emergency."

Henry did so, and the backup hospital emergency room nurse responded with, "Received. Over."

Maymie told Henry what to say, and he spoke her words into the radio. "'Three victims, multiple gunshot wounds. Two critical. Third, very critical, internal bleeding, possible sucking wound. Prep three rooms for emergency surgery. Repeat instructions and advise. Over.'"

The radio crackled. The nurse repeated the instructions then said, "Proceeding accordingly, calling in doctors and nurses. Stand by. Good luck, Maymie. Over."

Maymie coached Henry and Joey on putting in IVs for Tim and Greta. "You have to stick the needle in. Thataboy, Henry. Joey, stop gagging and push that needle into Tim's arm!"

Maymie rigged an IV and a plasma bag and pushed the needles into Maria's right arm. She wrapped a blood pressure monitor around the left arm and ran the test several times. First test: BP 90 over 50. Second test: 88 over 50. Third test: 85 over 45.

Maymie met Mary June's pleading eyes in the mirror, then shook her head. Maria's body was too damaged. She wouldn't make it.

Chapter 47

Ernie and Gunny ran along the creek with guns drawn. They paused when they heard an ambulance siren, then they resumed running. The siren dwindled in the distance and they slowed. They found Stresseman's body near a large Maple tree and a .45 pistol laying beside him. Then Ernie spotted another pool of blood and Tim's M-16 several feet away on one side of Stresseman. About fifteen feet on the other side of Stresseman, they picked up a cheap .22 revolver. They discovered another pool of blood about twenty feet downhill and northeast of the tree, and Maria's .45 Luger beside it. They found Maymie's .38 Smith & Wesson about twenty feet uphill toward the road.

"Must have been Maymie with the ambulance," said Ernie.

"Should we go back to the chateau?" asked Gunny.

"No. I've seen enough of Hans Peiper. Father Paul and the others can take care of things there."

There was nothing more to do but walk in the direction of town and hitch a ride.

Jimmy: Ernie, stop. You gotta piss.

"No I don't gotta piss."

Jimmy: Yeah you do. Tell Gunny to 'wait, I gotta piss like a Russian racehorse', then walk into the woods.

"Dammit, Jimmy, this isn't the time to play games!"

Jimmy: Ain't no game.

"Ernie, if Jimmy wants you to piss, then do it. It might shut him up," said Gunny.

Ernie and Jimmy entered the woods and stopped.

Jimmy: It's time, Ernie.

"Time for what?"

Jimmy: To leave you.

"Don't bullshit me, Jimmy," Ernie shouted. "You aren't going anywhere."

Jimmy: You don't need me anymore.

"Jimmy! Goddammit we been together since training in England. You can't just pick up and leave me!"

Jimmy: Hans Peiper is dead. You don't have him to worry about no more.

"But—but—the killing I done, Jimmy! The enemy. The boy and his mother! I didn't even try to save you, Jimmy, when you were under that tree!"

Jimmy: I know that, Ernie. And I know you think I've never forgiven you.

Ernie started to cry. "Then you gotta stay with me so I can make it right, Jimmy!"

Jimmy: Ernie, you don't get what I'm tellin' you. You couldn't have saved me. So you don't need my forgiveness. You're a good and decent man, Ernie. It's time you started believin' that again. You're nearing redemption. Get there, and you'll be okay.

"Jimmy! I need you to stay with me!"

Jimmy: No can do, Ernie. War's over.

"Then...then answer...me this. Were you ever really real?"

Jimmy only smiled. He never gave Ernie a straight answer.

Jimmy: Go now and attend to your family, Ernie. Goodbye.

"Jimmy, no!"

There was no answer.

"Jimmy? Jimmy!"

Silence.

"Jimmy!"

Nothing. Jimmy was gone.

Ernie turned, and Gunny embraced him as he sobbed.

"Ernie," said Gunny, "Jimmy's moved on because it's over. There, there. Let it out. It's over, Ernie. Mortain. The war. It's done and over."

Mary June, Maymie, Ernie, Gunny, the boys, and Father Paul Kessler sat in the surgery unit waiting area at St. Mary's Hospital. An Indiana state trooper had picked up Ernie and Gunny on the side of the road after they received news of shots being fired around a private residence. They'd driven to the Chateau where Father Paul joined them. The troopers had called in reinforcements once they started to get a full picture of what went down. Now, three Indiana state police troopers, one of them a detective, and an FBI agent, questioned them and obtained their statements.

A surgeon entered the room, pulled a chair in front of the group, then sat down and smiled. "It went well with Timothy. The bullet struck the pelvic bone and split into fragments. We repaired the bone and lower intestine and removed most of the bullet fragments. He's in satisfactory condition and will heal with time. We moved him to the Intensive Care Unit. He'll wake from the anesthesia in about one hour. Then you can see him."

"Thank you, Doctor," said Ernie.

"What about Maria Peiper?" asked Mary June.

"I can't say. She's in another operating room. However, one of the nurses told me that the older woman, Greta, is almost out of surgery. I got the impression that she'll survive. Must have been some battle out there in the woods."

No one answered. The surgeon left.

A nurse entered thirty minutes later. "Maymie, I've been asked to talk to Maria Peiper's family. Are they here?"

"We're her family," Maymie responded. "What do you need?"

"The doctors requested a priest to administer the last rites to Maria. Father Paul, will you please follow me? You have to scrub up and wear a gauze strip around your mouth."

Father Paul left with the nurse. He returned thirty minutes later.

"Well?" asked Maymie.

"She's hanging on, but just barely. They were moving her to the ICU when I left. One of the doctors pulled me to the side and told me that Maria remains alive only because she is young and was in good health before the torture and beatings. The bullet nicked her heart, missed her aorta, and part of it lodged in the left lung. They removed that piece, but it also means that the bullet broke into fragments after it entered her. Maria is so weak they didn't bother to look for the other fragments. Her blood pressure has stabilized, but she is on a ventilator. He told me that her chances are slim. It…it doesn't look good. He asked me to talk to the family and prepare them."

"What're we gonna tell Tim?" Ernie asked.

"Tell him the truth," said Paul. "Tell him it's in God's hands now."

Chapter 48

Maymie sat in the pew with her and Mary June's families and waited for the funeral mass to begin. At least for now, Maymie thought, we can have a small moment of peace after all this attention. Federal agents, backed by the Indiana State Police, had descended on the Peiper chateau the evening of the Battle of the Piankashaws, as the press soon dubbed the fight. Local, then state, then national media arrived the next day. The Feds arrested the local Dubain Nazis, including Alphonse Huff, Melvin Eichert and his wife, and Herman Streicher. They also hunted down and arrested three Skorzeny bodyguards. The Skorzeny men had escaped Ernie and his men, but not the government.

The Dubain prosecutor charged the arrestees with a spate of crimes, including murder, conspiracy to commit murder, and, for the American arrestees, high treason against the State of Indiana. The Feds had convened a grand jury to consider criminal charges of high treason against the United States of America, wire fraud, mail fraud, and criminal violations of the civil rights of others. The FBI and state police placed Greta Peiper under arrest and posted guards outside her hospital room.

It turned out that Hal, Peanut, and Gabe were escapees from an Idaho prison. At first, Idaho demanded Gabe's extradition. Then, yesterday, Idaho's governor bowed to political pressure and common sense and pardoned the three. Too late, it might be argued, for Hal and Peanut, who had died in the battle, but not for Gabe, who had lived through it.

The FBI soon realized that the Peiper chateau "Reich" was no one-cell gang of modern-day, neo-Nazi kooks. They quickly concluded, from the documents Maria stole and others they found in secret places in the chateau, that the Fourth Reich was a world-wide shadow government bent on universal rule under the guise of benevolence but with the reality of Nazism. The FBI instigated a nation-wide manhunt for Otto Skorzeny who, several days later, ridiculed them from the safety of Argentina. In spite of its extradition treaty with the United States, Argentina refused to arrest Skorzeny and return him to America to stand trial. The FBI possessed the information to dismantle the Indiana gaus and prosecute many other of its "citizens." However, they also discovered that each gaus, though part of the Fourth Reich or Great Reich, depending on whom you talked to, operated separately and independently from all the other gauses. The downfall of the Indiana gaus would not easily, if at all, lead to the dismantling of other gauses.

There would be no criminal charges against the Piankashaws. The state prosecutor and the federal district attorney criticized them for what they called "vigilante justice," but concluded that their sole aim had been to save the life of Maria Peiper. They said they were "stretching the limits of self-defense" but freely admitted that no jury would convict the Piankashaws.

The media picked up the story of Gunny and Ernie, starting with the SS massacre at Mortain, France, in 1944, and ending with the Battle of the Piankashaws. At first, the men refused interviews on the ground that they didn't want the attention and only wanted to enjoy their new found freedom with their families. They relinquished when Father Paul pointed out that their history in the war and experiences since then would give meaning to the monstrosity of the Great Reich and also expose the struggles of hundreds of thousands of war veterans the world over.

Maymie thought over all these things as she sat in the pew. She looked around the cathedral and pictured all that had taken place there. She pictured Father Hagemeyer lying on the floor right behind the altar. She had gleaned the first whiffs of sin and conspiracy right here, in these pews, and she now sat in almost the same spot as then. She saw Maria Reller—now Maria Peiper—enter the cathedral and pray over her lunch break. She saw the casket of Eleanor Wetzel before the altar. She watched Faulkenburg pray for Freddy Caldmeyer's soul. She looked to her left and watched herself enter the confessional, confront Hans Peiper, then leave in near panic. She saw so much sin, and some little good, right here in God's house. Did God intend such things? Maymie wanted to ask. But it didn't matter so much now. The war had ended, and her men had come home.

To Maymie, a measure of closure came with the funeral mass. The mass did not end grief, but it did recognize that a person lived, then died, was brought before God in the temple of the Church, and was commended to Him. But, Maymie thought, there must be lesser closures because there are other, lesser deaths. Two young soldier-boys with the same last name, enemies, then friends, battle bombs and bullets, then come before evil men who kill in cold blood. They and they alone escape and walk through the bowels of hell. One kills in a rage, both survive, then they are later torn apart by the same evil men. Another soldier-boy is sent by his government to fight in a war of futility. He kills as he must, then as he must not. These soldier-boys die more than a little inside, as do their wives and children. Are there closures for these lesser deaths?

There have to be, Maymie thought, but the soldier-boy and those who love him might never find the closure, or find it only after a good part of a lifetime. Closure appears in many forms, but what had happened this past week had been more than closure for her soldier-boys. They'd found redemption. Not just them, but their families and the other Piankashaws, both living and dead, had found their redemptions in their desperate battle against a diabolical enemy.

But Maymie waited uneasily. She, too, needed redemption, but redemption from what? She couldn't say. Could Father Paul answer the question and give relief in the rite to follow? No, it was asking too much of the man. You'll have to find your redemption on your own, Maymie told herself. Yet, she sensed that her fate was tied with another's. But whose? Was she losing her mind with all these strange thoughts? She remembered the day Eleanor and Freddy died and Timmy asking her if she was crazy. She'd said no then but felt herself slipping now. She took a deep breath and willed herself to stay calm.

Father Paul rang the bell and walked onto the altar to start the funeral mass. Maymie watched him spot and smile at the Balbach families—minus Tim—and Frenchie, Gus, and Gabe, the only black man in the cathedral. The choir sang "How Great Thou Art" while the pallbearers gently pushed the seven caskets from the back of the cathedral down the middle aisle and arranged them in front of the altar.

The families of Brute, Georgie, Wop, and Radius stood in the front rows. They not only insisted on a joint funeral mass for their dead, but were adamant that Hal, Peanut, and even Bernstein, a Jew, none of whom had any known family, be included. Georgie's family from Pennsylvania were comforted when they learned that their son, a Vietnam draft dodger, died heroically in desperate battle against a vicious Nazi group. They, too, insisted that Georgie join his companions at the foot of the altar. All the dead would be buried in the Piankashaw Cemetery. Other congregants packed into the pews behind them or stood along the back of the cathedral with the media.

Father Paul began, "In the name of the Father, the Son, and the Holy Ghost."

Neither Paul's unkempt and slightly daffy appearance nor his aura of mystery had changed since Maymie first met him. Father Paul, God bless him, had brought about the miracles of the past months with an uncanny instinct and internal motivation gleaned from...where? He'd pinned down the right people at the right times in the right places. He'd propagated their duties and then pushed them gently, then sometimes not so gently, to find courage, to move forward, to fight for themselves and so many others.

Maymie steeled herself against irrational displays of emotion.

The mass progressed into the readings and the Gospel, and then Father Paul's sermon. He thanked God for the heroics of the deceased. He pointed out that the celestial measure of a man was left to God, whose Son spoke for these deceased two thousand years ago. "Greater love than this, no man hath. That he lay down his life for his flock." He thanked God that such men lived and appeared here to lay down their lives to save others. But Father Paul also asked the congregation to pray for the enemies who had held the Piankashaw men and others in a thrall of fear, many of whom died, some of whom didn't die, and these latters now facing man's judgments.

"Certainly, all these people were, or remain, both tormented and lost in this life. Let us pray that they find the peace, love, and forgiveness of God, if not in this life, then maybe the next. Let us also remember the sacrifices of others: Father Chris Hagemeyer, Eleanor Wetzel, and Freddy Caldmeyer."

Maymie heard whisperings around her. Father Paul had forgotten to mention Maria Peiper.

Then Father Paul changed the normal order of the mass. "Today I will interrupt the sermon for delivery of the offertory gifts. I do this for two very special people who do not now sit among you but who risked all to expose and defeat the evil that stalked among you." Father looked to the back of the cathedral and commanded the delivery of the wine and water.

The congregation turned to watch two ushers pull back the large doors that opened to the middle aisle. The photo and television media scrambled for positions. Two people, a young woman in a wheelchair and a young man on a crutch, entered the cathedral and slowly made their way up the aisle. To Maymie, it felt as though all the air had been sucked from the cathedral. The young man pushed the wheelchair despite his injuries and the crutch. The figure in the wheelchair wore bandages on half her face while bruises lined the other side. Her right arm was set in a sling, and her left leg in a cast that was propped by an extension placed on the wheel chair. Her black hair shone. The young man whispered in her ear and both seemed to giggle. The congregation stood and watched in silence. Some stepped onto the pews to gain a better view. When the couple reached the midway point to the altar, the people started murmuring. There was sniffling, and then sobbing.

The two stopped at the caskets where Father Paul and two servers waited to accept the water and wine. Father asked them to turn around and face the congregation.

"Ladies and Gentlemen, I present to you Miss Maria Peiper and Mr. Timothy Balbach."

Father Paul led the congregants in clapping. Some in the crowd let out un-funeral-mass-like cheers and whistles. Tim and Maria handed the bread and wine to Father Paul who handed them to the servers. Tim, working his crutch, pushed Maria to the side to be next to his family. Ernie helped Tim into the pew.

Then Father Paul's demeanor changed. He dropped his role of the celebrant priest and took up another that was strange and unnerving, yet vulnerable and touching. Maymie felt a strange force pushing her to tears. It was almost as though someone had commanded her discipline to leave her. No! she told herself. Yet the tears started. Ernie gave her his handkerchief and squeezed her shoulders.

Father Paul started. "I have ministered to the residents of Piankashaw Rock as best I could. I prayed every day that they would find peace and return in good health to their families. I thank God for the bravery and sacrifices of these honored dead, and the safe delivery of those who yet live. I pray that they get the best treatment their government and medical science can offer.

"The living Piankashaws have given me permission to talk about the dread and torment that each of them has carried from his war. Ladies and gentlemen, what I am about to tell you is so stark, so real, and so horrendous that it cannot be sugarcoated. It cannot be hidden behind euphemisms. It cannot be softened by the simple cadences of a priest performing his earthly ministry. I must talk truthfully in plain but harsh words. And then I shall tell you about another who is imprisoned, who must be set free, who seeks redemption.

"These men killed in war. They killed enemy soldiers. They killed women and old men who supported enemy soldiers. They killed children. They killed their commanders who ordered them into battle one too many times. They killed prisoners in cold blood. They accidentally killed some of their friends in the chaos of war. There is nothing good or decent or heroic in killing others, no matter the circumstances. Yes, my friends, this is the cold hard truth of war. These men were raised with 'Thou Shalt Not Kill' and told repeatedly that a transgression of this commandment is a mortal sin that puts them at risk for damnation and eternal hellfire. I personally do not believe in the concept of hellish fire, but that is not the point here. What I do know is that these men have carried the most terrible fear that any human being can have.

"And what is that fear?" Father Paul asked, searching the congregation for some kind of recognition.

"It is the fear that God cannot forgive the sins of their wars, that God sees their souls as evil and dark, beyond forgiveness, even that of the confessional. They fear they will die in mortal offense to Him, and He will cast them into eternal hellfire."

Father hesitated. Many adults showed shock in spite of their best efforts to hide it. Maymie wanted to ask them, what do you people think war is? Do you actually believe that real war is like what you see in John Wayne movies?

Then Father Kessler blinked tears from his eyes and his voice stopped. He paused a few moments to wipe his face and regain his composure.

"I told you that there is another who must be freed. Who is that person?" Father Paul looked around the cathedral. "That person is me." He stopped again to wipe tears, then went on.

"I know of these things in a most personal way. I have my own confession, and I will give it to God and all of you now."

"My friends, I have killed. Yes, that's right. I have killed with guns and with my bare hands. Don't look so shocked. Some of you know that I was a marine chaplain with the 1st Marine Division in Korea. The division was at the Chosin Reservoir in North Korea when the Chinese attacked. I anointed dead boys and comforted those who were dying. Some…some pleaded with me to save them. 'I'm too young to die,' they cried. I could do nothing for them. For three days I did this job. Then I could do it no longer.

"There was evil at Chosin, and that evil was killing the boys I tried to help but couldn't. I lost my faith in God. I doubted His existence.

I went into a rage. I threw away my chaplain insignia and put on the combat jacket of a dead marine. I took up guns and started killing the murderers who were killing my kids. I killed again, and again, and again. The Chinese simply would not call off the attack. Some of the enemy made it into our foxholes and some of these I strangled. Yes. I pushed my thumbs into their windpipes and watched their eyes and tongues pop out in their last gasps of life. I took pleasure in this. God help me I did."

Father Paul paused.

"Since then, I have prayed every day for the souls of those I killed."

Father Paul struggled against his tears then continued in a surprisingly strong voice.

"'To everything there is a season, a time for every purpose under heaven. A time to kill and a time to heal.' We fought our wars and walked through the time to kill, through the fire. My friends, I have been wrong in all this and my shortcomings have added more grief and suffering to the Piankashaw men and me. I have chosen to tell you about my past so that I can now make it right. I have approached war from the standpoint of asking God to forgive we warriors, the Piankashaws and me, who killed. But there is no forgiveness from God because none is needed, and God has been trying to tell us so. In fact, it goes the other way.

"We must forgive God.

"Why is this?" Paul looked around the congregation. "Because God used us. God used us as His tools to end the scourges of those who sought to pervert his beautiful creation. Hitler, the Nazis, Mussolini, Fascist Italy, Tojo and Japan's Greater East Asian Co-Prosperity Sphere. He used us to try to end the soul-killing of Mao Zedong and his Red China, Ho Chi Minh and his armies, and Kim Tu Sung and his imprisonment of free people.

"And He used the deceased and many others in this cathedral to fight the evil of the Great Reich right here in Dubain. We defeated them as God commanded. So now is the time to lift the weights from our hearts and souls. It is the time to heal. It is the time to forgive God."

Then Paul looked directly at Maymie and smiled.

The scene that followed started with the stunned silence of a people lost in the epiphany of Father Paul's words and of perhaps the greatest sermon they'd ever heard or would hear. Maymie, crying, started the clapping. One by one, the survivors joined in, then the rest of the congregants. Maymie rose to her feet, and the others followed.

The standing ovation lasted five minutes.

And Maymie found her redemption.

Epilogue

He hid in the patch of foliage in the backyard of the house across the street from the home of Maria and Tim Balbach and watched the activities in their backyard through the telephoto lens. He snapped roll after roll of film, capturing each person and each activity, as his superiors had ordered. Ernie Balbach, Gunny Balbach, and Gabe Billups, the only African–American resident of Dubain, grilled hamburgers. Father Paul Kessler and Gus Striegel, along with several neighbors, played three-on-three basketball with the boys Henry, Joey, and Gabe Billups's son, Reynold. Mary June Balbach and Carol Billups, Gabe's wife, and two neighbors set the table in the backyard, while Maymie Balbach and Maria Balbach, visibly pregnant, placed picnic food on it. Maria's natural beauty had returned upon the healing of her injuries. He couldn't help but gawk at her from time to time, but he was careful not to snap an inordinate number of photos of her. His superiors demanded discipline and focus, and many times based promotions on such things.

A small battery-powered portable AM radio blared rock and roll. Occasionally, Ernie walked over and turned down the volume. Then, a short time later, when Ernie's back was turned, Henry or Joey or Reynold sneaked over and raised the volume. Paul, Gus, and the neighborhood guys laughed at the boys' hijinks, but not at their basketball skills. If he had to guess, he'd say the boys' team was winning big. Everyone came together around the table and prayed over folded hands. Then they ate. Several people drank beers, but most sipped soft drinks. It would be so much better, he thought, to have a recording of their conversations.

His superiors said that bugging the house and its phone would come soon. "Be patient," they said to him. "We must wait until the trials of the Indiana gaus citizens are done and forgotten, and the Balbachs and their friends feel secure. Americans' attention spans for these things are short, so this should last a few years at most. Then we will take our revenge, slowly and casually, and send a signal to other would-be traitors and enemies that the Great Reich neither forgets nor forgives."

He was thrilled when he recalled his last meeting with his superiors. "The Great Reich will endure," they said. "Why? Because it not only lives for the future, it lives in the hearts and minds of men who see the chaos that is the world, and want something better. These will become Great Reich citizens, like you. You," they said, "are talented and clever, and, it is plain to see, you already hold the Great Reich in your heart. You will go far. Perhaps you will rebuild the Indiana gaus as its next deputy."

He snapped more roles. At dark he would slip away, become just another pedestrian on the streets of Dubain, reach his apartment, develop the film in the darkroom he'd built there, and deliver the photos to his handlers on Monday.

About the Author

Tommy was born and raised in Jasper, a predominantly German descendant city of 14,000 located in Southwestern Indiana. His interests include the history of German and other waves of immigration to America. He reads novels and histories, and he studies cutting edge and futuristic science. He particularly enjoys fictional writing which includes real historical events and imagined future events. Tommy traces his fascination with woodlands back to his German forbears from Bavaria and the Black Forest. Tommy's family owns forested lands and these spark many of his ideas. But his writings go further. Tommy has been an activist of the type that embraces a changing world which struggles with new questions of right and wrong daily. His writings reflect these feelings. Tommy lives in Jasper, jogs and lifts weights to stay in shape, and indulges his passions for writing, law, government, and politics. He is a graduate of the Purdue University School of Engineering and the Vanderbilt University School of Law.